Rescued and Remembered

A Novel

by

Braxton DeGarmo

Christen Haus Publishing

COPYRIGHT

Paperback and eBook Edition
Publication Date: November 2013
Second edition: July 2015 (new ISBN)

Paperback ISBN: 978-1-943509-11-9
eBook (mobi) ISBN: 978-1-943509-02-7
eBook (ePub) ISBN: 978-1-943509-03-4

Cover design by Rocking Book Covers

For more information, go to
www.braxtondegarmo.com

i

DEDICATION

This book is for all of those people who work tirelessly against human trafficking. You *do* make a difference.

TABLE OF CONTENTS

ACKNOWLEDGEMENTS

As always, I wish to acknowledge and thank my dear wife, Paula, for her valuable proofreading skills, help and encouragement.

Once again, my thanks go out to my editor, Patrick LoBrutto, whose work always improves the final story. And to Lenda Selph for her proofreading expertise.

I'd also like to acknowledge Susan Prichard as the winner of my "Become a Character" contest on my Facebook page. You'll get to meet that character inside these pages.

Prologue

Ibrahim Jancic paced, experiencing an anxiety unfamiliar to him. Tonight, he would add to his "treason," but this time, his action could cost him his life.

He completed a light meal and returned to the front room of his austere apartment where he unfurled his *sajada*, his prayer rug. His father had given him this rug, and despite its daily use, its image of the Ka'aba in Mecca seemed as vivid to him as on the first day praying next to his father. The room was clean, which was Islam's only requirement for a place to pray, but he had not always had that convenience.

His use of the rug had become habit. Yet, instead of performing *wudu* before the *maghrib*, the twilight prayer, he rejoiced that he no longer needed the ritualistic washings before prayer. To his family and old friends, he was now *murtid*, an apostate. There were those in his extended family who would demand honor and his death. Certainly, his former employer, Darko Komarčić, would use that within their community to justify killing him. Yet, he no longer feared death because he was now washed clean by the blood of Jesus, not by washing his face, rinsing his mouth and irrigating his nostrils, or the rest of the ablution required of *wudu*, along with the hollow, repetitious prayers toward Mecca.

Danijela had shown him the fallacies of Islam—the violence, the monotonous ritual, the required works

1

that made him a slave to Allah—and the truth and freedom of Christianity. God, not Allah, had opened his eyes and allowed him to see that he had value as a human. Like the Apostle Paul, scales fell from his eyes, and the world he now saw was different. No longer did he seek to gain paradise through his futile, unworthy actions. The grace of God alone, through faith in His Son, would grant him eternal life. Grace was a gift he could not turn down.

He kneeled facing east. Some habits were hard to break. As he folded his hands in prayer, he first thought of Danijela. He had been assigned as security to drive the councilman, her "employer," whenever he wished to take Danijela out-on-the-town. "Arm candy" was a term he'd heard used about her. Yes, arm candy, with bruises and welts where no one else would see them. And a radiant smile but dead eyes, eyes that betrayed the slow death her soul endured.

Then, one day he saw new life in those eyes, and he knew deep inside that he had to know why. Nothing seemed to have changed, but it had, for her. He needed to know what that change was, because he, too, was dying. His cries to Allah had gone unheard.

He found his opportunity one evening when he was to pick her up first and take her to meet the councilman. He had faked car trouble and used that time to approach her. She had been wary of him at first, and he had been appalled to learn that she had become a Christian, *murtid*. Why? How? When? Over time, he learned the answers to those questions and more.

Ultimately, he rescued Danijela from the life of a harlot. She remained tucked away in his cabin, safe from those he now sought to bring down. It would not be easy, and tonight would reveal how serious he was—and how dangerous his former employer could be.

Danijela's rescue had been simple. When next assigned to drive her, they simply disappeared. The result, however, was that he no longer had the element of full surprise in his favor. Still, his former employer could not know which of his dozens of girls might be next, nor exactly when.

Danijela had insisted that Tatjana be next. Ibrahim saw that request as reasonable, for Tatjana was also "arm candy" and frequently escorted her "employer" to social functions. Although she would have a driver, who also acted as her guard, as Ibrahim had been to Danijela, he knew them all, and they knew him. He knew their weaknesses. To them, he had none. He knew their protocols, their behaviors. They knew him to act often outside the box. They were predictable. He was not. He felt confident that a "simple" snatch & go would gain Tatjana freedom as well.

It was time.

Ibrahim drove a rental car, secured with false ID, to Town and Country, an upper class suburb of St. Louis, and slowly cruised past the lawyer's home. The large two-story colonial sat at the back end of a five-acre lot on a road that looped back onto itself. Only one way in and out. The point where the road divided sat far enough from the main highway that nothing there could be seen by passersby. The homes nearby, too, were far enough off the road to pose no threat of observation.

His ex-boss' security crew would see that as the most vulnerable location, just as Ibrahim had. The driver would be most alert there. However, they would also anticipate he might avoid the location because he would know they'd be most alert and prepared for him there. So, using a bit of reverse logic, that's exactly where he prepared to stop the car and take Tatjana.

Parked nearby, he watched the car and driver enter the lane and take the branch toward the lawyer's home. There would be no delay. Tatjana would be waiting. The driver would show her to the car and they would leave to pick up the lawyer at his office.

Ibrahim jumped out of the car and pulled out a homemade net of chain and three-inch spikes. While spikes alone would stop a typical car, much like a police stinger or spike strip, they would not stop the run-flat tires on these cars. Instead, the spikes would embed themselves in the rubber, pull the "net" up to wrap around the axle, and stop the car.

Five minutes later, the net worked as planned, and the car rattled to an abrupt stop. The driver jumped out, armed, but Ibrahim was prepared and tasered the man before he could turn toward the back of the vehicle where Ibrahim stood. Ibrahim ran toward the back door and yanked it open. Tatjana sat there, bound, her face bloodied, duct tape over her mouth and fear flooding her eyes. A movement in the shadow just beyond her caught Ibrahim's attention and he pulled back just as a handgun spit its projectile. He recognized the gun and its suppressor at the same time he felt the burn in his upper arm.

Risto! He held no hope of taking Tatjana now. To move into the open doorway would mean death. They had been expecting him.

He fled to his car and sped off as two more shots bore into the hood and door of the car. How? How had they known he'd be coming for her and not one of the others? Determining the timing of the rescue took no advanced mathematics. Each of the girls had certain routines, schedules they followed. Again, they were predictable. Ibrahim could have chosen one of three dozen women to rescue. How had they known it would be Tatjana?

Then he remembered. Danijela and Tatjana came from the same town. They had been friends. Danijela's insistence should have been his first clue to stay clear of Tatjana until later.

As he passed the driveway to the home nearest the highway, he saw it. A black pickup truck, partially obscured by evergreen shrubs and virtually unseen by anyone coming into the lane. They had been watching. Risto had been there, acting on the knowledge Ibrahim had forgotten. The car picked him up on the way in, and Ibrahim would not have been able to see it. The seclusion of his attack point had worked both ways.

He had been over-confident. He'd neglected to do his research, to find that line of attack that lies outside the box. And now—Tatjana would pay the ultimate price. Her blood was on his hands.

One
୬◆◆ୡ

As the 206L-4 LongRanger IV helicopter circled the farm field a second time, the MedAir-12 crew knew they had a bad one waiting. In direct radio contact with the paramedic team on the ground, they surveyed the scene below and wished they were somewhere else. Amy Gibbs, the flight nurse, had had enough of the "bad ones." Her run-in with the "L.A. Rapist" three months earlier had shown her what she thought was the worst of what one person could do to another. She didn't want this case, or any case, to prove that wrong.

"They're setting up the LZ now," said Sanders, their new pilot on loan from MedAir-24, into the com system. Lyle Henderson, the crew's regular pilot, remained benched from the bilateral femur fractures suffered during the helicopter crash they'd experienced during that earlier, traumatizing case.

Amy gazed at the fallow field below. The remnants of an earlier light snow framed the fencerows where the wind could blow it no farther, and that day's sun had not melted it. In the dimming light of dusk, she could see a wide figure-eight etched into the dirt. At one end, the lights of the sheriff's cruisers and EMS vehicles lit up the field. Not far from them, she saw the first flare ignite. Within two minutes, all four flares illuminated the makeshift landing zone, and Sanders touched down with the typical finesse of a MedAir pilot.

Not. The jolt of landing almost knocked Amy from her seat.

"Sorry. The long shadows threw me off." Sanders powered down the bird as Amy and Reid McCormick, their paramedic, unbuckled and gathered their bags.

Upon entering the aurora of the headlights, Amy noticed that tire ruts formed the figure-eight in the rich, partially thawed topsoil of the Cuivre River floodplain. She saw the county paramedics working on the victim and hesitated. She saw no person there, just a mangled form. Images from three months earlier flooded her mind. She had to focus. The young woman needed her care, but nothing visually told Amy that this victim was female. She took a deep breath and fought the fear rising within. Her shrink had told her she was returning to work too soon after her ordeal. Until now, she'd thought Doctor Lange was the crazy one.

She had a job to do and rushed toward the scene.

"Hey, Amy. As we radioed, young female here. Can't tell her age. Feet were bound, and it appears she was dragged behind a truck for who knows how many laps around this field. Farmer was moving some equipment and saw headlights in his field. Thought it was joy-riders. Found her when he came to investigate. Saw a dark pickup leaving."

"We got here within five minutes of the call. Blood pressure was 40 systolic. Pulse barely discernible. Shallow breathing. Found one arm vein for an 18-gauge line. Had to do an I.O. into the marrow on the opposite side's tibia. We've squeezed in two liters of saline so far. Third and fourth are running. Blood pressure, maybe 60 now. Difficult reading it. Intubation was tough. Blood filled her throat every time we managed to clear it. But, Jazz there managed to snake in a seven. She's circling the drain and needs to get out of here STAT if we have any chance of saving her."

"Thanks, Paulie. Injuries?" A quick glance showed her that fluids were running easily into the cephalic vein of the woman's arm, as well as into the intraosseous line, the catheter going into the bone marrow of her tibia.

"Haven't had time to really inventory them. I mean, just take a look. What isn't torn up?"

Amy saw the form of a young woman but little else to identify the gender. Her hair had been shorn. Face, scalp, and exposed extremities appeared like ground beef, not human flesh. The generic jeans and t-shirt were as mangled as the flesh. Right femur appeared broken and angulated, as did the left upper arm. The wrists revealed wounds consistent with coarse bindings of some sort. Amy saw little oozing from the wounds, a good indication of the low blood pressure and of a body shutting down. Amy held little hope that this girl would even survive to the trauma center.

"Quick, let's get these extremities splinted. Reid, get the . . ." She stopped when she saw that Sanders had brought their stretcher to them and was preparing it for their patient. "Get the ventilator and hook her up."

Amy took her penlight and lifted the girl's eyelids. She gasped. The globes were flaccid, the corneas gone. She returned her focus to starting her initial assessment while the others immobilized the girl. The airway was good, but the lungs sounded full of fluid. Heart sounds were muffled. Tamponade? Her condition made the usual clinical signs of fluid collecting in the sac around the heart unlikely. Amy had little choice but to put a

8

needle into the pericardial sac to check it. To miss a tamponade would guarantee the girl's death while relieving one could prove the turning point in her resuscitation.

She grabbed an 18-gauge needle and pulled open the tattered shirt. Again, she startled. A large incision in the right upper quadrant of her abdomen gaped open, its sutures torn amidst the battered flesh. What had this girl gone through?

Amy's pulse quickened and her breathing seemed labored. Focusing on the patient became harder. Reid brought her back by swabbing the area just below the woman's breastbone with antiseptic. He'd read her mind. Amy unsheathed the needle, inserted it just below the xiphoid, the lower bone of the sternum, and angled it at roughly 40 degrees toward the heart. She felt the needle puncture the pericardial sac and immediately saw a return of fluid. With a large syringe, she removed 40 milliliters of serous fluid.

"Pulse?"

Reid was already on it. "Seems stronger. Good call." He checked her blood pressure. "Up to 80 systolic."

Amy felt mixed emotions. Were they going to save this girl to a life of disability? Blind and who knew what else. She slipped the plastic catheter off the needle and left it in the pericardial sac, burying the hub in a wad of sterile 4x4's to absorb further drainage in route.

She grabbed the antiseptic, doused the abdominal wound, and placed a bulky dressing over it as well. Then a sickening thought hit her.

"Guys, did you inspect her back?"

Both paramedics shook their heads. "Didn't get to

it yet," answered Paulie. "Higher priorities."

With the victim's extremities splinted and her neck immobilized, the team gently rolled the girl to her side. The ripped shirt fell away from her body except in the areas where it had been ground into her skin. Amy gagged at the site of two more gaping incisions, also torn apart by the trauma of being dragged behind the truck, the frayed ends of their sutures barely visible above the macerated skin.

Amy jumped up and ran, fighting the bile rising into her throat. Tears welled up and cascaded down her cheeks. As she neared the helicopter, she bent over and began to puke. She couldn't take it. She emptied her stomach, but the retching continued. Why? What had this poor girl done to deserve this? She kneeled, sobbing. What? The question would go unanswered.

"Amy!"

She turned to see Reid and the others loading their patient onto the bird. Sanders had started the engine. She knew she had to join them, do her job, but she couldn't move. Reid came, pulled her up, and helped her inside. By habit, she strapped in and donned the headset, but the tears continued as Reid managed the patient.

"W-we're not going to save her, Reid. She's not going to survive the flight."

Reid looked at her, questioning.

"She's been har . . . harvested, Reid. Corneas, liver, kidneys. Who knows what else! All taken." She bowed her head. They'd even taken her hair, a woman's crown of glory.

Two

"Richard?"

He looked up from his seat to see a slim woman, mid-forties, with shoulder length, light brown hair, wearing a brown tweed, skirted suit, approaching him with her hand extended. He stood to greet her and towered head and shoulders above her. Not that she was diminutive. His muscular, six-foot-three frame dwarfed most people. He gently shook her hand.

"I'm Leah Zalls. Pleased to meet you."

"Richard Nichols. Thank you so much for seeing me."

"My office is toward the back, so let me give you an abbreviated tour on the way."

She led the young man through the security door of the lobby, past a double wide, open stairway to the second floor, and into a main hallway that led to a large cubicle space. "Upstairs we have product presentation and meeting rooms. This is our marketing department."

As they passed through, several female heads popped up over and around cubicle walls. He heard whispers throughout the area.

They started to turn a corner when a young woman with sandy blond hair, carrying an armful of products, ran into him. Literally. Spilling her boxes to the floor.

"I-I'm sorry. Here, let me get those for you." Richard almost bumped heads with her as they both bent over to retrieve her items. He grabbed two-thirds of the boxes before she could claim them and stood up.

As she stood, she first stared straight ahead, into his chest, and then made a slow arc upward to see his face.

"Thanks. I, uh, wow. Um, thanks." She smiled.

"Richard, this is Stacey, one of our product managers."

He smiled back. "Nice to meet you. Where can I put these?"

"Um. Yeah. How about right over here?" She led the way to her cubicle and placed her load onto her desk. He added the rest of her packages and stood there, filling the entrance to her space.

"Right. Thanks, again. Nice to meet you, too."

"This way, Richard," Leah said, regaining control.

Richard backed out of the cubicle, smiling the whole time, and turned to follow the human resource director. Behind him, he could hear the whispers pick up.

"OMG. What a hunk!"

"Stacey, did you do that on purpose?"

"Whoa, he could be the Thor of *my* dreams."

Richard blushed at the last comment. He would have to have a face-to-face with his old buddy-in-arms, Clive. Sometimes, battlefield stories were meant to die on the front lines.

Leah walked into a corner office, its floor-to-ceiling windows partially covered with snow outside. A midwinter storm covering northern Illinois and southeastern Wisconsin had unloaded close to a foot of the frozen fluff over the previous two days. Yet, the chill did not penetrate the room. She offered him a chair and walked behind her desk to sit down.

"Well, my cousin thinks quite highly of you."

"I think Clive told you more than he should have." He didn't know whether to smile or not.

She laughed. "Oh, don't get mad at him. I have a unique way of getting him to talk. And plying him with liquor always helps when he won't."

Richard returned the laugh. "That's my buddy." He fidgeted in the chair.

"Since that's already out in the open, can I ask how you got the nickname, Thor?"

Richard sighed. So much for leaving that behind, he thought. "We were on patrol near a little town in southeast Afghanistan when our dog pointed on a possible IED on the trail. I saw where the dirt had been disturbed, where a bomb might have been placed, and happened to see an old hammer lying at the base of a nearby mud wall. As a lark, I picked it up, threw it at the IED, hit it, and blew the thing. Funny thing was the blast threw the hammer back toward me and I actually caught it before it nearly hit me in the face. It was like catching a major league fastball without a glove. My hand hurt for a week. Two days later, back at base, the guys presented me with a mock 'hammer of Thor,' and that became my call sign."

"Well, Richard, please don't take this the wrong way, but with a physique like yours, it's a fitting nickname. And that brings me back to business. I have to say, I'm quite impressed with your résumé, and we need someone with your marketing experience, but how do you see yourself fitting in here?"

Richard knew this question would be coming, just not so quickly, and he had struggled to come up with an answer. How could he fit in here?

"I understood that the position called for experience in social media."

"True. But, you will be called on to present our products to potential buyers like Walmart and Target as well. Someone like Stacey out there is a natural for us. She's one of our shining stars. How does Thor move from the mighty hammer to selling make-up brushes? We produce cosmetic and bath accessories, not tools or car parts."

And that was the crux of his problem. As much as he needed a job, and as few jobs as there were to be had, could he work with something so totally foreign to him? He knew he'd gotten this far only because Leah was Clive's cousin. It would end here.

"I can work with anything, Leah, but you're correct about perceptions. And that is the name of the game in marketing. I could do an excellent job for you on the social media and web presence aspects of your marketing, but I doubt I could be very convincing in personal presentations. If the job entails both, then I'm probably not the right guy for you. I realize I'm going against job interview 101 by not selling myself to you, but I'm not going to fake it just to get a job. There has to be a good fit for both sides. I thank you for your time."

He started to rise.

"Just a minute, Richard."

He settled back into his seat.

"I thank you for your honesty. And you're right. But I asked you here not because I thought you might be a good fit in our business. I never expected to offer a job marketing make-up accessories to a guy named Thor."

Richard was puzzled. Why would she waste his

time and hers?

"You probably know this. A venture capital group recently bought our company, and it has its fingers in many pies. I appreciate your service to our country and for watching Clive's back over there. I made some calls on your behalf. Here's a position I think you would be well suited for, and they're interested in you. It's in St. Louis. I don't know if that's a problem for a die-hard Brewers and Packers fan, but . . ."

He grinned. "I've lived in foreign territory for the past two years. I think I can handle the Cardinals fans. And anyone can handle a Rams fan for what that team's worth." He took the sheet of paper she held out to him. "Thank you. I didn't expect this."

As he took it, she added, "There is one other catch."

Three

❦❖❖❦

Jusuf. In the past three months, he'd become known as Jusuf, but his real name eluded him. As had most events prior to three months ago.

Yet, after weeks of frustration, he no longer felt disheartened. He'd made progress. Three months ago, he walked dragging his left leg. Now, his motor coordination had improved to the point he could jump rope, walk a wooden beam, and more importantly, chop the firewood they needed to warm the cabin. Two months ago, he still fumbled with dinnerware. Now, he could spin a fork in his fingers, not to mention that he actually knew the names of each utensil he used. Somewhere from the recess of his mind, he recalled how to set a table properly, a task he taught Danijela, while feeling surprised that she didn't already know how.

Danijela. He remembered his first night waking up in her cabin, with her holding a kitchen knife for protection. She had looked awful that day. 'Run hard and put away wet' was a phrase that came into his head, even though he didn't remember what that meant. The meaning would come to him at some point.

"Where am I?" he had asked.

"Here. This place," she had answered.

"Where is this place?"

"Is here." She had looked around the room and shrugged. "Ibrahim's home. He rescue me. Bring me here. Protect me. Good man."

"Where is Ibrahim? Can I talk to him?"

"Dead now." He saw the tears form in her eyes.

Danijela Durakovic. Ibrahim Jancic. Jancic. Jancic. The name kept tumbling through his brain. It seemed so familiar, yet not.

At the age of sixteen, Danijela had been promised a job as a nanny here in America. A place called Wildwood. Part of some bigger city. An American education was to be part of the package. Her best friend, Tatjana, had been offered the same opportunity. Together with a dozen other girls from surrounding villages near Tuzla, in Bosnia, they traveled to the port city of Dubrovnik, Croatia. She recalled the beautiful cruise ships at dock and imagined them taking her group to America. Instead, a battered launch with a smelly, leaking diesel engine took them to a rusty cargo ship where they joined two dozen other girls in a stinky hold outfitted with crude bunks and smelling of vomit. After two seasick weeks of contributing to the detritus in that hold, they'd been herded up top and, in smaller groups, pushed onto four old, sportfishing boats in the middle of the night and brought ashore somewhere near a city called Houston.

That was when the warning flags of concern began flapping in her head. She knew they were supposed to pass through Customs, to have work Visas and the papers needed to grant them entry into America. She was given no such documents. Instead, their passports had been confiscated, and she, Tatjana, and four other girls were hustled to a windowless white van. No food. One bottle of water to share. One lone bathroom break, at something called a 'rest stop,' while it was still dark.

They were allowed out of the van the next night, when each girl was turned over to her prospective "employer." She had been allowed to talk with Tatjana only once since, and that conversation had not gone well. Tatjana had been scared to talk, even in their native dialect, which Danijela did not believe her "employer" could understand.

Beyond that, Danijela refused to tell Jusuf anything more. Only that Ibrahim had rescued her from a life in hell, and that he'd gone to get Tatjana three weeks earlier. He had contacted her regularly until a week earlier. He never returned and she'd heard nothing more from him.

Jusuf emerged from the shower and stood in front of the small bathroom mirror, his towel wrapped around his waist. He took time to brush out his now shoulder length hair and to comb his full beard. Somewhere in his mental universe, his mind flirted with a memory of having looked like that once before. He certainly hadn't looked that way when Danijela fished him from the river and dragged him to the cabin. Danijela encouraged him, told him he looked more like the men of her village now. He supposed it made him look more like Ibrahim.

He walked to the bedroom that had been Ibrahim's and dressed. The blue jeans and flannel shirt he wore most days were nowhere to be found. He had wood to split and stack, so he needed those clothes. He searched the room only to confirm what he had begun to deduce, that Danijela had collected them to take to the laundromat. He started to leave the room in only his towel, but stopped. Once before he had approached her like that only to watch her begin to cower and shake. He donned the items he had found in the closet, a pair of chinos, as Danijela had called them, and a button-down oxford dress shirt. He slipped on some shoes that he'd learned were conveniently called 'slip-ons,' or loafers, and walked to the main room.

Danijela was sitting at the table and stood as he entered the room.

"Wow, you look beautiful." Her smile brightened the room. Jusuf stood there, stunned. Her black hair had been brushed to a luster he'd not seen on her and curled to hang loosely about her shoulders. Her cheeks were colored and black stuff coated her eyelashes. She wore a sleek knitted dress that accentuated curves he'd only assumed she had before now. Her dressy heels brought her to within three inches of his six foot, two-inch frame. She truly was beautiful.

He looked at her, questioning, and pointed first to her and then to his cheek. "Make-up?"

She nodded. "Yes. *Ruž*, in Bosnia." She spelled it. "Sound same in English, but spelled r-o-u-g-e. Also call blush."

He pointed to her eyes.

"*Maskara*. Sound same in both language. Spell different."

He nodded and watched her approach him. "So, what is the occasion?"

"We go out. Maybe dinner later."

"Umm." His confidence waned. "I, uh, I don't know if—"

"Is time. You must . . . how you say? Move along? No, not right. Anyway, is time you see more than this

19

cabin. Maybe help you with memory."

"But the cost? These clothes? Money for dinner? How?"

Her eyes fell to the floor. "I, I went back to . . . um, where I was before. I collect my things and some money."

"Danijela!"

"Is okay. I watch close. House empty. Turn off security. When return, they know I was there, but have no way to follow. Is safe."

"But what if they call the police?"

"They not do that. Get them more trouble than me."

Jusuf pondered that statement. Another clue? Even though she wouldn't talk about where she'd lived or what she'd been through before Ibrahim's rescue, comments here and there began to add up. Adding in the dressy clothes and the metamorphosis with just light make-up, Jusuf's brain recalled enough to form a picture of what she'd been forced to do. And it wasn't caring for children.

She grabbed his arm. "Come. We go out."

Jusuf pulled back in surprise. In three months of living under the same roof, they'd never touched. If he came too close, she'd pull back. If he reached across the table at a meal, she avoided his hand. There hadn't been so much as a brushing of shoulders or the graze of a hand. Yet, now she took his arm.

"Danijela?" He looked at her, puzzled.

"What?"

He put his hand on top of hers, and she didn't flinch.

"Okay, so I decide today that you good man, too. A

20

gentleman you have been. And, well, in way you save me, too. Like Ibrahim, but different way."

He waited for her to continue. She tugged at him to move. He planted his feet.

"Okay, so helping you, help me, too. Make me realize I am good person, not trash. Help me learn English, too." She held her chin up high and with a perfect British inflection said, "The rain in Spain falls mainly on the plain." She looked him square in the eye and said, "See?"

He didn't get it, and she started laughing. She playfully poked him on the shoulder. "From movie. 'My Fair Lady.' Watch it on TV many time. Dream I could become fine lady, too. Hey, maybe we get TV. That could be good way to get memory back."

The mention of the movie brought flashes, images, into his consciousness. "Rex Harrison and Audrey Hepburn. The story of a snobby professor and a flower girl."

Her eyes widened. "Hey, it work. Definite get TV." She pulled his arm again. "C'mon. Days a'wastin' pardner." She laughed, and with a Texas drawl at that.

The day started with shopping. A place called 'Home Depot' for hardware to make repairs on the cabin. Groceries at a store where the selection of foods overwhelmed Jusuf. He kept grabbing things from the shelves, and she kept taking them out of the cart and placing them back on their respective shelves.

"I get some money, not fortune," she told him more than once.

As she replaced the tenth item, she said, "You act like child."

He laughed and replied, "I guess I am. After all, it is the biggest grocery store I remember ever being in."

The cold weather allowed them to keep their groceries in the car while they enjoyed dinner at a chain steakhouse where Jusuf quickly relearned the parts of a cow, as related to steak, the pleasure of beer, and slang that he overheard in other conversations. He found he was a quick study. Rarely did he have to see or hear something twice. All the while, Danijela watched him, smiling and helping where she could.

And he watched her watching him. There was an obvious age difference between the two, yet he somehow believed that would make no difference should their relationship deepen. She was now twenty-two, and he was, well, older. Not a lot older he didn't think. He couldn't remember.

He finished his second dark, draught beer as the evening news came on the televisions over the bar. He caught glimpses of the video and overheard snatches of commentary. Comments about a murder in a farm field to the north and hunting a killer sent images spinning through his head. He couldn't stop them, or isolate any one impression long enough to study it. Yet, that, too, seemed familiar.

He glanced at Danijela to find her face filled with anguish, her skin pale, and tears forming in her eyes. Her gaze seemed riveted on the nearest TV.

"What's wrong?" he asked. "*Što je krivo*?" To use the phrase he'd heard her ask so many times.

With tears streaming down her cheeks, she could only point to the TV, to an artist's re-creation of a face, and whisper, "Tatjana."

Four

"As I told you, you're pushing things too fast, Amy."

Amy sat on the plush, light red couch with one leg folded under her, her hands folded in her lap. She looked across the room to Doctor Lange, watching the 40-year-old, strawberry blonde psychologist watching her. Amy became self-conscious about her body language. She was resisting, but she didn't want her body showing it. Yet, the more she tried to avoid that body language, the more resistant she appeared.

"Relax, Amy. I'm not the enemy here."

"Doctor Lange . . ."

There was a pause as the psychologist waited for her to continue. "Amy, please, as I've said before, call me Amanda. Go on."

Amy fought that, too. During her three years in nursing school, they drilled it into them that doctors were called "Doctor," whether M.D., D.O., or Ph.D. In her six years since, that continued to be the rule, broken only on rare occasion and never in a clinical setting.

"It's just that I've always been taught to get back on the horse after it throws you."

"That has some truth to it, but you don't climb right back on if you've broken a leg or arm in the fall. PTSD is like that. The mental trauma breaks something, and that has to heal enough to let you get back on."

She paused and sat there watching Amy.

"Are you still having the nightmares?"

A tear formed at the corner of her eye, and her gaze

fell toward the floor. She nodded. Every night, the helicopter suddenly drops from the sky and hits the water. Terror ensues at the sense of water starting to fill her lungs. She wakes up in the hyperbaric chamber, being attacked by a faceless killer. Except that her attacker had had a face and a name. And that face had practically exploded in the growing vacuum of the chamber where she'd trapped him.

"Every night?"

Again, she nodded.

"Flashbacks?"

Amy sighed and nodded. "Almost every time I board the helicopter," she whispered. "Sometimes when I see the patient."

"Do you think that's healthy? To make yourself revisit the event like that?"

"I thought it would get better. That each flight would help make it go away."

"Have they?"

"Maybe. A little. Until our call two days ago. The brutality that poor girl went through. It . . . it was too close to . . ."

Again, Amanda waited to see if Amy would finish.

"See? You're trying to get back on the horse while you're still broken." Amanda picked up a paper from Amy's folder. "I got a letter from your company. It asks me to determine your fitness for duty. How do you think I should answer this?"

"I-I can't just sit at home. I'll really go crazy then, with nothing to distract me, it will haunt me all day as well as night."

Amanda smiled and sat back in her chair. "Amy, I

think I understand you better than you give me credit for. I believe I've worked out something for you. They're going to put you in the training division for the next few months and let you attend my weekly group session."

"Group session! Oh, please." Amy groaned at the thought of baring all to a bunch of strangers. Maybe to a small group of close friends over a few bottles of wine, but to strangers? She couldn't imagine sitting in a circle, starting off with "Hi, I'm Amy and I have PTSD. I was almost killed, twice, by the 'L.A. Rapist'."

"Yes, group sessions." Amanda signed off on the paper and placed it into Amy's folder, which she closed.

Amy had learned that this was Amanda's signal that the session was over. She eased the leg she'd been sitting on back to the floor, where her shoes awaited.

"If you want to get released back to flying, you'll need to work with me. In the meantime, use your innumerable skills and experience to teach the paramedics and others. I hope you'll find that therapeutic as well."

She paused again. Amy decided that psychologists would never fare well in radio broadcasting. They were too content with dead air.

"Questions?"

"No, ma'am," replied Amy.

Amanda handed her a sheet of paper. "Here's the information and schedule for your sessions. I think you'll find the group diverse and interesting."

Amy raised her eyebrows and rolled her eyes.

"Honest. See you next Tuesday. Please don't be late. In consideration of everyone there, I really do try to start on time."

Amy sighed. "Okay. See you then."

What choice did she have? She wanted back in the air. Flying was in her blood. But, even that had soured, a fact she wouldn't share with Amanda because it would reflect yet another symptom of PTSD, a loss of interest in once-positive activities. Still, she hadn't taken up the Cessna 172 Skyhawk she shared with her dad since the memorial service for Lynch. *Oh Lynch*, she thought. She still mourned his loss. And she still blamed herself. After all, if she hadn't spotted the L.A. Rapist's motor home while flying and alerted Lynch to its location, he never would have gone there without backup, and he'd still be here, in her life.

As she climbed into her car, her cell rang with a familiar distinct ring tone—"I Like to Move It, Move It." Macy. Her timing was impeccably wrong, as always.

"Hi, Macy."

"Hey, girlfriend. Didja get cleared to fly?"

"No." Amy didn't want to delve into it but knew resistance was futile. On the good side, Macy was perfectly discreet. Whatever Amy told her would go no further without Amy's express, written, and notarized permission. She related her session to Macy.

"Aw, Amy. It won't be so bad. Heck, I've done it before, the group session thing. I met Tyrone there."

"Macy, you haven't dated Tyrone for two years. As I recall, you threatened to take out a restraining order against him."

"Nope, that was me just bein' dramatic. It was fun while it lasted." She paused. "Anyway, I'm not talkin' about goin' there to find a man. Believe it or not, those sessions helped."

Amy laughed. "Helped what, Macy? You still have your moments."

"True, but they's not as dramatic, and I'm not nearly as narcissistic." She laughed.

Macy had never been narcissistic. She claimed depression as her mental health issue of choice, although Amy had never seen any signs of depression in the woman for as long as she'd known her.

"I'm changing the subject," continued Macy. "I called for a reason. My cousin, Marquis, called."

Amy had to think. Macy compared life in general to that of her extended family. As a group, Amy was convinced Macy's family covered every possible fetish, philia, occupation, and general foible anyone could imagine. Which one was Marquis?

"You know, my cousin at the M.E.'s office," Macy said. "You were right, girlfriend. The gross showed corneas, liver, and both kidneys surgically removed no more than an hour prior to the EMS call."

Amy felt nauseated. She noted no pleasure at being proven right.

"Well, the Major Case Squad has it now. I need to distance myself from the case as much as I can."

"Sounds like shrink-talk, not my girl. What? You used to be someone who was gung-ho about helping the police, finding the perp. Like Nancy Drew's secret granddaughter, 'cause, ol' Nancy'd be an octogenarian by now."

Amy sobbed. "Macy, I-I . . ." Her tie to the police, her motivation to help, was gone, either blown up in a motor home explosion or hidden in the river waiting for the spring thaw to let his body loose.

"Oh, girl, I am so sorry. Those group sessions never helped my habit of putting my foot in my mouth and taking a hike. I am so sorry, Amy! Please, let me help somehow. I'll meet you at home."

"Macy, not now. Please. I just need some time alone. Please." Amy sniffled.

"Okay, you call if you need me. I can be there in fifteen minutes. You know that, right? I'm here for you."

"Thanks, Macy. I-I promise I'll call if I need you."

She debated heading straight back to Amanda's office and pleading for another hour of her time, but at the moment, that might lead to an involuntary commitment in some cuckoo's nest. An image of Jack Nicholson as a deranged psych patient floated in her consciousness.

She came to the realization that she was dealing with two issues. She needed closure about Lynch before she could really deal with her own emotional trauma. Too much of her clung to the unreasonable hope that he'd somehow survived the ordeal and was waiting to be found. Yet, while boating down the Big River looking for Lynch's body might help bring closure, the thought of doing so in midwinter, with another cold front barreling into the area that night, held no appeal and could only lengthen that 96-hour hold in the loony bin.

That realization, however, settled one thing in the turmoil of her current emotional state. She did, indeed, need help, group session or otherwise. That, in turn, brought her into agreement with Amanda. She had returned to full duty too soon. She resolved herself to be the best trainer MedAir had ever seen.

She started the car and drove home. As she neared home, she found herself daydreaming of turning the corner and seeing Lynch's car in the drive. She felt disappointment in pulling into the empty driveway of her home. As she turned off her car, her cell rang again, this time with the theme to *Top Gun*. Reid.

"Hey, Reid."

"Amy, just got the word that you're heading to the training ranks for a while. We're gonna miss you."

"Likewise."

"You doin' okay? Anything we can do? You had me worried the other night."

"Thanks, but, uh, I'm hanging in there."

"Look, I hope I'm not stirring anything up here, but I thought you'd want to know."

Amy felt her gut tighten. Maybe she didn't want to know whatever he was about to spring on her.

"What?"

"Jefferson County EMS just called for support from MedAir-23. A young woman found in a car on the Walmart parking lot in DeSoto. Harvested like our Jane Doe."

Five

Richard stood up as the owner of Darko Imports, Darko Komarčić, approached the small reception area at one end of the large warehouse in the Dutchtown neighborhood of St. Louis. The man appeared to be in his early fifties, but still held a commanding presence with a full head of ink black hair and mustache, and a muscular, six-foot frame. The man's face and eyes projected a cold, calculating demeanor, but like an actor on cue, his smile emerged and eyes brightened as he neared. Richard had met men like this in Afghanistan. He hadn't trusted a single one, and yet, this was the man he'd been referred to. Richard knew to be wary.

Komarčić held out his hand in greeting, and Richard returned the gesture, meeting force with equal force in the grip of their handshake.

"Mr. Komarčić, thank you for seeing me."

"Please. Call me Darko. We are like family here. And is I, perhaps, who should thank you for coming. I have trouble finding someone of your experience to fill need in my growing company. Maybe is just my perception, but it seem many hold prejudice against those of us from Eastern Europe. Fear, perhaps. I value someone with experience outside these borders. It gives you, how shall I say it, a different appreciation, a wider perspective, than these young people fresh from university. Come, let me show you around."

At their first stop, Darko showed Richard stacks of finely hand-woven, wool Persian carpets.

"Turkmenistani, but very nice. Some Turkish and Georgian here also."

"May I?" Richard examined the top rug on the pile. "Shorn wool, not dead wool from a butchered animal. Looks like, what, 200 to 250 knots per inch. Very nice indeed. And asymmetrical Persian knots, not Turkish. I would guess your source might tell you these are from the Caucasus or Turkmenistan, but I suspect they're Iranian. Khorasan province is a leading carpet producer and lies next to Turkmenistan."

Richard caught Darko scrutinizing him.

"No, no. They are Turkmenistani. I have been personally to source."

Richard nodded in approval.

"You have talents not mention in résumé, I see."

Richard smiled. "Not many, but I did learn something about Persian rugs during my two years in Afghanistan. Our unit interpreter was from a family of weavers."

"Ah. Please be assured these are legal. Since October 2010, U.S. law make import of Iranian carpets illegal. We are fully compliant."

Richard watched the man's eyes as he said this. He was lying, but then Richard knew this already. Mashhad, Iran, was known for a specific type of carpet, the type lying before them.

"Really? Rugs? Illegal? That seems so, um, minor. I guess that's something else I learned from my weaver friend. Sometimes the political moves of one government don't actually hurt the target government, just the little guy, the weaver busting his butt to make a living and being an exquisite craftsman in the process.

Don't know that I'll ever understand that."

Richard sensed that he was again being studied.

"Come, since you have appreciation of fine rug, let me show you something truly special."

Darko led Richard to a climate-controlled chamber behind an access-controlled door. Darko used an electronic key card to unlock it. Inside were antiques and three more Persian carpets, which Darko pointed out. "Feel free to examine, but please be careful."

Richard walked to the carpets, each lying on a raised platform, one next to the other with nothing on top of them. He unfolded the corner of the nearest carpet and took the material in his hand.

"Wow! Farsh, in silk! These must be worth a fortune." The "farsh" group of carpets simply meant they measured larger than six by four feet.

Darko smiled. "You know rugs. These are Iranian, from Kashan. I have held these since before embargo on Iranian carpets. The embargo only increase their worth."

"May I ask?"

Darko beamed. "Over quarter of a million dollars each. Only special customer will appreciate and afford this."

"This one is beautiful."

"As are others. If your marketing efforts work to sell even one of these beauties for me, your worth here will double. I am generous man to those who do well in their jobs."

The tour continued, revealing to Richard two things. The breadth of imports—from fine antiques and Persian carpets to Moldavian textiles and Georgian food products—offered a diversity that was no doubt profitable. It would also be a marketing challenge, trying to cater to multiple markets and economic strata. The second revelation was that the internal footprint of the warehouse did not match the dimensions of the exterior of the building. He saw nothing to account for the discrepancy and no obvious access to the additional part of the building. However, he had an inkling of an idea as to what might be stored in such a hidden area. If Darko had no qualms about importing contraband such as the Iranian carpets, what other illegal goods did he import?

Richard might look the "other way" for some things. Drugs were not among those things. Zero tolerance. He would surely become a whistleblower should he discover imports from Afghanistan's poppy fields or the like. He might even bust some heads personally for that.

"Come. Let us discuss the job."

Darko led them to the far end of the building and into a hallway leading to a smaller adjacent building. Here Richard saw one thing that surprised him— muscle. A man about his own size, nicely dressed, sat near the main entrance. The man stood as they approached, but Darko waved him off with the subtle shake of his head. The man turned to sit back down, but not before Richard saw the bulge of a concealed handgun under the man's left armpit.

"That is Risto, head of my security. He will run background check on you, should we come to agreement."

"No problem there," answered Richard. "I have

nothing to hide."

Richard followed Darko into a plush office suite after first walking between two rows of cubicles housing a dozen raven-haired beauties, some speaking perfect English, others in a language that sounded East European. One he recognized as speaking Italian, and he suspected all were multilingual. In addition, not one could be described as plain, and none appeared to be American by birth. He saw no jeans or casual clothing, and of the faces he saw more fully, each was perfectly made-up. They could step from the office to nightclub at the blink of an eye.

He confirmed Darko's appreciation of the finer things as soon as he stepped into the man's private office. Fine woods paneled the walls. Antiques, likely worth tens of thousands of dollars, lined the walls. Archeological artifacts sat on shelves and inside glass cases. The man's solid oak desk appeared worthy of European royalty. To top it off, a large silk Persian rug covered the floor under a formal sitting area.

Richard glanced around the perimeter of the room. More than one security camera covered the area. The large plate glass window overlooking a private garden appeared to be reinforced, perhaps even bulletproof. An electronic panel on the wall next to the door revealed other hidden levels of security. Considering the million dollar contents of the office, Richard would not have been surprised if lasers, pressure plates, infrared sensing or a combination of all guarded the room.

"Please have seat," Darko said, pointing out the chairs in the sitting area. His chair in the group was obvious. Richard slipped off his shoes before walking onto the carpet and sat opposite that one.

Darko returned from his desk and laughed as he spied the shoes. "Thank you for consideration, but for future, is not necessary. I have expert to care for all my carpets." He sat down in his chair and opened a folder on his lap. He perused what Richard recognized as his résumé.

"So, magna cum laude from University of Wisconsin in business administration and marketing. Internship at Proctor and Gamble—an excellent opportunity, I hear. A year at S.C. Johnson Company following graduation and then you join military. May I ask why?"

"My buddies and I felt it was the patriotic thing to do. One of my best friends has a family legacy of service. I guess that played a lot into it also."

"I see you were Ranger and Special Forces. That include special talents you not mention here?"

Richard shrugged and smiled. "I guess so. Other than knowing rugs, I can talk wine with the best of them. The other talents, as you call them, don't have much use in civilian life."

"Perhaps."

Richard found that to be a curious reply.

"Any problems with law, here or overseas?"

"Other than an hour in jail over getting too rowdy when we graduated college, no, sir, as Risto will no doubt discover." He smiled at Darko.

"Okay. So, tell me how you think you help my business."

Richard spent the next 20 minutes describing what he saw as the marketing challenges of the company, as well as the use of the internet and social media to promote their products. He talked of featured ads on search engines and Facebook, maximizing search meta-tags for the same, direct internet marketing, email, and more.

Darko waved his hand to stop Richard.

"I not know these things, meta-tags, SEO."

"That's okay, because I do and I know how to get the biggest bang for your buck in those areas."

Darko smiled at that.

"The biggest problem I see is finding the market and advertising your highest end products, like those silk rugs. The very rich usually have people who scout out and buy such items on their behalf. That group tends to be very protective, not just of their clients, but of their own privacy as well. Plus, I'm sure you are not alone in offering such items. We need to identify the competition and how they market their wares, if we wish to make inroads into their clientele. It may take some very special advertising. Give me a month to research that issue and maybe another to present a marketing plan and budget."

Darko sat back in his chair, steepled his fingers, and smiled at Richard. After a moment, he leaned forward and pointed to his head. "Yes, yes. I know you the one for this job as soon I read this." He held up the résumé. "So, how much?"

"Well, like I said, I should be able to give a preliminary marketing budget in two months."

"No, not that." He pointed at Richard. "How much do you ask for? We give full benefits, plus some." His smile became mischievous then. Richard wasn't sure what to make of that.

Richard had prepared a salary range to ask for that many might find too low. Now, he felt emboldened to ask for the top of that range. He gave Darko a figure.

The man laughed. "No, no, no. Too low." He countered with a figure ten percent higher. "You have car?"

Richard nodded, but he didn't want to admit that he drove a 1996 Accord with over 200,000 miles on it.

"What kind?"

Richard gulped and told the man.

Darko laughed again. "Also, give you lease car. New Lexus of your choice. If your effort increase sales by ten percent in one year, car become yours. Also, fifteen thousand for moving expense." He knitted his brow. "Anything I miss?"

Richard didn't know what to say. "I-I don't think so. Thank you, sir."

"Hey, none that 'sir' stuff. You be family now, too. When can you start?"

Richard gave that a quick mental rundown. "Next week. Tuesday."

Darko thought for a moment. "Tell you what, make it two week. Start first Monday of March. Easier for accountant."

"Not a problem for me."

Darko stood and clapped his hands together. "Good. We drink toast. Name your poison."

Richard hadn't expected this. He was cautious about drinking. Not that he couldn't hold his liquor. He'd seen a buddy let slip on some intel after a drink too many and almost end up with a court martial. He reminded himself to be wary of Darko Komarčić, never to ease up on his guard. Still.

"Whatever you like would be fine with me, I'm sure."

Darko went to an adjacent bar and pulled up a bottle of Johnny Walker Blue Label. He replaced it with a bottle of single-malt Laphroaig. "No, no. Is special occasion. Ahhhh . . ."

He retrieved a bottle Richard had never heard of before. "Badel Stara Šljivovica, the traditional plum brandy from where I grow up is world renowned." He opened the bottle and poured two snifters. "You say you know wine, but probably not wine from Eastern Europe. Now you get to know this."

Richard took the glass and sniffed the heady bouquet. Darko had already taken a sip, so Richard followed suit. The brandy was much stronger than he'd prepared himself for, but he suppressed the cough triggered by the sweet burn in his throat.

"Hmm. This is good, Darko."

The businessman held out his glass. "To business and profit."

Richard held up his glass as well, avoiding direct contact between the fragile antique crystal glasses. They savored the brandy while Darko told Richard a little about himself—where he grew up, how he came to America, and how the business started. Richard realized this was all for his benefit, material to use in marketing. Moreover, sanitized for the high-end client.

Richard and Darko shook hands as the man opened the door for his new employee. Risto was already standing there.

"He will show you some things you need to know and get your security credentials. I look forward to your return."

"Thank you. I know I can do a great job for you."

Richard glanced back at the door as they approached the far end of the cubicles, to find Darko closing his door while all of the ladies were standing and watching him. He suddenly felt as if he'd been walking a runway and actually felt a bit disquieted that several were smiling quite seductively at him. He didn't know what to make of that, but then, he recalled the stir he'd created at his previous "interview." He'd never worked anywhere with so many women. However, if these were his co-workers, he could get used to it.

As Darko closed the door and walked back to his desk, a side door opened.

"So, you hire him."

Darko looked up at his wife. Although ten years older than any of the women working outside the door, she remained as beautiful. Her shiny ebony hair fell in waves below her shoulder. Her high cheekbones and almond-shaped eyes dominated her Slavic face. Her curves were natural and alluring. After all, she had captured Darko's heart, and he could have had any one of hundreds of beautiful women.

"Yes, Sonja, *moj dragi*. He will do job and do it well."

"And you trust?"

"*Mi ćemo uvesti vrijeme, najdraži neki.*" We will see in time, dearest one.

"He is good looking. That could be problem, with girls."

Darko smiled and approached his wife, stroking her cheek gently.

"But not with you, I hope." He stopped, kissed her on the lips, and returned to his side of the desk. "Girls could prove to be asset with him, too. Right now, I use money to buy loyalty. If not enough, one of girls might be insurance."

"And if he learn too much?"

Darko shrugged. "Same girl become blackmail. Has work before." He paused and glanced toward the door where Richard had exited. "On other thought, let us not to wait. Tell girls there is bonus to girl who can seduce him and get goods on him."

"What kind bonus?"

"I am sure you can think of something."

"We receive another call from our friend in Wildwood. Danijela return to the house."

"Yes, *moj dragi*. I know of this. She took clothes, jewelry, and all cash she find."

That Danijela had slipped by them so easily bothered Darko. He had always counted on finding her to lead him to Ibrahim, the *murtid.*

Sonja nodded. "And we still not find Ibrahim."

Darko thought about that for a moment. He had already ordered the destruction of Ibrahim's apartment. St Louis held the largest Bosnian community outside of Bosnia, and he had put the word out there, as well as in surrounding immigrant communities, that anyone seeing Ibrahim should call Risto. A simple spotting could garner a reward, but a tip leading to his capture would be worth thousands to the informant. Yes, the word was out, and the heat was on. Ibrahim had nowhere else to go, no friends to rely upon. He couldn't hide forever.

"Time we double the price on both heads."

Six

❧ ✦ ✦ ❧

Amy spent her first day in the training division of MedAir, pouring over their current manuals. Trauma resuscitation, ACLS, procedural skills, ATLS, and more. Most were severely outdated. She knew that most of their providers kept up with changes. Those changes just had never made it into the paperwork. Yet, an accreditation audit would start with the manuals, and likely end with the manuals, given their current state.

She got up and walked down the hall to the COO's office. She knocked on the doorpost.

"Hey, Craig, about these manuals . . ."

He frowned and held up his hand, palm to stop her.

"I know. Dreadful, aren't they? Did you notice the revision dates?"

Amy shook her head.

"Bottom left corner of the first page of each section. I think most of them are at least five to eight years old."

This could keep her busy 24/7, and it hit her that maybe Amanda did understand her better then she believed. And had been in cahoots with Craig before making her recommendation.

Amy shrugged and sighed, and returned to her workspace. She opened one manual and perused the revision dates—all in early 2K. She decided to prioritize the manuals by problem acuity and then by frequency encountered in the field. As she started her list of manuals, their topics, and their revision dates, she heard a knock at her door. This time, Craig had come to her.

"By the way, you did get the memo about tomorrow's EKG class, right?"

Her mouth dropped open as she shook her head. "Um, nooo. No memo here."

"Sorry. Look, no pressure. Just a refresher on EKG reading. You know, STEMIs, bundle branch blocks, non-STEMI infarcts, ischemia, A-V blocks. The usual stuff. You can do that in your sleep." He started to turn away, but stopped and looked back. "Oh. Nine a.m., in the classroom. Should be about 20 to 30 people. We'll have a sign-in sheet for you in the morning, and there's a PowerPoint presentation on the computer. That should be up-to-date at least." He turned and left.

Amy sank back into her chair. "In my sleep. Right," she muttered.

At nine a.m. the next morning, Amy was ready to go. Craig had been right, fortunately. The material she could recite in her sleep. She could take a quick glance at an EKG and know what she was looking at. Myocardial infarcts, both ST-elevation and not. Blockages of the electrical conduction system of the heart. All of it. Her dilemma had been one of how to teach the material. She'd never been a teacher before, so organizing her thoughts took some thinking. At least Craig had been right about the computer presentation being up-to-date. She just had to reorganize the slides to match her way of presenting the material and add some new things.

As she watched the paramedics and nurses filing

into the room and signing in, she realized something else. She'd been so preoccupied with this task that she did not experience her recurrent nightmare last night. She'd fallen asleep exhausted and had slept uninterrupted until her alarm urged her to wake. *Thank you, Amanda*, she thought.

An hour later, she began to wind down the course. She presented one last slide with an EKG revealing deeply negative T-waves in the precordial, or chest, leads, prolonged QT intervals, and U waves, an unusual finding on such tracings.

"Can anyone tell me what this tracing suggests?"

She saw numerous puzzled faces. One hand began to go up tentatively, but quickly fell back to the table. With no takers, she continued.

"I thought I'd throw in a couple of unusual EKG findings. This one, with . . ." She pointed out the diagnostic findings. ". . . highly suggests a subdural bleed in the head, possibly from a stroke or tumor, anything that could cause increased intracranial pressure. They don't really know why, but one hypothesis is that the increased pressure could cause a catecholamine storm, which would affect the heart this way. Of course, you still need to consider things like medications, ventricular flutter or fib, or torsade."

She waited for the positive murmuring to die down and felt good that she'd given them something new.

"Okay, one last one. Do you all know what hypospadias is?"

There were a couple of chuckles and several raised eyebrows. One of the nurses raised his hand.

"It's a minor birth defect where the urethra opens

on the bottom side of the penis instead of the tip."

"That's right. Now, can anyone tell me what EKG finding is suggestive of that defect?"

She noted a lot of furrowed brows and heads shaking. She waited, as Amanda waited on her. Finally, she said, "An inverted P-wave." When the groans, moans, eye rolling, and tongue wagging finally stopped, she added. "That's it. Have a great day."

The nurse sitting directly in front of her, looked at her and said, "You're bad!" as she stood and laughed, shaking her head.

Amy received several compliments on the way to her office. At her desk, she thought, *That was actually kinda fun.* Again, she realized that not once had her ordeal from months earlier intruded on her thoughts.

Craig stopped by right before lunch. "Hey, I hear that went well. Good job! What was that last diagnosis again?" He laughed and handed her two pieces of paper, stapled together. "Here's the list of upcoming training classes. I figured I'd better hand deliver this so I don't surprise you with one day's notice again."

"Thanks. And thanks for the positive feedback."

After a quiet lunch, Amy resumed work on the training manuals and got lost in time. She looked up at a knock at her door to find Craig there again. This time he simply pointed to his watch and raised his eyebrows.

Amy looked at the time on her computer screen and panicked. Two-thirty! Her first group session started at three. She shut down her computer, grabbed her purse, locked her office door and ran for her car. *Please, please. Let the traffic be light.*

Seven

❦ ◆ ◆ ❧

"Man, did my cousin score for you or what? This guy . . . what's his name? Darko? What kind of name is Darko? Sounds like something out of *Star Wars* or *Twilight*. So, he need any more employees?"

Richard sat in the driver's seat of the 20-foot U-Haul, resting both hands on the wheel, fighting the occasional wind gust as they rode south on Interstate 55 toward St. Louis. In the back sat all of his earthly possessions: a sofa bed that weighed as much as a Humvee; a water-stained coffee table, three upholstered chairs handed down by his parents; a king-sized bed set and mismatched bedroom furniture; three boxes of beat up kitchenware; boxes of books, DVDs, and CDs; a 40-inch HDTV; other assorted electronics; and his clothing. On the tow hitch behind the truck was his car.

Clive, looking like the starving artist he was, sat next to him, riding shotgun.

"I mean, you'll need graphic arts and stuff, right? You can throw some of that my way, can't you?"

"I can try. I don't know enough about this business yet to tell you anything. I just got the job. Remember? That's why you're helping me move. Remember?"

Richard glanced at his buddy, who sat there with his feet on the dash as he fiddled with his iPhone. He chuckled.

"I thought you didn't want a full-time job, the bondage to a desk somewhere producing crappy art that someone else told you to create."

"Yeah, well, the real world intervenes once again. My parents are riding me to move out of their basement, and I can only use the 'there are no jobs for veterans' excuse for so long. I've already started putting out my résumé and portfolio to find something."

Richard laughed. "I hope it's not the portfolio you showed me. That kind of front-line war coverage stuff went out of vogue somewhere about the time of the daguerreotype. I think that was the Civil War. Don't get me wrong, the sketches are amazing, but they have this thing called a camera nowadays. And Photoshop."

Clive waggled his head about as he said, "Ooooo, Thor made a funny." He sighed. "Go back to Valhalla, will you?" His phone chimed and began to vibrate. "I have a very professional portfolio." He checked the text on his phone. "Oh wow, you are NOT going to believe this." He began feverishly fingering a reply to the text.

"What?"

"Alright!" He pumped his fist in the air.

"Job interview?"

"Better. Redman, Capt. A, and Hassle are going to meet us in St. Louis. They're driving in tomorrow." He squirmed in his seat like attempting some touchdown dance. "Oh yeah, oh yeah. The boys will be on the prowl tomorrow."

Richard laughed. *Oh yeah*, he thought. A celebration with the old squad was just what the doctor ordered.

Three hours later, Richard pulled up to an old, brownstone-styled building less than a block to the

47

west of Lafayette Park in South St. Louis. No one walked the sidewalks, and only a few cars sat parked along the dead-end street in the early afternoon. The two-and-a-half-story home's brick was painted a muted, almost mustard yellow while the trim provided contrast in brick red. Lace curtains filled the tall, first floor windows while white shades covered the upper floor windows.

"What's this?" asked Clive.

"We're here," replied Richard.

Clive looked at Richard, then the building, and back at his friend. "You're kidding, right? Where's the clubhouse, the fitness center, the pool where the babes congregate in the hot, hot summer?"

"I wanted something quieter to start, more private. This place is just ten minutes from work. Plus, I don't know this city. I need time to scout it out, find the best place for me."

A wizened, gray-haired woman with a cane emerged from the front door and waved. Clive went pale when he saw her and simply pointed her way.

"Mrs. Bowles, the owner. She lives on the first floor. I'm renting the top two floors."

Clive looked sick. "Oh great. Not only do we have to move that monster sofa bed up those stairs, but you're, like, movin' in with your grandmother. What's gotten into you?" He furrowed his brow while scrutinizing his comrade. "Okay, I get it. You're doing that Boy Scout thing again, aren't you? Helpin' out little old ladies, retrieving kittens in trees, that stuff again."

Richard laughed. "Yeah, kinda. She could use the money, and I think she sees me as her private security.

She seems like a nice old gal. Widowed. Her husband was retired Army, and she's got some funny stories about places he was stationed."

"Yeah, I bet. Looks like a laugh a minute."

"Hey, be nice. I've only committed to three months. That should give me time to find something I like."

"Committed is about right," Clive murmured. He sighed. "Well, let's get this done."

Richard went to the front door, greeted Mrs. Bowles, and introduced Clive. Then, together they unhitched the car, and Richard parked it far enough behind them to leave room to work. Later, he would drive it around to a parking spot off the alley behind the house. Clive grabbed some tools and removed two doors from their hinges, leaving only the main front door, which they debated removing but left in place because of the cold.

Two hours later, Richard swept out the back of the truck while Clive replaced the doors he had removed. As Clive approached the truck, Richard tossed him his car keys. Thirty minutes later, the sky grew dark as they finally pulled into the alley behind the house after returning the truck. They collapsed on Richard's couch.

"Thanks, buddy. I owe you one," said Richard.

"Hell, you owe me more than one. I stopped counting years ago."

Richard chuckled and noticed a paper on the kitchenette's refrigerator. He stood and walked over to it, to find a note pinned to the door with a magnetic church key bottle opener. He smiled and opened the fridge. Inside was a case of cold Schlafly beer, in a variety of styles. He grabbed two bottles of pilsner, popped the caps, and walked back to the couch.

"Here you go. Compliments of the landlord."

Clive grabbed the bottle eagerly and took a long draught.

"You know, she does seem like a pretty nice lady." He took another sip and looked about the room. "And this place does have character. You said there's an upper floor, too?"

Richard nodded. "One big room, up those stairs." He pointed. "It'd make a great office and media room."

"Yeah, for someone staying longer than three months."

Richard grinned. "Right." As he arose to get two more beers, his cell phone rang. He glanced at the caller ID and took a deep breath. "Hey, grab another beer. I, uh, need to take this call, um, privately."

Eight

"Amy, girl, I am sooo glad you decided to join us. We haven't had a girls' night out in months, and Sammi's been itchin' to try this place." Macy practically pulled Amy from the back seat of Erica's car after they parked on Locust. Erica and Sammi rounded the front of the car and joined them on the sidewalk. The parking meter still showed fifteen minutes, more than enough time to avoid a ticket before parking became free.

"The Bridge has gotten rave reviews. Great atmosphere. Fabulous food in the small plate style. Over 200 beers and wines. This'll be fun," said Sammi.

Amy had agreed during a moment of weakness. Life had been a roller coaster over the previous 48 hours since a tumultuous group session. Amy's nightmare had returned and had worsened with the addition of images of the victims Amy had cared for. In addition, of course, there was work. More work than one person could possibly manage within the determined timeline.

Amy looked about at her friends—all nurses from the trauma center—and smiled. Maybe this would be good for her. Macy was right. It had been months.

The bright interior lights spilled through the tall glass windows and doors onto the pavement. The place appeared busy for midweek in winter, but some tables remained open. Behind the long oak bar sat an equally long line of taps for 40-plus beers and behind that, bar-to-ceiling oak shelves held hundreds of bottles of wine

51

and spirits. Wooden-backed barstools sat filled with patrons in front of the bar, while tables for four sat scattered across the room and above them on a loft that they could reach by a wide, open stairway to their left. An eclectic collection of chandeliers and track lights guaranteed no dark nights there.

Erica led them up to the loft where they found a table at the end nearest the stairs, by the rail overlooking the main floor. Amy glanced around to see couples laughing and talking, larger groups doing the same, and a group of guys cutting up at the back end of the loft. They appeared to have been there a while, but they were obviously having fun.

Sammi interrupted Amy's attention to the surroundings.

"Look at this menu. Should we get a charcuterie plank to share?"

"Wow, over 300 types of beer and wine," said Macy.

"That's more than I thought," added Sammi.

"I think I want to try the roasted pork and ruby grapefruit salad," replied Erica.

Only Amy sat quietly. "What do you want, Amy?" asked Macy, nudging her with her elbow. "They got all kinds of martinis. Get your fave."

Amy opened her menu and began to review it. *Why is this so hard?* She asked herself. She knew she needed to move on. Her relationship with Lynch had been rocky at best. Would it have improved? *Loosen up. Have some fun,* she told herself. She glanced at the beer list and quickly homed in on a local brew.

"I'm going to try the chocolate ale and the Pork

Bolognese pasta pot," replied Amy. "You know, I'm hungrier than I thought. Why don't we get one of the boards, like the cheddar crisps, a couple of salads, and a couple of pots, maybe the Bolognese and the mac and cheese, and share them all?"

The ladies uniformly agreed, decided on their order, and signaled the server. By the time the waitress returned, Amy had caught up on the happenings at the medical center and half a dozen absent friends.

"Whoa, did you guys hear what Sasquatch is doing?" Hassle took a deep gulp of Gouden Carolus Noel, a strong, dark Belgian ale, and leaned over the table. "He actually got a date to the Military Ball with Ashley Greene. You know, from the *Twilight* movies. He said if some leatherneck could get a date with Mila Kunis, he ought to be able to get a date with someone just as hot. He wrote her, she accepted. Can you believe that? Man!"

Richard sat back laughing. "Does she know he's nicknamed Sasquatch for a reason?" His thoughts drifted back to the women at Darko Imports. He finished off his Hop Head Red—an American Amber he'd first tasted in San Diego—and set it down on the table a bit harder than he'd planned. The resulting noise caused everyone seated on the loft to look their way. "Oops!"

Clive, Hassle, and Capt. A all laughed. Clive popped Richard on the shoulder. "He's got nothin' on our buddy Thor here. He was telling me he's about to be surrounded by beauties at his new job."

"Yeah, right," replied Capt. A. "Probably a bevy of overweight peasant women wearing long wool skirts, embroidered coats and scarves, with half their teeth missing. He just *wants* us to be jealous."

Richard shook his head, smiling. "You only wish. Next time you come back, I'll prove it to you."

"Hey, careful there Cap'n," added Clive. "If he's telling the truth and we miss out on some great dates 'cause of you, the 'A' won't stand for 'America' anymore."

"Hey, anybody heard from Snarky or Walts?" asked Richard, looking to change the subject. Hassle obliged him, and soon they were discussing the current status of other squad members. The talk drifted back to women, occasionally to the politics behind Afghanistan, and then onto sports or yet another old comrade-in-arms. Fifteen minutes later, Richard felt a bit dry.

"Anyone seen the waitress lately?"

The others all shook their heads and held up empty glasses. Richard gave a thumb up and stood, nearly knocking over his chair. He caught it before drawing attention to them yet again. "Everyone getting the same?" They all nodded.

Richard walked toward the stairway and noticed again the table of young women nearest the steps. All four of them followed his every step. He smiled and nodded at them, which made every one of them turn away. He could hear them whisper as he started down the steps.

As he reached the top of the steps, Capt. A's voice rang out behind him. "Hey, Thor, get some snacks, too."

Richard raised his hand in acknowledgment. At the

bar, he ordered and paid for another round, plus snacks, a round for the women, and arranged for the server to deliver everything.

Back at their table, he sat back down. "Drinks are coming."

Clive chimed in, "Hey, we need some company. Why didn't you stop at that table of ladies at the other end and invite them over? They watched every move you made."

"Patience, old buddy, patience. You know my style."

Clive settled back into his chair and waited. The three men turned their gaze toward the stairs.

Richard sighed. "For crying out loud, guys. Don't be so obvious, and quit drooling, Hassle."

A few minutes later, the waitress appeared with a tray filled with beverages and bowls of beer nuts, pretzels and popcorn. She stopped first at the women's table and began to place glasses in front of each lady, to their surprise. Well, three looked surprised and pleased. Richard noticed the fourth, the tall one, frowning and looking his way. Her task done there, the server headed for their table, and he couldn't see the tall one anymore.

Clive slapped him on the shoulder. "Smooth move, Thor."

By the time the waitress emptied her tray onto their table, Clive was up and moving an adjacent empty table into line with theirs. Richard could see the women glancing their way, chatting. No, it looked more like debating, a discussion that only included the three. The tall one apparently wanted no role in what might be coming.

Clive walked down to their table and began to talk. Richard saw him nod back toward their table. The three women had one, last brief discussion and then, as a group, stood and followed Clive, who introduced Ben, a.k.a. Capt. A; Richard, a.k.a. Thor; and Jim, a.k.a. Hassle. The shorter brunette introduced herself as Sammi and introduced the other two as Erica and Macy. Macy walked over to Richard and tossed a $5 bill onto the table in front of him.

"My friend back there says, thanks, but she doesn't accept drinks from strangers."

"So, why don't you introduce us then?"

"Un-uh, not me. I am not going to get into the middle of this one. BFF or not, I've been down that road before." She moved to the other end of the table and sat next to Capt. A.

Richard fingered the bill while trying to decide what to do. He would be satisfied staying there and getting to know some local ladies, particularly with his being new to the city. However, he hated the idea of the one gal sitting alone, deserted by her friends. Still, watching her, she seemed content with that fact and she hadn't really resisted when the girls left the table. He crunched the fiver into his palm and stood up. She was watching the crowd below them on the main floor when he arrived at her side.

"Sorry if I somehow offended you. Your friend says you won't accept drinks from strangers."

The woman looked up at him. "That's right." She took a swig of her drink.

"Well, we can fix that. I'm Richard." He held out his hand. "Why don't you join us? Hate to see you sitting all by yourself."

She didn't accept his handshake, but a sly smile crossed her face. "I thought your name was Thor."

"Yeah, well, to my friends. If we get to be friends, maybe I'll show you my hammer." His eyes widened and he tried to continue, "Wait. That didn't come—"

She huffed. "Of all the disgusting, lame . . . You want to show me your what?" She stood up and, in her heeled boots, stood nearly eye to eye with him. "Get lost!" She grabbed her glass and tossed its contents into Richard's face before Macy could intervene.

Nine

～◆◆～

Jusuf didn't know what to do. Danijela had been inconsolable. For ten days, she had remained holed up in her room, eating only small portions of what food Jusuf could prepare for her. She looked awful, a ghost of the beautiful woman she had been that day of their last and only outing.

He paced the front room of the cabin, frustrated. He not only felt incapable of helping her, but his own "re-education" now stood at a standstill. He had found the stimulation of going out shopping and eating overwhelming at first, but soon realized how much more he remembered afterwards. Now, he felt even more conflicted, between his concern and caring for Danijela and his motivation to return to the man he sensed he had once been.

When he ran low on food, he took the keys to Ibrahim's car and dared to venture out on his own. He had remembered the way to the large grocery store and, surprisingly, found that he knew how to operate the car. Like the inbred instinct of a baby bird knowing how to fly, he sat in the driver's seat, turned the ignition, and drove as if he had done so all of his life.

During that trip to the store, he splurged and bought the local newspaper and half a dozen magazines that he found on display near the cash register. He found reading to be an effort, but like so many things, the more he made that effort, the easier it became. It wasn't until he had returned to the cabin that he noticed the local newspaper's front page and winced at the headline below the fold. A second woman had been murdered, like the first. The front page carried an artist's portrait of a young woman. More conflict. He was afraid to show it to Danijela, but knew he should. In his gut he knew this woman had to be someone else Danijela knew, another woman smuggled into America by human traffickers. Maybe he was wrong, but he didn't think so. He tucked the paper away in a safe place. Maybe, in time, he would show it to her.

He had noticed something else in the paper. The article had displayed a map showing the locations where each woman had been found. Something in Jusuf's brain clicked. An emerging pattern perhaps. Using a larger map he'd found in the car, he located each spot. Something in his head told him that when, not if, another body was found it would be—his finger pointed to the spot on the map.

He needed to do something, with or without Danijela's approval. In fact, he knew she wouldn't approve, so he decided not to mention it to her. After checking on her, he snatched the paper from its hiding place and took the car to the closest convenience store. At the one remaining payphone, he dialed the number listed in the article.

"Major Case Squad, how may I direct your call?"

Jusuf hesitated. Was he doing the right thing?

"I, uh, I have information on the first Jane Doe, the one from Cuivre River."

"Just a minute, I'll connect you to a detective."

There was a delay and finally a brusque voice came on the line. "Lieutenant Janick. I understand you have information on one of our cases. What's your name, please?"

Jusuf again hesitated. "It's Jusuf, and I know—"

"Jusuf what? And where are you calling from?"

"Just Jusuf, calling from a payphone. Look, the first victim, her name is Tatjana Alic." He spelled the name as Danijela had spelled it for him. "She is from Bosnia, from a town near Tuzla."

"How do you know this?"

"My friend, Danijela, was her friend. They were smuggled into America from a boat anchored near Houston four years ago. They had been promised jobs, but I think they were forced into being servants or maybe even prostitutes. Danijela recognized the sketch on TV last week."

"Where is this Danijela? Can we talk to her, to you both? I can send someone to get you."

The quarreling emotions within threatened to suffocate Jusuf. He knew they should go to the police. More women could die, and the murderer remained on the loose. Yet, what would happen to Danijela? Had he already jeopardized her by revealing her name? What would happen to her since she was in the country illegally? And what would happen to him? A whole range of 'what if' possibilities flooded his brain. Would they lock him up, too? Would they subject him to a myriad of merciless tests aimed at restoring his memory?

"N-no, she won't talk or come forward, that's why I'm calling. I think—"

The detective interrupted again. "Do I know you? Have we met someplace?" The urgency in the man's

60

voice frightened Jusuf.

"I, uh, I don't think so. I don't remember much. Look, Danijela is afraid of the authorities because she is here illegally, even though that's not her fault. And I think the people who brought her here are after her. I think the second girl is also from that group."

"Cully? Lynch Cully? Is that you, Lynch?"

Jusuf began to panic. "I, uh, uh, my name is Jusuf." He felt a need to hurry, but he didn't understand why. He rushed on. "One more thing, I think there will be another girl, maybe not soon. But the map, check the map. The dump sites are equidistant from south St. Louis and 90 degrees apart. When the next girl is found, I think it will be near a town called Marissa, in that state next to here. I have to go."

"Damn it, Cully, this has to be you. Where are you? We need to get you."

Jusuf hung up.

Janick looked at his partner, Susan Prichard. "Did we get that trace?"

Prichard was a fifteen-year veteran of the St. Charles Police Department, the last five spent in their detective bureau. The timing of that promotion couldn't have come at a better point in her life, as it allowed her more flexibility and time for the activities of her four kids. That included the unexpected oral surgeon appointments for her eldest, Riley, who had fallen and knocked out his front upper incisors. The drawback came with these increasingly frequent call-ups to the MCS. As interesting as the cases sometimes were, they interfered with the family time she had come to expect.

She shook her head. "We didn't start it in time for a direct trace, but give me a few minutes. Phone company should be able to tell us since it came from a payphone."

"Did you hear that voice?"

"I only met Cully once. He sure didn't seem to know who you are. There was fear in that voice. You really think it's him?"

"That or his ghost, and I don't believe in ghosts. The whole call's recorded right? Can we put it on a flash drive? I need to take this back to my chief."

A minute later, Susan handed him a flash drive. Janick picked up the phone and made two calls. The first he made back to his own office. On loan to the MCS from the Ladue Police Department, he needed to report back to his boss. If Lynch really was alive, they had to find him. Colonel Halbert would be waiting for him. He placed the second call.

"Dandridge."

"Chief Dandridge, it's Bob Janick."

"Hey, Bob, good to hear from you. Why's an old fuddy-duddy retired policeman like me deserve getting a call from you?"

"Nothing fuddy-duddy about you, Chief. Got a missing person's case I need your opinion on. Can you meet me at the Ladue station in, say, 20 minutes?"

The retired police chief chuckled. "A missing person case? What? You guys stretched too thin? Calling in reinforcements for the mundane stuff?"

"Doubt you'll find it mundane, sir. Twenty minutes?"

"Okay, you've piqued my interest. Who is it?"

"Lynch Cully."

Jusuf ran back to the car, pulled out from the parking slot, and sped away from the store—in the opposite direction that he needed to go. He didn't understand why he did that. It seemed like the right thing to do. He would circle around using a couple of back streets he had discovered.

The names whirled about in his head like a hurricane. Janick. He recalled the feeling of familiarity when Danijela told him Ibrahim's full name, Ibrahim Jancic. Now, the voice on the phone. He knew that voice. Janick. And the man seemed sure that he knew Jusuf, but by the name Lynch Cully. That name, too, seemed familiar. In fact, it seemed right. Was his name Lynch Cully? If so, what had happened to him?

He realized he was speeding and slowed down to the posted speed. Maybe Janick was right. Maybe he would find his answers by meeting with this detective. Yet, he couldn't do that. Not yet.

Danijela. He needed to get back to her. Despite her attempt to act normally around him, up to ten days ago, he knew it was a front. She feared for her life more than she feared the authorities. Learning of Tatjana's death drove that fear to new heights. He would protect her, not abandon her. She had saved his life. He would return the favor.

As he drove back toward the cabin, a helicopter flew overhead. At first, he worried that it was looking for him, but it kept flying toward the city. Still, its appearance started another avalanche of images falling through his mind. Helicopters. Hospitals. A woman. The name 'Amy' flashed into his head. For whatever reason, that was important. She was important. He struggled to recall more, but the more he fought, the further away the images flew.

Janick and his boss, Colonel Halbert, were huddled over the colonel's computer when Chief Dandridge walked in. Janick looked up.

"Thanks for coming, Chief," he said. "I think you're going to want to hear this."

"Cully was like a son to me," replied the retired chief. "You know I want to hear what you've got if you really think he's still alive."

Colonel Halbert moved his mouse and clicked on the media player. The recorded phone call filled the room with a voice they all knew well.

"I'll be. You're right; it's him. It's got to be him. He even saw an emerging pattern in this case the MCS is working on."

Janick spoke up. "Got a call from Susan Prichard. The phone company says the call came from a rural payphone, at a Maw and Paw's Convenience Store on Highway 47, south of Richwoods."

"Just miles from where the motor home exploded and he disappeared." Dandridge looked out the window. "Have we sent someone out there, yet?"

"I'm going personally," replied Janick. "Just waiting for you to make it unanimous. It'll take me just over an hour to get there."

"Let me come with you, Bob," added Dandridge.

"It'll be a pleasure to have your company, sir. Let's go."

Ninety minutes later, the two men pulled into the gravel lot of the decrepit convenience store, a store that had apparently gone out of business years earlier. At one end of the desolate building sat two old payphone stalls, one phone missing, while one still looked as if someone maintained it.

"So much for hoping a clerk could identify him, and I never expected a place called 'Maw and Paw's' to have video surveillance, even if they were still in business," said Janick.

"No, but with some luck we'll find fingerprints on the phone," answered the retired chief.

Janick nodded and opened his trunk to retrieve his gear. Together they walked to the working payphone, and Janick carefully dusted the receiver. Dozens of prints appeared, some more recent than others.

"This could take a while, and then getting the crime lab to compare them all, well, we might have something in a few weeks."

"Not to worry," replied Chief Dandridge. "Get me an exemplar of Lynch's prints and I'll do it, the old fashioned way."

"And if it's a hit?"

"Then we look at county property records for anything listed under either name. If that strikes out, we start staking out the area. He and that Danijela gal have to eat. We start watching the nearest grocery stores, showing his picture around."

"Chief, we don't have that kind of manpower. We maybe could get some of the off-duty guys to help, but that'll be limited, too."

Dandridge looked at Janick with a gleam in his eye. "I'll do it. I'll spend days down here if that's what it takes."

Janick shook his head. "Chief, you don't—"

"Bob, look at me. My wife died three years ago. My kids and their kids live out of state and visit me twice a year. I visit them twice a year. That leaves me with 48 weeks of puttering around my house, retelling war stories over beers at Gillies or the club, trying to find something useful to do. Let me do this."

Ten

❧ ✦ ✦ ☙

Amy sat in Amanda's outer room awaiting an "emergency" session, thanks to Macy. Amy didn't know whether to thank her friend or wring her neck. Probably the latter, after Macy called Amanda and squealed on her.

Amanda poked her head through the door to her office. "Amy?"

She stood up and slowly walked across the room to meet the psychologist and follow into her inner office. Amy took her customary place on the couch, but Amanda took a chair directly across from her instead of sitting behind her desk.

"Soooo . . ." sighed Amanda.

Amy gazed at the floor for a minute before meeting the psychologist's eyes.

"You are aware that impulsive behavior is another symptom of PTSD, aren't you?" Amy nodded. "Have you ever thrown your drink on anyone before?" Amy shook her head. "Sounds like a lack of impulse control to me. What happened?"

Amy related her side of the story to Amanda.

"So, the guy had a lame line. I've heard worse. I usually just walk away, not throw my drink in his face."

"Y-you're right. I should have . . ."

"What happened after that?"

"Umm . . ." Amy tried to gauge what Amanda already knew. What all did Macy tell her? "After Macy stopped me, the guy, Thor, apologized profusely. He said he knew as soon as the words came out how it sounded, and that wasn't at all what he meant."

"What else?"

Amy started to fume. Macy had spilled the beans.

"What else?" Amy replied.

"Yes, what else? I'm sure there's more to the story. There always is."

Okay, so maybe Macy hadn't said anymore.

"Macy dragged me to the restroom and told me what the guys had told them about Thor's nickname and that he really did have a hammer, something his friend, the artist, had constructed. When we came out, the men had left, and I apologized to my friends. We finished our drinks and left for the night."

"And?"

"And?"

"Amy, I think you can hear well enough. And?"

"And I went home and barely slept."

"How did you feel?"

"Half crazy. Embarrassed. I didn't have the nightmare though. I'm not sure why."

"I talked with you once before about the process of psychodynamic psychotherapy and that one of its goals is to help you recognize triggers for the memories and symptoms. I think we both understand that climbing aboard a helicopter is an obvious trigger. What about last night? Can you identify what might have triggered your impulse to douse the guy with your drink?"

Amy tightened up on the couch, drawing her feet under her and her knees to her chest. She didn't want to talk about that.

"Amy? You're getting defensive again. I think you

know why."

Amy hesitated and then nodded. "I-I felt guilty. Like I was somehow cheating on Lynch."

Amanda sat back in her chair and watched Amy. After a moment, she asked, "Why?" Amy shrugged. "Hmmm. I see we're getting into some new territory here. You've not mentioned Lynch before now. I can see that his loss has a more crucial role in all of this than I might have guessed. Did you feel guilty just because you were talking to a man who seemed interested in you, or because you found him interesting, too?"

Amy didn't want to respond because she knew her answer was "both." And that made her feel guilty all over again.

The final half hour of Amy's session centered on Lynch, and afterwards, Amy had to admit that some of her thoughts had changed. She thought about some of the things Amanda brought up as she drove to work. Lunchtime came and went. The afternoon breezed by as Amy dove headfirst into her project of revamping their training manuals. Once again, she had to be reminded that it was time to go home.

She picked up some of her favorite Greek dishes from Zorba's carryout and headed for home. Halfway there, her cell rang—"The Army Goes Rolling Along." Her father.

"Hi, Dad."

"How's my favorite daughter?"

She was his only daughter, but somehow that line never got old.

"I've had better days. What's up?"

"I need your help. Hostessing."

Her mother had died over a decade earlier, and Amy had learned the role of hostess quickly as a teen. Her father's position prior to retiring as an Army aviator had required a certain amount of social interaction, and more often than she could count, that planning had fallen into her lap. She found she enjoyed it. At first, it made her feel grown-up, but later, since college, that skill had made her the "go-to party planner" in her circle of friends. This marked the first time her father had asked for her help since the accident. She decided on the spot that she could use the diversion.

"If I can. When?"

"Friday evening." There was a brief pause. "Whoa, that's tomorrow already. Sorry, this is really last minute."

"Sure, I can help. What'd you have in mind and for whom?"

Her dad chuckled. "Remember General 'Ulcer?'"

"Oh no, Dad. Please. Not him."

Her father had worked for General Aaron Hessler when Amy was three. She never could pronounce his name and continued to call him "Gen'l Ulcer." The General got mad and thought it was because her father called him that at home, until he personally tried to get Amy to pronounce it correctly and couldn't. Then it became an ongoing joke that Amy never could live down.

He laughed loudly. "No, not him. His grandson is in town and promised his grandfather he would pay his respects to me. He's coming by just for dessert and drinks, at seven."

"Dad? You're not trying to—"

"No, Amy. Never. I promised I'd stick to praying for the right guy to come your way, not to meddling directly."

"Okay, but I won't get home from work until six, and by the time I change, pick up dessert, and drive over, it might be a little after seven before I get there."

"Not a problem. I appreciate the help, as always."

Janick sat in the medical examiner's lab, sorting through the scant evidence from their two cases with the lead tech. His mind tried to entertain multiple scenarios, but unlike Chief Dandridge or Lynch Cully, he just couldn't manage the "what if" game like they could. It didn't help that he felt distracted by the possible reappearance of Lynch Cully, one of his own, whose memorial service just two months earlier had been a statewide spectacle. He needed to head home, grab a beer, and clear his head so he could refocus on the case at hand. Still.

"So, the second victim wasn't torn up like the first, and we found this small tattoo at the base of her neck on the right," the tech continued. He handed a photo to the detective. "We went back to the first body and examined that area more closely. The flesh was heavily damaged, but we found tattoo ink in a small tissue sample under the microscope."

Janick worked to focus on that piece of information. "So, if this is a case of human trafficking, could this be some kind of brand?"

The tech shrugged. "Can't say. All I can tell you is, there were tattoos in the same area of the bodies, not that they were identical. At least we have an intact one, you know, for comparison in case this happens again."

"Anything found to suggest where either girl came from?"

"You mean, like, ethnic origins?"

"Well, that and maybe where they was livin' before they died."

"DNA might suggest ethnic origins, but that's a good three, four weeks away. We don't have anything in trace yet to suggest anything other than they drank county water, so they probably lived in the county. Of course, the first vic was contaminated by everything the Cuivre River could deposit on that field, so we can't glean much from her."

The tech stood up and stretched. "Anything on the name Tatjana Alic, yet?"

"Nothing. That information has been forwarded to Interpol, for what that's worth." Janick stood as well. Time to head home. "Thanks. Let me know if anything new comes to light."

"As always."

Janick emerged from the M.E.'s building as a jet roared overhead on takeoff from the airport. He felt his phone vibrate more than he could hear it.

"Janick."

"Bob, he's alive. I've got positive matches on a thumb and two fingers." Janick could hear the glee in the Chief's voice. "I think we need to rethink what we discussed the other day. I'm still more than willing to work this, stake out the area, but we need more manpower. Maybe release this to the press."

Janick reflected on the fear he'd heard in Lynch's voice, not to mention his apparent lack of recognition of both Janick and his real identity. Some kind of amnesia? Maybe brain damage from that psycho Koettering's anoxia chamber? What if the damage was more than Lynch could handle, and he wouldn't recover from it? He also recalled the grief shared by his family and girlfriend, Amy. They had already been through losing him once. What if something happened? He didn't want to put them through losing Lynch twice.

"Chief, I hear you. And I understand your motive, but I think we need to keep this low key, keep it in the family, so-to-speak." He explained his rationale. There was silence on the other end.

"Maybe you're right," replied Chief Dandridge. His reluctance and disappointment were audible.

"Chief, I'll pass this along to Halbert and see what resources he's willing to offer. Then we'll see about volunteers to help. But, no press, no police alerts, nothing on the day sheet. I don't want to drive him underground."

Eleven

Jusuf carried a load of firewood into the cabin to find Danijela sitting at the table sipping a cup of tea, a worn Bible open on the table in front of her. She had emerged briefly from her self-imposed hibernation the day before to eat what he had prepared for her. She had taken a shower and sat at the window staring outside for maybe an hour before returning to her bedroom. She had said nothing.

He was pleased to see her up and about. He had grown to care for her and hadn't liked seeing her hurting. He had been frustrated that he had no way to help her through the anguish. Now, he saw that she was working through it on her own. That revealed a strength in her that he only recently began to appreciate.

He unloaded his arms and twice more walked back to the woodpile for another stack until the pile inside was sufficient for the day. If the weather warmed as predicted, he might not need any more for the weekend. Finished, he removed his coat and work gloves and placed them on their hook beside the door. She still sat at the table.

"Thank you," said Danijela.

He shrugged. "For what?"

"For, how you say, give me space. Tatjana was best friend. I think they kill her for try to escape, like me."

"I can see that possibility." He debated telling her about the second woman. Maybe in another day or two.

"You're afraid, too. I can tell."

She nodded. "No doubt I am target. But I know that since leaving with Ibrahim." She then gave him a look that confused him. "Thank you also."

He furrowed his brow and looked at her, questioning. She pulled a folded newspaper from her lap and opened it on the table.

"For not telling me of other one."

So much for waiting.

"I find paper yesterday while you outside. Her name Jelena. She on ship, too, but not from Bosnia. Croatia. I do not know last name." She pointed to the phone number circled on the article. "You leave here three day ago. You call police?"

Jusuf nodded. "I did. I told them what you told me, about Tatjana, your being smuggled here. The man wanted us to come to them. I-I refused. The man got upset on the phone and started calling me by another name, as if he knew me." Jusuf noted the puzzlement in his statement matched the confusion he felt.

He'd spent the last three days replaying that conversation over and over in his head. He tried to block it by reading the magazines he'd picked up. He'd read each, cover-to-cover, twice, and found the infatuation with so-called celebrities inane and trivial, irrelevant to real life. They had not been enough of a distraction.

Danijela fidgeted in her chair and drew her knees up to her chest. She looked agitated.

"What name?"

"Lynch Cully."

"I not know that name. Is name you know,

remember?"

Lynch approached the table and sat in the chair to Danijela's left. He reached over and placed his hand on hers. She did not flinch.

"I-I think so. I don't so much remember the name, but it seems familiar. And it feels right, like that is my name. I don't understand that. It also triggered other memories that I don't understand. I don't know why that man thought he knew me, but he became insistent. It, uh, scared me." He figured he should tell her everything. "Also, as I drove home, I saw a helicopter, and that triggered memories, images in my head." He stopped short of mentioning the image of a woman named Amy.

She put her other hand on top of his and stared at him. "Are you police, too?"

Jusuf tried to place that comment into the jigsaw of thoughts, images, and memories he'd had over the previous three days. He just couldn't see enough of the final picture to know where that piece needed to go. "I honestly do not know. Maybe. Maybe not. I wish I could remember."

"Why else he know you good enough to know your voice?"

Lynch had wrestled with that very thought. He had tried for hours on end to recall the voices of his parents and the woman named Amy. He had not succeeded. Even images of his parents' faces seemed more like mirages. He couldn't trust what he saw in his mind any more than the wavering image of a distant road in the summer heat.

"Maybe we're friends? Maybe I'm a criminal he's

looking for. I just really do not know."

She huffed, and the first slight smile he'd seen in over a week eased across her face. "You no criminal. Criminal I know. Not you."

He felt a bit of relief at her comment. He'd been worried about the possibility of being someone hunted by the police. He could still feel the tension in her hands, the tightness in her body. There was something more bothering her.

"What's wrong?" he asked.

She glanced away and took her hand off his. After a pause, she replied, "I still grieve my friend."

He eased his hand to her chin and turned her to face him. She did not resist.

"No, that's not all. I can sense it. Something else worries you."

A tear formed in her eye. "Phone call. Police can trace. I am afraid they find us. And . . ."

He took her hand and kissed it. She did not pull away.

"And?"

"If police can find, so can Risto."

Risto? What, who is Risto? thought Jusuf.

He saw her begin to tremble and pulled her toward him. She eased off the chair and climbed onto his lap, like a child seeking security in the arms of a loved one.

Darko entered a final locking code on the vault door and turned to find Risto waiting in the hallway. He placed some documents in his briefcase and approached his security chief.

"Da? Risto. Imate neke informacije?" You have some information?

"Da. Major Case Squad *zna Tatjana ime."* They know Tatjana's name.

"Kako?" How?

"Telefonski poziv. . ." Phone call. "Maybe Danijela, or Ibrahim. I have paid our contact in the phone company to find out."

"Excellent. If he succeed, give him bonus." He motioned for Risto to follow and walked to his office.

"Tell me. What is status of search for Ibrahim?"

"Have man watch apartment building all hours. Storeowners know to watch for him. Client with girls Danijela know have more security."

"What about car?"

"Only car I know still outside apartment. I have man at DMV looking for others, but find none so far. I have put GPS tracker on mother car, but it has not move, and she is not home. I think he hide her already."

"And sister?"

"Still look for her."

"Phone?"

"Ibrahim too smart for that. Always use throw-away, even before betrayal."

Darko understood the difficulties of finding someone who didn't wish to be found, even in this day and age of surveillance. Even the NSA might have trouble finding Ibrahim. If their efforts did not soon turn up the stone where this traitor hid, he would call upon influential friends for help. He did not like calling in favors, but then again, perhaps they wouldn't see them as favors but as a means of self-preservation.

78

After all, if Darko fell, so would they.

As her workday ended, Amy developed second thoughts about her fast-approaching hostess gig. True, her father had never before attempted to set her up with sons of friends. Moreover, he denied doing so now. Still, this meeting just had that feel about it. After all, he could have picked up a dessert as easily as she.

With the loss of Lynch, maybe he had decided to intervene, to try to help for a change, despite his denials. No, he wouldn't do that to her without being more forthcoming about it. She hadn't shared any details of her battle with PTSD with him. She didn't want to worry him. However, he was ex-Army. He'd seen soldiers and aviators dealing with PTSD before and had to recognize it in her. Was he trying to cheer her up? Her mind tossed back and forth. Was he setting her up? Not likely. Maybe? No.

If she managed it just right, she could just drop off the dessert and hightail it home. With some luck, she could even get it into the kitchen without being seen and call him when she was nearly home to make sure he'd found it.

Vacillating, she drove home and changed clothes before heading to her father's house. At the nearest Dierberg's grocery, she picked up a cheesecake sampler, pre-sliced in four flavors. As she pulled onto his street, she took a deep breath and devised her plan for sneaking into the kitchen. An unfamiliar car sat in her dad's driveway. She parked at the curb in front of a neighbor's house and walked around to the back of her father's home so no one could see her from any of the front windows.

As quietly as she could, she unlocked and entered the back door, easing it shut. She listened for voices and, satisfied they were in the front room, she tiptoed into the kitchen and set the box on a counter.

"Woof! Woof, woof, woof!"

"What the . . ." Amy about jumped onto the counter with the cheesecake at the unexpected appearance of a shaggy English Sheepdog at the door to the front, wagging its tail.

"Willie, come here!" commanded an unfamiliar voice.

The dog turned around and bounded back to the front room, its position replaced by her father.

"Amy, I didn't hear you come in. Glad you could make it. We're in the front room." He laughed. "I see you met Prince Willie, Jim's dog. Come, come." He motioned for her to follow him.

Amy sighed and walked in behind him. The young man kneeling and holding his dog looked familiar.

"Amy, this is Jim Hessler, the General's grandson. Jim, this is my daughter, Amy."

Jim glanced up and his eyes widened. "Uh-oh. Umm, hi."

Amy nodded in greeting, still trying to place his face.

"Jim brought a friend with him. He's in . . . Oh, here he is now. This is Richard Nichols. He just moved here from—"

Amy blanched at the sight of Thor, and her father astutely noticed. He looked at Amy and back to Richard.

80

And back to Amy.

Richard made a point of looking at both of her hands. "You don't have a drink, do you?" He smiled mischievously. "Hello again."

Amy's pallor flamed to crimson.

"Um, hi."

Her dad chuckled. "Obviously, I'm missing something here." He looked back and forth between them again and eased backward a step. "I . . . I think I'll go get another round for the guys. Amy?"

"Any, um, crow to eat?" she whispered.

Her father stared at her for a moment. "I'll just fix your usual." He left for the kitchen, walking behind her to avoid getting between the two.

Amy noticed Jim and Willie had moved to the far chair. She stood alone facing Richard. He smiled.

"I guess I need a new opening line. Let's see. Come here often? No, wait. Obviously, you must. Hmmm, how about—"

Amy stopped him. "Look, I owe you an apology. I, uh, I'm sorry for my, for the way I acted."

"And I apologize for my unintentional crude comment. It certainly didn't come out like I meant it."

"So Macy told me. It was more of a lecture actually. I've not been myself lately."

"So Macy told me," he replied, still smiling. He gestured toward the couch and waited until she sat at one end. He stood at the other end and asked, "Will I be safe on this end? It's still within arm's reach."

Amy nodded. "I promise to be on my best behavior." She leaned forward and gently clapped her hands toward Willie. Jim released his hold, and the dog loped over to Amy and gave her hands a sloppy kiss. She laughed. "He's wonderful. I don't think I've ever seen an English Sheepdog in person. That is right, isn't it? The breed?"

Jim replied, "Yes. My mom loved the breed, so we grew up with them. My sister breeds them now, and Willie here came from one of her first litters. Purebred. His registered name is 'Prince Willie of Tails.' She gave him the name, not me."

Amy smiled and noticed that Richard, Thor, sat there watching her. A moment later, her dad returned with dessert and beverages—beers for the guys, two fingers of scotch on the rocks for himself, and something unexpected for his daughter.

"I thought you were fixing my usual. This isn't a margarita."

"No, it's not."

She took a sip. "Hmmm, it's good. What is it?"

"Well, I sensed something brewing as I left the room, but the air seems to have cleared."

Amy rolled her eyes. "Dad?"

"It's called a 'Dark and Stormy.' Dark rum and ginger beer." He grinned. "By the way, you might want to stick to just one, unless you want to spend the night in your old room."

She heard Richard stifle a laugh and turned to him. "Careful. I am in range."

"So," her dad continued. "I take it you two have already met. Do I get to hear how and where?"

"No!" answered Amy and Richard in unison.

He jerked back slightly at the prompt rebuttal and said, "All right then. Jim, I hear you and Amy have something in common."

"Oh?"

Amy furrowed her brow, suspecting what was coming. "Dad, I don't think we need—"

Her dad ignored her and continued. "Jim's grandfather told me he couldn't pronounce their name any better than you did until he started school. That's how he got his nickname, Hassle."

Jim laughed. "That's right. Embarrassed my parents no end."

"So that's how you got that nickname. You never told us that," said Richard.

Jim shrugged. "And relax, Amy, Granddad already told me the story."

Lt. Colonel Gibbs slowly shook his head back and forth, and said, "Yep, embarrassed her father no end."

Richard held up his hand to stop the conversation. "Wait a minute, I haven't heard this story."

Amy sank into the couch cushion as her father repeated the General 'Ulcer' story, embellishing it as a true storyteller would. In turn, she coaxed the story of 'Thor' out of Richard, with Hassle embellishing that story. The evening continued with stories of the two men's Afghanistan experiences and one or two old war stories by her father. Richard told how he came into his new job and about his new apartment.

Amy soon learned that her father was right about her drink. One was just enough. She hadn't relaxed this much in months, and she found herself enjoying the company of both young men. She eyed Richard as he talked and realized that even though she hadn't gotten past Lynch yet, she could enjoy Richard as a friend.

As the evening neared ten o'clock, Amy felt the day, or maybe the drink, catching up with her. "Dad. Guys. I'm going to have to excuse myself and head home. It's been a long day at the end of a long week."

All three men stood as she did.

"Hey, take some of that cheesecake with you. I don't need it sitting around here," said her father as he kissed her on the forehead.

"Not me, but I'm sure two guys named Thor and Hassle would enjoy more later."

"Sure, thanks," replied Jim.

Richard looked at Amy as she slung her purse over her shoulder and said, "I'm glad we got to hit the 'Re-do' button. Um, would you be willing to show me around town sometime? I could use an expert guide."

Amy lowered her purse and opened it, retrieving a business card. She handed it to him. "That might be fun, as long as it doesn't involve any hand tools." She smirked. "I'm sure you'll need time to get settled into your new job. Give me a call when you're ready."

She shook hands with both men and kissed her dad on the cheek. She left through the front door, with Willie bolting outside with her. She watched the dog head for the nearest shrubs as she walked down the front walk. Behind her, she overheard Hassle comment to Thor, "When you're ready? Why don't you just set something up right now?" He laughed and started calling for Willie as the dog caught up with and followed Amy to her car.

Twelve

Jusuf awoke with a start. The eddy of thoughts and memories that had started with his phone call to the police had accelerated to a whirlpool threatening to suck him down into . . . into what? He didn't know, but the more his mind spun, the more "right" the name Lynch Cully seemed to be. How could he be sure?

Yet, that's not what woke him. Risto, he had learned, was a who. When Danijela had commented about knowing criminals, Risto was the first to come to her mind. But, she also told Jusuf that Risto worked for someone worse. Risto was hired muscle. Dangerous, resourceful, remorseless, hired muscle.

She did not know this man, the boss, but she knew he traded in many things. And his most profitable trade was in young women like her.

He had looked forward to Sunday. He had wood stocked inside for the weekend. They had enough groceries to last a week or more. He had wanted to use the day to learn more about Danijela and, maybe, himself. If they could find a library nearby, maybe they could make a discreet trip there to find out more about Lynch Cully.

For three months, they had worked together through local papers, popular magazines, how-to books, and anything else Danijela could buy at the grocery that she thought could be useful in reconnecting his memory. Some had helped, some hadn't. He had asked for, and she purchased, an inexpensive radio, and he spent hours listening to talk radio. As his vocabulary returned, his reading skills did as well, although until recently, he preferred the ease of listening to the struggle of reading. Now, reading would provide the only answers he sought.

However, instead of waking to the pleasant anticipation of a day with Danijela, he woke up in a sweat, his heart racing. Danijela's worry had coalesced into the realization of his mistake. If this was Ibrahim's place, purchased in his name, Jusuf's phone call would have alerted the authorities—and anyone else with the right resources—to the county where they were. A simple search of county records would find Ibrahim's name and property, and lead them right to their front door.

Even without Ibrahim's name, the area's sparse population would make the search of a one, or even two-mile radius around the old convenient store's pay phone an easy one. With so many weekenders' cabins in the area, someone searching for them needed only to look for occupied places and watch for a while. Why he knew this, he didn't understand, but it had now been four days since that phone call. The idyllic life he'd imagined living with Danijela had become a fantasy on borrowed time.

He raced to her bedroom and pounded on the door.

"I am awake," she replied, but her voice came from the kitchen.

"Quickly, we must leave. We must pack everything; take everything except what someone would expect to find in a weekend cabin that has not been used in weeks. Pack your clothes, valuables, anything you need.

And we must pack our food and some essentials. We have to make this place look like no one has been here in a long time."

He could see his fear snake across the room like a tentacle, wrapping itself around Danijela and etching itself onto her face like a death mask. She gave him no second look. She did not ask why. She ran from the room and pulled out two canvas duffels from a closet. By then, Jusuf was behind her, and she threw one to him. She ran into her room, peeled off her robe and nightgown, with no hint of modesty, and dressed quickly in jeans and sweatshirt. Jusuf watched her begin to pack and ran to his room to do the same.

Ten minutes later, he had his bed made and room straightened up. His clothing and toiletries only filled half the duffel. He began unloading the refrigerator and placing everything into two boxes he'd found, as well as two black plastic trash bags. Danijela joined him and unloaded the cabinets. As they finished, he turned off the refrigerator and left the door ajar. The few dirty dishes he washed, dried and put away.

"I tidy up. You pack car," Danijela said.

That was a good plan. He'd have to do the heavy lifting anyway. Jusuf nodded and, within ten minutes, moved their meager belongings and supplies to the car. He returned to the cabin to find Danijela dousing the fire in the woodstove.

"With luck it will be cold before anyone finds it," he said, not expressing his concern that someone would find it warm and know someone had been in the cabin.

"I should do something more?" asked Danijela.

"No. It might damage the wood stove, and we might

have to come back here. We'll need it." .

He found the main water line and turned off the supply to the house. He then opened faucets in the kitchen and bathroom to let any water under pressure out and to allow room for any freezing once they left. He shut off the propane line to the water heater and from there he scurried about the cabin.

What else? What else? he asked himself silently. If he wanted the place to look unoccupied, what else did he need to do? He felt frantic, like he was missing something, something critical.

The electric panel. He found it inside the hallway closet and flipped off all breakers except those to essential lights. The exterior floodlights were on motion sensors, to keep prowlers from working unseen. They would need the front room lights just to find the breaker panel if they returned after dark. More than that was unnecessary.

"Can you think of anything else?" he asked her.

"*Ne.*" She shook her head, and she wandered around the main room and then peered into each bedroom and the bathroom.

"Let's go."

He followed her from the cabin and locked up behind them. After turning the car around and driving several yards, he stopped.

"What wrong?"

"Nothing," he replied as he jumped from the car and checked the drive behind the car. The ground remained frozen enough to prevent any tracks. No one would be able to tell that someone had driven down that drive recently. He looked back one more time, still feeling like he'd overlooked something. Time was up. They needed to leave.

Once on the main road, Jusuf felt the first sense of relief since waking that morning. He turned to Danijela, to find her staring at him.

"So, I take time now to ask, why we do this?"

He explained his reason and saw that she understood.

Nodding, she asked, "So, where we go?"

Maybe it was the adrenaline rush wearing off. Maybe it was her question. He felt defeated. He had no answer. He hadn't thought that part through.

"I, uh, I don't know. I just know we had to leave."

As he said that, a car passed by them. The driver was an older man, someone Jusuf would have sworn he knew. But how? And who was it? He experienced no flashbacks, no swirl of memories. Maybe he'd been mistaken.

"May I suggest?" Danijela looked at him, both brows raised.

He shrugged his shoulders. Why not? He recalled enough to drive to the grocery and gas station. He'd be lost in a St. Louis second trying to drive anywhere else. "Sure. I'm open to all suggestions."

"In movies, hunted man sometime hide in plain sight, I think they call it. I know such place."

"Okay."

"Cabin across river, up higher on hill. Old man die month ago. Children try to sell, so no one there. We can watch for Risto. See if threat real."

Jusuf thought about that. Her idea made sense, and his mind told him that claiming higher ground was a good defense. Logic told him that being across the river would also give them time to escape should they be spotted from Ibrahim's place. He nodded.

"Take next left and first left after. I show you."

The next left-hand turn was ten miles down the road and the following turn was a mile after crossing the river. That road eased through farmland before traversing the crest of the hill along the river. After fifteen minutes of driving, Danijela poked him on the shoulder.

"There. Next gate." She pointed ahead to a metal farm gate stretched across a gravel drive.

He pulled up to the gate and glanced at it. There was a locked chain wrapped around the end. Had they driven there only to have a chained gate thwart them? He had no tools. He started to comment, but Danijela opened the door and jumped out. In a minute, she had the gate open. Jusuf pulled the car through, and she closed the gate behind them. He watched her replace the chain and return to the car.

She smiled as he began to ask, "How—"

"Just look locked. To keep people out. Old man not manage lock so chain just attach to nail on back of post."

"How'd you know that?"

"Old man, Charley his name, invite Ibrahim and me for meal three, four time before he die."

Jusuf drove another quarter mile before the cabin came into view. He pulled up to the house and got out of the car. The cabin wasn't much, showing the signs of neglect he might expect from an elderly owner, but the view of the river valley was spectacular. He tried to imagine it fully leafed out in the summer. Under other circumstances, he would have loved the location and the serenity that the isolated perch above the river provided. Today, not so much.

He walked around the corner of the cabin and saw Ibrahim's place below them across the river. He stopped and eased up next to the cabin. Danijela came up behind him.

"Over here is—"

He grabbed her close and put his finger to his tight lips. Her brow furrowed as she followed his finger that now pointed across the river.

The car they had passed on the main road sat in the drive. They could see the older, white-haired man walking from window to window, peering into each. They had left the curtains closed, so the man was not going to see much. It appeared as if he was trying to determine if anyone was inside. When he got to the back door, he stopped and pounded on the door. "Jusuf! Danijela! Lynch?" He paused. "Anybody inside?"

Jusuf stood there, stunned by the clear transmission of sound across the valley. He hadn't thought about that. Without leaves on the trees to soak up and muffle the sound, any noise would echo down the valley with ease. They would have to be extra quiet to avoid detection. Had the man heard their car? He watched the man for a while and felt comfortable that he hadn't. The man remained focused on Ibrahim's cabin and moved to the trash cans outside the back door.

Rats! thought Jusuf. He hadn't thought about the trash. Their recent discards would give away the fact that someone had been there within the past few days.

He was so absorbed in watching the man that Danijela's pokes to his ribs went unnoticed until her jabs became punches. He turned to look at her.

"What?" he whispered. "And keep it down. He might be able to hear us as easily as we heard him."

She nodded. "Yes, yes, I understand. You know him?"

Jusuf thought about that sense of familiarity he'd felt as they passed on the road. In answer, he shrugged.

She pointed with a nod of her head toward the man. "He maybe know you."

Darko gazed out across the barren, wintry landscape of their home just south of St. Louis in Jefferson County. While he and Sonja maintained a small, modestly appointed apartment in the city, near his business, they spent the bulk of their off-hours at their more "substantial" estate in the country. The six-acre clearing where their twelve thousand square-foot home sat was beautifully landscaped with gardens and entertaining space for the warmer months, and was surrounded by forest, which provided a natural isolation that suited their "special tastes."

Darko's efforts to find Ibrahim continued to come up empty. He had doubled the rewards for information. He had re-emphasized his desire to find the man to his legion of pimps and the girls they controlled. He had installed cameras to monitor the traitor's old apartment and his mother's home, so he could free up the men assigned to watch both places to hunt the turncoat more aggressively. Still, Ibrahim had become a ghost.

Sonja, dressed only in sheer, black lace Parisian lingerie with thigh-high stockings held by a garter belt, walked up behind him and began to massage his shoulders as he stared outside, covered with a towel wrapped about his waist. "She is ready for us. *Dodi, moja ljubav.* She will provide us with special afternoon."

He took a last puff from his unfiltered Russian cigarette and snuffed it out in a nearby ashtray. He turned to follow his wife back to their bedroom. "She is favorite of yours. I have notice how you choose her again and again."

She turned to face him again, smiling. "Do you object?" She paused and laughed. "I think not. She is compliant to bring us both pleasure." As she resumed her course toward the bedroom, the phone on Darko's desk rang.

"Go on, *moj dragi.*" He kissed her on the back of her neck. "I be there in a moment." Only one person, besides his wife, had that phone number. He answered the phone on the fourth ring.

"*Da*, Risto."

"*Imam adresu. Ja ću voditi brigu o problemu večeras.*" I have the address. I will take care of the problem tonight.

"*Izvrstan.* Excellent. Call when you are finished."

He hung up the phone and smiled. Now he could relax and truly focus on a pleasurable afternoon.

Jusuf and Danijela had watched the older man throughout his stay on Ibrahim's property. He made no attempt to enter the cabin, but tried unsuccessfully to

93

use his cell phone. He moved about the property a little, but did not appear to find anything of interest.

Jusuf mulled over Danijela's comment. She was correct, of course. The people Danijela had escaped from didn't know of his existence, much less the name mentioned by the policeman. The detective had not sounded as old as the man appeared across the river, and the voice of the man as he called at the door was distinctly that of an older man. Still, the man had appeared at the property and knew both of their names. So, who was this man?

"He gone now," said Danijela as the car disappeared up the drive. She pulled at Jusuf's sleeve. "Here." She reached into some lattice covering the opening to a crawl space beneath a portion of the cabin, but came up empty-handed. "He keep key in here someplace."

Jusuf took her place next to the lattice and began to feel behind it. He moved from one opening to the next and found nothing at first. He moved down to the next row of openings and in the middle of the lattice, felt a hook fastened on the inside of the vinyl trellis. It was empty, but that prompted him to check the dirt below the hook. In the second opening, he found the key buried beneath some leaves. He pulled it out, brushed it off, and handed it to Danijela.

A minute later, she had the door open, and they entered the empty cottage. Built to take command of the spectacular view, the place had a large great room stretching across the length of the building facing the river with floor-to-ceiling plate glass windows. The room sat six steps down from the entry level with stairs for access at both ends. On the uphill side, Jusuf found a functional eat-in kitchen, two bedrooms, and a bath between them.

What they didn't find was a single stick of furniture. The barren rooms would not give them a comfortable place to stay for even a night, much less for the time needed to formulate a new plan. Adding to the misery, there was neither electricity nor water. A wood stove might provide a source of heat, but Jusuf knew that using it might draw attention to the cabin. They would also need to avoid the large windows overlooking the river.

He returned to the car and feeling assured it could not be spied from anywhere across the river, he retrieved the single sleeping bag they had collected from Ibrahim's place. He found some foodstuffs that required no cooking and moved them all inside.

"We won't be able to stay here long," he said to Danijela. He moved the items from the car into the bedroom furthest from Ibrahim's cabin and placed them in the room. "You look cold. Here, take the sleeping bag and wrap up inside it. Stay away from any windows."

She looked at him with concern. "What you do? It get colder tonight."

He shrugged. "I'll figure something out. Hungry? I can make a few sandwiches and the sodas are certainly cold enough."

"I make. You . . ." She looked about the cottage and grinned. "You make self at home." With that, she laughed and took the food from the back room to a kitchen counter where she could work on a surface other than the floor. With sandwiches and sodas in hand, they sat together on the stairs to the main room and ate while gazing out across the valley.

"Good thing it's not supposed to freeze tonight. We'd have to empty a bunch of the food from the car," he said after several minutes of silence.

"Yes. Good thing," she replied.

The silence felt awkward. Until now, their conversations had revolved around reteaching him names and trying to stimulate his memory. Their interactions had a similar purpose, helping him to regain his motor skills. He was willing, but unable to share anything of his past. She was able, but unwilling.

He had wanted this day to learn more about her. He realized now was as good as any time to do so. They needed some distraction from the cold and discomfort.

He placed his hand on hers, and she looked at him. "Danijela, you know *everything* I know about myself. Please tell me about you, your home, your family." He paused and looked into her eyes trying to determine her mood. "Nothing you would be uncomfortable with."

Silence followed for a few minutes and then, having taken the last bite of her food, she gazed across the river valley and smiled. "I grow up in little town . . ."

Danijela finished long before dark engulfed the cabin. Wistful at times, she told Jusuf of her parents, her one sister, and what it was like to grow up in the mountains between Tuzla and Sarajevo. Her family had largely escaped the war in the 1990s, but many families she knew had felt the ethnic cleansings of both the

Lašva valley and Srebrenica. She had been but a toddler at the outbreak of the war, but by its end, she had seen things as a small child she wished she could forget. The lure of something better, a new life, had led to her current status. Her story ended as it had before, with her arrival in St. Louis.

As the chill of dark seeped into the cabin, Jusuf took her by the arm and retreated to the small bedroom, closing the door in hope that it would help contain what body heat they emitted into the room.

"Here, let me help you with the sleeping bag," he said. He unzipped it and laid it out in a corner of the room. "C'mon."

She removed her shoes and coat, and stretched out into the bag. As he tried to zipper the bag, she stopped him. "We share."

He faltered. "I, um, I'm not sure that—"

"Yes, is good idea. I promise, no hanky-panky. That is right, yes? Hanky-panky?"

He chuckled. "Yes, that is right." He hoped he could promise the same.

Nestled together inside the bag and sitting upright in a corner of the room, they quickly fell asleep, her head on his shoulder, his head on hers.

Sometime later, Jusuf started awake at a loud popping noise that reverberated through the valley. Loud voices followed. He hastily unzipped the bag and crawled to the door, easing it open, fearful of what might be waiting on the other side. He peered through the crack to find the cabin empty. He belly crawled to the railing above the great room and peered out the windows. Something was happening at Ibrahim's cabin. Two vehicles' headlights flooded the drive and sides of the building. The motion controlled floodlights revealed the vehicles to be dark colored SUVs. He saw flashlights darting about inside, intermittently lighting up the curtains. Three men emerged from the doorway, yelling in a language he recognized as similar to Danijela's. Another man emerged from the SUV furthest from the cabin. In the headlights, Jusuf saw enough to know it wasn't the police and that he wouldn't want to tangle with the man in an empty alley.

"Risto," whispered Danijela, on the floor behind him.

Risto walked up to one of the men and slapped him hard across the face. More yelling.

"Risto angry. Man he hit startle by cat, shoot it. That noise wake us. Risto unhappy about noise."

Risto marched to the door of the cabin where another man handed him a powerful flashlight. Several minutes later, he emerged and said something to the man at the door. He walked to his vehicle and soon it sped away.

"They not find us. Risto angry about that, too."

The second SUV stayed put. Would they be there all night?

"Maybe leave soon. We go back."

"Not a good idea. They might watch the place for days. We can't trust staying there."

The man at the door stayed there for another ten minutes, by Jusuf's rough calculation. The man poked his head inside for a moment and signaled something to whoever waited in the SUV. The vehicle crept forward into the parking apron and then turned around and eased back toward the driveway. The face of the man at the door suddenly lit up, illuminated by the flare of his cigarette lighter. He appeared to light a cigarette and then opened the door and flicked it inside. He darted for the vehicle.

As the SUV began to speed up the drive, the cabin exploded in a ball of blue propane flame that turned yellow as it rose into the trees above the cabin. They had no choice but to find a new hiding place now. Risto had forced their hand, making them move, increasing their chance of being discovered.

Thirteen
❧ ✦ ✦ ❧

The hooded figure eased along the leafless hedgerow dividing the landscaped yard from the adjacent woods. The multi-million dollar home near the heart of Chesterfield looked little different from any other McMansion that contractors had scurried to complete in the building boom of ten years earlier. Nine out of ten of those builders had gone bankrupt with the housing crash. Still, the homes endured, and their occupants, for the most part, had stuck with their mortgage payments even though many of the homes now held values far less than when they were built.

Ibrahim Jancic, while healing from the bullet graze of his arm, had spent the last three weeks studying the home, its occupants, and their habits. He had failed to do so for Tatjana Alic, and she had ended up as a black market organ donor. With Jelena Kordić, his third attempted rescue, he'd tried a direct approach, calling the police. She was dead and dissected, and her room cleansed long before the authorities acted on the tip and arrived at the house. Darko Komarčić's long tentacles held many informants, protected his clients, and never missed a chance to make a profit.

The home had a series of motion-sensor-controlled lights around its periphery, but Ibrahim had found a flaw in the layout. A narrow corridor between sensors would allow him to approach the house and sneak around to the back corner, under the bedroom window where he needed to be. In that bedroom, three floors up, lay another young woman, Raifa Bukvic, locked into the room whenever the owner left. And raped in that same room at the owner's whim when he was home.

Like the others, she had been promised an education and a job, only to become a slave. Unlike some of the others, she had been spared the drug addictions and beatings that forced those girls into whoring for Darko's legion of pimps. Darko controlled the pimps, and each pimp managed two or three girls.

Ibrahim studied the home and crept toward it, careful to remain undetected. At the foundation plantings, he bent low to the ground and eased toward the back of the house. Beneath the window, he reached up and found a nylon line dangling in the air.

Good girl, he thought. Although closely watched, her duties as the maid required that she accept deliveries at the door. All such interactions were videoed, and any deviance from her instructions led to punishment. Ibrahim knew the drill. Prior to his own life-changing experience, he had been one of the deliverers of such punishments.

It was because of this knowledge that he had been able to deliver a terse message to Raifa. She had followed through.

He tied a smartphone to the cord and gave it two gentle tugs, followed by a third after a fifteen second pause. The phone quickly disappeared above him. Twenty seconds later, her first text came through.

"I collect what you ask me to. What now to do?"

He replied, "Patience, please. Ready almost. Must check again safe house. When will boss be gone next?"

"Two night."

"Good. I return then. Same time."

A minute later, the dangling cell phone almost hit him on the head. He knew how hard it must be for her to give up the phone each time, and how tempting it must be for her to use it to call for help. She understood the danger of having it discovered in her room. From previous conversations, he knew she had seen the newspapers. She had seen what had happened to two of her "friends." He had told her the police could not be trusted because he did not know who did and did not have ties with Darko. His only hope was to collect enough of the girls to present them as a group to the press and police at the same time.

He untied the phone, placed it in his pocket, and left the property just as stealthily as he had entered it. A few minutes later, he was back at his truck, but he didn't rush to it from the secluded spot where he had stashed some emergency supplies. Headlights had appeared down the street, a police cruiser. It slowed down and stopped behind the truck. The officer got out and studied the pickup using his flashlight to light up the cargo bed first and then the inside. He stopped at the driver side windshield.

Ibrahim had hoped never to run into this scenario, but he knew to be prepared, particularly in such a well-heeled neighborhood where anything and everything suspicious would be called in to the police. The sign on his dash read, "Out of Gas, Back ASAP." He collected his things, doubled back to a point in the road where he would not be seen by the officer and walked out onto the road and toward his truck.

"Yo! Officer! Sorry, I get back as soon as I could."

He walked up to the man, carrying a full gas can, a small backpack, and a grocery bag containing snacks and a receipt for the gas from the nearest convenience store, two miles away.

"I thought I never make it back here with this load. This stuff get heavy."

The officer's flashlight lit up his face. "Can I see some ID, please?"

Ibrahim obliged him with a professionally produced fake ID.

"What's in the bag and backpack?"

Ibrahim made no effort to hide anything. He pulled an iPad and books from the backpack. "I could not leave this in truck while gone." From the bag, he pulled out a few candy bars, a Coke, and the receipt showing his gas and sundries purchase from 40 minutes earlier. Just enough time to validate his story of walking to get gas.

Satisfied, the officer wished him well, but watched as Ibrahim emptied the gas can into his truck. He climbed in and started off, the police cruiser "escorting" him to the main road. Thirty minutes later, he pulled into an alley parking spot behind a non-descript building a block away from the Bevo Mill in south St. Louis, in the very heart of the Bosnian community.

At the building's basement door, he first carefully surveyed the area around him and then reached through a heavy steel gate to unlock the chain securing it. After sliding it open, he unlocked and opened the steel security door. Then he closed and locked the gate and door and walked up the short concrete incline into the main room of the basement of the old building. Ahead of him sat donated furniture and household items. To his right sat a room full of donated clothing. Upstairs, the building held the offices and classrooms of Desert Well Ministries.

Ibrahim was of Bosnian origins. His father and uncles had been killed by the ethnic genocide of the war fifteen years earlier. Like many in this St. Louis conclave, he had escaped to America with his mother and sister as political refugees. Although Muslim by family tradition, he had come to Desert Well to learn English and prepare for American citizenship and instead, at Danijela's urging, learned more about Christ as his Lord and Savior. After three years of serving a warlord, meting out punishment to whoever Darko said deserved it, he now served the one true Lord of all creation. Desert Well became his de facto home after his apartment "mysteriously" went up in flames the day after his attempted rescue of Tatjana.

Ibrahim moved through the racks of clothing and at the back of the room slid between two of dozens of women's dresses hanging on a rack. Hidden behind the rack was a small doorway to a seldom-used storeroom. There he slept on a cot and read his Croatian Bible. From there, he plotted out his next step for saving these women caught up by human traffickers.

Fourteen

❧✦✦❧

Richard arrived at work early, only to find the doors locked, and he had no key. He pounded on the door hoping there might be a security man on duty. No response. He glanced around and found a sign regarding after-hours deliveries and pointing to a phone inside a case. He opened the door and picked up the receiver. No dial tone. He was about to hang up when he heard a voice.

"Hello?"

"Good morning. I'm sorry. This is Richard Nichols. It's my first day of work here, and I didn't realize I wouldn't be able to get in."

There was a pause before the voice said, "Come to loading dock."

He sighed as he hung up the phone and closed the door on the enclosure. He clicked his remote to make sure his car was locked and turned to walk around the building. As he approached the back parking area, he found a man-gate in the tall chain link fence surrounding the lot. It was locked. He looked about and spied a security camera. As he looked directly into it, he heard a buzz on the lock and was able to push it open. He climbed the steps to the loading dock, and there, too, the locked man-door buzzed as he approached.

Inside, he came face-to-face with a muscular man about five-eleven, carrying what looked to be a 9mm handgun in a shoulder holster. The man didn't smile, didn't extend his hand in greeting, but did point to a rickety plastic office chair sitting next to an adjacent wall.

"Risto say you wait here for office to open. Not too long. He say not to come early in future."

Richard smiled and extended his hand. "I'm Richard."

The man did not reciprocate. "Yes, you say that already." He used his thumb to point to himself. "Hasan. Night guard." He lit up a crude unfiltered cigarette that Richard guessed was Eastern European in origin. It smelled awful.

Richard wished he'd picked up a cup of coffee at Dunkin' Donuts and watched the clock on the opposite wall above the receiving desk as it slowly ticked toward 8:20. The office opened at nine. *Yeah. Not long*, he thought. *In terms of glacial ages.*

At 8:30, a woman with long, dark hair entered the area and walked straight toward him. She appeared older than the women he'd encountered in the office, but they were no more beautiful. She walked up to him, smiling, and extended her hand.

"Richard, I am Sonja, Darko's wife. I am please to meet you. Darko got phone call soon as he arrive. He will meet you in office later. Come."

Richard shook her hand and replied, "Very nice to meet you. I came early to get a head start on things before your husband arrived. I guess that didn't work."

She laughed. "Not like you think, but he was impress. Trust me. Most worker before you not have much work ethic."

She led him through the call center, where the women were collecting and beginning their day. She stopped halfway through.

"Ladies! This is Richard. He is to work to develop online market, Facebook, um, thing like that." After a brief pause, she continued, "Social media. That is term I wanted. Also, new website, to make your life easier. So be nice."

The women all smiled, several more seductively than Richard was comfortable with, and each came up to greet him and introduce herself. With the foreign names, he realized it might take him a couple of weeks to remember each one.

Sonja turned to him. "Richard, we have tradition here. New guy take all girls to lunch on first day. Their choice."

Voices saying "Yay!" greeted Richard's mouth dropping open. Not that he had any reservation at all to paying for lunch. It was just, well, um, why couldn't his friends be at that restaurant when he walked in the door with this bevy of beauties surrounding him?

Sonja leaned toward him and whispered in his ear, "No worry. We reimburse. Is our way of getting people to know each other."

He smiled. "I would be honored to take you ladies anywhere. Thank you for the privilege."

Sonja took his arm and led him away. Richard could feel the women's stares penetrating his back and wasn't sure how to feel about it.

"Here is your office. We have T-1 internet cable. Darko want to install own server farm when time come. Maybe upgrade to T3. Is that right term? He talk over my head sometime."

Richard began to comment that he wasn't a

computer guy and couldn't do that kind of set-up, when she continued.

"We have man to do that when is time. We also have man to make actual website. You will work with him when time come. Now, is time to work. I will leave you to start. Darko say he will stop by later." She turned to leave, but stopped. "Oh, and we will make arrangement for early work if you see need. Let us know."

Amy looked at the clock on her computer screen. One hour until her next class. She returned her focus to her presentation, but that focus had failed to assuage the grumbling in her gut. This wasn't hunger. She'd eaten her lunch. Her gut reflected the emotional chaos she found escalating inside over this topic.

Regional authorities had asked all EMS services to provide a refresher course to its paramedics, nurses and other personnel on the Department of Homeland Security's Blue Campaign on human trafficking. The case that resulted in her personal meltdown had prompted the call for these courses. Word was out that an anonymous tip claimed that the young women whose organs had been taken had been victims of human trafficking, and recalling that first case now caused the turmoil she felt. She could still see that poor girl's mutilated body in her mind, and her anger over that injustice flamed.

She picked up the phone, dialed Amanda's number, and left a message. With a little luck, her therapist might call back before the course started.

Her boss poked his head into her door. "How's it going?"

She looked up. "How do you think it's going?" That came out a bit more sarcastic than she'd meant it. "Sorry. I'm a little on edge."

"Hey look, I have an idea what this is doing to you. I am fully aware what precipitated the need for this class, and I've worried how it might affect you. But you're the only one I have to do it. With this viral bug going around, we're running short of personnel here, in the field, everywhere. That's the other thing I wanted to see you about. I might have to put you back on your crew for a time. I need you to pass that by your therapist."

"Thanks, Craig. Again, I'm sorry. I—"

He held up his hand. "Understand. As I've said before, if I can help in any way, let me know."

Richard looked up at the knock on his doorpost. A stunning display of feminine sexuality stood at his door. Never before had he been anyplace with such a collection of beautiful women. While in the military, unforeseen circumstances led to his missing a chance to be an escort for the Miss America competition. Maybe this was some cosmic redemption for that missed opportunity.

"Richard, hi, we are ready for lunch."

Three others, standing next to the woman who spoke, waved, smiling.

"Okay, um, you're Irina, right?" He reached desperately into his memory for the ladies' names. It had only been three hours earlier, but the introductions had all come at once.

"Very good," Irina replied.

"And, let's see, Aida, Nina, and Miloska."

They all smiled and giggled. "Almost. I am Aida, but *this* is Miloska, and this is Emira. Nina is behind us, in the hall with Carina,—"

Richard held up his hand. "Please, I'm going to need some time to get everyone straight. Give . . . me . . . one . . . second." He closed down his computer and placed a marker in the paperwork so he could find where he left off when they returned.

He stood, grabbed his coat from a nearby chair and joined the women in the hall. Introductions were made yet again, more slowly this time.

Irina added, "And over there are Katarina, Ivanka, and Kristina. They drew the short draws and have to stay with the phones. We will bring them something from the restaurant."

He nodded toward the three women who smiled and winked back as they worked their phones. "So, are all of you from overseas? Your English is excellent."

Aida laughed. "It should be. Half of us were born here. Our parents were in the first wave of immigrants from the old Yugoslavia. The others have come more recently, from Croatia or Bosnia. We were all recruited to work here because we're multi-lingual and have some kind of tie to Eastern Europe, mostly family."

Richard had no doubt that was true, but he could see that Darko recruited for reasons that were more obvious as well. How had the man found so many women who were both talented and beautiful? He resisted the temptation to pinch himself, afraid he

110

would wake up and find it really was but a dream.

Aida and Irina seemed to take control as they took up positions on Richard's right and left and took his respective arms in theirs. They led him out of the building, followed by the seven others, and Richard exited the door to find another surprise. A limousine awaited them.

"Darko has a small fleet of cars and limos," Irina said. "Rentals. They're used mostly at night, or on weekends for weddings."

Richard beat the driver to opening the door and allowed the women to precede him into the vehicle. As he climbed in, he found they had saved him the seat between Irina and Aida. He found that somewhat curious. If he'd been Spiderman and not Thor, he'd note his spidey-sense tingling. However, he was Thor, and as his nose filled with a mixed perfume of womanly scents, and his eyes saw a sea of long, shapely legs emerging from short skirts, and his hands felt the innocent caresses of Aida and Irina on both sides, he found it difficult to focus on anything else.

Amy stood before a packed classroom and clicked the remote for their projector. The PowerPoint presentation's title screen with the DHS logo and website information filled the screen at the front of the room.

"Before we get started, I'm a bit curious. Before the two cases that triggered this class, have any of you ever run across someone you thought might be a victim of human trafficking?"

Only two hands went up.

"Sean."

"Six months or so ago, we were called to the scene of a MVA. A young woman was injured and needed to be flown to the city. She was dressed to the nines, but had track marks of varying ages. The man with her insisted that he had to accompany her, but, of course, he couldn't. Our crew commented later on how protective he seemed to be, but as it ended up, she had no ID, did not speak English well, would not tell us anything, even her name. She seemed scared to death. When we arrived at the hospital, another man was there to meet her, but security wouldn't let him into the E.D. We heard the next day that her exam revealed sexual activity just before the accident, and later that afternoon the nursing staff found her dead in her bed. Probable OD. In hindsight, we think she was being drugged and pimped, and that these men somehow got to her to give her that fatal overdose to protect themselves. Neither man was ever found. The girl was never identified. The whole case, the possibility of a crime, just kind of died with her."

Amy heard several sighs from the room, sighs that echoed her own frustration with that story. Had she missed one or more telltale signs of human trafficking in the past?

She pointed to the owner of the other hand that had gone up. "Our story had a better ending."

"Good," said someone in the crowd.

"This was before I joined MedAir, when I worked with a ground crew. We got called to a domestic disturbance, and the patient was a young girl whose dress and make-up was far older than we suspected her to be. At the scene, she would say nothing, and she literally trembled in fear. The man insisted on going with her, but the police intervened, and we managed to get her alone in the back of the rig. Then she started spilling her guts about having been picked up off the street, drugged, and forced into prostitution. She was only fifteen, but had been held captive for almost two years. Folks at Children's Hospital got her care and protection, found her family back on the East Coast. The police eventually found the pimp, and he's serving time. He was suspected of just being a low-level scumbag in a bigger operation, but he would never say anything. I heard he simply pled guilty and took his lumps."

"He'd probably be dead now if he'd said anything," said a voice from the back of the room.

"Too bad," replied someone from the other end of the room. "We'd have one less dirt-bag being supported with our taxes."

Amy quickly asserted control over the class. She didn't want the class to head down that track.

"So, those two examples show us several key factors for recognizing human trafficking. A minor involved in sex trafficking is always considered a victim, even without force or threats. But, with the first case, the presence of a controlling person, the lack of ID, the fear, the appearance of being forced to do sex acts, the presence of track marks and drugs in her system, all can be clues to someone being a victim of human trafficking. Does anyone know other signs?"

Several hands went up. She called on them in turn.

"Someone being coached on what to say, especially

to police."

"Not having freedom of movement, like, not being able to socialize or go to church. Not being free to contact friends or family."

"Threats. Someone threatening the victim with harm or harm to their family, or threats of deportation or arrest."

"That's right," said Amy. "Don't forget signs of neglect or physical abuse, like not being fed or given water, not being allowed to sleep or get medical care. Also, bruises, burns, and other evidence of repetitive injury, like we watch for in child abuse cases."

They went on to discuss other signs and the size of the problem. She breezed through the PowerPoint presentation to pick up a few things not already mentioned.

"Remember, as many as 30% of these victims will encounter a healthcare professional at some point. We need to be aware, and we might save a life by being alert. Any questions or other comments?"

Amy glanced around the room. No one spoke up.

"Okay then, we've got laminated index cards listing things to watch for. They're in the back as you leave. And if you want more info, you can find it on the dhs-dot-gov website. We're done. Have a great day."

Amy collected her things and headed back to her office, uninterrupted. Amanda had been right. In her call back, right before the class, she had told Amy, "If you want to make a difference, focus your emotions into a positive force. Make it a point to do your part to stop people like human traffickers. You can't save the world, Amy, but you might save one small part of it, one person. Channel your energies like you used to do on the basketball court in college."

Amy had done just that. She had refused to let the class take a toll on her emotions. She had refused to yield to the PTSD and had instead focused her mind on helping to stamp out human trafficking. She felt good. She felt pumped up.

Lunch had been surreal for Richard. The limo had pulled up to the front of the restaurant, and nine gorgeous ladies emerged, followed by Richard. Two of the women immediately latched onto his arms, and he walked into the place like he was a movie star or pro athlete surrounded by his "ladies." He caught more than one guy's jaw dropping in envy. He'd also noticed the women in the restaurant eyeing him, as if asking, "What's he got to make those women flock to him?"

In addition, lunch itself was delicious and fun. These women knew how to have a good time. No doubt about that.

Yet, back in the office, he realized that Aida and Irina had actually "fought" for his favor, and he found that odd. They'd only just met that morning. Surely they had boyfriends or husbands. They were too attractive, intelligent, and fun to remain unattached for long. In fact, it appeared that not one of these women was attached to someone. That wasn't just strange. The odds were astronomically against it.

He put his musing aside and returned to work. By the end of the afternoon, he'd barely made a dent in the company's product listings. He needed to figure out a more efficient way to achieve his goal.

There was a knock at his door, and he looked up expecting Irina or Aida. Darko stood there smiling. Richard stood to greet his boss. Darko pumped his hand up and down.

"No, no. Is okay, please sit. So, what you think?"

"I can't say yet. There's a lot of material here."

Darko laughed and raised his hand to wave it back and forth in front of him. "No, no, no. Is only first day. I do not expect opinion yet. You say two month to create plan. That when I expect your opinion." He nodded his head toward the phone bay and its women. "What you think about them? Isn't it rush to go out surrounded by such beauty? You should go to club with them sometime. Wow! Is fringe benefit I not mention."

Richard gave him a funny look, and Darko answered as if he'd read Richard's mind.

"Yes, yes, I know you meet my wife. She go, too. Fit right in and keep me in line." He laughed. "But, you! Ha! Red-blood American boy could have great time, yes?"

Richard nodded, but the thought, if it's too good to be true, floated through his head.

"Anyway, I fix thing for you to come in when need to." He reached out and handed Richard an electronic key card. "This go to lock at loading dock door, but not to special vaults. If you need access there, it must be Sonja or me to go with you. I am sure you understand."

Richard took the card and added it to his wallet. He would make a point of testing it before leaving for the day, although he now debated the need to come early just to impress the boss.

"Thanks. I know there'll be times I need to get in

outside of the usual hours. This will save me from bothering your security guys. Speaking of which, they, uh, know who I am, right? I mean, I don't want to get shot if I stop by after dark just to get something I forgot in my office."

Darko laughed again. "You watch too much TV." He turned to leave, but turned back. "Have great night. Why not you take Irina to dinner tonight. I hear she . . ." He grinned. ". . . is hot for you. Or maybe Aida if you like better."

Richard took a deep breath. *This is awkward.* In most companies, the management bends over backward to avoid anything even hinting at sexual harassment. Yet, here, his boss is a lascivious old goat who's encouraging him to seduce a co-worker. Of course, as he thought about it, he had to admit the co-worker already seemed willing, even after having known Richard for all of seven hours. Nothing added up.

"Tempting, Darko. Very tempting. But, I can't tonight. I have other commitments." Well, he hoped he had another commitment. He didn't want to start his job "lying" to his boss, but he still had a phone call to make about that.

"Well, another time perhaps," replied Darko. His visage darkened as he turned away, as if his personality switch flicked off, but Richard caught the change.

The diuretic effect of his lunchtime beer caught up to him, and he needed to answer nature's call. Now would be a good time to test his key card, as well as explore the office a bit. He needed some supplies.

He left his office and turned away from the phone

center. Darko's office sat at that end of the hall, and he saw only two offices similar to his between them. One was empty, and in the other sat the first "normal" employee he'd seen in the building. Neither beauty— the ladies—nor a beast—a gun-toting security man. The grey-haired woman appeared to be in her fifties, maybe early sixties, and was dressed nicely for her age and somewhat overweight physique, but certainly not in a style comparable to Sonja and the ladies. More matronly, grandmotherly. She sat at a desk pouring over some type of catalogs. Richard couldn't make out the company or type of products. He poked his head into the doorway.

"Hi, I'm Richard. First day today, for marketing."

She looked up and smiled. If you could call it a smile. Several front teeth were noted for their absence.

"*Da*, Reechard. *Ne govorim engleski.*" I don't speak English.

He took a step closer in an effort to understand, and an earlier whiff of garlic became a heady stench. He noticed the catalogs contained a variety of bondage and sex toys, and he quickly stepped back into the doorway.

"Naomi," she said as he retook a position of escape.

"Well, uh, nice to meet you, Naomi. I'm sure I'll be seeing you around." He gave a quick wave and retreated to the hall and back toward the phone center. As he neared the women, they all smiled and waved. Irina quickly removed her headset and intercepted him. Aida, busy talking to a customer, frowned.

"Richard."

"Hey, um, where can I find a restroom?"

"Uh, sure. Down the hall that way and take the hall

118

to the left. We just have one unisex restroom so please help keep it clean. Or there's one in the warehouse, where the security guys and warehousemen have their break room." She paused, smiling, and fingered his collar. "Um, by the way—"

"Hold that thought. I'll be back."

He rushed off to the restroom, answered the call of nature, and followed that by going to the loading dock where he successfully tested his key card. On the way back, he again noted the discrepancy in building size between the outdoor footprint and indoor layout. That made him curious.

He walked past the "vault" where Darko had shown him the silk rugs and antiques. He wandered back toward his office and glanced into various rooms along the way. He took the hallway past the restroom. All of these rooms held more inventory, and Richard wondered how efficient their order fulfillment operation was. Who could make heads or tails of all of these rooms and their contents? Just as he thought that, three workers with various items on small carts emerged from three different rooms and entered adjacent rooms. They seemed to know what they were doing.

At the end of the hall, it turned back toward the warehouse. Maybe this would take him to the space he couldn't account for. Twenty feet down the hall, it ended at another access-controlled door. He tried his key card, but it didn't work. Maybe it was another "vault" that required Darko or Sonja. He wandered back the way he came, and as he neared the turn in the hallway, a security man coming from the other direction nearly bumped into him. The guard sized him up.

"You new guy?"

"Yeah, hi. I'm Richard." He extended his hand, but the man did not take it.

"What you do down here?"

"I was looking for a supply room. I need some things for my office, and no one ever showed me where I might find them. Can you show me where they keep office supplies?"

"Not down here. That door private. Not use your key card in it again. Okay?"

That revelation surprised Richard. They tracked the use of his key card. But then, he thought of Darko's office and the security panel he'd seen there. He should have expected they could track his card.

"Ask girly girls, on phones. They show you supplies." He turned and retreated toward the warehouse. Richard followed until he hit the main hallway where he turned the other way toward his office. Irina was gone from her phone, and Aida approached him without hesitation.

"Richard. Say, would you like to join me after work for a drink? I could show you around town a little bit." She gently stroked his arm with her fingertips.

"Thanks, Aida, but I have a commitment tonight. Sorry." He thought her frown a bit histrionic. "Hey, where can I find office supplies? I need a whiteboard, a presentation easel and pad, and some other things."

She grabbed his arm and led him to the other side of the phone bay, where she opened what appeared to be a closet door. Inside was a small walk-in closet holding notepads, pens, and the like.

"Make a list of things you need that we don't have and give it to me. I'll have Naomi order it for you."

At the mention of Naomi, Richard was more than glad to let Aida interact with her. Yet, he wondered how the woman could order supplies when she couldn't even speak the language.

"Thanks." He started looking through the shelves, but Aida stopped him, leaned up against him and kissed his cheek.

"You're welcome. Maybe we can do those drinks later this week."

She left, and he finished grazing through the supplies to find what he needed. He emerged with an armful of supplies and saw Sonja standing in the phone bay talking with Miloska. She glanced up at him and gave him a smirk. With her finger, she pointed to her own cheek where Aida had kissed his cheek. He blushed at the realization that Aida had marked her territory, him.

At the end of the day, Darko and Sonja watched Richard leave on the building's front security cameras. Darko frowned, while Sonja gave him a mischievous smile.

"Still think you can trust him?" she asked.

"If, by that, you really ask if I think he is police. No, he is not police."

"But he is ex-military."

"Yes, and maybe could be trouble, but I think not. He come to us by reference I trust and have no police background."

"But he snoop around today."

"Sure, but just curious. Try to find way around building. I would do same in new job."

Sonja nuzzled up to his side, draping her arms over his shoulder. "Yet, you frown *moja ljuba*. Why?"

"He not take bait, Aida or Irina. What normal man could resist?"

"Maybe he is gay."

"No, no. Not gay."

"Maybe he have girlfriend."

Darko nodded, and then turned his head toward her and kissed her on the forehead.

"Yes, that might be it. He is honorable man. Loyalty to girlfriend could make him resistant." He thought for a moment. "I will have Risto put man on him. Watch him. Find out. Might have to rethink my insurance about him. In meantime, double bonus we offer to girl who can compromise him."

Fifteen

Jusuf and Danijela had awakened with the dawn, and Jusuf wondered whether he'd slept at all. His back ached. His neck felt stiff and sore. And his mind worried. Where could they possibly go and remain safe? They couldn't stay in this empty, cold cottage. The cabin across the river was the only "home" he could recall. Now, it lay in a smoldering ruin.

Danijela moved as if stiff and sore as well, but she voiced no complaint. She arose before him and made first claim on the bathroom.

"One flush only. No water pressure," she announced as she rejoined Jusuf on the walkway above the sunken great room.

He walked to the bathroom, emptied his bladder, and used that single flush.

"I find bucket. We use water from river for flush," said Danijela as he returned.

"No. First, we can't stay here. Risto's men might be watching the area. Second, if we go near the water, we could give ourselves away."

"Only me. You not give yourself away because they not know you."

He furrowed his brow. She was right, of course, but he continued, "Third, I don't think I could do more nights like last night. I'm so sore I feel like a truck hit me. We need to find a better place to hide. A place with water, heat, a way to cook."

Danijela shrugged. "All ears. Is that right? All ears

123

for ideas, right?"

Jusuf looked toward the floor. "I don't have any."

She went to the kitchen and retrieved several energy bars to eat, plus a partial bottle of orange juice. They sat on the steps and gazed towards the river. That's when they first noticed the activity across the river. The fire department had obviously been called and responded to the structure fire. They had extinguished the fire so completely that no smoke arose from the site. Two men wandered about the area, a fire department SUV parked where the black SUVs had been the previous night. Yellow tape extended across several areas.

One man walked up to the other, who was talking with a police officer. As they talked, the man pointed toward the cabin where they sat. The deputy looked up, nodded to the man, and headed for his patrol car.

"Uh-oh," said Jusuf. "C'mon. We need to leave."

"Why hurry?"

"I have a feeling that sheriff's deputy over there is going to be knocking on this door in as much time as it takes him to get here. We gotta clear out."

With no argument, Danijela picked up their trash and food, while Jusuf grabbed the sleeping bag and other items. She peeked out the door and turned to him.

"Is clear."

They scurried to the car, and Jusuf loaded up while Danijela replaced the key to its hiding spot. A minute later, they eased out the drive and turned toward the main road.

"If I'm right, we'll pass that deputy about the time we hit the main road."

He was right.

Half an hour later, they pulled into the parking lot of the grocery store where they shopped previously. As they sat in the lot, Jusuf scanned the area. Not too busy, as he might expect for early morning, early in the week. No one seemed suspicious.

"Do you have a road map in this car?"

Danijela shook her head. "I not know. Never look." She opened the glove compartment in front of her and rummaged through an assortment of mostly trash. "None here. Maybe trunk?"

"No, I would have found it when we packed. Okay, I'm going to go inside and get a map and a few other things. Do you need anything?"

"Yes. I come, too."

Jusuf held up his hand. "No. Too dangerous. If I were Risto, I'd pick the two or three closest groceries and place people there to watch for you. Like you said before, they don't know me."

Danijela said nothing, but gave a slight nod of her head. Jusuf checked his pockets. He had enough cash.

"Be right back."

He walked into the small AG Market store, alert to everyone around him. Once inside he moved quickly to get the items he needed. At the checkout lane, he made small talk with the clerk, who gave him an odd look at some of the things on the conveyor. "Wife," was his curt answer. As he paid, he noted an older man out of the corner of his eye and an alarm rang in his head. A quick look revealed the man to be the same one they had passed on the road the day before, who later appeared at the cabin. The man glanced at him, but moved his gaze to someone else.

He took his change and asked, "Hey, do you know where the nearest public library is? We're new here, and I don't know the area very well yet."

"Sure. The Jefferson County Public Library has a branch in High Ridge just a few miles north on Highway 30. Take a left at Highway PP."

"Thanks." He gathered his bags and watched the older man. Should he approach the man? No. Not yet. He couldn't risk exposing Danijela if he wasn't this Lynch Cully fellow. The man could also work for Risto, but then Jusuf realized the man wouldn't know the name Jusuf, or Lynch for that matter. Still, Jusuf reasoned even a policeman might work for Risto, too. He could take no chances. He slowed down until he saw the man turn to look the opposite direction and then eased past him toward the exit. The man turned to look again, but Jusuf had already passed by and gave the man just the back of his head. At the door, he took off and sprinted for the car.

He tossed the bag into the back seat and climbed into the driver's seat. He needed no map to find the library. Highway 30 was at the next intersection. He started the car and peeled out.

Danijela raised both hands, questioning, and asked, "Again, hurry, hurry. Always you hurry. When we slow down?"

"When you're safe."

She put her hand on his shoulder.

As they neared High Ridge, they passed a bank, and Jusuf noted the hour. The library wouldn't be open this early. He felt a new anxiety born of anticipation. Was

126

this the day he would rediscover who he was? He had grown comfortable with Danijela, being Jusuf. Was that about to change?

He passed the turnoff and kept driving toward the city, looking for a place to eat. Nothing but pizza joints, Chinese carry-outs, and bars. Further up the road, they came to a "Jack in the Box," and he pulled into the drive-thru lane, ordered breakfast sandwiches plus coffee, and pulled back onto the highway. He found the library and parked in the lot.

"We can eat here and figure out our next move."

Danijela sat still, holding the bag of food. "What we do here?"

"I need an answer to a big question. I hope I can find it here."

After a second of thought, Danijela's face registered her understanding. She opened the bag, passed Jusuf a steak and egg burrito, and then unwrapped her breakfast croissant.

"That old guy was in the grocery store, the man we saw at Ibrahim's yesterday."

"But he not recognize you?"

He finished chewing and replied, "No, he didn't. So, that makes me wonder, if he really knows this Lynch Cully, why didn't he?"

"Ummm, maybe beard, long hair disguise you. Duh." She rolled her eyes.

"Okay, okay. Maybe it's that simple, but I need to find out more about Lynch Cully. This is the only place I can think of where I might find that answer." The question he didn't state was, "Did he *want* to find that answer?"

They ate in silence, and Jusuf simply stared out the window as he chewed. Jusuf finished his second burrito and turned to the back seat, where he retrieved the bag from the grocery store. He took out the map and laid it on his lap. Then he removed a comb, scissors, and a box of hair color.

"How'd you like to become a blond?" he asked, a mischievous smile easing across his face. "And maybe short hair?"

She furrowed her brow. "You cut hair before?"

"Not that I remember. How hard could it be? I'd just shorten it, not style it."

She said nothing for a moment. "Blond, maybe. Not sure I want you cut hair. Hair is special to woman. Do not want, how you say it, hatchet job."

Jusuf smiled and held up the scissors. "They're just scissors, not a hatchet."

Danijela pouted. "I think about it."

Jusuf placed the items back in the bag and dropped it behind Danijela's seat. As he exited the car to dump their breakfast trash in a nearby can, he saw two cars, a woman driving each, enter the lot and pull behind the building. A few minutes later, he saw another car, with a woman and young child, pull into the lot. It was almost time. He hoped the answer to his big question waited inside. He still hadn't decided what he hoped the answer would be.

Ibrahim had finished his morning's Bible reading, eaten breakfast, and discussed his work with a confidante at the mission. Now, he had work to do. He donned his hooded sweatshirt and added an outer jacket over it. His head covered, he eased out the back door into the alley and sauntered toward his pick-up, alert to every sound and movement around him. His former comrades could be anywhere.

An hour later, he turned off the highway onto the road skirting the river. For three months he had worried about Danijela. He had had to go into hiding and couldn't risk coming to the cabin. Since there was no phone there either, he had sent her a note with money weekly and, as planned, had received no replies. However, he realized that his instructions to contact him only in case of emergency had a flaw. He'd had no way of knowing if she was okay.

It didn't take long to realize something was very wrong. Yellow police tape crossed the drive leaving him just enough space to pull his truck into it.

Ibrahim gazed down the drive and saw nothing but rubble. The cabin was gone, and his heart raced in fear that Danijela was now dead as well. He ran toward the battered, rusty mailbox and nearly pulled it off its post as he pulled open the door. Inside he found a notice from the rural fire protection district, and all of his letters. She had never checked the mailbox, or hadn't been able to. What had she thought of him? He stroked his mustache with one hand and took a deep breath. What next? *Dear Lord*, he thought. *Please let her be okay.*

He had one remaining long shot. They had previously discussed the use of a warning system, a failsafe plan, should trouble arise when they weren't together. He found the "Reward for Lost Dog" flyer in his truck and posted it on a tree near the driveway opening. Innocent enough to warrant no second glance. Common enough to evoke no suspicion. Yet, on the back, he had printed a contact point. She was to do the same, had she posted the flyer. If she came back, if she remembered the plan, she would see the flyer and find a new place for refuge.

As he returned to the truck, he heard a branch break on the hillside above him. Instinctively he dropped to the ground. The single crack became a cascade of rustling leaves and snapping branches. Someone was coming down the hillside at him.

He crawled as fast as he could to the passenger's door, opened it and climbed in, staying as low as he could. He pulled a 9mm S&W from under the seat and sat up quickly on the driver's side. He shifted into reverse and his wheels spun before gaining traction and catapulting the pickup onto the road. He looked up as one of two men raised a handgun toward him. His gun was up first, but having no time to aim, he could only fire a shot their way through his open window. It was enough to make both men duck and give him time to shift into gear and lurch forward. He was gone before they could clear the road.

Yet, now he faced a new dilemma. Had they seen him post the flyer? Were they retrieving it even now? Had he placed someone else in danger, someone willing to step up for Christ and do the right thing by providing sanctuary to women he rescued from these scum?

He downshifted into second gear, gave the wheel a quick Scandinavian flick and turned it into the opposite lane, performing a fast bootleg turn to take him back toward the cabin's ruins. Within seconds, he raced past the drive. The flyer remained tacked to the tree, and the men were nowhere to be seen. He sighed in relief. The only way to find the new contact location was to remove the flyer from the tree. So far, his friends were safe. He also noted the leaves on the downhill side of the road remained undisturbed, so it appeared they had retreated uphill back to their vehicle. With a bit of luck, he would soon encounter them racing toward him in pursuit along his original track.

He was not disappointed. In fact, he found a vicious delight in having the element of surprise. He recognized the black SUV barreling toward him. He had once been its driver. He moved to the center of the road, forcing them into a game of chicken. He had no doubt who would flinch first.

He shifted his gun into his left hand and extended it out the window, firing once at the oncoming vehicle. A puff of shattered glass flew off the windshield, likely taking out the center rearview mirror inside. He gunned it. He knew the men inside, and they knew him. He had no fear of dying to protect his friends.

The passenger tried to rise up through his side window, but appeared to have trouble turning toward him. He would get no shot. With seconds to go before impact, the SUV veered off the road into the wooded ravine toward the river. The passenger's hands flew up into a protective position, but the trees won. To say he was half the man he used to be was now the truth. The SUV's path ended squarely on a large sycamore tree, shattering the windshield fully before the driver flew out headfirst into the tree's embrace.

Ibrahim slowed, and continued on. Someone else

would have to "stumble" upon the accident and report it.

Jusuf and Danijela gave the mother and child a chance to enter the building before following. He looked around the interior and spotted some tables holding desktop computers. He frowned. He knew that at one time he knew everything about these machines. They seemed so familiar, and yet now they weren't. The frequent irritation he felt over realizing he should know something permeated him again. He'd felt that exasperation so frequently over the past weeks that he thought he'd be used to it by now. He wasn't. In fact, as his memories returned, that annoyance hit him doubly hard.

Danijela led him to the tables.

"Okay. Now we Google this Lynch Cully man."

Google. Yes. He remembered that.

Jusuf sat down in front of the machine and tried to launch a browser. A window popped up asking for his name and library card number. He sat there, stymied, and the frustration mounted. He found himself navigating through the Control Panel to the User Accounts. Here he discovered the administrator's account name, but he again faltered at needing a password.

He wanted to pound the table, but knew that would only attract attention and risk their being asked to leave. He knew that he once could hack this. Easily. Public library computer security was beginner's stuff and a low-budget rural system was even more basic. He began to breathe faster, racking his brain trying to remember. He needed to remember.

He felt a tap on his shoulder.

"Here. Quick, before she miss it." Danijela handed him a library card.

He returned to the main screen and entered the name and number. Danijela swept up the card and walked casually toward the mother. The child had just returned to her mother with three books she had checked out.

"Here is card. She drop this at desk," Danijela told the mother as she handed the card back to the woman. The woman smiled and thanked Danijela before chastising her daughter to be more careful.

Jusuf smirked as Danijela returned to the table. "Dropped it, eh?"

Danijela smiled back and shrugged. "With little help maybe. So, she learn good lesson from this—to be careful. To little girl, is bridge over water now."

Jusuf chuckled. "That's water under the bridge."

"Same thing."

Grinning, Jusuf turned back to the computer and pulled up the internet browser. He called up the Google website and typed in "L-y-n-c-h C-u-l-l-e-y." The browser met his request with the question, "Do you mean Lynch Cully?" A list of references to Lynch Cully followed.

He clicked through to the first item, his obituary. He certainly fit the age of the man.

"Wow," said Danijela, reading over his shoulder. "I not read English good, but he look like super cop."

Jusuf nodded. The credits for cases solved, his

pioneering work in computer forensics, and undercover drug work had been topped by his last case, stopping a vicious serial assailant and murderer. He'd disappeared after that last case, presumed dead at the hand of that killer. The memorial service had been quite the event, disrupting traffic more effectively than a presidential visit.

This didn't satisfy him. He learned what the man had done, but not who the man had been.

Back to the search page, where he clicked on a second reference. This one detailed the memorial service and showed pictures of the motorcade and the man's parents—and girlfriend? The caption identified her as Amy Gibbs. Again, images of this woman swirled through his head. He had known her. Of this, he was now positive. In addition, she had been important to him. That, too, was certain. The pictures of his parents triggered memories from a childhood that could only be his. He had no other frame of reference for synthesizing a childhood.

He glanced at Danijela. She had a look of distaste carved onto her face and her eyes seemed set on the picture of Amy Gibbs.

"Go to next one," she said.

He navigated to a third citation and found what he'd been looking for. He heard Danijela let out a breath, and he turned. Her eyes were wide now, as she pointed to the photo of Lynch Cully.

"I call you Lynch now. That is you, clean shaved. That is man I fish from river."

He saw tears well up in her eyes.

"What's wrong?"

134

She pointed to a picture showing a large group of politicians gathered at the memorial service. She put her finger on the face of a man, third from the right.

"H-he," she whispered, "is one I escape from."

A quiet anger seethed inside Lynch as he noted the man's name and position. It was a name he felt he had known in the past, but the memories didn't surface. Perhaps it was best that they didn't. Knowing what the man had done to Danijela, he wanted to hunt the man and cleanse the earth of his presence.

"Don't worry, we'll get him," he said. He navigated back to the previous article and focused on the photo of his parents and Amy Gibbs. While he focused on his parents, he sensed increased anguish in Danijela. Again, with a glance, he saw tears flowing down her cheeks. "There's something else, isn't there?"

She didn't answer, but turned on her heels and made a straight path for the door.

Jusuf—Lynch—quickly signed off the computer and followed her to the car. He opened the door for her and quickly took to the driver's seat.

"What's wrong?" he asked again.

She looked away, hesitated, and then answered. "You have life to go to. You have girlfriend, parent who mourn for you. To them you must go back. I . . ." She stopped and sobbed.

Lynch took her hand. "Danijela, I—"

"No. You go back to family. I do not. I have parent and sister who mourn, who I not see, or talk to, or hear about for four year. I am sick in heart to see them."

Her comment surprised Lynch, though it shouldn't have. He thought he had seen jealousy in her eyes when she saw the photo of Amy Gibbs. He knew he had fantasized about a future with her. Had he simply projected those feelings onto her, believing she had wanted a future with him as well? Maybe he'd been wrong to assume that. Maybe he'd been wrong to consider any future with Danijela.

"Not yet," he replied.

She turned to him. "What mean, not yet? Yes, you go back."

"Not yet. I told you before I'm not going anywhere until I know you're safe."

She had no reply except to lean into him and kiss him on the cheek.

He found the map he had purchased and opened it to find their location. To keep heading north would take them into St. Louis County, closer to Risto's network of eyes and trouble. Heading back the way they came made them more remote, harder to find, but where could they stay? He voiced his thoughts to Danijela.

"Go back to cabin. Keep past on road. Is another cabin we might use, but owner might be there. If not, we break in. I have no key."

Lynch turned off the main road onto the river road to the cabin. As they neared Ibrahim's property, flares and flashing lights slowed their progress. Two sheriff's cars, an ambulance and tow truck lined one lane of the road. A deputy waved them on, and off to their right, they could see a crumpled black SUV. Two men, paramedics, carried a body bag up from the ravine. Lynch saw enough and focused on passing the scene as quickly as possible to avoid scrutiny. The tow truck, last in the line, blocked Ibrahim's drive. As Lynch passed it and began to speed up, Danijela suddenly screamed.

"Stop! Stop!"

There were no cars behind him, so he safely screeched to a halt. Danijela jumped from the car and ran toward the driveway to the cabin ruins. He lost sight of her for a moment, but within seconds, she was running back toward the car and jumping into the passenger seat. She waved a paper flyer back and forth so quickly, he couldn't make out what it promoted.

"Ibrahim! Alive! Ibrahim did this. He is living." This time her tears appeared as tears of joy.

He grabbed her hand and stopped it midair. She released the flyer, and Lynch saw only that it offered a reward for a lost dog. How did that mean Ibrahim still lived?

She took it back and showed him the front. "This, this was warning signal. For trouble, we agree to post one of these on tree next to driveway." She flipped it around to reveal a hand-printed address and phone number. "Here is new contact point. We find Ibrahim here, and place to stay."

Sixteen

❧ ✦ ✦ ☙

Amy arrived home feeling emotionally tired. The drive from Amanda's office consumed 30 minutes in typical traffic, but her mind had been so focused on her session that the half hour seemed like just a few minutes. In the course of that time, she'd come to two conclusions. First, she needed more time with God. Second, she had to move on and stop living with a ghost that was more fantasy than reality. Amanda had been right. She lived with a fantasy of what life with Lynch might have been like, not with the reality of what their relationship had been. Still, the loss of Lynch seemed to play a larger role in her 'problem' than she'd admitted.

She entered her kitchen from the garage and plopped her purse down on the counter. She retrieved a glass from the cabinet and filled it with cold water from the front of her refrigerator. Suddenly, she felt famished. As she took a sip of water, she pondered what to do about dinner. She turned to lean back against the counter and noticed the message light blinking on her answering machine. *Work or Macy?* she wondered.

She pressed the button on the machine, and Caller ID revealed the answer. Macy. Her best friend had been working a string of night shifts in the E.D., something she disliked and did not have to do with her seniority, but had agreed to do because of the maternity leave of another friend. Already their paths had diverged with Amy no longer on flight status and not visiting the E.D. with patients. The night shifts added to their separation.

"Hey girlfriend, haven't talked in over a week. I'm back on the sanity shift, so call me."

She deleted the message and found a second, a hang-up with a number she did not recognize. Delete. A third message, ten minutes after the second, queued up with the same phone number.

"Amy, this is Richard Nichols. I hope you remember me from your dad's place, um, and not from the restaurant." There was a pause, and Amy could almost see his grin. "Hey look, I know this is last minute, but if you're free for dinner tonight, I'd love to treat you to a meal, anywhere you'd like to go, to make up for Thor's faux pas. Here's my number." He recited his cell number. "If I don't hear from you by seven, I'll assume the worst and have to start a hunger strike in penance. But I'm already hungry, so hope to hear from you. Bye."

Amy smiled. It was Tuesday, but dinner out would be okay. She picked up the portable phone and froze. Her breathing accelerated, and she forced the phone back onto its charging rack. What was she doing?

She took a deep breath and forced a sense of calm upon her soul. Hadn't she just concluded that she needed to step out, to move on, to re-enter reality? She bowed her head, said a quiet prayer for boldness, and picked up the phone again. *Okay, let's do this!* she thought as she dialed.

"Richard."

"Hi, Thor." She heard a deep basso laugh on the other end.

"Oh no, am I in trouble again already? What's a guy gotta do to catch a break here?"

"I'm sure I can come up with a list of things, but I'm willing to start with dinner, as promised."

"So, tonight gonna work okay?"

"I called back, didn't I? But, I'm not going to take advantage of your offer by suggesting someplace really upscale. I don't have time to get ready for that. You, uh, didn't plan it that way, did you? Because we can postpone this to a date when I have plenty of time to get ready." She smiled at the idea of seeing him squirm on the other end.

"Never even crossed my mind. We can do dinner tonight *and* get ritzy this weekend. Your choice both nights."

He certainly didn't seem to need any prayers for boldness. He had already twisted his invitation into a twofer. That was a definite, and not unpleasant, change compared to her dates with Lynch. She shook her head at that thought. Maybe she wasn't ready. She shouldn't start by comparing Richard's every move, every turn of phrase, his sense of humor, to Lynch. No, she had to approach this fairly, openly.

"Do you know where the Galleria is? There's an Italian place across the street, Maggiano's Little Italy. I can be there in 30, 40 minutes."

"I can pick you up."

"No. This place is in-between us, closer to you actually. It makes more sense for me to meet you there."

"Well, okay. I haven't been to the Galleria, or this restaurant, yet, but I'll find it. Why don't we plan on seven o'clock? I'll meet you just inside."

"Okay. Seven o'clock. See you then."

Amy took a deep breath as she hung up. That gave

140

her an hour to get ready and get there.

Richard's cell phone rang again just as he clicked off with Amy. His first thought was she'd changed her mind, but a glance at the Caller ID showed a now familiar number. He walked into the bathroom, turned on the shower, and answered the phone as he sat on the closed commode.

"How's it going?"

"As planned," he answered quietly. "I have to move slowly 'cause his security guys are armed and well-trained. They move like seasoned pros, and the security system is top notch. I think the women are trained, too, but in a much different art. They make Mata Hari look like an amateur."

"Be careful."

"I know. Hey, there is one thing you can do for me." He went on to explain the rare, silk farsh rugs. "Find me a legitimate buyer for one of them."

Seventeen

It was dusk as Lynch circled the block slowly for the third time and meandered along adjacent streets. The neighborhood in north St. Louis County was one of the original inner ring suburbs for the city. Beginning in the 1850s, William Ferguson convinced the Wabash Railroad to put a line through his property with a permanent stop at the new Ferguson Station depot. He then sold tracts of land to businesses and people interested in a country home. By 1894, with a population over 1,000, the city of Ferguson Station incorporated as a fourth-class city. Ferguson, later becoming one of the first Charter Cities in the county, had seen its share of changes throughout its 100-plus years.

Lynch sensed no hint of trouble, and the community seemed relatively quiet. Plus, from what Danijela had told him, it lay at the opposite end of the county from Risto's base of operation.

With no one visible on the streets, he finally pulled up to park on the side street next to a large, well-restored, two-and-a-half-story, white frame home bearing a Century Home plaque. Smoke rose from the chimney. Someone was home.

Lynch looked at Danijela. "You stay low. Don't let anyone see you until I clear this place and come get you."

She looked at him as if he'd gone crazy. "No way. I go with you."

She jumped out of the car before he could protest, taking the "lost dog" flyer with her. Lynch raced along the sidewalk and up the driveway after her.

"Danijela! We don't know—"

She stopped and swirled to face him. "Yes, I do know. Ibrahim do this." She held up the flyer and flapped it in Lynch's face. "I trust." She turned and resumed her walk toward the home's front door. "Beside, they expect woman, not man."

Lynch stood his ground on the driveway, but he had no counter-argument. She was the one in danger, the one whose face was known to her captors, and the one who held the key to bringing down these human traffickers. All along, he'd been an unknown factor, the ace-up-the-sleeve, an unintended guardian.

As Danijela mounted the first step to the broad, covered front porch, she turned back. "Come, come."

Lynch shrugged and shook his head, before racing to join her. Together they rang the bell and waited. A minute later, an older woman, mid-sixties with a short cut hairstyle, came to the door.

"May I help you?" she asked through the closed door.

Danijela held up the flyer, showing the woman's address on the back. "Ibrahim send me."

The woman's eyes widened. She turned for a second and yelled into the house, "Honey, come here!" She then opened the door and ushered them inside. "Quickly, come inside." She appeared a bit flustered as she took their coats and hung them on a bentwood coat rack just inside the main door. "I'm Mary Southworth, and my husband is Mike. W-we expected a bit of advanced notice, but welcome. Please have a seat." She pointed to an adjacent room holding two couches, an antique piano, and a large screen TV.

"I am Danijela, and this is . . ."

Lynch saw the puzzle in her mind. How should she introduce him?

"I'm Lynch."

Mike joined his wife in the wide doorway. "Welcome to our home. Can we get you something to eat or drink? Water, tea, soda. A beer if you like. We can fix you some dinner. Are you hungry?"

While Danijela accepted water, Lynch really wanted a beer, but took a tall glass of iced tea. Their hosts brought some cheese and crackers as well.

Mary sat in an antique chair opposite the couches. "We have friends at church who run a ministry in south city, Desert Well Ministries. Through them, we volunteered our home for young women rescued from trafficking, but we never expected someone to just appear on our doorstep. How . . . when . . . um, I don't even know what question to ask. I don't want to get too personal if it's uncomfortable."

Danijela did not appear inhibited. "I taken from Bosnia over four year ago. Ibrahim rescue me . . ." She proceeded to tell her story, in abbreviated form, to the couple. She mentioned only that Lynch had joined her after Ibrahim's disappearance.

"What happened to bring you to our home?" asked Mike.

"Can I trust you both to keep a secret?" asked Lynch. The couple nodded in unison. "I'm Lynch Cully, formerly of the Ladue police." The couple's jaws dropped in unison, too.

"B-but you're d-dead," stammered Mary.

Mike added, "The local news was filled with your story for weeks. Even the national news outlets picked up the story."

He proceeded to tell them what had happened, filling in gaps in Danijela's story from the point where she had dragged him from the river. He explained his amnesia, the large gaps in his memory that remained, that Ibrahim's cabin had been discovered and destroyed, and how they had ended up on the couple's doorstep in Ferguson.

"I bring this all up because your taking us in puts you in a position of some danger. If that's a problem, we need to find someplace else."

"Why don't you just go to your police chief, or the Major Case Squad, let them know you're still alive? I'm sure they can help."

Yes, why didn't he do just that? Now that he'd confirmed his identity, wasn't it easier to go that route? He could get Danijela into protective custody and set the ball rolling to go after this trafficking ring. But . . .

"I, uh, I can't do that. Yet. I have my reasons," Lynch replied. "Please trust me on this one." He could see the couple still had concerns. He leaned forward and placed his elbows on his knees, his hands folded together. "Look, my first priority is keeping Danijela safe. I owe her my life, and I'd give it up to protect her. Plus, we have no hope of taking these men down without the direct testimony of victims like her."

He noted Danijela's countenance, but couldn't quite figure out the emotion behind it. He suspected she was experiencing a whirlpool of feelings that maybe she couldn't identify herself. He knew he was going through that kind of turbulence. He would protect her with his life. Was that love or simply gratitude? He also felt something rise within when he saw the photo of Amy. Was that love or something else?

On a personal level, he didn't want to expose himself to the authorities because he knew he would immediately be removed from the case. He would become the subject of a dozen doctors and who knows how much medical and psychological testing. He might no longer be considered a police officer and might have to re-qualify to regain his badge. In the meantime, Danijela would be at the mercy of men he no longer knew, including one ranking politician *she* knew all too well.

"Well, let's get you both settled in. Any luggage, bags? We have two spare bedrooms on the third floor, our main guest room on the second, and this couch here folds out to a queen-sized bed."

Lynch pondered that layout. The two rooms on the third floor seemed to make the most sense, but now he had to think about the safety of this couple as well. If they were discovered and Lynch was on the third floor, Risto could take out the couple before Lynch was even aware the home had been invaded. He hadn't considered how adding more people to the mix could complicate matters. Protecting the two of them was easy, in a relative sense. Adding in the Southworths, or even Ibrahim if he showed up, multiplied the potential for problems.

"If it's not too inconvenient, I think I'd like to settle

in right here, with this sofa bed. I want to be the first line of defense. Not that I expect trouble." They hadn't expected to be found in Jefferson County either. At least here there were no property records linking it to Ibrahim. "We have a few things in the car. I can get them."

"I'll help," said Mike.

Mike led Lynch through the kitchen and garage to go to the car. Once outside he asked, "We might need more protection. Do you have a gun?"

Lynch shook his head.

Mike replied, "I have a 9mm S&W and Mary won't part with her Beretta. So, I'll get an extra handgun from my son. You do remember how to use one, right?"

"I think so." Images flowed into Lynch's head, memories of many hours spent on a firing range.

"Yeah, kinda like riding a bike. You can handle mine later to see what you recall."

They started unloading bags of clothing from the car.

"We've got a few perishables, food-wise."

"We can put 'em in the spare refrigerator, in the garage."

After a second trip to the car, Mike asked, "Do we need to hide the car?"

Lynch paused. He wasn't sure. "I'm not sure. If it's registered to Ibrahim, I guess someone might recognize it or be able to trace it. But it seems unlikely these men would have such a large network to cover this far north in the county."

"We'll hide it. I'll pull one of our cars out of the garage, and you can park in there for now. We'll figure out something more long-term."

They switched cars and re-entered the kitchen.

Lynch looked at the man, appreciating his decisiveness and noting his calm demeanor. "Sir, I apologize if we've put you in a spot. I don't like putting you and your wife at risk."

Mike smiled. "Son, not much scares us anymore. Our trust is in the Lord. He's our protector, and should our time come to join Him, we know it will be a much better place. Besides, we've been in worse situations. Something else to drink?"

"Oh?"

"I'm a retired full bird, Army. 101st Air Assault from Ft. Campbell. My career started in VietNam with the battle for Hamburger Hill. I was at Firebase Ripcord when the North Vietnamese Army attacked. I've been to Kosovo, the first Persian Gulf War, and too many places to count in-between. Retired shortly after the Gulf War. Mary worked for a local police department. Saw a lot of dirtballs come through their doors. If we need to, we can handle ourselves pretty well."

Lynch suddenly felt much more secure.

Eighteen

Richard had checked himself in the mirror, brushed his teeth a second time, and looked up Maggiano's three times on his smartphone's GPS map. Now he paced outside the Crate & Barrel across the street from the restaurant, and it was only six-thirty. He'd failed to grab a heavier coat and the cold ate through his inadequate outerwear. He didn't want to enter the restaurant so early, but he couldn't give himself a good reason for that decision. Instead, he walked into the trendy home goods store and pretended to shop.

He wandered through the dinnerware and found himself looking at new living room furniture. He needed something other than the hand-me-down sofa bed and coffee table given to him after college by an aunt, and his parents' old chairs. He liked what he saw. He ran his hand across the material of several sofa beds. He sat on two selections. Comfortable. The design was a bit more traditional than he'd envisioned. He flipped over the price tag and felt relief that he was sitting down. Maybe he'd put up with Clive's complaints about the old sofa bed a little longer.

"May I help you?" A pert, young salesclerk stood in front of him. She looked college age and stylishly dressed.

"I was just . . ." He suddenly remembered why he was there and glanced at this watch. Six-fifty eight. His heart began to race. *Oh no, the time!* he thought.

"Actually, I need to run. I lost track of time. Sorry."

He jumped up and brushed past the girl. "Sorry," he said again as he passed by. He raced for the door, ran into the street, and saw Amy ahead of him, just fifteen feet from the restaurant's main door. He sprinted.

HONNNKKK!! He slid past the car that almost hit him and made it to the door in time to open it for Amy.

"Allow me!" He tried to avoid sounding out of breath, but doubted his success. As she stepped through the door ahead of him, he took in a couple of deep gulps of air and brought his breathing under control. If only his heart rate would follow suit quickly.

"Two, please," he said to the hostess.

"Well, I see you found the place okay."

Richard debated how much to divulge and quickly decided openness was the best policy. He never had been one to play games.

"Actually, I, uh—"

"Right this way, please," said the hostess. Richard played the gentleman and held Amy's chair for her. As he sat across from her, she said, "You were saying . . ."

"Right. Um, I got here at six-thirty." He felt a faint blush rise to his face. "I decided to kill time across the street and then lost track of the time. I need a new sofa bed. But, I caught the time just in time for a timely opening of the door for you." He grinned.

"Yeah, and you almost had an untimely accident with that car. That could've put a damper on the evening. Timing is everything."

"Oh. You saw that."

"And heard it. I, um, saw you racing through C&B for the front door."

He laughed. "What? And you didn't just stop and wait for me?"

She smiled. "And just what would be the fun in that. I wanted to see if you could beat me to the door." Now she was being coquettish.

"Do you like red, white, or rose?" he asked.

"Imported beer, but a good red sounds wonderful."

Richard worked through the wine list, but grinned as he got to the list of beers. "Ah, then we have the best option right here." When the server returned, he ordered two Irish Red Ales.

Amy gazed at Richard and realized how easy he made it to be with him. She had indeed seen him rush through the Crate & Barrel. To her it was obvious that he hadn't been on time. He'd gotten there early enough to take time to shop. Lynch rarely had been on time for anything, except work. Lynch would have ordered two Bud Lights without asking Amy's preference. Richard had been open and forthright about getting there early, even at the risk of embarrassing himself. Lynch always seemed to be holding something back. At that point, Amy realized two things. One, she was comparing Richard to Lynch again. Two, she needed to stop.

Actually, she realized one other thing.

"Richard, before we get too far into anything, there's something you need to know."

Richard's countenance became somber, but not downcast. "Sounds serious. I'm already sitting. Should I finish my beer first?"

Amy frowned. "I am being serious."

"Okay. Sorry." He made no more wisecracks and waited intently on her to continue.

"I just want you to know that I was in a serious relationship not too long ago, and well . . ." How should she continue?

He put his hand over hers. "Amy, you don't have to go there. Your dad already told me, us -- Hassle and me that is, when we were at his house, about the detective you had been dating. He sounded like quite the guy."

Amy didn't know whether to strangle her father or hug him. "He was, in some ways. Look, I'm moving on. Despite our, say, rocky start at The Bridge, I really enjoyed the evening at my dad's. That's why I'm here. But . . ."

"Hey, no pushing. I promise. We're just getting to know each other, and I don't know where it will lead any more than you do. Let's just promise to have some good times together. Okay?"

She gave a little shrug of her shoulders and nodded.

"By the way . . ." He grinned. ". . . after dinner, can I show you my hammer?" He wiggled his eyebrows 'a la Groucho Marx.' She grimaced and punched him in the shoulder. "No really, I brought it with me. It's in my car." He started to laugh, as he rubbed his shoulder, and then added, "Ouch, you sure don't hit like a girl."

She punched him in the other shoulder.

"Hey, I don't think I can move my arms. You're gonna have to feed me now. And I need a straw for my beer."

She laughed. Yes, Richard Nichols was definitely fun to be around.

152

Richard had taken what he'd learned from Lt. Col. Gibbs that evening the week before and checked out Lynch Cully on the internet. He had been quite the cop. He seemed like the kind of man Richard could have been good friends with, if he had known how to loosen up. His whole platoon had been comprised of such guys. His best friends, though, were the ones who could let go of the job long enough to have fun. Had this Cully been like that?

Although they'd never met, Richard felt a loss at the man's death. Not the depth of loss he'd felt in losing friends on the battlefield, but that distant sense of losing someone people admired, someone who actually had made a difference. However, Richard also acknowledged, in a selfish way, that he was glad he didn't have to compete for Amy's attentions.

Dinner went better than he could have expected. They shared stories of growing up. He explained why he'd joined the service and shared some stories of his time in Afghanistan. She told him of the sudden death of her brother, Chad, just over a year earlier in Afghanistan. He hadn't known her brother, but it was a loss he understood and by the end of the meal, he felt they had bonded over several common interests and life events. Yes, the first date had gone well.

"Wow, it's later than I thought. I think they're locking the doors," he said.

He watched Amy as she glanced around the restaurant, which remained packed. Still, it was late, after eleven, and now he understood the looks they'd

153

been getting from the wait staff. The bill had been lying in front of him for over two hours, during which time they'd tied up the table, and the staff had lost out on additional tips. He'd make it up to them.

He picked up the tab and inspected it.

"Let me pay my part," Amy offered.

He shook his head. "No way. I asked you to dinner, and I'm just chauvinist enough to insist on paying."

She scrunched her mouth sideways and then said, "Sooo, if I ask you to dinner, you expect me to pay?" She smiled.

"Um, sure, if you're liberated enough to ask." He had pegged her as a traditionalist.

"Then, I have to work with my flight crew on Friday, but will you join me for dinner this weekend, Saturday night?"

"Un-uh, no fair. I already asked you. Tonight part of a package deal, remember?"

"Oh, I'll still let you keep that part of the deal. I was thinking more along the line of dinner at my place. Say, six-thirty. It's been a while since I put my cooking talents to use, and I love to cook."

He smiled inwardly. A traditional gal, just as he thought and just as he liked.

"I accept. I'll bring wine, unless you really want to stick to beer."

"Wine would be nice. What kind of food do you like?"

He laughed. "Do I look like there's any type of food I don't like? Surprise me." He stood and helped her with her chair. "Now, for the highlight of the evening."

He led her back to the parking garage, to his car.

154

"I don't know if I'm ready for this," Amy said, laughing. "The infamous Hammer of Thor. And here we all thought it was a myth."

Richard moved his hands, palms down, out over the trunk and spread them across the top. "Are you ready to be amazed?" She laughed again. "Close your eyes."

"Oh, come on. Are you kidding?"

"Nope, close 'em."

She complied. He pulled out an authentic looking replica of the comic book hero's mystical weapon. He held it in both hands. "Okay, you can open them."

She opened her eyes and upon seeing it for the first time, her eyes widened. "It looks just like in the movie. It's better than I expected. Clive is quite the artist."

"No, he's more than an artist. You don't know the whole story. Clive made this with layers of scrap Kevlar and hand carved the handle for it. See this?" He pointed to a small jagged piece of metal embedded in one of the broad sides of the hammer.

"Looks like a bullet."

"You're right. Clive and the guys thought it would be funny to make me carry this on patrol. They stuck the handle into the top of my pack, with the hammer resting on top, behind my head. We were on patrol outside a small village, and a sniper decided to take out the point man, me. Bullet hit the hammer instead of inflicting a fatal neck wound. It saved my life."

Tears welled up in his eyes at the memory, but he felt no shame in that. Amy, too, had tears in her eyes as she leaned up and kissed him on the cheek.

Nineteen

Ibrahim took time during the daylight hours to scout the neighborhood and found a small gravel turnout that led into a lightly wooded area about a half mile from the house. Parking the truck there, he navigated to a spot where he could watch the house. The sun had long ago descended below the horizon, and the air smelled of snow, although the forecasters predicted otherwise.

He waited and watched the house. According to the information Raifa had given him, her captors had a gala event that evening at the Ritz-Carlton. He watched for any unexpected guards, knowing that Darko had been spooked and Risto had been charged with additional security of their "assets." Fortunately, Risto did not have the manpower to cover every home of their clients, a situation helped recently by the loss of two of his men in that unfortunate motor vehicle accident. Ibrahim would have no problem relieving Risto of more men, should that become necessary, although he sometimes labored to justify those feelings with his new faith.

At seven-thirty, he watched the decked-out, white Cadillac Escalade back out of the garage and ease up the drive. Its owner held a prominent title and was known for his supposed intellect, yet he was so predictable. The usual "we're away" lights lit up their usual rooms. He watched for a while to make sure no one else was in the home. Satisfied, he flashed the laser of a standard classroom pointer at the window three floors up from the backyard patio. In response, the curtain drew back, and the light inside flashed three times.

Ibrahim moved along his practiced path until he stood beneath the window. On cue, the window opened enough for Raifa to lower the string, and he tied the phone to it. A moment later, he texted, "Ready?"

"No! I cannot do it."

"I have the rope. Knots make climb down easy."

"I cannot make it. He beat me. I have no strength. I will fall if I try. Plan B?"

Ibrahim hesitated, trying to think. "Give me minute to think," he replied. If the home's security system was on par with those recommended by Darko, he had no easy way to disable it. Cutting the power or phone lines would alert the monitoring company. The police response time would be a gamble, dependent on the location of the nearest patrol car.

What choice did he have? To leave her in the home would be like leaving her to die. He would have to break in, retrieve her, and carry her to the truck as quickly as possible. The time between the house and his truck would be the most vulnerable. Moreover, carrying her would not only slow them down, it would also make them all the more suspicious to neighbors.

He mentally reviewed what he knew about the security layout. Motion sensors starting along the driveway just 20 feet from the street. Video surveillance at the front door and garage. Inside, Raifa had told him there were door and window sensors as well as motion sensors at the expected traffic points on the lower floor. There were video cameras in the main entry hall and the man's study. All were linked wirelessly to a main panel in the master bedroom. That panel no doubt had wireless backup for contacting the monitoring company.

"I will break in. Get you. Need diversion and must get truck in better position first. Keep phone. If someone else come, throw into backyard."

He started to move back toward the truck and a thought struck him. He texted Raifa. "New plan. I take out power and phone. Police come. Find home secure, watch for a while and leave. Then I come get you. I text then."

He walked along the perimeter of the property until he came to the utilities. Had this been a densely built development, those lines might have been underground. Fortunately, the semi-rural location and large lots made overhead lines the economical choice for the builder, and those lines came through a wooded easement behind the homes. He walked along the lines and smiled as he found the ideal place to disrupt the power and phone.

He thanked God for the foresight to bring his backpack and a variety of supplies. From inside he retrieved two small explosive charges, originally prepared to take out locks on reinforced metal doors. Linked by a fuse, he placed them at 90 degrees to each other on the lower trunk of a medium-sized tree, possibly an oak by the bark, which held the slightest lean toward the utility lines. He lit the fuse and stepped out of the way.

With a slight pop and flash, each charge removed a hunk of tree, much like an ax in the hands of a skilled lumberjack. Nothing more was required. The tree creaked and groaned and slowly, at first, began its descent onto the utility lines. In its hurried finish, the tree lay on top of the crackling power lines, along with the innocuous cable and telephone lines. He waited long enough to feel assured there would be no fire. They didn't need a full-fledged emergency response with police and fire.

He crept deeper into the woods and waited.

Five minutes later, a patrol car rolled along the street, its searchlight scanning the area as it crept along. A minute later, a second car arrived. Ibrahim watched the officers check the house. He knew they'd find it secure. They moved away from the house, and one of the men followed the lines. His light flashed along the lines until he spotted the tree. Ibrahim held his breath, and released it slowly when the officer chose not to inspect the trunk and turned around. Joining up to the other patrolman, he used his flashlight to point toward the fallen tree. They returned to their cars, and Ibrahim could see well enough to note that the first officer to arrive was on the radio. The second officer resumed his patrol.

Ibrahim grew impatient as the officer remained in the home's driveway. *What he wait for?* Ibrahim began to calculate other options, but the car finally pulled away. In a flash, Ibrahim began to run through the woods toward his truck. He had a small window of opportunity and needed to take advantage of it. The police would likely step up their patrols of the area, and he had to act fast.

As he pulled onto the street, he saw that the area

remained clear. He quickly texted Raifa to be ready and sped into the driveway as close to the front door as possible. Leaving the vehicle running, he donned gloves and a dark balaclava and grabbed a heavy fence post driver from the bed of the truck before sprinting for the door. Using the post driver as a battering ram, he broke the locks on the front door with one quick thrust of the driver. He raced up the steps and straight to Raifa's door, where he required two strikes to break through the metal door's locks.

"Phone?" he asked. She handed the cell phone to him and he shoved it into his pocket. "Come! Quick! Police come."

She struggled to walk, and he wasted no time in snatching her up with one arm and placing her over his shoulder. Carrying her over one shoulder and the post driver in his other hand, he descended the steps and ran for the truck as quickly as he could. Out of breath, he tossed the post driver into the bed and lowered her on the seat. She pulled herself to the passenger side and he slid in behind her. He had the truck in reverse before he had the door closed behind him. Once on the street, he cruised away at the speed limit, careful not to attract attention. They were safely on the main road, heading toward the interstate before he saw a patrol car, lights flashing, heading the way he had just come.

Lynch and Danijela sat with their hosts in the room with the couches and television—the parlor, as their hosts called it. The clock showed it was after eleven, and the couple's son, Mike Jr., had just left, leaving behind a 9mm S&W like his father's. The two Mikes had worked with Lynch to make sure he felt comfortable with the handgun, although they had no place to test shoot. Satisfied he could handle it, Mike Jr. left and the four adults discussed future plans.

"Is your room okay, Danijela?"

"Yes, thank you. So high up. Look out window like being in cloud."

Mike laughed. "Our grandkids say the same thing."

"Is lonely though. Only me up there."

"That's what our daughter used to say. You can still move down to the second floor if you'd like."

"No, please. I'd like her to sleep up there. It's more secure," interjected Lynch. Lynch realized his statement came out more as a command than a simple statement that showed his concern.

Danijela eyed him and started to say something, but stopped.

"Do you have any plan of attack? There must be some way to stop these people."

Lynch looked at Mary. "I really haven't had time to think this all through. My biggest worry is not knowing how well connected these people are. They haven't been caught yet, and we know they're connected to two recent deaths. The Major Case Squad knows what we know, but I'm obviously not in their loop. I don't know if they have more info."

Mike cocked his head and looked at Lynch. "I thought you weren't ready to go to them."

"I'm not, and I didn't. They received a call from a man called Jusuf, the name Danijela gave me before I learned who I was and what happened to me. Parts of those memories are starting to come back." Lynch had long ago realized that he would never be able to say *all* of his memory was back. After all, how would he ever realize what he didn't remember?

"So, how do you want to do this? At some point, you have to go to the police. Is there anyone you remember whom you trust?"

"Maybe. I . . ."

The phone rang, and Mary answered. "Hello? . . . Right now? . . . No, it's a good time to come. In fact, someone you know is already here." Even from five feet away, Lynch could hear an excited voice on the other end. Mary smiled. "We have lots of room. How long? We're up, talking. See you soon."

"Let me guess. Ibrahim is coming," said Lynch. At this statement, Danijela's countenance lightened, and Lynch felt like he'd taken a punch in the gut.

"And he's bringing another woman, . . ." Her smile faded. ". . . but she's not in great shape. She received a beating before he got her out tonight."

"But he got her out," Lynch replied. "That's the important part. Maybe now we can decide how to proceed."

Mary looked at Danijela. "He was excited to hear that you were here."

Danijela replied with a wan smile. "Did he say name? Other woman name?"

"No, no name. We'll find out soon enough. He was less than 30 minutes away."

After 25 minutes of more silence than talk, Lynch heard a vehicle pull up next to the house. He stood and saw a man carrying a young woman up the drive. He rushed to the front door and went outside to assist.

Once inside, they sat the woman on the couch. It was the most she could do to remain upright in the corner of the couch.

"Raifa?" Danijela eased over to the girl. Raifa opened her eyes and gazed at Danijela before nodding. Tears welled up in Danijela's eyes. "Oh, Raifa." She whispered in her native dialect, as she stroked the other woman's hair. Raifa replied softly.

After a few minutes, Danijela stood up and looked at Ibrahim. "*Hvala.*" Thank you. She walked to him and gave him a hug. "*Hvala.*"

Lynch had anticipated a warmer, more joyous reunion between Danijela and Ibrahim. Perhaps the presence of Raifa had tempered that, but it was just as likely that his presence was the moderating factor. Lynch surveyed Ibrahim. They were of similar size and build, although Ibrahim was more muscular, his hair was trim, and he wore a full mustache. He had the confident bearing of a man well trained in military, or perhaps, police arts.

"She will heal, with time and care," said Ibrahim. "Now, she sleep. Where?"

"We share room," said Danijela. "I care for her. Come, Ibrahim. *Dolaze na ovaj način.*" Come this way. Ibrahim lifted the young woman with ease and followed Danijela from the parlor and up two flights of stairs to a bedroom on the third floor. Lynch watched them disappear at the top of the first flight and returned to the room.

"We have a doctor friend at the church who will come to check her out. We'll call him in the morning and cover any expense for supplies or medications," said Mike.

Lynch mulled that over a bit. "Be careful about any prescriptions. Using her real name might make her traceable."

Mike nodded as the sound of heavy footsteps descended the steps. Ibrahim appeared at the door.

"Danijela good nurse. Raifa is friend from child days. They taken together and brought here. She will care good for her."

Mike repeated his offer.

"Please not use real name. Darko has pharmacist client who watch computer for names," Ibrahim replied.

Lynch smiled. "Just said the same thing." He held out his hand. "I'm Lynch." He watched as Ibrahim scrutinized him. Were they competitors for Danijela's attentions? Lynch had once thought they would be. Now, he wasn't so sure. For one thing, there was a girl named Amy he would soon meet again, for the first time, in a manner of speaking. Second, they would be more successful as partners working against these slavers.

Ibrahim shook his hand, but continued the scrutiny.

"Who is this Darko you mentioned? Danijela only gave me the name, Risto."

Ibrahim sat on the nearest couch. Lynch noted the clock above the piano had ticked past midnight. He was exhausted, but knew he wouldn't sleep until a few answers became clear.

"Darko Komarčić. Boss. Was mobster in Croatia and Bosnia, but used war there as way to escape to

164

America. He own company that bring goods from Eastern Europe to America for sale. Import is word I want. Legitimate side sell thing like rug, antique, food, and wine. Other side, sell people. Some girls become house servant. Slaves with no wage, no passport or ID, no way escape. Most girls force into prostitution. Best girls, prettiest girls, work company in day and as high price escort at night. These girls loyal out of fear. Darko will kill girl and her family if she snitch. Some girl come from old countries. Other from families here. Some families owe Darko. Some sell girl to Darko."

Lynch felt a sudden fear. "Tatjana Alic and the other girl—"

"Jelena Kordić." Ibrahim's face turned grim.

"Sorry, Danijela didn't know her name. Have their families—"

Ibrahim interrupted again. "No. They have no family. That why they chosen as example." He paused and stared at the floor. "They killed because of me. I save Danijela. They die as example. I fear another die now, because I save Raifa."

The two men, and their hosts, sat there silently.

"Why haven't you gone to the police?" whispered Mary, who had tears in her eyes. "Why can't they save these girls? And stop this man?"

"And who is Risto?" asked Mike.

"Risto Dudakovic, head enforcer. Ex-military. Cold, cold man." Ibrahim took a deep breath and let it out slowly. He looked like a man about to gamble with his life. "I not go to police because, like girls, I forced to work for Darko. Mother still live in city, but I hide her right before I take Danijela. Hide sister, too." He started

165

to say something more, but stopped and glanced at the floor before continuing. "Risto and other men, all mobster at home. I work with him, do things I not proud of. By Danijela and your friends at Desert Well, I come to know Christ. Have repent. I willing to lay down life to make thing good, but not willing to give it up without reason. Darko like octopus, many tentacles stretch in all direction. Many friend in high place. I go to police, I end up dead, or my mother, or sister. They not hesitate to find them. Even now, there is price on my head, and they hunt for family."

He paused and gazed from one face to another. "As brother in Christ, I ask your help, not, as you say, throw me under bus."

Silence once again commended the room.

Mary was first to break in. "Will another girl die because of tonight?"

Ibrahim sighed. "I pray not, but very possible. And maybe family member, too, this time. May already have happen. Risto will act with no feeling. None of girl safe." A tear formed in his eye. "If so, I very, very sorry."

Twenty

Risto sat in Darko's office, a lone, low wattage lamp casting a soft light across the furnishings. Darko sat opposite him, in his usual chair, unhappy at the late hour disruption in his life. He had reason to fear Risto. The man was remorseless, lethal, and had a heart of dry ice. Yet, he was a man trained to know his place, to serve his masters. Should Risto ever mutiny, Darko's colleagues in Croatia would repay him his rebellion by exterminating every trace of family, something even Risto would regret. Besides, he kept all of Risto's appetites appeased.

"So, Ibrahim strike again. You tell me you have all under control, but he take Raifa. How? Judge Wallace now under investigation because of what police find when they answer alarm at his house. Not good. Not good at all, Risto."

"*Moje isprike, gospodine.*" My apologies, sir. "You know I give no excuse, but understand I lose two men yesterday. Ibrahim was best man we have. He know to strike before new men start. Clever. He make diversion and then make direct front assault. Even if we have man there, that man likely be dead now. Then police have more question."

"We must find, stop Ibrahim!"

"Agree. If you have idea how, I listen. We pay people all over city to watch for him. We burn his apartment, his hiding place. Even pay for credit card trace. Nothing, he must use cash or new card. He have vehicle, maybe more, we don't know. How we cover whole metro area with current resource?"

Darko sat back in his chair, his fingers steepled, and pondered the problem. Ibrahim was indeed clever. His strikes had been perfectly placed. First, a county councilman's home and now a judge. Darko had friends, and clients, in positions of authority. Two were now compromised.

He had only one option, to return fire with fire. Fear was his best weapon.

"Crosscheck our friends' medical needs with girls on list. Select girl with local family if possible. I make call to Dubrovnik to see if Ibrahim, Danijela, and Raifa have family still in homeland. And try again find Ibrahim's sister. We send stronger message this time."

Richard walked into work with a bounce in his step and whistling a mindless tune. The threat of snow caused no concern. The meteorologists could conjure up a tornado to go with it, and he wouldn't care. That wind would only lift him higher than he already felt.

As soon as he passed through the front door and hit the main hallway, he could sense a difference. Silence. He stopped and listened. No. Not really silent. He could hear deep whispers and muted sobs. What had happened?

As he approached the call center, the women immediately quieted. Two or three picked up their handsets and proceeded to make calls, but it looked more like show than real work. For some reason, their calls did not seem to go through. One woman was missing, Aida. Had something happened to her?

Richard started to ask, but stopped. Something in their demeanor warned him off. He simply nodded in greeting and walked into his office. An hour later, a text message came through on his phone that made him smile. His contact had come through. He copied the name and contact information onto a sheet of copy paper, and, after laying a convincing computer trail to the subject, he left to find Darko. As he passed the call center, half of the women were talking quietly on their phones, but the others were absent, Irina among the latter group.

"Come in, Richard," said Darko in answer to the knock at his door.

The man seemed somber, but not as distraught as the women.

"Am I coming in at a bad time? I, uh, noticed the ladies were upset this morning."

"Aida is missing. We not hear from her this morning. She was out at club last night. Is all we know right now."

"Wow. I hope she's okay."

Darko nodded. "What have you?"

Richard smiled. "Hopefully something to lift your mood. I've been working to determine the potential markets for our high-end products. I'm just beginning that, but already I think I have a potential buyer for one of the silk farsh rugs." He handed the name and contact data to his boss. "I thought for such a buyer, that you, the owner, should be the one to call, to make the sale."

Darko's eyes lit up, as they only did when talking profits or lovely ladies. "In just two week? Amazing."

Richard shrugged. "Beginner's luck."

"That I doubt," replied Darko. "I will call today. Thank you."

Richard nodded and left the office. As he neared the call center, he noted that all of the women, except Aida, were at work. The mood seemed cautious but not as emotional as first thing that morning. Perhaps Aida had called, just hung over from a rough night on the town.

An hour before closing down for the day, Irina knocked on Richard's doorpost. As he looked up, she held up a sheaf of papers and smiled. Her eyes, however, revealed the emotions of the day.

"You are Darko's favorite now."

"Oh?"

"You are cute when you play coy. I think you know why." Her words said 'flirt', but her eyes remained troubled.

He suspected the answer, but simply shrugged his shoulders.

"Darko sold the peach-colored, silk farsh. He said you would be getting the ten percent sales commission."

Richard sat back. His main purpose in finding a buyer had been to get in good with Darko. He'd forgotten Darko's comment of being generous to those who did well, but now realized just how big his bonus might be. Plus, he was on his way toward owning that new Lexus IS C he found in his parking spot earlier in the week.

"Perhaps, now you can afford a night on the town." She walked over to his desk and circled behind it.

"I-I'd love to take you ladies out again. Maybe next week sometime."

She came up to him and sat on his lap. "No, just us. You and me. I have work commitments Friday night, so maybe Thursday night. Not next week."

Richard felt his pulse quicken, and his mind kept pace with it. Thursday night would work. His dinner date with Amy was two nights later. After all, Darko *had* been encouraging him to go out with Irina. That had been plainly spoken to him. And he was trying to curry favor with the boss. And she was incredibly beautiful, and willing, and so sexy. And the perfume she wore was intoxicating.

Twenty-one

Janick stormed into the MCS workroom, currently at the Richmond Heights Police Department, after a way-too-early morning phone call. He found the coffee pot empty and felt like throwing the carafe at the nearby wall. He resumed grumbling after realizing no one would be making the java any sooner than he could. At least he would be able to make it the way he liked it. Let the others complain for a change.

For the past two weeks, his mind replayed and replayed the phone call from Jusuf. The prints were a match, according to the Chief. How could it be anyone but Cully? Yet, Chief Dandridge had spent days canvassing the area around the Jefferson County property listed to an Ibrahim Jancic. He saw no one closely resembling Lynch Cully. Who was this Jancic character? They found nothing on the man. The social security number on the real estate records was conveniently missing. The man had paid cash. Sounded like drug money to Janick.

Susan Prichard walked up behind him. "Oh no. Please don't tell me you're making the coffee."

"Grrrr," mumbled Janick.

Susan laughed. "Yeah, good morning to you, too."

"I hear we got another one."

"That's right. Ready to go? Metro Air Support is giving us a lift to the scene."

Janick's face fell further. "Flying? Why do we have to fly?"

"Hmmm, let me think. Could it be you're an hour late, so we're last to go. We'll meet up with the others and ride back with them."

"We didn't fly to the last scene."

"We were the first ones called on that one."

"I got my car right out back," Janick replied, extending his protest.

"Hey, do what you want. I'm just following orders. They want us there ASAP."

Janick sighed. "Just need some coffee. I can take coffee, right?"

Susan shook her head and sighed. "C'mon, car's waiting to take us to the helipad."

Five minutes later, and nine stories up on top of St. Mary's Health Center, they stood huddled against the wall as a cold westerly breeze numbed their noses and chilled Janick's coffee.

"Crap, you didn't say nothin' about falling off the top of a hospital." Janick didn't like flying because he didn't like heights. This was too much.

"Hey, closest place they could land. What can I say?" She rubbed her hands and then cupped one hand over her nose and mouth. "At least the E.D.'s just a short step away," she mumbled. She laughed at her partner's squeamishness.

"Yeah, one step over the side. Didn't know they had a rooftop entrance." Janick looked up to see the police MD500E helicopter making its final approach. They wasted no time boarding the aircraft and appreciated the warm cabin as they strapped in.

Fifteen minutes later, Janick opened his eyes long enough to see a circle of emergency vehicles in what looked like a landfill. He closed his eyes and held his breath as the helicopter descended to a cushion-soft landing. Janick said a silent thanks to heaven and a verbal one to the pilot before jumping from his seat onto solid ground. He was tempted to kiss the ground, but it was a landfill, and who knew what was just beneath the surface.

He and Susan met up with other MCS members near an ambulance. State crime lab technicians still worked an area a dozen yards away. Uniformed Illinois State Police conferred with a couple of plain-clothed men. Janick couldn't hear the conversation.

"Where is she?" he asked.

Another detective nodded toward the ambulance. "They've already put her inside. Pretty much the same story, but with a difference." He handed a digital SLR camera to Janick.

He squinted to see the 2-inch screen. Viewing the scene photos on a laptop would be preferred, but that option hadn't been offered yet, so he made do. First thing that struck him was that this woman was gorgeous, with nice hair, manicured nails, and stylish clothes. She appeared posed, fully clothed. She'd look like she was asleep except for the damage to her eyes.

"Beautiful lady," Janick said.

"Yeah. So much for beautiful people having it easy in life. Under the clothes is another story. Corneas, liver and kidneys gone, like the others. But, so are her heart, lungs, and one thighbone. Paramedics called it the femur."

Janick worked through the rest of the photos.

"Why a bone? What can you do with a bone?" asked

another detective to no one in particular.

Janick had no idea. He moved back to the first images.

"Definitely posed. This woman was of a higher status than the others. Someone special."

"But still someone who pissed off the killer big-time."

"Maybe. Maybe not." Janick thought it through a bit further. "If these deaths are related to a trafficking ring, there could be several reasons they were killed. Maybe, like you said, they pissed off their killer, or someone who controls the killer. Maybe they're having some rebellion in the ranks, and the first two women were meant to be messages to the others. Women from the rank-and-file, so to speak. But, the message wasn't being heeded, so they needed a stronger message. Someone with higher status, someone the rank-and-file might see as untouchable."

"Or maybe this has nothing to do with trafficking, and this poor lady was just in the wrong place at the wrong time and this crazy killed her."

Janick shook his head. "Nothing crazy here. This takes planning, contacts, and skill. And medical records. You can't just take a kidney and put it into anybody who needs one. Maybe we need to approach this from another angle. Danny, see if you can find anything on the black market for organs. Maybe we can work backwards. Find where these organs are going and trace them back here. Will, you help him."

The two detectives headed for their car to begin their task as a uniformed officer approached. Introductions were made.

"Okay, we're going to release the body to your medical examiner. Some of my higher-ups weren't happy with that, but reason won out over politics for a change. Having the same M.E. do the posts on these ladies makes sense and she is willing, or so I was told."

Susan nodded. "She's never turned down a case that I've heard about."

Janick was happy with that turn of events. It would be a definite time-saver to work with the St. Louis County M.E. instead of a lab in Springfield. He knew no better forensic pathologists.

"By the way, where exactly are we in Illinois? What town is nearby?"

"This is the Cottonwood Hills landfill. Marissa."

"Damn." Janick felt his heart drop. Cully, a voice from the dead, had called it. The *wunderkind* still had it, wherever he was. And wherever that was, Janick was convinced it wasn't a realm beyond this one.

"By the way, we have an ID," said the trooper.

"Oh?" Janick was surprised. This was another definite turn for the better.

"Aida Tadić. She was booked in Belleville for soliciting a year ago. Gave a St. Louis address, in the Central West End. Here's the details."

He handed Janick a sheet of paper, but Susan snatched it first. "I'll call it in. See what we can find."

Janick discussed the case with the state policeman and his chief technician. Susan appeared ten minutes later. "Janick, we're going to need more help. A Božena Tadić, age 47, at this Central West End address, was the victim of a home invasion and burglary last night. She's still alive but barely, in critical condition in the ICU at

Barnes. She's not expected to make it. And a Manojlo Tadić, age 26, died in a hit-and-run just 30 minutes ago on Grand. If these guys are sending a message to someone, they're doin' it big time. They just wiped out an entire family."

Twenty-two

Richard had been a little surprised when Irina suggested he pick her up at work rather than at her home. Not that he had any strong desire to know where she lived. This "date" was mostly to appease her aggression and score points with the boss, who seemed intent on setting the two up as a couple. Not once, but twice that day, Darko had expressed his favor of Richard's date that evening. Strange.

Yet, despite her beauty, Darko's encouragement, and the allure of that perfume, he knew he had to control his hormonal surge. He had made up his mind that under no circumstance would he sleep with her. He could only hope that he could live up to that commitment.

He pulled into his usual parking spot, half expecting to find Irina waiting in her car, but realizing he'd never actually seen any cars that might have been owned by any of the women. He waited a few minutes, to see if she arrived. He walked to the door. Not waiting there either, so he used his pass card to enter the building. She wasn't at her desk. His office remained locked. He started to leave when he heard footsteps, a woman's heels, clacking down the intersecting hall. Had she been in the bathroom? Then a thought hit him. Was she coming from the door he couldn't access? He walked toward the noise and made it to the junction in time to see her round the distant corner beyond the bathroom doorway. What was behind that distant door?

"Oh!" She startled at seeing him at the other end of the hall. "Richard. I am sorry to be late. I thought I had time to finish a quick task for Sonja. I meant to meet you at the front door."

"Hi. Didn't mean to scare you. I didn't know where you'd be and didn't see a car outside. I'm parked in my usual place."

"I am ready. If you like, we could take limo. I just make a call and driver will be ready."

Richard thought about that offer. He preferred driving, but he didn't know the city and with a limo any parking issues would be the driver's problem, not his.

"I, uh, don't know. I expected to drive, but I admit I don't know the city yet. Do you know your way around?"

"I am always passenger, and I am directionally impaired. Do not count on me to get us anywhere." She laughed as she stepped up to him. "Beside, driver is very discreet." She stroked his cheek with a fingernail.

There was that perfume again.

"Okay."

Within two minutes of her call, the limo pulled up outside the front door. Richard suspected she had that planned all along. Or, perhaps Darko had set it up.

He climbed in after her, and no sooner had he settled in, she had the bar open. At least she wasn't trying to pull his pants down. He'd come prepared for just about anything, but he wasn't that kind of guy. How far would he have to go to make Darko trust him?

They settled in with a drink. He didn't recall ever mentioning his favorite "every day" beer to anyone at work, yet the bar was adequately stocked with Warsteiner Verum. Had that fact slipped from him at lunch that first day? If so, someone had taken notes. He needed to be more careful.

The first leg of their drive filled quickly with small talk about growing up and school, as well as previous jobs. Irina talked of home in Croatia. She missed her home, but her family had died in the war, and she had no one to go home to. She had done well since coming to America. How it was that she came to the States was part of her story she failed to mention, missing along with why it was that she wasn't married or somehow spoken for. Richard kept his own mental notes.

Her first glass of white wine gone, Irina snuggled closer to Richard and leaned into him, kissing his neck. Richard took a deep breath.

"Hey, look, I, uh, don't want to spoil the mood, but I need to know something."

She looked into his eyes, with longing in her own. "No husband, no boyfriend. Yes to birth control," she whispered.

"Um, any word from Aida?"

She sat back as if hit with a bucket of cold water, as he had hoped. Instead of jealousy or anger, her eyes filled with anguished tears. Curiously, he caught a subtle few seconds of eye contact between the driver's face in the rearview mirror and Irina. As if directed by some telepathic command from the front seat, she stifled her sniffles and composed herself.

"No, no word. We are worried. Very worried." She grabbed a tissue from a nearby dispenser and dabbed her eyes. "I am sorry. She was, is a good friend."

Again, Richard caught the driver's eyes in the mirror.

"And I'm sorry," replied Richard. "I don't want to ruin the evening, but I needed to know. No one would talk about it at work. I wanted to ask earlier, but, well, didn't really have the opportunity. Is there any way I can help?"

Irina smiled, and Richard suspected he'd asked the wrong question. She climbed onto his lap and cupped his face in her hands before kissing him fully on the lips. She leaned to one side and whispered in his ear, "Yes, help me forget what happen to her. I do not want to end up dead like her. Help me escape." He felt a tear drop onto his neck.

In that instant, he understood that Irina and the others had known of Aida's destiny all day. And that Aida's fate had been a date with eternity. The limo wasn't a perk. It was an extension of her prison, and the driver was her guard. What kind of company had he gotten involved with? He had been forewarned about what to expect from Darko Komarčić, but Darko was proving to be far worse. Still, he had a job to do. There was still a game to play.

At that moment, he also understood another thing—that Irina, and the others, were damsels in distress. They needed a personal superhero. He'd been raised to protect women and children. Now, he'd have to walk a narrow line between the job and being that superhero.

Amy stared at Macy as Macy wove in and out of

traffic heading toward downtown St. Louis. She'd seen Macy's maniacal driving before, but tonight's drive crossed into the realm of Xtreme Sports and a potential trauma admission at the nearest Level 1 center.

"What has gotten into you, Macy? Slow down for heaven's sake."

"Uh-uh, girlfriend. I'm not giving you time to change your mind. Like you did last time."

"I'm not going to change my mind. It's a new me, remember? I'm even going out tonight despite having to get up for work in the morning. The new me."

"More like the old you. B.L. Before Lynch. Something's going on, and you need to fill me in, girl."

"I came to realize that a lot of my problem wasn't the patients I had to deal with, but that the loss of Lynch affected everything. And I realized much of that sense of loss centered on a fantasy of what life with Lynch could have been like, not the reality of our relationship."

"Finally, the girl has come to her senses."

Amy smiled. "I had a date Tuesday night."

"What?!" Macy nearly hit the car she had started to pass. "I need to get there fast so I can focus on the details you been holdin' back from me."

"Focus on your driving, please. I want to survive tonight so I can cook him dinner Saturday night." She enjoyed taunting her friend. Macy loved being up-to-date on the latest and greatest gossip, although she never passed anything to others without express permission. She was a great friend that way.

Macy accelerated, and Amy cried, "Slow down, or you won't get any details from me." Macy complied.

Ten minutes later, Macy backed into a spot outside

the City Museum that Amy thought was clearly marked '15 Minute Loading Zone.' "Um, Macy? This is a loading zone."

"Sure, during the day. Who's gonna be loading anything this time of night?"

"I don't think that really makes a difference."

"I'm okay. My cousin, Amira, is parking enforcement, and she's working this zone tonight. I checked. We're good."

Amy shook her head and laughed. Macy's 100-plus cousins made for great entertainment and had come to their rescue on more than one occasion. Amy tried mentally to count the number of cousins she'd met over her years of friendship with Macy. She only made it to a dozen, but she had certainly heard more stories than that.

Europe Night Club was packed for a midwinter Thursday night. Macy and Amy swerved and swiveled their way to the first floor bar and ordered drinks. Amy always thought their drinks too expensive, but the dancing was fun, and she didn't drink enough to make a major dent in her budget.

Macy nudged her. "Hey, quick! Over there. Before someone else grabs it."

Amy followed Macy's point to see a couple picking up their coats and leaving their table. Macy elbowed her way through the crowd, while Amy followed more politely. Macy claimed the table a split second before another couple.

"You missed your calling!" Amy had to shout to talk over the music.

"What?"

"You missed your calling. You should have gone into roller derby, not nursing." She laughed.

Macy smiled. "You mean I'm better at whipping butt than wiping them?" The pair laughed and sipped their drinks. "Okay, girlfriend, time for all the chilling details. Spill it!"

As Amy leaned toward her friend's ear, she felt a tap on her shoulder. She turned to see two guys standing next to them. They pointed to the nearby dance floor.

"Would you like to dance?"

At least it wasn't some lame pick-up line. She was ready to dance, even if it meant holding Macy in suspense a while longer. She stood and realized she had about six inches over the tallest of the two. She shrugged mentally. It was only a dance. She had started toward the floor when Macy tugged on her arm.

"You aren't getting out of it this easily, girl. One dance. Then you talk."

Amy nodded. The DJ played a Lady Gaga song that Amy had heard, but couldn't recall the name. Chris, her impromptu partner's name, made up for his shorter stature with his confidence and great dancing. After the first song, she watched Macy head back to their table, but she stuck it out for a second dance, thanked Chris, and ignored his request to give him her number.

The odds of someone having slipped rohypnol, or some other date-rape drug, into their drinks was remote, but they were always cautious about leaving their drinks unattended at a club. Amy had kept an eye on their table throughout the first dance, knowing that Macy would "guard" it during the second. Still, she checked it closely upon returning to the table.

"It's okay. I was watching," said Macy.

Amy took a hesitant sip. If anything happened, they each had the other's back.

"Okay, give me all the glorious details."

Amy leaned close to her friend to avoid yelling. She decided to have a little fun with Macy and started by telling of her meeting this guy at her father's home. She moved on to their phone calls and finally dinner at Maggiano's.

"I invited him to my place for dinner Saturday night," she said in ending her story.

Macy finished her drink and laughed. "Is my friend Amy moving a little fast with this guy?"

"It's just dinner, Macy."

"At your place, with you cookin'." Macy scrunched up her mouth. "Soundin' like rebound to me, girl. Be careful."

Macy waved down a waitress for another drink. Amy put her hand over her glass. She was good for now.

"And you're tellin' me you met him at your dad's house, there with the grandson of one of your dad's old commanders."

Amy grinned. "Well, we met once before. You met him, too. Sorta."

Macy eyebrows flew to the ceiling.

"You are holdin' out on me, girl. You know Macy doesn't like that. What's this miracle man's name?" She paid the waitress and took a sip.

"Richard Nichols."

Macy spit her drink across the table. "Wha? Whoa, girlfriend. You're tellin' me the guy you doused at The

Bridge, Thor, is the guy you're seein?"

Amy's grin grew as she nodded. "And he really does have an amazing hammer."

Macy choked, but waved off Amy before she could apply the Heimlich maneuver.

"Kevlar. Saved his life in Afghanistan." She sipped her chocolate martini. She went on to detail the ways he was different from Lynch—his openness, honesty, and considerate nature among his many traits. Macy soaked it all in, all the while focusing on Amy's eyes as she spoke.

When Amy stopped, Macy sighed and said, "Rebound. You are definitely on the rebound." She shook her head.

"No, I'm not." Amy said that without confidence though. Was she? She was about to argue the point, when two more guys approached the table.

"Ladies, we saw you dancing earlier. Looks like you enjoy it. Ready for another spin? I'm Dallas and this is Preston. May we have the honor?"

Amy surveyed the pair. At least they were a better match for height. Could they dance as well as Chris and Alex? She and Macy had come to dance, so after a quick glance to see Macy's approval, they headed toward the dance floor. Their glasses were empty, so this time Amy focused on the dancing more than their table.

The guys were as good as the previous pair, so both ladies agreed to a second dance, but some lame Justin Bieber song started up. The third song was better, retro disco. Amy glanced at Macy, whose face suddenly morphed into a serious frown. Macy stopped dancing and said something to Preston, before moving toward

Amy. She grabbed Amy's elbow.

"C'mon. I think we need to leave." She tried to steer Amy toward their table.

"Hey, what's with you? We're just getting warmed up."

Amy caught Macy's glance to something behind her. She started to turn to see what had spooked her friend, but Macy stopped her, and gently pushed her toward the table. Amy resisted.

"C'mon, you have to work tomorrow."

"Stop! What gives?"

She tried a second time to look toward whatever had started this and, again, Macy stopped her. Macy grabbed Amy's coat and literally threw it at her.

"I've had enough, Macy! What is wrong with you?"

Macy took a deep breath and released it slowly. She shook her head and raised both hands, palms up, as if silently saying, "I tried."

Amy looked back in the direction Macy had been watching. At first, she saw nothing. The crowd ebbed and flowed with the beat. Then the sea of dancers parted and she saw him. Richard Nichols, with some supermodel babe practically giving him a lap dance. *He's a player?* She clutched her coat to her chest and stormed ahead of Macy toward the exit.

Richard had been careful with his drinks. Irina? Not so much. She was on him like a horny, drunk sorority girl at a frat kegger. He had resisted dancing so far, but if that would keep her off his lap for a while, he'd take to the dance floor. While he took care to pay attention to Irina, he also had one eye on Sergei, the driver, who had taken a stool at the bar and made no effort to hide.

Twice Irina had glanced Sergei's way and quickly seemed to redouble her effort to seduce Richard. Once, Richard noticed him on a cell phone. How he could hear over the din was something Richard couldn't fathom. However, he did have a pretty good idea who might be on the other end of the call.

The situation posed a dilemma. He didn't want to take advantage of Irina, nor did he trust her "health status," for lack of a better term. The night would be over in hours, but herpes was forever, and the clap was nothing to applaud. He again reminded himself that he had no intention of sleeping with her, despite her apparent readiness.

Yet, he also didn't want to jeopardize her. What fate would befall her if she failed at her obvious seduction? And why was he the target of this same seduction? He lifted her off his lap and steadied her on her feet before leading her to the dance floor. He would have time to think there. He had to find a way to convince Sergei she had succeeded without letting her succeed.

Twenty-three

Darko watched Sergei leave the office, backing out as if afraid to turn his back on his boss. However, Sergei was just a messenger. Darko had learned long ago not to kill the messengers. Mostly.

A few minutes later, Sergei appeared at the door with Irina in hand. The man waited at the doorway, and when she hesitated to enter the room, he gave her a not-so-gentle push.

"So, Sergei tell me you succeed in seduce Richard." He could see fear in her eyes. "Well done. I want you keep it hot and heavy. Get him wrap around little finger."

She nodded. "Yes, Darko."

The fear persisted. Surely, she would not lie to him. Yet . . .

"Yes, Darko, what?" He gave her a menacing look, not that he felt he needed to.

"Yes, Darko. We had sex in the back of the limo, and I will keep him interested."

"And?"

"I will wrap him around my little finger."

He smiled and nodded. "Good girl. You go, get ready for work."

He gave a contented sigh as she turned and left his office. He still had Ibrahim to deal with, but at least he felt confident that Richard would not cause him trouble.

The week had been so bittersweet and quite the emotional roller coaster. Ibrahim's successful retrieval

189

of Raifa had been a cause for great anger. And concern. Darko had had to call in a few favors to help sidetrack the investigation of Judge Wallace. He hated to use up favors.

Nevertheless, then came Richard's sudden discovery of a buyer for the farsh. At first, he'd been suspect of that turn of events. Despite Risto's report that the man had a "clean" background, he harbored suspicions that Richard wasn't who he seemed to be. Yet, the second, deeper background check only verified the first. Even then, he had his computer expert retrace Richard's computer activities for the past week. His work had been exactly what he was being paid to do. His online behavior showed no "improper" use of the system. Darko could forgive him the occasional "recreational" surfing as most of it seemed appropriate for a man trying to learn a new city. They had retraced a series of websites regarding markets for the rugs, and Darko could see a logical trail leading to the discovery of the man who ultimately bought the $350,000 Iranian farsh. Even with that, however, Darko would only be comfortable when he had something, anything, to hold over Richard.

So, a week that started in loss, anger, and mistrust moved on to one of an incredibly profitable sale. Then came Aida. She had been one of his favorites. Even her brother had shown potential in Darko's enterprises. Their mother had been one of his many lovers prior to his marrying Sonja and their taking on new avenues of pleasure. He'd had serious misgivings when Risto's list revealed only one candidate, only one girl whose organs could meet a need and bring a profit, while delivering a crucial message to the rest of his "staff." That message had been heard.

Now, the week that had moved from down to up, to down again seemed to continue the pattern. He smiled as he reflected on Irina's success. He would have preferred something more tangible: incriminating photos or a sex tape. Yes, he thought, a sex tape would have been ideal, something he and Sonja could enjoy in several ways. Yet, he had nothing so physical. Instead, he had Sergei's report that Irina had proven herself irresistible to the young man and Irina's confirmation. Richard's innocent annunciation of his growing love for Irina, made in the quiet of the limo's back seat, had been sincere, according to Sergei. Although the window cover had been drawn so that Sergei could not witness the act firsthand, Sergei's report backed up Irina's confession that the act had been consummated. Darko believed Sergei, mostly. So, now, instead of photos or a video, maybe he could hold Irina herself over Richard.

Darko settled into the chair at his desk. Although the hour was early on a Friday morning, he had details of the farsh sale to finalize. He completed and gathered up the insurance papers on his desk and left the office for the secure room where the carpets were stored. He would oversee the packaging and crating of the rug. The secure mover would be there in less than two hours to pick up the cargo.

As he walked down the hallway, he was surprised to see the door to Richard's office open and the light on. He peeked through the doorway, but didn't see Richard. Had Sergei known the man was in the building?

He continued toward the secure room. He had to

open the vault to let his packers inside. Any delay could jeopardize the timing of the shipment, and his payment. Outside the room, he found Richard leaning against the wall. He looked as if he hadn't slept all night. Then Darko realized the man hadn't.

"Good morning, Richard. It is surprise to find you here so early."

Richard nodded. "Darko. I need to talk with you."

Three men appeared behind Darko with crating materials. A fourth appeared with additional supplies.

"I must get these men started. Would you like to see the farsh you sell? One last time?"

Richard nodded and yawned.

Darko opened the vault and directed the men inside. They first unrolled the carpet onto a larger piece of clean, simple cotton sheeting. The fourth man would inspect and carefully spot clean the rug while the other three built a custom crate for shipping.

"Wow," said Richard. "I've never seen it fully laid out. It is beyond doubt a beautiful piece."

"Yes, it is. And I thank you again for finding buyer who will truly appreciate it."

"Thank you, sir. For the generous bonus."

Darko waved his hand. "Is least I do. Commission is commission." He stepped aside to give additional directions to the man inspecting the rug. Once finished he returned to Richard's side. "So, have good night last night?" He grinned his usual lecherous smile.

"That, that's what I wanted to talk with you about." Richard appeared nervous.

"Come. We step outside." Richard followed him to the hallway, which remained deserted for a weekday.

"What is it you want talk about?"

"Well, sir. I, uh, know you were encouraging me to go out with Irina and, uh, we had a great time, a really great time. It's just that, well, I've never been one to date a fellow worker and other companies I know frown on it. I, uh, just want to make sure it's okay if I continue to see her."

Darko laughed. "No problem. Not at all." Sergei's instinct had been right on the target. He could see more than fatigue in the man's eyes. Richard really was smitten.

"I, uh . . ." Richard's cheeks flushed. "This is embarrassing. My boss is the last person I should mention this to, but . . ." Richard stopped and studied Darko's face.

Darko's curiosity peaked. "But?"

"Sir, can I ask a personal question?"

Darko raised his eyebrows, but he couldn't resist. He had to hear what was on Richard's mind. "You may ask, but I chose to answer or not."

"Well, sir, you seem to be a man of the world, very cosmopolitan. And a man who truly enjoys the finer things of life, especially women." He paused. "I, uh . . ." Richard let out a long, tired sigh. "Are you sure you don't mind?"

Darko flipped his hand as if to say, "It is nothing, continue."

"If you had a new girlfriend and she, uh, she. . ." His cheeks flushed again. "She wants me to join her and two of her friends for, well, you know what. I mean every guy I know has fantasized about a threesome, but a foursome? With three beauties like Irina? I don't know

193

what to tell her."

Darko paused a moment and then began to laugh, a deep belly laugh. Irina would indeed get that bonus. She had played Richard better than he'd expected. Now, he would get that incriminating evidence to hold over Richard. A sex tape of a foursome? He felt a tingle in his own loins.

"Hell, Richard, what? You would turn down offer like that? I tell her yes, before she change mind."

Twenty-four

Lynch startled awake at an unexpected noise. He took a second to orient himself to the new room, where the extended sofa bed filled two-thirds of the open space, but he became fully alert within that second. The front door was ten feet to his immediate right. An invasion of the home would likely come through that door. He heard the noise again. It came from the adjacent room.

He eased up onto the edge of the sofa bed as silently as possible, retrieving the 9mm S&W from beneath the nearby cushion. In the gloom of early morning, he saw a figure moving about the room. A few seconds later, newspaper flared up to start a wood fire in the fireplace. By that flash of light, he saw that the figure was Ibrahim, who now settled into a chair next to the fire.

After replacing the gun in its hiding place, Lynch walked over, sat in the adjacent chair, and stared at the growing flames. "A fire sure can be mesmerizing."

Ibrahim, too, gazed into the blaze. "Do not know this word, mesmerizing."

"Like hypnotizing."

"Ah, yes, in fireplace. In house all around you, not mesmerizing at all."

Lynch gave a quick laugh. "No, I guess not. Do you know this from experience?" Ibrahim offered no answer. "In my case, it was water. The trickle and flow of water can be just as relaxing, but not when you're about to drown."

The two sat in quiet and watched the fire.

"Thank you," said Lynch, breaking the silence.

"For what?"

"Lots of things, I guess. These clothes. A place to stay. Food to eat." He paused. "For having Danijela at your cabin. Had she not been there, I probably would have died."

Ibrahim broke his gaze from the fire and looked at Lynch. "Do you love her?"

The question took Lynch aback. He'd not been prepared for such a 'direct assault' by Ibrahim. He'd thought about it off and on for weeks. Did he? "Yes, I guess I do, but maybe not in the way you're asking. You have to remember there is a lot I don't remember. In a way, I don't know anyone else. She is beautiful, compassionate, easy to be around. She saved my life, nursed me back to health."

He stopped and watched the fire. Ibrahim, too, returned his gaze to the flames.

"But now, thanks to her, I've started getting my memory back. I'm beginning to recall another woman who was important to me, before my accident. I think I loved her, too."

"Must feel confuse."

"Like you can't believe."

Ibrahim looked at him directly again. "You are welcome."

"Huh?"

"For food, clothes, place to stay. Special people give to me. I give also. So, you are welcome. And to answer next question, yes, I love her. She is whole reason I give up life I know. She is one lead me to Lord Jesus. Darko, Risto laugh at her. The councilman abuse her without mercy, mock her new faith when she become Christian. Now, God will have His vengeance through me."

Lynch stared at Ibrahim and then at the fire.

"You go to police now?"

Lynch shook his head. "I'm not sure."

"Why not? Make sense."

Lynch pondered that for a moment. "In some ways, I agree. Tell me more about Darko and Risto."

"What way you not agree?" Ibrahim shifted in his chair to face Lynch and looked him squarely in the eyes.

Lynch took a deep breath. "Well, if I go in, I'll be unable to help. They'll put me in the hospital for a check-up, most of which will include a bunch of shrinks and neurologists."

"What is shrinks?"

Lynch tapped his head. "Psychiatrists, like for crazy people. Plus, the neurologists will want to scan me and check my brain. And when all those tests are done, I'll be forced to stay home, see doctors every week until they say I'm fit for duty. Even then, I might have to re-qualify for my badge, if I want to be a policeman again. During that whole time, Darko will still be operating because it will take weeks, maybe months, for a task force to form, investigate, and press charges. From what you've told me, Darko has influential friends who will do whatever it takes to save their own hides by creating as many obstructions as possible. He could disappear before any charges are ever produced."

Ibrahim nodded in understanding. "Yes, friends in high places."

"That's why I need to know more about him, and his friends. I already know about the county councilman and judge. Who else is in the guy's pocket?"

"There is state senator, local mayor, one, maybe two high rank policeman, two more judge, and two big-time businessman with much money."

"Any others?"

"Many small-time player, but they not possible help Darko much. I not know of anyone else with money or power after I leave him." Ibrahim watched Lynch carefully. "You have plan?"

"Maybe. Tell me about Darko's setup, his business, home, anything else about what he likes and where he goes."

Ibrahim started in the order Lynch had asked and described the import company's building, complete with squalid housing quarters. He described Darko's country home and its security measures. The city apartment held nothing useful to them. He talked about the man's kinky sex habits, the individual women, the limos, the escort service, the guards, and more. Lynch asked questions, and Ibrahim answered all as best he could. By the time they'd finished talking, the sun had crept up just over the horizon, and they heard footsteps on the floor above them.

"Do you know the Greek myth of the Hydra?" asked Lynch.

"Yes, I learn this myth. We not want two heads appear for one we cut off."

Lynch smiled. "True, but Hercules defeated it with the help of Iolaus. It took teamwork to cut off the heads of the monster, and now there are two of us."

Ibrahim studied Lynch in silence for over a minute. "Thing could go wrong. Might be killing. You have much lose if you kill."

Ibrahim was correct. Lynch felt, no, he knew that he'd killed before, but that was in the line of duty. Without legal authority, how could he justify killing a bad guy for any reason other than self-defense? He could even be charged for unlawful gun possession and breaking a host of other laws. Yet, in the world of Darko and Risto, gun laws meant nothing, and murder ensured survival of the fittest. If he wanted his old life restored, he'd have to be cautious.

Lynch nodded in agreement. "You have much to lose as well."

Ibrahim shrugged. "I deserve much, too. There is chance I end up in jail no matter what happen."

Lynch contemplated that. Maybe he could help there. Maybe there was a way to go to the police without physically showing up on their doorstep. He needed to find someone he could trust in the police ranks.

Both men turned to the sound of footsteps in the hall and saw Mike at the doorway. "Did I miss something?"

Lynch shook his head.

"I'm willing to help."

Lynch shrugged. "You could help with a computer and internet access. I need to do some more research."

Mike looked disappointed. "Sure, but I was thinking of something more active. Kinda miss the battlefront."

"Different kind of war. Different rules and laws."

Lynch stood and moved closer to the fire. "But if I come up with something you can help with, believe me, I'll come get you."

"Coffee?"

Both men nodded, and Mike turned to leave. Lynch started to follow when Ibrahim, with a certain gleam in his eyes, grabbed his arm. "I cut off heads. You put torch to wounds."

Twenty-five

Lynch sat in the parlor with Mike's laptop linked to the home's wireless network. He rubbed his eyes and yawned, and although early in the afternoon, the dark clouds threatening snow muted the sunlight and made the time seem much later. Not enough sleep and up way too early.

Yet, the time spent had been productive. He felt as if he'd made good headway in his quest to recover his identity. He had searched for information on everyone in local law enforcement who had appeared at his memorial. Some he began to remember, recalling details that only later in his research did he confirm. Others still drew a complete blank. He wondered if he had ever truly worked with them. Perhaps they had attended the service only to enhance their own image.

Danijela entered the parlor and handed Lynch another cup of coffee. "*Hvala*, Danijela." He took a sip, then another, and hoped for a caffeine jolt that never came, even as he closed in on finishing the cup. He yawned again. "Guess I need a break more than I thought."

"You finish?"

"Not really. But I think I'm closer to finding what I want."

"What is what you want?" She sat on the adjacent couch to his left. She looked tired, too.

"I've found out some more about myself, and it triggered some more memories. But what I'm looking for is a name. I need to find someone I can trust with the police."

Danijela looked at her feet. "More memory of girlfriend?"

He looked at her and saw her eyes misting. "Yes, and no. I have regained some more memories of her, but not because of what I'm doing now."

Was this a topic he wanted to discuss now? In his mind, this was much too soon. Yes, he had regained some memories of Amy, but only casual things, nothing that clued him into their relationship. He wished Danijela had not brought up Amy.

She reached for his hand, but hesitated. "Do you love her?"

Lynch felt a wave of intense confusion sweep through him. No, he definitely wasn't ready for this discussion.

Before he could say anything, she continued, "I-I love you, Lynch."

The wave curled over him and pounded him into the sand. He took her hand. "I love you, too, Danijela. But I suspect you love Ibrahim, too." He received silence as her response. "I'm right, aren't I?"

She waggled her head in indecision. "Is very confusing."

"I know. Think how I feel. You're confused between two people you know. My confusion involves a memory. I don't really know that woman anymore, yet I feel I owe something to her. Think what will happen when I go public with the fact I'm still very much alive. How will she respond, and how will she feel when she realizes my memory of her is limited? I don't know her favorite color, what she likes to do, or anything. I know all of that about you."

Danijela looked him straight in the eyes. "So, do not make public. Go back, become Jusuf again."

Could he do that? He'd already contemplated that option, and realized he had already moved beyond the point of no return.

"Is that really what you want? I saw how you reacted when we learned Ibrahim was alive, and again when we learned he was coming here. Besides, how could I, we, live? I need a social security number to get a job, and I need a real identity to get that number. I think there are a lot more complications to becoming Jusuf than returning from the dead as Lynch."

He heard Ibrahim's distinctive heavy footfall on the second floor as the man approached the stairway. Danijela turned toward the sound as well and quickly withdrew her hand from Lynch's. "It's okay to be confused, Danijela. Time will sort everything out. For both of us." He thought, *I certainly hope so.*

Danijela arose as Ibrahim descended the nearby stairs. "More coffee?"

Lynch shook his head. "No, thank you. I need to take a break, not take in more caffeine." She started to leave the room. "Hey, wait a minute." He grabbed the laptop and entered a few keystrokes. An image appeared on the screen. "Does this man look familiar to you?" He turned the screen toward her.

Without hesitation, she replied, "Man from cabin. Before Risto find it."

Lynch nodded. "I think so, too."

Danijela scooted from the room as Ibrahim entered

it, but not, as Lynch noticed, without taking a good look at the man. Ibrahim walked up to the computer and gazed at the screen. "So, is this man to trust?"

"Maybe. From what I can determine, he and I worked together closely. He is quoted in the papers on several occasions after my disappearance that I was like a son to him, the son he never had. He was Chief of Police in Webster Grove and commanded the Major Case Squad for a number of years before retiring a few months ago. The articles on his retirement detailed an exemplary record of police work starting as a military policeman in the 60s."

"Name?"

"Dandridge. Albert Dandridge. His wife of 40-plus years died two years ago from complications of a bad breast cancer."

"Not know name. Sound good."

Mike turned the corner from the dining room and joined them as Ibrahim spoke. "What sounds good?"

"Lynch find policeman he trust."

"Well, sort of. He's retired now. He and I worked together on several major cases. At least that's what the newspaper and internet articles show. He already suspects I'm still alive. He managed to track down Ibrahim's cabin hours before the bad guys burned it down. I saw him there."

Mike furrowed his brow. "I don't know. I'm getting a bad vibe here. I think we should pray about it before you move ahead."

Ibrahim nodded, but Lynch stared at them both. He was unaccustomed to praying about every little thing. Okay, so this wasn't a little thing, but he still felt uncomfortable. Was God going to give him a direct answer? Somehow, he knew he'd trusted his own gut for years, and a flash of memory told him others had placed their trust in his instincts as well. Before he could say anything, he saw Mike and Ibrahim close their eyes.

Mike prayed, "Lord, Your Word says that while the naïve believe everything, the sensible man considers his steps. You also say that although the mind of a man plans his way, You direct his steps. Please help us to recognize the right path and show us the steps to take to help set the captives free. In the name of our Lord, Jesus, thank you. Amen."

The two men opened their eyes and looked at Lynch. He nodded. *That wasn't so bad*, he thought. *I can still plan my way.* He looked at Ibrahim. "Have you considered my earlier request?"

The man nodded. "Yes. I agree, need more girl as witness."

"And I have a friend at church who can help us with making the video," Mike added.

"Good. Any thoughts about who we should go after?"

Ibrahim nodded again. "Two, maybe three girl, from house familiar to me. One from house in Ladue. Big businessman. Much money. Other girl in Kirkwood. State senator. Final girl in Jefferson County. Darko's estate. Most difficult, but place I know best of three."

"Tell me about the first two."

"House in Ladue sit on ten acre. Fenced. Two dog loose at night. Bandog. Full-time housekeeper. This girl from Ecuador. Came to America to live with family and get education, but they sell her to be forced labor for man in Las Vegas. He sell her to Darko to get money to pay mob. Name is Agata. Speak little English and no passport. Once a week she leave house with housekeeper and male escort to shop."

"That would be the time to grab her."

"My thought, too, at first. Easy job. Bad news is since Danijela rescued, do not see her with housekeeper. She is at house, and I cannot get onto property to set up communication. Make it hard job. Rescue of Raifa will add to problem."

Lynch thought about the task. Somewhere inside he knew he'd been good at finding people. Could he be just as resourceful at kidnapping them?

"Tell me how you rescued Danijela and Raifa."

"Danijela easy. She often force to be escort."

Lynch frowned. He couldn't see Danijela as a prostitute. Ibrahim must have seen his thoughts on his face.

"She much different woman then. Now is free. Has hope." He paused. "I assigned to drive one night. When she went to bathroom at restaurant, we walk out together. Darko and men on alert after that." He gave a brief description of his failure with Tatjana and then explained in detail how he managed to free Raifa. "Now, Darko on high alert. Might take more than damage to property."

"Are you afraid of dogs?"

Ibrahim shook his head.

"Good. They'll be easy to deal with, but we'll have to let them attack to disable them."

Ibrahim shrugged. "Have silencer. Just shoot them."

Lynch recognized that might have to happen. He hated the thought, but these dogs weren't pets. They were trained killers. Still, he preferred disabling the animals. The situation wasn't their fault. Besides, shooting them at a distance, with a handgun, in the dark, was harder than it looked, and shooting them at close quarters presented other risks, to each other.

"What about the house?"

"Do not know. Security set up by someone else, not Darko's team. I do know where to find room they keep her in. I help take her there first time."

"They might have changed it."

Ibrahim tossed his head back and forth a couple of times. "Maybe, but doubt. Servant quarter built away from family and guest area. In basement. Bigger chance they add security man. Must prepare for extra guard."

Ibrahim and Lynch discussed the task in detail, and Lynch realized they needed better surveillance and more recon visits. After settling on a plan for that, they did the same for the state senator's home. This home presented another potential conflict, the possible presence of state police. He also reflected on Ibrahim's earlier comment. At a minimum, he'd be violating numerous property laws. He might actually have to hurt or kill someone to get this girl out. Would he also find himself in direct conflict with one or more state police officers? What kind of jeopardy was he placing himself in?

Twenty-six
❧ ♦ ♦ ❧

Darko sat behind his desk, his hand rolling and clicking the computer mouse to scroll through the images on the screen in front of him. He smiled as certain images flickered past. Some he knew well. Some were new to him and he wanted to linger on them, soak in their eroticism. He sighed at the sight of a younger, more acrobatic Tatjana Alic, nude and compromising a certain police captain. Another image caught the officer at the height of ecstasy. Other images showed Jelena Kordić, while additional photos revealed the side of Aida Tadić not seen in the office. Pornographic photos of five other women in Darko's stable, including Irina, rounded the "evidence." Last, but not least, were images of organs being harvested on the three dead women.

"Excellent work, Robert. Excellent. And these files you have hidden on the computers?"

"Yes, sir, as instructed. Here and at his home. I used the keystroke caching software to capture his password and used it to protect these folders. It will look like he put them on the hard drive himself. Then I removed and wiped the keystroke software so no one can tell it was used."

Darko smiled. "There was no problem at his home?"

The man shook his head. "None. Everyone loves a free upgrade."

"Well done, Robert. Your usual good work always

appreciated." Darko handed the man an over-stuffed envelope. "Risto to show you out and arrange for night of pleasure."

"Thank you, Darko. Please, call me anytime." He stuffed the envelope into an inner coat pocket and headed for the office door.

"One last thing," Darko said, placing his hand on the man's shoulder. "Destroy copy of CD you keep." His tone was cold, threatening, and obvious.

Richard arrived at his apartment ready to down a cold brewski and kick back. What he really needed was to get out, to have some guy time. Where were Clive, Redman, Capt. A, and Hassle when he needed them?

He felt like he'd spent the day in a mortuary. He hated it. After his early morning talk with Darko, he'd staggered to his office to find Irina was AWOL, which was probably a good thing. He didn't have to pretend around Darko. She had played her role well. Darko had not seemed at all suspicious, but, at first, he'd been concerned. Had Darko discovered that she'd lied about their growing relationship? However, the others reassured him she was okay. Still, the others might as well have dressed in black, hidden behind inky veils, and sung dirges all day. The tension over Aida's death hung over the office as a blinding fog and he'd heard whispers that Aida's family had been killed, too. He found online stories about a home invasion and a hit-and-run, but names had been withheld by the authorities.

He tossed his briefcase on the couch and headed

straight for the kitchen. Seconds later, he popped the top on a Schlafly Pale Ale and mentally thanked his landlady for introducing him to the local craft brew. He took two large gulps, as much from stress as from thirst. He reached into the refrigerator to grab a second bottle to take with him upstairs, so he wouldn't have to return to the kitchen just minutes later. He was about to pop the top when he heard a knock on the door.

His landlady stood in the stairwell, her cane propped against the wall and a glass in each hand. "Ola! Time to celebrate. You do like margaritas, doncha? I make a mean one." She held one glass out to Richard.

He couldn't help but laugh at the elderly woman standing before him in a timeworn sombrero offering him relief after his miserable day. He took the glass and stepped aside to allow her into the apartment. As she ambled into the front room, he grabbed the cane from the hall and closed the door. She sat on his couch and raised her glass. "To technology!"

He laughed again and joined her in the toast. "Whoa," he exclaimed after his first sip. "Mean isn't the word I'd use for this margarita. Are you going to need to be carried back downstairs after finishing this?"

"Shush! Takes more than this to pickle me. *Un brindis por la tecnología!*" She took another drink, and Richard reciprocated.

"So, what are we toasting?"

"What? You don't know? I thought you set it up."

"Set up what?"

"The technician came around today and upgraded my, our, internet service. Super duper high speed now. All those bits, or bytes, bandwidth, whatever. I can download my TV shows in seconds now. Well, okay, maybe a couple of minutes, but it's sure better than what we had yesterday."

Richard felt a tingle of concern. He hadn't ordered any upgrade, but he didn't want to worry Mrs. Bowles.

"Oh, that. It wasn't really me, but probably my work. My boss had asked if I needed high speed internet at home, but I told him probably not. I guess he decided to go with it anyway, just in case. Do you have the technician's card or receipt? Something with the man's name on it? That way I can make sure it was my employer and not some error by the carrier. We sure don't want to pay for an upgrade we didn't order."

She looked deflated. "Wasn't any charge on the receipt, and it looked like it was all paid for."

"Maybe, but it's the monthly fee that kills you."

She nodded. "I like the speed."

"But at two, three times what your current bill is?"

He could see an aura of concern cross her face. He knew her funds were limited.

"Let me look into it. In the meantime, *saludamos*." He raised his glass.

She hesitated. "Party-pooper. I'll just take my drink back downstairs and brood about the bill."

Richard made a subtle grimace. "Sorry. I'm pretty sure it was my employer, so enjoy it." He cut his sentence short.

"You were going to add, 'while I can,' right?" She slugged back half of her glass. "Well, darn it, that's just what I'm going to do. Drink up, buster. I hate drinking alone."

Richard laughed, but only to hide his growing

unease. Lots of things at Darko Imports were beginning to add up, and he wasn't sure he was equipped to handle the sum.

Fifteen minutes later, he assisted Mrs. Bowles back down the stairs, claimed the receipt for the internet service change, and walked out the front door. Standing outside his car, he pulled out a prepaid cell phone and dialed.

"Problem?" The man on the other end seemed surprised at the call.

"I think I'm getting in way over my head." Richard explained the unexpected service upgrade and his fear that his apartment had been bugged and computer tampered with. He went on to describe the situation at work and how uncomfortable he felt there. "Look, I feel like I'm being scooted out on a limb waiting for a chainsaw to cut it off at the trunk. I have no authority. I'm not police, or FBI, or Justice Department, or whatever. You are going to protect me, right? That's what we agreed to, right?"

"Absolutely. So, what do you want us to do?"

"Well, check out my apartment and computer for starters."

"Sure, but realize we won't remove what we find. That might tip him off. He might have ways of knowing if anything has been removed."

Richard thought about that. He didn't like that, but he realized that was probably the right move. After a pause, he replied, "Understood."

"Look, we still need something on that area of the building you can't account for. Without something solid, we can't get a warrant. And until we can bust the place, we need you there."

Richard liked that even less, but he had agreed to that "one catch" about the job, that he was going into Darko Imports as a mole. Undercover, but with no legal authority as a law enforcement officer.

"I know. The place is too well guarded, and my key card doesn't work that door. I've told you that already."

"Yes, you have. You also told me you have a plan."

Richard returned to his apartment and plopped into his threadbare, hand-me-down chair. He had no idea how to check for listening devices. However, he had a good idea how to check out his computer. He walked over to the table holding it, sat down and booted up. The security and system logs confirmed someone had turned on and accessed his system while he was gone, but nothing more.

Twenty minutes later, he found what they'd placed on his hard drive, and ran to the bathroom to empty his gastric contents.

Twenty-seven

Lynch drove Ibrahim to the property in Ladue and let him off so that an abandoned car wouldn't arouse suspicion. He then took off to locate and purchase some of the items they might need to battle the homeowner's defenses. With Mike's help—money, a map and an address list—he tried small, local hardware, sporting goods, and pet stores. What he couldn't find there he found at the big chain stores. Yet, there remained one set of items they might need, and Lynch wasn't sure where to obtain them.

Shortly after lunch, he returned to the rendezvous point and retrieved Ibrahim.

"How'd it go?" he asked.

"Much same. Count two dog. Fence easy climb, but I fix anyway. I not see any motion sensors, but cannot know for sure. They not install any when set up security first time, but my action put scare in Darko. They maybe beef up security. How about you?"

"Starting to remember how to get around. Lots of these streets sure look familiar to me. Anyway, got everything we talked about except the baton stun guns. I found hand stuns and stunners combined with flashlights, but not the batons, and I think we need the added length."

Ibrahim nodded. He pulled his phone from his pocket and opened up his contact list. "Here is place, but you must do it. They call Risto if they see me." He showed the information to Lynch.

Lynch copied the number into his borrowed phone and dialed. Using a story about needing protection for him and his girlfriend when jogging, along with the name of a police officer reference—a name that came to him out of the blue but seemed to be recognized—he was told to stop by within the hour because they would be closed for two days after that.

"It's a go. Fifty dollars apiece for 300,000 watt stun batons."

"Good. Work on these dogs. For big, big dog, need more juice to put down. We deal with two Bandog. Maybe only 150 pound each."

Lynch winced at the thought. Only 150 pounds of angry dog in attack mode. What was he getting into?

"I drive now."

Lynch responded by putting the car in gear and starting off. It seemed the more he drove these roads, the more he remembered about locations and roads in the area. Like a map unfolding in his brain. He didn't want to stop that process now.

Ibrahim shrugged. "Go west, to Lindbergh, then north. I show you to this place."

Ten minutes later, Lynch found himself in an apartment complex twisting and turning between buildings and finally pulling into a parking spot near the end of the street. Lynch was expecting a storefront or, at least, a commercial building.

"Go around corner. Last building. First apartment on ground level. I stay here so not see me."

Lynch got out of the car and approached the first door on a lower apartment. An attractive woman, 30-ish, answered the door.

"Hi. I called about two baton stun guns just a while ago."

She nodded and stepped back to let him into the apartment. The front room was filled with boxes of security equipment—cameras, stun guns, batons with and without stun capability, pepper spray, Tasers™ and replacement cartridges, and more. The only open space remaining consisted of two paths, one leading to a kitchen counter where they'd set up a small office, and one leading to another room.

"Hey. I'm Jerold. You the guy who called a little while ago?" The young man had emerged from a room in the back.

Lynch nodded. "About needing two stun batons."

"Yeah. Put them aside. They're over here on the counter. Please excuse the mess. We lost the lease on our store when the owner sold the building. Still trying to find the right place."

Lynch chose not to say anything. Ibrahim had already told him that this couple had been working out of their apartment for the past five years. Five minutes later, his cash transaction completed, he walked out with the last items on his shopping list. He tossed them onto the back seat and started to climb into the driver's seat, but Ibrahim had taken it.

"I drive now. Not good to risk problem with police since you have no license. One thing to drive when necessary. Another to take risk when not necessary."

Lynch sighed. The man was right, as much as he wanted to argue the point.

"Okay, but let me try to get us back to the house. I think I know my way around now. As we leave the apartment complex, take a right, and at the light take another right." He paused in thought. "Then, at the second light, take another right."

He sat back to enjoy the ride. At the second light, Ibrahim turned left.

Amy's mind wandered as she unloaded her groceries from the car. Was she crazy for going through with this? No. She had only just met Richard, and they had agreed to be friends. If he wanted to go out with some bimbo who offered lap dances, why should she get upset about it? Why indeed. If he wanted to go out and make a drunken fool of himself, was that any of her business? No. Umm, maybe? Yes?

She could feel her blood pressure rising. She *was* crazy for going through with this.

Macy had warned her about being on the rebound. Macy had tried to prevent her from seeing Richard at the club. Richard and that gyrating, supermodel gorgeous slut! Macy had her best interest at heart. Why did she find it so difficult to listen to Macy?

She returned to the car, retrieved the third and final bag from the trunk, and released a huge sigh as she lowered it onto the kitchen counter. She had to get her mind in gear and her emotions in check. It was already past three in the afternoon, and he would be there before she knew it. She was determined to wow him with an amazing meal.

"I bet what's-her-name can't even boil water," she found herself saying out loud.

She placed the pork tenderloin, cheeses, cream and

more in the refrigerator and proceeded to lay out her ingredients. Richard was expected to bring wine, but she bought three bottles anyway—one for deglazing her sauce, and the others just in case he forgot.

She thought through the timing of her preparations and decided she would have time to sit down and relax for a little while, after prepping the pork and starting the marinating process. She pulled out her cutting board, cut open the bag holding the meat, and placed the tenderloin on the board. She grabbed her knife and noticed her hand shaking a bit.

Why am I nervous? she asked herself. *This won't do.*

She opened one bottle of wine and poured a small glass of the rich claret liquid. She savored a sip, letting it coat her taste buds before sliding down her throat. She took another gulp and picked up the knife again, feeling steadier.

Fifteen minutes later, she had the meat prepped, covered with the dry rub, and placed into a zip-lock bag to marinate in the refrigerator for the next couple of hours. That task accomplished, she grabbed her wine and moved to her small office where she signed onto the internet and checked her email and Facebook newsfeed. Nothing exciting there.

She headed for her bedroom, after topping off her glass, and began rummaging through her closet for just the right outfit. She would have time to change clothes right before Richard arrived, but only if she had everything laid out and ready. She showered and, before fixing her hair, glanced at the clock. Plenty of time. She sipped the last of her wine and stretched out on her bed to relax for a few minutes.

When she opened her eyes, she again checked her bedside clock, and panicked. Five o'clock! She had fallen asleep. Her heart raced as she rushed to the bathroom, brushed out her hair and pulled it back. She jumped into jeans, pulled on a sweatshirt and sprinted to the kitchen. Her thoughts galloped in six different directions. *What first?*

She grabbed a pot for water and filled it. Her hands were shaking again. The pasta was ready, waiting for the water to boil. She took that time to walk to her bedroom and reclaim her wine glass. With it full, she began to grate and prepare the cheese for her four-cheese penné. She added the cheese to her cream and tomato bisque preparation. By the time she began to mix the cheese sauce and pasta together, her glass was three-quarters empty. But, her hands were no longer shaking, and her anxiety had calmed.

With the pasta in the oven, she turned her attention to the bacon for her roasted asparagus with goat cheese and bacon. That would stand at room temperature until roasting it, after the pasta had baked. She poured another glass of wine before pulling the pork from the refrigerator to let it come to room temp.

The clock read five-fifty. Her heart began to race again. She hoped he wasn't a big dessert fan because she no longer had time to make the chocolate lava cake she had planned. She took another gulp of wine. Was the meat ready? It still felt cold. She should have taken it out at the beginning. What should she do?

She imbibed another swig of wine and raced to the bedroom where she dressed, applied a light touch of make-up, and worked on her hair, which would not cooperate. After the fourth attempt at something more stylish, she gave up and pulled it back into the original ponytail. That would have to do. She had to get back to the kitchen.

The pork hadn't come to room temperature, but she couldn't take more time. She sliced it into filets, added olive oil to the now clean frying pan, turned on the gas cooktop, and began to sauté the meat. She added her onion and a sprinkling of various herbs and finished the meat. Removing it to a dish, she reached for the wine to deglaze the drippings and create her sauce. The bottle was empty.

She huffed in frustration as she opened a new bottle, refilled her glass, and completed her sauce. It just needed to thicken a bit. She was "cookin'" now. In the zone. The meal was coming together as she'd planned, with fifteen minutes to spare. As the buzzer sounded for the oven, the doorbell rang. Early?

She ran to the door and yanked it open. There stood Richard, smiling, flowers in one hand, and a bag, presumably holding wine, in the other.

"Hope I'm not too early."

"Hi there." She couldn't think of anything else to say, as she stood there smiling and looking at the flowers. Her mind had gone blank.

A minute later, Richard broke the silence. "Um, may I come in, or are we . . .?"

"Oh, sorry." She stepped back to let him inside.

Richard stepped into the foyer and quickly furrowed his brow. "Is something, uh, burning?"

A funny smell snared her attention. Without another word, she turned and ran to the kitchen, where she pulled the pan with the sauce off the cooktop. Was it ruined? It was definitely thicker than she had planned. However, that wasn't the smell.

With a quick glance into the oven, she saw the top of her pasta dish browning more deeply than she wanted. The buzzer had gone off, and she had ignored it to answer the door. She grabbed her mitts and removed it from the oven. Inwardly she sighed in relief. Brown but not burnt. She adjusted the oven temperature for the asparagus and stepped back.

She turned and started at seeing Richard standing in the doorway. In her frustrated rush, she'd momentarily forgotten him.

"Hello again," he said.

"Hi." She gave him a loopy smile. "I hope you like dinner. It's not every day I get to make dinner for a Norse god." *Did I just really say that?*

He gave her a curious look. "Smells wonderful." He held up the flowers.

"Oh. Yes. Something to put those in." She went to a cabinet at the other end of the kitchen and rummaged through it for a minute. "It's been so long since I had fresh flowers, I have to think about where I put my vases." She realized that time had little to do with it. The wine was taking its toll on her thought processes. She found a plastic pitcher and removed its lid. "This will have to do for now." She filled it halfway and plopped the bouquet into it, making no effort to arrange the stems to best show off each flower. Her hand started shaking again.

"So, do you like red wine or white? I didn't know, so I brought two of each."

Richard held up a bottle in each hand, and Amy could see from the labels that they outclassed the bottles on her countertop.

"Yes," she replied. She grabbed her glass of red and took a sip.

Richard laughed. "I guess we start with the cabernet. May I?" He pointed to the refrigerator with a bottle of chardonnay. Amy nodded, and he placed each bottle on its side on the shelf. "Opener?"

Amy walked around him to a cabinet and retrieved a second wine glass, which she placed next to her already open bottle of inexpensive Norton. "We might as well finish this one first." She took another drink from her glass and checked the oven. Time for the asparagus. "Hungry? Ready in six minutes." She set the time again.

Richard picked up the open bottle and inspected it. She saw him glance at the nearby empty bottle. He gave her another quizzical look. "Sure. Where should I put these?" He poured his glass of wine and held up both bottles of red.

"Dining room." *Oh shoot*, she thought. She hadn't set the table. She quickly gathered up utensils, fumbling them as she collected the cloth napkins she rarely used, and nearly dropping the water glasses before walking to the dining table. Fortunately, it was empty of the usual clutter that found its way to that large flat surface. She quickly set two places and found a glass carafe, which she filled with ice and water and set on the table.

Richard followed her with the flowers and added them to the setting. "There," he said. "That's okay, isn't it?"

Not exactly classy with a plastic pitcher, she thought, but she replied, "Um, sure. Make yourself at home." She pointed to one of the chairs just as the timer sounded. She returned to the kitchen and within minutes returned with two plates that would make any challenger on the Food Network program *Chopped* proud.

"Wow! This looks really good." He held up his glass. "A toast to the chef."

Amy dipped her head in modesty and smiled. She raised her glass to realize it was almost empty, a temporary problem as Richard filled it halfway after they clinked glasses. "Just half?"

"Yeah, I think that's best right now."

Amy giggled. And she knew at that moment, he was right. She was, after all, drunk enough that she giggled. She never giggled. At least she felt relaxed. Normally, she would have stressed out at the combination of the buzzer sounding, the doorbell ringing, the realization that her guest had arrived early, and the threat of her food burning all at once. Maybe she needed to drink wine whenever she cooked for company.

"Sorry. I guess I did take a head start on you."

He nodded as he chewed. After swallowing he said, "This is really good."

"Thanks. I love cooking . . . and baking."

As they ate, they shared tales of favorite foods and restaurants from across the globe. Her experiences came from following her Army aviator father across Europe, while his came from traveling with buddies on leave. His favorite ethnic cuisine was Lebanese, hers, Greek. Very similar.

Richard had finished the open bottle of Norton and started the bottle of red wine he'd brought with him. He poured himself a glass, and offered Amy another half a glass as she finished her Norton.

"Here, try this one. It's an Enira 2006 Thracian Lowlands Bulgarian red wine, a mix of cabernet sauvignon and merlot. The oenophiles would describe it as a spicy, red wine boasting flavors of plum and black currant. It's produced and bottled by the Bessa Valley Winery in the Bulgarian village of Ognianovo. It's really good."

Amy felt her mouth pucker as she sipped it. She knew that drier wines were the heart-healthier ones, but sometimes her taste buds rebelled as the tannins seemed to absorb the saliva from her mouth.

"Too dry?" he asked.

"No. It just takes me a mouthful or two to get used to a drier wine, but I like them. From work?"

Richard smiled and nodded. "As my boss would say, '*Živjeli*.' That's the Croatian equivalent of 'cheers' and he's quite the partier. From what I hear."

"So, how's work going?"

"It's been a challenge." He went on explain how many items they imported, the price ranges of those items and the difficulty in developing marketing plans for the multiple markets those items aimed for. "I set a two-month goal for myself, which Darko thought too restrictive, but I think I can make it."

"Darko?"

"Oh, sorry. He's the owner. Darko Komarčić. He's really a character." He finished his last bite of food and took a sip of wine as he sat back a bit from the table.

"He might be eccentric, but he sure is generous. He, uh . . . I, uh . . ."

Amy noticed his hesitation.

"He, you, what?"

"I, um, stumbled upon a buyer for a rug he had. He closed the deal and did all the work, but he gave me a commission anyway. I was really surprised."

That didn't compute in Amy's hazy mind. Surprised? Over a commission for some rug? Big deal. But, she played along.

"So, that's what we're drinking tonight? Your commission?"

Richard smiled, but hesitated again. He clearly didn't want to say anything more, but he was the one who brought it up.

"I sense there's more to this story," Amy added.

"Um, yeah, well, it was a rare silk rug, Iranian, from before the restrictions on importing Iranian products."

"And . . ."

"Okay, I didn't want it to sound like I'm bragging. He sold it Thursday for $350,000 and gave me a ten percent commission."

Even Amy's wine-fogged brain could make that calculation easily enough. "You've been there, what, a couple of weeks and got a $35,000 commission? That sounds like a cause to celebrate." It took her fuzzy mind a few more minutes to connect with the day. Thursday. The club. She'd done well keeping that memory submerged beneath the Norton and cabernet, only to have it come up for air at that moment.

"So, are we celebrating now, or have you already done that?"

225

His countenance reflected the change in her tone. He seemed to sense a sinkhole was about to open up beneath him.

"Oh no, we can celebrate with the fancy dinner I promised. You invited me here. I-it wouldn't be right, you know, to have you do all the work on this fabulous meal and for me to . . . to, well, say this is my, our celebration."

Amy stood up, crossed around the table, and sat on his lap. "So, perhaps I should put on some music and we can dance. Or maybe you'd prefer a lap dance."

"Amy! W-what's gotten into you?"

She stood up, frowning at him.

"Seems to me you did plenty of celebrating already."

He looked at her like "what are you talking about?"

"Thursday night. Macy and I were at Europe Night Club. We saw you with whatever-her-name-is. You certainly seemed to be having a good time." She stormed back to her chair and sat down, with arms crossed in front of her.

"Wait a minute; you've got that all wrong. That was work—"

"Work? Sure didn't look like work to us, except maybe she was workin' it pretty good. Where'd you pick her up?"

"Work. She—"

"What? I thought you worked for an importer, not a pimp. I . . ." She stopped when she saw his face blanch. She had no doubt he played a lousy game of poker because his face was all an opponent needed to read him.

226

"I can't say anymore. I've already said too much."

"Said too much? You haven't said anything."

"And you haven't let me." He stood up and threw his napkin on the table. "But, as I think about it, I can't tell you anything more."

"Can't or won't? Have another hot date with the supermodel? I don't care. We're just supposed to be friends, right?"

"Actually, that's . . ." He stopped. "Sorry, Amy, but I think it best that I leave. Thank you for a delicious meal."

With that, he retrieved his coat from the couch in the front room and let himself out. Amy watched him leave, and poured another full glass of wine. *Maybe I shouldn't drink wine when I cook for company.*

Twenty-eight

Darko had spent yet another Saturday in his office, something he did not enjoy. Events involving Ibrahim and the whores he "imported" required his attention. As he prepared to leave for their country home, he heard a knock on his office door. He lifted his head to see his security chief's head peer around the doorpost. He motioned for the man to enter.

"*Da*, Risto?"

"*Ibrahim je uočena.*" Ibrahim has been spotted. "He use homeless bum to buy two stun baton. Jerold watch parking lot cam, see Ibrahim in car, waiting."

"Homeless bum? Is he sure?"

Risto nodded. "Da. Ratty beard, long hair. Clothes not fit right. Use cash. Ibrahim driving. Could be. Easy money for bum."

Darko thought about that for a moment. Had Ibrahim solicited help? If so, from where? The man's only contacts in the city were Darko's contacts. At least they had been. He had lived exclusively in the Bosnian conclave since coming to the U.S. Whom else could he have turned to? One of Darko's competitors? No, their men would not look like that, but they might have recruited some bum to help. That was more their style than Darko's.

"Maybe not. We must be alert. What is he up to?"

Darko contemplated their predicament. They were shorthanded and resources were stretched thin.

"*Pasa*," Risto answered. Dogs. "He is concern about

dog."

"Oh?"

Risto nodded confidently. "Man you take down from distance. Taser or gun. Dog small, hard to hit until dog get close. If miss, dog go for gun, so protect with stun gun. Baton give you more distance to dog. Can use on man, too, but bet on dog."

Darko could agree with that, except for Ibrahim. "Not like Ibrahim. He just shoot dog. And, why two baton?"

Risto shook his head. "Ne. He like dog. Only shoot if have to. Second baton backup. Maybe need if lose first one or it damaged."

Darko thought about that for a moment. That didn't sound like the man he knew, but he respected Risto and his knowledge of their men. So, the batons were likely to be used on a dog. That assessment helped. Only a handful of their clients used guard dogs. So, which one was Ibrahim's target?

"We have three, no, four client with dog. Which is best target, and how many men we have to move?" he asked his security chief.

"Only two man. One available now. Other watching Richard." replied Risto. "Target? High value first. That has been his way."

"And?"

"State senator at top of list. Flip coin for number two. Ladue or Town and Country. Ladue have three dog. Other have only one."

"Put man with senator and with client in Town and Country," replied Darko. "Even Ibrahim cannot fight three dog and win. Not those dog." Darko knew those dogs. Even with help, Ibrahim would meet his match with those dogs.

Risto nodded. "*Još jedna stvar.*" One more thing. "Richard visit her again. Take flowers and wine. Wine he buy from us. Enira."

Darko smiled inwardly. At least the man had good taste in wine. Nevertheless, his visit to this other woman, Amy Gibbs, meant what? Had Richard lied about Irina? In turn, that meant he lied about other things. What had they missed on his background check? His apartment and his car held no clues, and his life outside of work was ordinary, boring in fact. The man's work was excellent and Darko needed the result of those efforts to expand his business. He could not afford to make Richard disappear. Yet.

Or, was he more of a player than Darko had taken him for? His eagerness for the foursome with Irina seemed real. Yes. In reflection, that emotion *was* real. Darko was sure of it. Richard was no actor, and he had actually blushed. He would have to be well trained to do that over a lie. Such training would have come to light in their background check.

Well, he had a way of fixing this quandary and getting the leverage he wanted over the man.

"Irina offer Richard a foursome. We make that happen, at the country house. I have Sonja instruct Miloska to join the party. And please extend my 'invitation' to this Gibbs woman. She will make nice number four."

Twenty-nine

"We must move tonight." Ibrahim paced the dining room of the Southworth home. He rubbed his hands together, as if itching to put them to work.

"I don't know. I think we have to rehearse this somehow. Make sure our plan is sound," replied Lynch. He sat in an upholstered chair tucked into the room's bay window. His hesitancy was born of uncertainty in his abilities. Yes, according to the papers, he had been an outstanding police officer, but were those skills lying latent somewhere in his mind and body? His assurance in those skills was MIA.

"No luxury of time. Agata could die. I see her this morning, but Darko might cut loss, regroup later. Also, tonight is symphony. This man and his wife support symphony. Will go to concert, no matter what."

Lynch was not convinced that they were ready, that he was ready. He had no confidence in his ability to think quickly on his feet and improvise should the plan go awry.

"I still don't know."

"Is okay. I go anyway. Without you. Time is critical." Ibrahim stopped pacing and checked his watch. "I go now."

Mike and Mary sat at the dining table watching the exchange. Mike had his head bowed and eyes closed until Ibrahim announced his departure.

"I'll go with you, to drive. A parked car will arouse even more suspicion at night than it would have today."

Lynch looked at his host with his mouth agape. He had come to appreciate the retired colonel's insights and commitment to helping these women. Was he going too far? Or, was Lynch being too insecure in his own abilities and transferring that upon Mike? He had to face the fact that he didn't remember much about police tactics, weapons, or self-defense. As with the handgun, Mike would say it's like riding a bicycle. Even so, Mike's eagerness to help showed his willingness to risk everything. Lynch wondered if he ever had been that selfless.

"Are you sure?" he asked Mike.

"Yes. You need a driver, and I'm the guy. I won't sit on the sidelines on this one."

"But what if something happens? You have a lot to lose."

"If something happens, I might be your only saving grace."

Both Lynch and Ibrahim looked at him quizzically.

"Think about it. An immigrant and a dead man. You get caught, and they might just throw away the jail key for you . . ." He pointed to Ibrahim. ". . . and lock you up in a hospital room." He pointed to Lynch. "Having me there might make the world of difference. Don't get me wrong. I'm nothing special, and I don't have a ton of political strings to pull, but I can add a certain level of credibility. They can't ignore my distinguished record." He emphasized the words 'distinguished record' as if spoken by some news anchor. "And, again, you really need a driver. A parked empty car is going to invite the police. At the least, they might tow it and leave you without wheels. At the worst, they set up surveillance and catch you."

Lynch and Ibrahim looked at each other. Ibrahim shrugged and nodded. Lynch couldn't argue the logic behind Mike's statement.

"Okay. Let's roll." He stood up as Ibrahim tossed his car keys to Mike.

Mike shook his head. "My car."

Eighteen minutes later, they rolled down a side lane near the Ladue property. Lynch sat in the back seat while Ibrahim rode shotgun. Both men struggled in the tight quarters to prepare. Lynch wished they had body armor, but the cost and difficulty in obtaining it on short notice eliminated that option. Besides, they were preparing for dogs, not armed men. They had modified, and padded, baseball shin guards front and back for their calves, wrapped in place by ACE bandages. Catchers' chest protectors, cut into strips, were taped onto their thighs. Likewise, their forearms were padded, the right one less so, to allow better use of their dominant arms. Lynch couldn't come up with a way to protect their butts; they needed some mobility.

Each man carried duplicate rucksacks containing tools to disable alarms, break locks, and more. Fifty feet of nylon rope, duct tape, and plastic ties added to the list. And last, but not least, each man carried a dog muzzle.

"Ready," said Ibrahim.

Lynch nodded. "Okay." He took a deep breath. Ready or not, the time had come.

"Up there. White stake next to road. Cross fence there. Meet back here in 30 minute."

Ibrahim seemed confident, but Lynch expected

that, considering the fact that he'd been successful on his previous missions. Lynch was a rank amateur in comparison, with years of police training he couldn't remember. Maybe some of Ibrahim's confidence would rub off on him, before they crossed the fence and entered the dogs' domain.

The overhead compartment light was turned off, and each man slid out his door into the chill of the night. Despite the 38-degree temperature, Lynch sweated profusely. He donned his rucksack and picked up the baton with a white-knuckle death grip. He had a date with a large dog and wasn't about to let go of his only defense. As the car eased away down the lane, he followed Ibrahim to the ten-foot-high, chain link fence hidden by a tangle of leaf-bare shrubs. There was a gap in the woody barrier, and they moved through it in single file. At the fence, Ibrahim began to unwrap wire that held together the chain link that had been cut.

"I fix this early. Much easy than climbing."

A minute later, he rolled back the chain link to reveal a short but wide opening that a man could easily duck through, even with a pack on his back. Seconds later, Lynch was in dog territory. Fortunately, the dogs weren't waiting. They would have some warning. He hoped.

Lynch watched Ibrahim move through the fence and struggle to push a similar white stake into the near frozen ground. Satisfied with it, the man gave Lynch a thumbs up, followed by a signal showing the direction of the house which was supposed to be about 200 yards away from that portion of the fence. That signal was followed by one telling Lynch to remain quiet.

Ibrahim began to move toward the home in a crouch. Lynch followed. They used the trees and landscape for cover as much as they could. Halfway there, Ibrahim began to move toward a long arbor bordering a landscaped patio in what looked like a swimming pool complex. On the opposite side of the closed pool sat a small building, which Lynch guessed to hold changing rooms and perhaps a party room.

Three steps later, Lynch heard a menacing, guttural growl from behind, echoed by a similar snarl ahead. Ibrahim backed up until they touched. Like Spartan warriors, they eased upward into a fighting stance, covering each other's back. Lynch heard the buzz of Ibrahim's baton as he flipped the switch to engage his stun baton. His moves were slow and measured to prevent provoking the animals. Simultaneously, the two men extended their left forearms outward, as bait.

What next? The dogs seemed content to hold the men at bay.

Suddenly, Ibrahim let out a deep growl and stomped one foot toward the nearest dog. The next thing Lynch knew, both dogs, now provoked, lunged for the attack. He waved his left forearm in front of him. In their planning discussion, they had agreed the dogs would likely go for that forearm, an obvious, easy target and heavily padded in anticipation. The dog went for his right arm, the one holding the baton, the one lightly padded for increased mobility.

He heard Ibrahim's baton discharge, but the second dog continued to attack his companion. Lynch planted his right foot and launched a kick into the rib cage of the dog as it tried to pull him down by his right forearm. The weight of the dog almost toppled him, but the dog let go of his forearm and went for the leg. That gave Lynch the moment he needed to regain his balance. Lynch could feel the power of those jaws against the plates of the shin guards, squeezing his calf. He could only imagine those teeth burying into his calf and was thankful they had decided to cover both front and back of their calves. He quickly moved the baton toward the dog, but the animal saw the weapon and responded.

Lynch kicked again and used that moment to apply the stun points to the animal's chest. The dog yelped, but did not go down. He heard a similar burst from Ibrahim's baton, followed by a thud. Lynch focused his attack on the animal's neck and triggered the baton again. As he did so, he saw Ibrahim's baton join his and the animal received a double shock. It quickly dropped to the ground with no sound, its breathing shallow.

"Muzzle quick," whispered Ibrahim.

Each man worked swiftly to pull the muzzle from the side of his rucksack and strap it onto an animal's head. Lynch cinched his tight and took two plastic ties from his pack, using one to bind the front legs and the second for the hind legs. He looked at these dogs in the dim light from the house. Bandogs. He'd never heard of the breed before Ibrahim's report earlier that day. He was glad he'd never faced one before. The dog lying before him was every bit of the 150 pounds mentioned by Ibrahim. Maybe more. And ugly? The animal was stereotypical of a junkyard dog.

"Do not let look fool you. Bandog is great dog for family. Love family and ferocious to protect family.

Much loyal," Ibrahim whispered as he finished immobilizing his animal. "We must move fast now."

Staying in the shadows, the pair ran toward the house and located a set of French doors leading from a patio into what appeared to be a family area. The only lights appeared to come from a kitchen and basement window.

"Basement light Agata's room. Stay here. I check kitchen," whispered Ibrahim.

Lynch sat against the house and noticed four large dog bowls, two each for food and water. He wondered if the animals had shelter to use during foul weather. He calmed his heart and breathing. The next part should be easier, according to Ibrahim. He subconsciously rubbed his right forearm and realized he needed to inspect it. The light padding had protected him from the teeth, but not the crushing pressure of the bite. His forearm hurt. He had no doubt that significant bruising would be evident by morning's light.

Ibrahim eased up next to him. "Housekeeper alone in kitchen. See no sign of more guard. Check garage, too. Car gone. To symphony, like I say. God watch over us."

He stood up and faced the French doors. With a few deft movements, he had the lock open. Lynch stood, prepared to enter the home. They had but fifteen minutes remaining before the rendezvous with Mike. This would have to be a dash and grab.

"What about the alarm system?"

"More luck. Panel inside kitchen door show green. Housekeeper not set until she go to bed." He eased open the latch and the door silently moved inward. No clarions. No armed guards rushing into the room.

Lynch saw light at the end of a hallway and heard the rattle of dishes being stacked. He saw three closed doors before reaching the kitchen. Each one could hold a surprise, but maybe Ibrahim was correct. Maybe they'd gotten lucky.

"Okay. Go take care of housekeeper, like we talk about. I get Agata."

Ibrahim turned toward the kitchen, but disappeared through a door in the hallway. The one to the basement, thought Lynch. Only two potential surprises remained. He crept toward the kitchen where the noise continued. A few seconds later, he peeked around the corner. The woman appeared in her forties and more athletic than the stereotype of a housekeeper he had in his mind. She had her back to him. Maybe his luck would continue, and she'd be compliant, so he wouldn't have to zap her.

At the moment he entered the kitchen, she turned, saw him, and let out a scream.

"Quiet! And I won't hurt you," said Lynch.

She lunged at him with a large kitchen knife in hand. He instinctively raised his left forearm in defense, feeling glad he hadn't removed the padding. But, the padding wasn't needed as he lifted the baton and connected with her before she could swing her arm down. The knife clanked onto the tile floor as she fell, twitching, on top of it. So much for the 'Easy Button.' Lynch quickly taped her mouth and bound her wrists with the plastic ties. He wrapped her ankles in duct tape. She wouldn't be going anywhere until her employer released her.

He stood and glanced down the hallway. Where

was Ibrahim? He should have been upstairs with Agata by now. They had maybe seven minutes left and needed to leave the property. He looked at the three doors leading off the hallway. Which door had Ibrahim used? He wished he'd paid closer attention at the time.

He walked up to the first door and then the second—identical, as was the third. Nothing about each door indicated where it led. He could hear no noise from behind any of them. No light shown beneath.

He decided to open the first door nearest the kitchen, although he felt sure Ibrahim hadn't gone that far down the hall. As he turned the knob, he heard a muted growl. Where had it come from? Had one of the dogs gotten loose somehow? How could that have happened? He looked behind him. No dog in the hall. He started to turn the knob again and heard nothing. Expecting the worst, he eased open the door to find an empty laundry room. One door down.

Which door next? The story of the lady and the tiger flitted through his mind. No eenie, meenie, miney, moe. No flipping of a coin. He had a 50-50 chance of opening the right door, so nothing like the closest one. He moved to the adjacent door and slowly eased the knob to open the latch. Grrrr! The door flew open as the latch gave way and a mass of canine terror launched through the door, fangs bared, hot breath pouring from its nostrils.

Lynch's padded forearm flew up in reaction, but the mass of the animal tossed him onto his back and he dropped his baton. The dog was larger than anything he'd ever encountered and the snap of its jaws onto his left forearm made the Bandog seem like a puppy.

Although the padding had protected his forearm from being ripped open, the pain was incredible, and its fangs were quickly shredding the padding. He didn't have long before his skin would be exposed.

He violently kicked the dog's belly, its flanks, anywhere he could land a foot, but the close quarters prevented him from delivering much force. The monster did not relent, nor did it drop his forearm and go after a leg where Lynch had better protection from the animal's teeth. With his free arm, he fished around for his baton. He touched it once, but the dog nearly yanked his arm from his shoulder, and he lost it again. He pushed back along the floor, trying to drag the dog with him toward the baton. Finally, he landed on it and reached under his back to grab it.

He thrust the baton against the beast's throat and discharged it. Nothing. The creature bit down harder. Lynch felt as if the bones in his forearm were about to break. He moved the baton closer to the dog's head and triggered it again. The baton was so close, he felt an electrical tingle in his forearm. This time the animal seemed to lessen its grip. He stunned it again and kicked it. This time the animal let go but attacked his leg. Lynch had instant relief in his forearm, but now the dog had a different type of leverage and was out of easy reach with the baton. The brute strength of the animal tossed Lynch back and forth and it dragged him into the family room where they'd entered the house. Every time Lynch tried to lean forward to reach the dog with the baton, he was jerked a different direction and lost his balance. He tried to kick the dog's head with his other foot, but that, too, was far from effective.

Suddenly, the dog stopped. Lynch thought he'd heard the spit of a muffled gunshot. The dog toppled over, its eyes glazed and drool dripping from its mouth. Lynch turned toward the hallway and saw Ibrahim standing there with his silenced 9mm in one hand, but a Taser in the other, its wires leading to probes in the animal's side. A frail young woman stood next to him.

Ibrahim rushed toward him, but the woman backed against the wall as if to remain unnoticed.

"You okay? Can walk? We must go."

He reached down to assist Lynch, who offered his "good" arm. He stood and tested his legs. Good enough, but his left forearm was going to keep him awake that night. He inspected the padding and saw how close the dog had come to shredding him. He winced with every movement. He looked down at the monster and saw that without Ibrahim, he would have lost this battle. The thing appeared twice the size of the Bandog outside.

"English Mastiff," said Ibrahim. "Baton stun like bee sting to this breed." He turned and motioned to Agata to join them. "Come. We must be quick. Even Taser charge only last minute on Mastiff. If he wake up, I must shoot."

The three left the house, closing the French doors to keep the mastiff inside, and Ibrahim led them back past the pool. The guard dogs, now alert, struggled to free themselves and growled at the trio. Ibrahim pulled his gun and aimed at the first animal's head. Lynch stopped him before he could pull the trigger.

"They're no danger to us right now. Let's go."

Thirty
❧ ✦ ✦ ☙

Darko and Sonja had spent the last few hours enjoying their perverse fleshly delights. Darko relaxed on the silk covered Turkish bed, its colorful turned-wood posts towering above each corner. Costly wall tapestries and subdued light from antique brass lamps provided a seductive, old world atmosphere suitable for a sultan. He took a drag of hashish from their antique hookah, and watched as Sonja slept next to him, their concubine lying at their feet. He would let her sleep a bit longer before demanding her services again.

Quiet music of Croatia—*Tamburitza* bands and native instruments like the *gusle* and diple—provided a soothing remembrance of home. He also loved the small orchestras of violins, *cimbule*, *tamburice* and *harmonike* playing the folk music of Zagorje. At the moment, a melancholic tune from *Međimurje* lilted through the room. Perhaps next would be a partially diatonic melody in the Istrian scale unique to his homeland. This was his playground, his escape, his release from the pressures of business, both legal and illegal.

In the ideal world, nothing would intrude upon his time in "The Harem." Unfortunately, the real world lay just outside the door. He allowed no phones, no intrusions into the room, except for one. A small, muted light sat just above the door and was tied to a single phone line, a line only known to a handful of people. One of those people was trying to reach him now.

He took one additional drag from the pipe and

stood, unhappy at being forced back to reality so soon. He took one more look at the two women sleeping and left them be. He hoped to return within minutes.

He entered his office and picked up the phone.

"*Oprostite*, Darko." Pardon me.

"*Da*, Risto." The man's call meant only bad news.

"Ibrahim hit Ladue house, take Agata. He have help. Description sound like same homeless bum at security store." Risto provided more details.

Darko pounded his fist into the desktop and swore like none of his men, even Risto, had ever heard. His usual confident, calm manner had dissolved like cocaine in a spoon of water over an open flame. He wanted to hurt someone, anyone, at that moment, yet felt relief that Sonja was not in the room with him. He saw his empire crumbling, his good life becoming entrapped by bars. He hated that one man, a man he had once trusted with his life, was evading him and worse, besting him, outplaying him. Even more, he hated that he had called it wrong. He had not foreseen the damage Ibrahim could cause. Overconfident, he had not called for reinforcements, and now he was shorthanded, with angry clients demanding protection and restitution. His self-esteem roiled at this revelation of his shortcoming.

To make it worse, he had a battle brewing on a second front. Richard. If he really wasn't who he said he was, then just whom did he work for? What was his goal? However, Darko had nothing to suggest that Richard was someone other than what his background showed. Nothing except his gut at this time.

Even more concerning, if Richard was a fake, what had Darko done to find himself on some unknown

243

group's radar? At least Ibrahim was a known threat, his resources limited. How could he battle the unknown, with perhaps unlimited resources? He needed to cut off this second threat at its knees, and Richard was the key.

"Get the Gibbs woman now! When you have her, send proof to my phone. Photo best. Have Hasan get Irina and Miloska. Bring here, to estate. We give Richard test. If he pass, good. If not, we eliminate threat. Then we focus on Ibrahim. Call Toma in Pittsburgh. Send dozen man. I cover expense, plus bonus."

Darko paced in front of his desk as he thought through his dilemma.

"Keep man at senator house and Town and Country house. Bring dog from Ladue to estate. Move Hasan and Goran from warehouse to Richmond Height and Webster Grove. When Toma's men arrive, scatter where need is. Find Ibrahim!"

Amy tossed and turned. Her bed felt like a bag of rocks, but her real problem was a combination of wine and regret. Too much of both. The former flowed all too easily to form the second. Why hadn't she kept her mouth shut? They'd been having such a good time. Dinner was as good as she had hoped, and she had impressed him with the food. Unfortunately, the after dinner impression was the one likely to linger.

She turned again to check the time. One a.m. On the good side, the flight nurse she had replaced had returned to work, and Amy was back to being an instructor. That gave her a day to recuperate. She would need it. Maybe she would be able to contact Richard and apologize, ask for a do-over.

She rolled onto her back and stared at the ceiling. The nearest streetlight cast a dim glow through the curtains into her room. In a couple of hours, she'd be getting up to prepare to go to work with her aircrew, if she were on flight status. With all the rubbish filling her mind, would she be able to go back to sleep? She needed to. Richard's comment about the other woman being somehow related to his work stood front and center in that mental junk pile. He had been about to clarify that when she had interrupted and he decided to leave. Maybe the situation wasn't what it looked like.

No. What she and Macy saw was indeed what they saw. There was no mistaking that lap dance for something else. Still, maybe the circumstances leading to such an action wasn't what it obviously seemed to be. Maybe he was an innocent victim. Maybe she was the boss' daughter, and he was too polite to reject her advances. Yeah, right.

An unexpected shadow crossed in front of her window.

Richard woke up in his car, freezing. He had taken off driving after walking out of Amy's house. His mind wandered, and his car followed. He found himself in the boonies of some adjacent county, with no cell service, no light, and no idea where he was. Having pulled into the gravel lot of some defunct tavern, he had tried to reconstruct in his head how he had gotten there and had fallen asleep.

Good thing I turned off the engine, he thought. The

cold had wakened him. Had he left the car running, he might have stayed warm and slept until he'd run out of gas and then got cold. As it was, he didn't have much gas and couldn't afford to head out blindly, or simply to run the car for the heater.

He rubbed his hands together, followed by rubbing both arms and thighs for warmth, but it wasn't enough. He climbed out of the car and did a few jumping jacks to warm up. He gazed in all directions looking for lights on the horizon, hoping to get some bearing back toward people. The clear sky held a full array of heavenly lights that allowed him to locate the North Star. At least now, he knew which way was north, but was he now north, south, or west of civilization? More importantly, north, south, or west of an open gas station? He still didn't have enough information to make a good decision.

He glanced at the abandoned eatery and noticed what looked like a dilapidated bulletin board in the dim light. He reached into his glove compartment and found a small LED flashlight, which he shone in the direction of the building as he walked toward it. It was a decaying notice board that had caught his attention, and fastened to it was the top half of an old menu. Standard American fare at prices he hadn't seen for a decade. More importantly though, at the top right corner, there was a simple, faded map showing the tavern's location between a town called Clarksville and the larger city of Louisiana. He was on State Route 79, and the Mississippi River was within spitting distance just to his east.

Confident he'd find gas to his south, he returned to his car and took off in that direction. Now his thoughts returned to Amy –and Irina. He shouldn't have run out on Amy without telling her more. Yet, he couldn't place her in danger by telling her what he was doing. She was far safer not knowing. The more he thought about it the more he realized he simply needed to finish this job. He needed to find out what lay behind that locked door at Darko Imports, find Irina and make sure she was safe, and notify his handler to tear into the place.

Forty-five minutes later, Richard found himself back on Interstate 70, not as far from Amy's house as he'd imagined. For a second he thought about doing something bold, driving back to her home, pounding on the door until he woke her up, and explaining everything. Then he realized just how crazy that would be. She'd kill him, or worse, never talk to him again.

After filling his tank, he took off for south city. Hasan would be on duty, as usual, at the warehouse. Was he prepared to deal with the man?

Darko finished dressing in black jeans and turtleneck, and slicked back his hair in front of the mirror on Sonja's dresser. Long ago, this had been his "uniform" of the day, back when he performed special ops for his militia in Croatia. His crepe-soled black leather shoes, his "brothel creepers," had sat in the back of his closet for so long that he had to clean a thick layer of dust from them. The outfit brought back memories, but did he still have the skills those memories required?

"Trouble?"

He turned to see Sonja in the doorway, walking into their bedroom.

"You not need wear such clothes in long time."

Darko explained their situation. He held nothing back from Sonja. He never had. Many times, she had given him new insight into solutions to a problem. She nodded often as he talked. A wan smile crossed her lips as he mentioned Richard.

"You suspected all along, yes?"

She eased up next to him and caressed his neck. "*Da, moj najdraži.*" Yes, my dearest. "Call it woman instinct." She kissed him on the cheek. "Do not underestimate that man."

"Not again. Still, he do good work, work I need and cannot afford put off."

Darko nodded and kissed his wife on the lips. "I must go to warehouse first. Then I have loose end to deal with. Irina and Miloska will be coming here. Also, other woman Richard like. Risto bring her. Put her with other girls, but not touch." He smiled. "That time might come later, but for now, not touch. And no drug."

Sonja gave him a seductive pout as she let him go.

"Be good."

"I'm always good," she purred. "Cannot Risto deal with this loose end?"

"He have other tasks to do, and I wish to deal with this councilman myself."

Sonja kissed him before he left, and Darko saw her watching him from a front window as he drove off in his SUV. He was not surprised to find his Czech CZ-82, with an extra magazine, sitting on the passenger seat. She always looked out for him.

Thirty-one

❧ ✦ ❧

The trip back to the Southworth's home had been a quiet one. Agata cowered on the back seat against the door. Neither Mike nor Lynch knew Spanish. Ibrahim knew a few words, but they were words from his previous employment, not exactly words of assurance or encouragement. From the young woman's reaction, Lynch was convinced she believed she was being taken from one hell to a new one. Mike assured them that Mary would be able to talk with her, and he had alerted his wife to that need.

Ibrahim spoke little, and Lynch, for his part, was in such pain he wanted only to focus on "happy thoughts" to try to keep his mind from the damage done to his forearm and legs by that monster called a mastiff. He did thank Ibrahim, twice, for saving his life. Each time the man simply shrugged and nodded as if saying, "no big deal," not "you're welcome."

Mike pulled into the garage, and immediately Mary was at the car, opening the door to Agata. Lynch and Ibrahim removed their gear and placed it aside, while Mike aided his wife in helping Agata inside. The woman seemed confused. She kept shutting her eyes and shaking her head as if what was happening wasn't real. Mary explained that she was safe. There were others with them who had been rescued from Darko's clutches. Agata had trouble taking it in.

Danijela and Raifa waited in the kitchen and attempted to welcome the newcomer with hugs and food. They, too, spoke no Spanish. Agata withdrew from physical touch, but gingerly took a cup of tea and some cookies. Mary continued to talk, but, as she explained to the others, there were some significant differences between Mary's formal, schooled Spanish and the young woman's dialect. The woman avoided the men when they passed through.

Lynch and the other men stood in the parlor where Mike examined Lynch's arm. Lynch looked to the doorway as Danijela walked in.

"How is she?"

"Still scare. Not sure of us. Mary show her to room upstair. Will take time." She leaned past Mike's shoulder to look at Lynch's arm and winced at the sight.

"Yeah. Pretty sight, isn't it?" His forearm looked twice its normal size and already displayed a variety of red and purple hues. He wondered if he'd be able to use it later that day, after a period of rest. His calves, too, were beginning to feel the same—stiff, sore, and swollen.

Mary walked down the main stairs and joined them. Mike looked at her and asked, "How's Agata? Is she settling in?"

"She's still unsure. She wanted to leave and was surprised, I think, when we said she could and wouldn't stop her. But, when she was reminded that Risto had informants all over the city and that her photo would be in their hands by morning, she backed off. Maybe she was testing us. Maybe she really hadn't thought it through. She did seem amazed at the nice bedroom where she'll be staying. Evidently, her room was little more than a closet and a cot."

Ibrahim nodded. "Yes. Very small. Cold and dark."

Mary excused herself, but returned a minute later with a gel ice pack for Lynch. She sat down on the couch, crossed one leg over the other, clasped her hands around her knee and sat forward, attentive. Danijela followed and sat next to her. "Okay, boys, you know how women are; Danijela and I want some details."

The others took a seat, and Lynch started relating the tale. Ibrahim mostly grunted in agreement, but filled in what happened when he left Lynch to find Agata's quarters.

As Lynch finished, the room went silent for a minute as if no one knew what to say next, but Mike filled the void with a question.

"Lynch, why do you do this? I know, we asked you before why you didn't just go to the police. You only gave us a partial answer. But tonight, you could have been killed. Look at you. You've got some significant injuries. Why not go back to your friends and family now? I'm sure your family is missing you greatly. Isn't it kind of unfair to them to keep them thinking you're dead?"

Lynch thought for a moment. He'd given Ibrahim a deeper explanation. However, he answered Mike's query with his own.

"Why do *you* do this? Why does Ibrahim do it? He's put himself at risk several times now and has a bounty on his head."

Ibrahim did not hesitate to answer. "Penance." He raised his hand to stop Mike, who had started to comment. "I know salvation is gift of God through

Christ. I know I am new creation in Christ. Head know that, but heart still act like in Islam. In Islam, it is work and penance get me to paradise. I admit I still try to work through that, to understand Christian way better."

Mike smiled. "Penance won't help you, but the Bible does say that we show our faith by our works."

Mary added, "Ibrahim, you already show better understanding than most Christians who think everybody goes to heaven." She turned toward Lynch. "Lynch, do you have an answer?"

"I, uh, honestly don't recall if I went to church or not. But I *do* know that freeing these women is the right thing to do." He took a deep breath and continued, "And I really respect you guys for what you're doing. Maybe you can tell me more later."

"Be happy to do that, Lynch," replied Mike. "But, we also have a saying, 'You're only one heartbeat from eternity.' The Bible tells us that Christ is the *only* way to God, and that *today* is the day of salvation. Not tomorrow, because tomorrow never comes. You get to choose your eternal destination while alive on earth. Once you die, that opportunity is gone. So, if you're going to put your life on the line to help these women, you need to make a decision sooner. Not later."

Thirty-two

❧✦✦☙

Amy's mind became alert as the shadow passed her window. Had the wind blown something across the yard? Was the wind even blowing? It hadn't been when she watched Richard leave. She stood up from bed and walked to the window where she lifted a corner of the curtain to look outside without being too obvious. A strange car sat parked across the street in front of a neighbor's home. Had it been there earlier? She'd been so focused on Richard she hadn't noticed.

A moment later, she felt a sudden cold draft. She turned and rushed to her nightstand. After her experiences with the L.A. Rapist, she had purchased a 9mm Glock and mastered it at the firing range. She pulled it from the drawer, followed by the magazine, which she inserted into the handle. Safety off, she eased toward the bedroom door and stopped. She tried to control her breathing, to listen for any unusual noise within her house. Was that footsteps in the hall?

Maybe. She couldn't be sure. Her heart beat so fast all she seemed to hear was its thrum. Where was her phone?

In the kitchen, recharging. If someone was there, she'd not get to it, power it on, and dial 911 in time. Or could she? Maybe she could run fast enough to grab it and keep going out the door. Not likely. It was double locked. Did she dare to call out? If no one was there, she'd be doing nothing more than talking to herself. However, if there was someone there, could she cast some confusion on the scene? Or, did she just hunker down in the far corner of the room and wait? She was armed. Anyone coming through that door would be toast.

She decided to do both. She eased open the door a crack and yelled out, "Dad? Are you here already? Thanks for coming over in the middle of the night. I'll be out in a minute." If someone was out there, they might think twice about being there if someone else was expected and, fingers crossed, leave before being discovered.

No response. No creaky boards. No rush of cold air from a door opening again. No dad, either, not that he would ever show up unexpectedly or unannounced like that.

She eased to the far corner of the room and sat down, her knees to her chest and the Glock in both hands resting on them, aimed at the doorway. Five minutes. Ten. Fifteen. She began to feel ridiculous. Twenty minutes. Her imagination would be her downfall, keeping her awake all night when she really needed a good night's sleep. Well, the chance for that was already gone.

She began to relax. She took her left hand off the handgun and held it to her mouth as she yawned. How much longer would she sit here?

She felt foolish. It had just been a shadow. Maybe an owl had swooped across the yard between the house and nearby streetlamp. Despite the cold weather, she'd heard the neighborhood hooter just a few nights earlier so she knew it remained in the area. Maybe the wind had blown something in front of the window. Was there any wind?

She arose and turned to peek out from behind the curtain. That car was still parked in front of the neighbor's house. She tried to find a tree or some other reference point moving to prove there was a breeze. A couple of doors away, she saw a flag on their porch post. By its flutter, there was definitely more than a light breeze out there. She turned back toward her bed.

Suddenly the bedroom door burst open, and a dark figure in a black ski mask rushed into the room. Reflexively, she raised the gun and fired. The figure stopped, but did not fall.

Had she hit him? Before she could pull the trigger again, the man ran from the room. She followed to the bedroom door and watched as he dashed toward the kitchen. Again, she felt a rush of cold air.

She found the hallway light switch and flipped on that light. The bath off the hall was empty. She had a clear view of that area. The small bedroom she used as an office was next. She could see a portion of the room. Two-handed, she held the gun out in front of her and started into the room, only to quickly pull back. What was she thinking? This wasn't a TV show. To hold the gun like that invited someone to knock it from her hands. Instead, she held it closer to her body. If someone rushed her, she could fire straight ahead even if he was right on her. She cleared her office that way. And the living room.

A few nerve-wracking minutes later, she was in the kitchen with her cell phone in hand, dialing 9-1-1. That's when she noticed drops of blood on the vinyl floor.

Thirty-three

Richard made a single pass in front of Darko Imports and paid special attention to the fenced yard and loading area. He saw a limo and a black SUV pulled up to the steps coming down from the dock. Sergei was the limo's driver, but he saw no one with the SUV. Several women emerged from the limo and started up the steps. The clock in his car said it was 2 a.m., and he nodded to himself. The bars had closed.

As he drove past, he noticed Irina and Miloska. They stood separate from the others at the top of the dock. Irina glanced his way. Uh-oh! Did she know his car? Probably, even though they had used the limo for their one "date." He debated whether or not to just head home. Was he inviting trouble to go inside? Abort the mission or not? He needed to find out what was going on before making a decision.

At the next intersection, he turned and found the alley that ran between the buildings adjacent to the warehouse. He turned off his headlamps and crept down the lane, hopeful that nearby road noise would hide his car's engine. He didn't need the guards paying attention to the alley. He said a silent 'thank you' for a new car with an engine that purred. There would have been no hiding his old car's clatter.

He pulled as close to the warehouse fence as he could without being spotted and eased open his door, leaving it open for quick ingress. He slinked up to, embraced the corner of the building, and peered around it. The limo was gone, but a black pickup truck had joined the SUV vehicles. Dog kennels sat in the cargo bed, holding not dogs but beasts. He'd never seen a dog as big as the largest one, and he shivered at the thought of meeting up with any one of those brutes without a weapon. They seemed to be looking his way, but had made no commotion. He felt relief that they were kenneled, but he needed to make sure they weren't being taken inside. Even one dog inside would be a scenario that would end all thoughts of exploration.

Irina and Miloska stood with Hasan on the dock. Sergei reappeared with another dark SUV. The other women had gone inside. Both women clutched their arms to their chests and appeared cold, but Irina kept looking around. Was she looking for him? As Hasan looked away, Richard saw her remove something from her clutch purse and drop it next to the building. She looked nervous, but Hasan hadn't noticed her action.

A moment later, Risto emerged along with Goran. Goran's right upper arm was bandaged, and he held the extremity in a sling. What had happened?

Risto talked with the three men, and Hasan led Goran to one of the SUVs. They left through the main gate. Sergei jumped down from the dock and took the second SUV. Now Risto addressed the women and pushed them into moving toward the steps. Irina hesitated on the third step, and Risto cuffed her on the back of the head and said something. Both women now hurried to the truck and climbed into the passenger side. Risto took the driver's side and a minute later, the lot was clear.

Richard stood away from the building, surprised.

All of the security men—at least all that he knew of—had left the building. They'd left no dog behind to roam the area and Goran was injured. So, to the best of his knowledge, only the women had been left behind. That piece of information, along with his experience picking up Irina a few nights earlier, gave him a good idea what was behind that secured door.

He pulled out his prepaid cell phone and placed a call.

Darko listened to Risto's report. There had been a complication getting the Gibbs woman. She had been awake and armed, and managed to shoot Goran in the arm. Risto had correctly abandoned that mission and had taken Goran to the warehouse for medical attention. To persist going after the Gibbs woman might have left one or both men dead, not to mention the Gibbs woman, and that would have been a worse complication for Darko. At this point, the action would appear to be a random home invasion. Nothing would tie it to Darko.

Still, Goran's usefulness was now limited, so he would assist Hasan in Richmond Heights and Sergei had been tasked with guarding the Webster Grove client. That left the warehouse with only his electronic security system to guard its contents. The women were secured inside their quarters and could not leave without someone opening the door from the outside.

Darko clicked off his cell phone and laid it on his car's console next to him. Risto was on his way to the estate with the dogs and the two women. As he shifted gears and accelerated, he smiled at Risto's resourcefulness. The warehouse was fifteen minutes away. Once there, he would check the women's quarters to make sure it was secure. Then he would retrieve several necessary items from his office. The councilman was becoming squeamish. He had become a whiner after losing Danijela, but the investigation of the judge was taking a toll on his sanity. He feared it would lead to him. If and when he heard about the Ladue incident, he might break. His silence was required. Besides, Darko's other clients needed an object lesson, as had his girls.

Thirty-four

Amy paced in her living room. Her father was on his way. The police had responded within two minutes of her 9-1-1 call. She figured something about her saying she'd shot the guy had motivated them. As for the debate about gun control, she had no doubts now about where she stood on that issue.

She heard movement on the front stoop.

"I'm sorry, sir, you can't go inside. It's a crime scene."

"I'm her *father* for crying out loud. What do you mean I can't go inside? Is she okay?"

Amy stood and walked as far as she was allowed toward the kitchen. "Detective, my dad's here. Do you think you could get your officer to let him in?"

The man stopped his work and turned toward her. "Um, sure. Same restrictions as you, though."

Amy nodded. "No problem. Thank you."

The detective approached the door and opened it. "It's okay, Sam. He can come inside with his daughter."

"Thank you!" her father replied.

The detective stepped aside to let him inside.

"I'm Detective Hoskins. You can join your daughter, but right now you're both limited to this section of the living room." He waved across the corner of the room where Amy stood.

"Thank you, again, detective. I'm Colonel Gibbs." He extended his hand, but stopped as the officer held up his gloved hands.

"Sorry, don't want to be impolite, but . . ."

Lt. Colonel Gibbs nodded as he put his arm around Amy's shoulders. The detective resumed his work in the kitchen.

Amy and her father sat down on the couch.

"Are you okay?"

"Yes. Mostly."

"What happened?"

Amy proceeded to give her father the same story she'd told the officers.

"You're shaking. Are you sure you're okay? I can take you to the E.D. or . . ." He paused. "Never mind the E.D. I already know that answer. Do you want me to call Macy or anyone?"

Amy shook her head. "I've already called her. And my boss. Who then contacted Doctor Lange. So, I've already talked with her, too. I've had a busy half hour since I called you."

"Has the detective said anything?"

Amy shook her head. "There's a crime scene tech in the bedroom. They haven't told me anything directly, but I overheard them talking. They found the slug from my Glock in the doorframe, along with a few bits of tissue and blood. I noticed blood drops in the hall and kitchen leading to the back door. So, my best guess is that I wounded the guy with a through and through of the arm or shoulder, maybe a grazing wound. A solid enough hit for the bullet to take some tissue with it, anyway."

Amy felt a cold rush of air again, followed by the detective exclaiming, "I'll be. Didn't expect this."

Amy and her father stood and walked to the

boundary of their permissible area. The detective walked into the room.

"I'm done in the kitchen. You can walk in there now, if you need to." He was holding some type of electronic device. He called out toward the bedroom. "Ed, come look at this. Found it outside the back door." He showed the gadget to the tech.

"Hmmm, haven't seen one of those used in an invasion before."

"What is it?" asked Lt. Col. Gibbs.

"An infrared scanner. Kinda like the utility guys use to look for heat leaks when they assess a house's insulation." He held up the clear plastic bag holding the device and showed it to them. He looked directly at Amy. "Did you have your back door locked?"

Amy nodded. "Definitely. I rarely use it this time of year, so it's locked pretty much all the time. The door *and* the dead bolt."

"Well, it looks like the guy picked both locks. There are some tool scratches on the dead bolt. This guy knew what he was doing. He's done this before."

"So, what about this sensor thing?" asked Amy.

"I'm thinking he used it to pinpoint you in the house. When you yelled out, he knew you were awake. At first, I figured he used it to make sure he knew where you were while he looked for stuff out here. But nothing was disturbed out here, so I'm thinking maybe robbery wasn't this guy's motive."

Amy's eye widened, and she began to tremble.

"Y-you think he was here to rape me?"

The officer shrugged. "Maybe. But we haven't any problems like that out here."

"But, he *did* attack her," added Lt. Col. Gibbs.

"Yes. I think he used this thing to watch you. He could tell you were tense and not going to be an easy target while you were huddled in the corner of the room. He attacked after he saw you up and about, figured you had relaxed your guard."

"I had," admitted Amy, rubbing both temples with her fingers.

"He just hadn't expected you to be armed. And he wanted to stay alive, so he took off." The detective turned toward Amy's father. "Sir, do you come here often? I'll need a set of your fingerprints so we can rule your prints out."

"Here often enough my prints are probably everywhere. I tend to be her handyman, as well as her father." He smirked at Amy. "I've got a full set of prints in the military database, but if you need 'em again, let's do it."

The crime tech stepped forward. "Thanks. That would speed things up." He led the colonel aside to collect his prints. Amy had already provided hers.

"Miss Gibbs, can you think of anyone who'd want to hurt you?"

Amy could, but that monster was dead. She thought back to her conversation with Macy. Although trying to lighten the mood with emergency department humor, Macy made a comment that seemed to be increasingly true. Amy had become a super "poop magnet." Why did these things happen to *her*?

Thirty-five

Richard moved his car to a more accessible position, yet still removed from easy viewing. He used his access card to open the gate and walked into the loading area, alert to the slightest noise. He felt like he was back on patrol in Afghanistan, except without body armor or a gun. He had had the foresight to grab the car's tire iron, not that it would help him against a bullet. *Next time, he'd bring the hammer,* he thought. Next time? Was he crazy?

He climbed the steps to the loading dock and glanced around. Quiet. He took a couple of steps toward the door and remembered Irina dropping something. He looked around and saw it next to the wall. Her access card. "Yes!" he whispered.

Okay, he thought. *I need to adjust my attitude. I work here, and I just stopped by to grab something I left in my office. I need to act like it, in case there's a security guard inside I don't know about.*

He pushed the tire iron up his coat's inside left sleeve to hide it. He then steadied his nerves and took a deep breath. Using Irina's card, he unlocked the door and walked in. A single light cast a dull glow across the area, enough to see to walk around safely. The door to the security and dock office was open, and the room was dark. He heard nothing other than the fan of an auxiliary heater working against the chill of the night.

Richard quickly moved out of the bay into the hallway toward the offices, his office. The hallways were similarly lit by the soft illumination of night-lights. The same units would activate and light the halls in case of a power outage. He avoided the hallways to the secured rooms, knowing they held motion sensors and video surveillance, and walked confidently toward his office. Once there, he stopped and listened. Still nothing more than the subtle hum of air blowing through the ducts. He moved farther down the hall toward Darko's office, but stopped short of being in range of the security video camera he had seen there. No lights or sound there either. He felt strange sneaking around the building in the middle of the night.

Satisfied that he was alone except for the women he saw enter earlier, he sauntered toward the mystery door. As he passed the small employee lounge, he made a brief detour as he noticed the box of day-old donuts still on the table. Curiously, someone had wrapped the remaining two donuts in aluminum foil instead of plastic wrap. Fortunately for him, this was just what he needed. Besides, the sneaking around had made him hungry. *Why not?* He devoured the first of the two leftover cake donuts, and took the second, foil and all.

He had finished the second donut by the time he arrived at the door. As before, his access card did nothing to unlock the door. He glanced around and noticed something he'd not seen in the daytime. Besides the red and green lights on the lock mechanism, there was a small red light shining solidly at the top of the doorframe. That meant there was more than just a card access lock on the door. He would have to be careful.

He used Irina's card and the light on the lock changed from red to green. There was no audible click.

He eased the handle down to release the latch and opened the door an inch, pulling it toward him. Again, he listened, but this time he heard sobs and women whispering. He peered through the door and saw no guard. He glanced about the doorway and saw that the small light at the top of the frame now flashed. With the door open, he could see the metal contacts of the alarm system's sensor. He examined the latch and finally moved through the door. Looking up he saw a second small red light at the top of the inside frame. It, too, flashed. It wasn't until the door eased shut that he realized there was no handle on that side. The red light stopped its blinking and become solid red again.

He gulped. Was he now trapped inside?

He walked through a short hallway into a small living area holding a rickety wooden dining table with eight mismatched chairs, two worn couches, several single chairs and an ancient television set. Numerous small rooms opened into the space, each containing two old twin beds and a battered chest of drawers. At the other end of the larger room, a doorway appeared to lead to a large bathroom and dressing area. As he neared the door, he heard a gasp.

"Richard."

Suddenly five women were upon him.

"Richard, what you do here?"

"How did you get in?"

"Richard, you shouldn't be here."

He put his finger to his lips. "Shhhh . . ."

Ivanka stepped forward. "Richard, they will kill you if they find you here."

Suddenly, the women began to babble among

themselves, shaking their heads. Nina rushed down the hall to the door and returned, shaking her head.

"Is too late, he shut door," she said.

"I've come to get you out," Richard replied.

The women looked puzzled.

"Get us out?"

Richard nodded. "Yes, I know you're here against your will. Irina told me what they make you do. We have to leave. Now."

"How? Door only opens from outside or from control panels in offices. You shut the door, and now you are trapped with us. When guard find you in morning, you will disappear."

"That's why we need to leave while the guards are gone."

Fear flashed across the women's faces. They began to shake their heads and all talk at once.

"No."

"I cannot leave."

"We must stay. We have to stay."

"Richard, you must leave us alone."

"I-I don't get it. You're prisoners," he replied.

Ivanka again took charge. "Richard, you do not understand. Darko controls our families, too. We leave, he hurt them, maybe kill them like Aida's family. Plus, he have Irina and Miloska at his estate. They would die for sure if we disappear. And there are dozens others at homes across metro area. Darko, Risto, and other men. Must deal with them first. For safety of all."

"We will. There are federal agents preparing right now to get them in the morning."

"Morning is too late."

"Must protect families first. Get Irina and Miloska back. Then come get Darko and Risto," said Ivanka.

"We must figure way to get you out. Now," added Katarina.

"Don't worry, I can—"

Nina interrupted. "*Sranje!* Someone opening door." The red light began to flash.

Ivanka pulled Richard into the dressing room while the other women scattered to their respective rooms. "Quick! Hide behind dresses!" She shoved him into a rack stuffed with perfumed finery.

Richard found the clothing rack to be two rows deep. He nestled against the wall, but realized his feet still showed below the short garments. He grabbed a sundress, and a second, and dropped them around his legs and shoes. A third one he held in front to hide his legs. It would have to do. He doubted the guards would search the women's closet. Unless they knew he was here! Suddenly his heart began to race.

Darko arrived at the loading dock and saw that all appeared in order. He walked through the loading area to the guard's office and scrutinized the security panel. All was in order.

On the way to his office, he decided to stop and check on the women. He approached the door and saw all of the security lights in order. He used a wireless fob to access the lock and pulled the door open.

Upon entering the hallway, he heard a flurry of feet. *Curious*, he thought. The women should all be in bed by now. Tomorrow was a busy day. With the Rams playing in town, their services would be needed all day and into the night. He came to a stop in the middle of the central living area.

"What is going on?" he demanded. He looked into the nearest room and saw Nina combing out her long hair. Kristina appeared to be asleep already. Katarina and Emira were sitting on the edge of their beds.

Ivanka walked out of the bathroom, brushing her teeth. "Nothing is going on," she mumbled around the toothbrush. "We get ready for bed."

"Good," replied Darko. He looked into the bedrooms, noting how empty the place seemed with Aida dead, and Irina and Miloska at the estate. He made a mental note to ask Sonja to find a replacement for Aida as soon as possible. He stopped short of the bathroom and dressing area. He turned back toward the exit. "Big day tomorrow. Get rest."

Ivanka, toothbrush gone and mouth rinsed, played up to him. "You not stay?" She ran a finger along his cheek.

He scowled and brushed her off. He sensed her behind him, following him to the door. He used his fob to unlock it from the inside and pushed it open. He kept walking, stopping only long enough to turn and make sure the security lights confirmed that the door was locked. He rushed to his office, retrieved a folder of photographs, several packets of cocaine, and sex paraphernalia that he would leave behind at the soon-to-be-deceased councilman's home, all of which would tie him to Aida, a dead hooker from a police perspective. Ten minutes later, he was out the back door and heading for Wildwood.

                                     *   *   *

Five minutes after Darko left, Nina pulled back the
dresses to reveal Richard hiding behind the dress he
held up in front of himself. She looked him up and
down. "Hmmm, is not your color." She quickly grabbed
another from the rack and said, "Here, this better."
Katarina laughed, and the two women helped Richard
from the closet. His grip on the tire iron relaxed, and it
remained hidden in his coat sleeve.

"Is it safe?" he asked.

Nina nodded. "Unlikely he come back. He never
stay back here for long. I think he afraid we gang up on
him and kill him."

Katarina nodded in agreement. "He never let his
guard down in here. Never."

"But, he is probably still in the building, so even if
we could let you out, I would not leave yet," said Ivanka.
"The big question is, how we get you out?"

"I was starting to tell you that's not a problem."
Richard led the five women to the door and proceeded
to slip the tire iron from his sleeve.

"What? You beat door down with that?"

"No."

He reached for the door, but Ivanka stopped him.

"Not yet. Darko may still be here."

She led him back to the dining table and sat down.
The other women followed.

"We must have assurance that family is safe, before
we go against Darko."

Richard thought about that for a moment.

"I think I can set that up, but it might take a few

                                     270

days."

"Some family still in Europe," added Nina.

"Oh." Richard didn't know what to do now. "Look, I'm not a policeman or federal agent or anything like that. I was just asked to spy on Darko. I don't know what they can or can't do about people outside this country, but I can ask." He paused and glanced around the table as the women looked at each other, questioning with their eyes.

"Look, do you have any paper and a pen? Write down who you need to get protection and where they live, and I'll pass it on. It's all I can do."

All five women looked defeated.

Kristina responded, "Darko gives us nothing that we could use to pass a note or communicate with."

"They even inspect our purses when we go out," added Nina.

"Okay. Then slip them to me on Monday at work." He looked toward the door. "Do you think it's safe to leave now?"

Ivanka shrugged. To kill a little more time, each woman gave Richard a brief history of how she became entrapped by and forced to work for Darko. By the time Emira finished her story, Richard knew he had to do more than just play the mole. He would do whatever he could to help these women escape their bondage, as well as those women less well off in private homes around the city. He had no idea so many women, some just young girls, were subject to such abhorrent conditions, forced labor, and sexual trafficking in St. Louis. The women sitting with him were the "lucky" ones, if such a term could be used.

271

"Okay, I need to leave." He stood and walked toward the door.

"I not see how tire thing open door for you," said Nina as they came to the door.

"It won't. That's in case someone is waiting on the other side." He placed his hand on the door and gave it a gentle push. It opened right up. No one waited on the other side. The women's eyes widened. "It's an old trick from college. We liked to play basketball in the gym after it closed. We learned that aluminum foil stuffed into the latch hole would keep the latch open, and it closed the electrical loop to the security sensor in the latch. I think the only security sensor on this door is that one, up there, but I couldn't be sure."

He started to pull the foil out, but Ivanka stopped him, smiling. "Please leave it. We will remove when ready."

"You sure? If they find it, it will cause trouble."

"Yes, sure. We will take care of it." She leaned forward and kissed him on the cheek. "Thank you."

Richard smiled. "See you Monday. Remember, act normal. And tell Irina and Miloska what is going on."

The women nodded, and Richard could feel them watching him as he crept down the hall toward the first turn. But now their stares didn't make him feel like he was walking a runway. This was more of a gauntlet.

He made it to the loading area without a problem and was about to exit when he noticed a trash bin adjacent to the door. It had been hidden by the door on his way in. At the top of the pile sat a small pile of bloody gauze and an empty bottle of hydrogen peroxide. He used the tire iron to lift the gauze and

272

discovered a man's bloody shirt underneath. Closer examination revealed what looked to be a bullet hole in the right upper arm. That was the focal point of the bloody stain. Goran's injury. It seemed likely that Goran had been shot in the arm. He wondered how, and who might have done that.

He eased open the door to the outside and peeked out. The coast appeared clear, and he ran to the man-gate, and after clearing it, to his car. He pulled out his burner phone and started to dial his handler to update him on the latest turn of events. That's when he noticed the man standing next to his car, gun in hand.

Thirty-six

Darko returned to their city apartment on Monday morning with Sonja, but while she went to the office, he stayed home. He hadn't slept in three nights, since being told of the latest rescue. Even now, sleep evaded him. He paced the floor of their living room and glanced occasionally out the window. He didn't expect to see anything helpful. He just didn't like feeling caged.

Darko took pride in his family roots in the Varangian Rus'. By the early 7th century, these Viking tribes had migrated from the Baltic States to Eastern Europe and engaged in a mix of trade, piracy, and mercenary activities that earned them the description as warrior-merchants. For hundreds of years they controlled the vital trade routes of the Volga and Dnieper Rivers. By the tenth century, they had become valuable mercenaries of the Byzantine Army, with the elite Varangian Guard acting as the personal bodyguards of the Byzantine Emperors. Darko traced his roots to these men, men who would not hesitate to take what they wanted if trading did not work.

His mind held flashbacks of Croatia and Bosnia. There he had been a young man in control of much. He liked the feeling of control. Then came the war. He'd played both sides—Croat allied with the Bosniaks against the Serbs, and then Croat allied with the Serbs against the Bosniaks. He learned the finer aspects of the black market. If he could find a way to make money, he did. And the most profitable had been the flesh trade.

He again took control, until he crossed a Serbian general who thought he should have the girls Darko had taken. Darko found himself on the run. Then, too, he had found himself caged, pacing, and glancing out windows, looking for any sign of trouble.

The phone rang and caller ID showed it to be Risto.

"*Da*, Risto."

"*Loša vijest.*" Bad news. "Toma has only two man he spare and not send until Friday."

Darko plopped down onto the nearby chair. This was not the news he expected.

"Darko?"

"*Da*. Still here. Trying to think."

"Other bad news. Councilman skip country. That why you find house empty. Office say he in Mexico. Back in two week."

Darko buried his head in his hands. Taking a deep breath, he lifted his head and replied to Risto.

"At least he not easy for police to talk to. *If* investigation get to him. Okay, so how we cover men until help come?"

The two men discussed strategy and timing. Hasan and Sergei would sit tight. Risto would cover another high profile client who now clamored for protection. Goran could cover the estate, despite his injury, now that the dogs were there. They would move the women from the office to the estate and consider doing the same with the women owned by his more prestigious clients. Risto had recruited another man to guard the warehouse, another to drive and assist Goran, and two more to beef up the search for Ibrahim. They were prepared to start that day.

But, what about the Gibbs woman? He told Risto to stop their surveillance of her. They needed that man looking for Ibrahim. Plus, she would be doubly alert now and likely armed at all times. Darko took it as a sign that he should avoid her, for now, and perhaps find another way to influence Richard.

Darko felt better. His level of control wasn't as tight as he'd like it to be, but at least he was no longer at the mercy of random disasters. He hoped. He had no doubt that, soon, Ibrahim would get the information, the news that would lure him out.

As instructed by the man with the gun, Richard arrived at the warehouse at his usual time, stopped into the break room for his usual cup of coffee, and found the women preparing for a usual day of work. He opened his office and powered on his computer, allowing it to boot up as he hung up his coat, opened his briefcase, and retrieved some paperwork he'd never had time to scan, much less work on, at home. Again, his usual routine, hiding his anything-but-usual anxiety.

No sooner had he sat down at his desk, Irina, looking more gaunt than normal, walked into his office, partially closed the door, and proceeded to sit on his lap. She placed her hands on both sides of his face and delivered a full mouth kiss that was definitely not usual.

At first, he felt shocked. They were at work. Anyone could walk in. He could be fired.

Then he realized, no, he wouldn't be fired. Moreover, it was Irina. She was back. Did that mean Miloska was with them as well?

And that perfume! He had concluded that perfume amounted to chemical warfare—and he always lost.

Irina nibbled his ear lobe and whispered, "Thank you. Thank you."

Richard was about to reply when the door opened. His eyes bugged open to see Sonja standing in the doorway.

"I, uh . . . we, umm . . ." He jumped to a standing position, steadying Irina as she landed on her feet next to him. "I-I'm sorry. I, uh, we, uh, don't usually . . ."

"Yes? Maybe you should shut door all way." She didn't look happy. On the other hand, had the corner of her mouth eased upward toward a smile for just a second?

"Sorry. It won't happen again."

"Good. Save for after hour. Now, I need see Irina." She wiggled her finger at the woman, to say, 'Come with me.'

As Irina headed out the door, she turned back toward Richard and mouthed, "Thank you." She then made a look on her face that made Richard realize she had seen Sonja coming and had played her part. Perhaps too well. "Down boy!" he told himself.

As the time rolled toward the official start of the workday, Richard wondered how the women would get the information about their loved ones to him and how soon. He wanted to be done with this job. Despite being a perfect fit for his education and experience, and exactly the type of job he'd love to have, even without the beautiful co-workers, he had come to see Darko for what he was. As well as Sonja, and Risto, and the others. He didn't know how much longer he could play the game of "dedicated employee."

A few minutes after nine, the power suddenly went out, and the emergency lights lent their soft glow to the room and the hallway outside his door. His computer's uninterrupted power supply unit clicked on, and he took a moment to back up what little he'd already accomplished that morning. He then powered down his computer the correct way.

That done, he stood up and walked to the door to see what the ladies were doing and to discover what might have happened. The women's cubicles were empty. Their purses were gone. Panic flooded his mind.

He stepped back into the doorway and noticed a small piece of paper on the floor. It appeared to have been slid under his door. He bent down and retrieved it.

At that moment, a man he didn't know turned the corner of the hall and entered the area. "Darko say power out all day. Transformer blow up. He say go home. Enjoy day off."

Richard nonchalantly slid the paper into a pocket and tried to act pleased at the free day off. Yet, as he turned back into his office to collect his gear, happiness was nowhere to be found. If Darko hadn't already found out what he was doing, he was at least suspicious. Coat on and briefcase in hand, he proceeded down the hall, ever alert. He debated a detour toward the women's quarters, wondering if the foil was still in place to let him open the door, but the new security guard followed ten paces behind.

Once again, he left through the loading area, with the new security man following him out the door. Richard stopped at the top of the dock's steps, glanced around, and took a deep breath, as if happy to be outside. Smiling, he turned back to the man and held out his hand.

"By the way, I'm Richard. And you are . . .?"

The man did not smile or shake his hand. "Darko say we call you when power back on."

"Okay then." He put his hand in his coat pocket and walked down the steps. Once in his car, he pulled the paper out of his pants pocket and read it. The message confirmed his fear. "Darko suspects. Taking us all away."

Thirty-seven

Amy fought her way through the early morning "rush hour" toward Amanda's office. The psychologist had insisted on seeing her before the start of her scheduled day. At the time of their conversation right after the break-in, Amy had agreed that they should meet. Now, after spending the previous day in the air with her father, flying their Cessna 172 Skyhawk to lunch at Flying Jake's Steaks, their favorite steak house sitting next to the runway of a small community airport not far away, she figured she'd already had her therapy.

Arriving ten minutes late because of traffic, Amy pulled into what appeared to be an empty car lot. She collected her purse and walked to the building's entrance, which she found to be unlocked. She proceeded down the hall to the doctor's office, where Amanda waited and led the way toward her office.

"Come in, come in."

Amy took off her coat and laid it across the arm of the couch. She placed her purse on the floor below it and sat in her customary position. Amanda took up her place in an adjacent chair.

"So." She gave Amy a curious stare. "Just how are you this morning?"

"Fine."

Amanda shook her head and chuckled. "Well then, I guess that ends this morning's session. You can call back later for your next appointment."

Amy's mouth dropped open and then she sighed.

"Okay, so I'm not really fine, but I'm doing okay. Really."

"Amy, after all that's happened, are you sure? You had someone break into your home, and you shot that person. How do you feel about that?"

Amy glanced at the ceiling and then around the room and out the window. Until that moment, she had done a remarkable job compartmentalizing those feelings.

"Amy?"

"Sorry." She turned her eyes toward Amanda. "I was scared to death at the time. Now, I'm angry and a little sorry I only wounded the guy."

"Really?"

She looked toward the floor. "Yeah, really. But I also know I would have felt awful if I'd really hurt him or killed him." She paused. "How is it possible to feel both ways? It seems contradictory."

Amanda leaned forward. "It does, doesn't it? But that's not unusual, and a very human response. You have every right to be angry with the intruder. And anger can cause a desire for retribution, justice. As for how you might feel if you'd killed him, that's only speculation. Depending on circumstances, your real feelings might be different from what you imagine. More importantly, though, is what should a Christian's response be?"

Amy felt the pang of conviction. Amanda was right. The women discussed this for a few minutes, and then Amanda changed course. "Nightmares?"

Amy shook her head. Despite the incident, her nightmare had *not* returned. "No, no nightmare. That actually surprised me a little."

"Any insights on why?"

Amy replied with a subtle shrug. "Maybe."

"And?"

"My feelings of loss about Lynch. Like we talked about before. I feel like I'm finally moving on."

Amy realized where this line of thinking was headed and wanted to stop. "My dad and I went flying yesterday, to one of our favorite restaurants, next to an airstrip. That was great therapy. Plus, he's already cleaned, patched, and repaired my home. You can't even tell anything happened there the other night."

Amanda furrowed her eyes and pursed her lips. "Why do I get the feeling you're avoiding something, Amy?"

Amy gulped and replied, "Um, because I'm so adept at changing the subject?"

Amanda laughed. "That must be it."

Following a deep sigh, Amy said, "Okay. I'm embarrassed for anyone else to know this. I had a little too much wine and made a complete and utter fool of myself with Richard." She went on to describe what had happened at dinner. "So," she concluded, "Richard probably won't want to have anything to do with me now. But, that's okay. I'm moving on from Lynch, and I'm confident the right guy'll show up. Eventually."

The therapist cocked her head a little and answered, "Don't write him off so quickly. You never know. However, one thing does come to mind. The Bible says that 'God causes all things to work together for good to those who love God.'"

Amy nodded. "Romans 8:28. I know that verse."

"What if you had had a wonderful meal and

everything went well, would you have had trouble getting to sleep? If you'd been sound asleep, what might have happened?"

Amy's eyes widened at the thought. "So, you're saying God protected me by letting those things happen with Richard?"

It was Amanda's turn to shrug. "Sure is one way of looking at things. He might have given you a lousy aim, too, 'cause he knew how you'd feel if you killed the man." She smiled.

Amy's time was over, and she continued to marvel at the idea that God used her getting drunk for some purpose. By the time she reached her car, she realized that this also meant God had let her see Richard at the club with that, that . . . oh, she still didn't like thinking about that woman. That's when God slapped her upside the head. She knew nothing about the woman, or what the woman was about, or what the woman might be going through. As a Christian, she needed to "remove the log from her own eye," as it was written in the Gospel of Matthew. She found herself praying for that woman as she drove to work.

Thirty-eight

Lynch awoke late that morning. He hadn't slept well; the aching in his left forearm and both legs appeared to be no better, but at least they didn't feel worse. He dropped his legs over the side of the bed, noting that 'dropped' was the right term. They felt like they were made of concrete this morning. He attempted to make a fist with his left hand, but his muscles did not want to cooperate. His fingertips felt numb.

His groan must have been louder than he'd thought. The sliding door from the front hallway creaked as it slid into the wall, and Danijela appeared in the opening.

"You make sound like you hurt. You okay?"

Lynch shook his head. "Not really. What time is it?"

"Almost ten. You not sleep well. I check in night, and you making awful moans."

Lynch didn't need her to tell him that, but he appreciated that she'd checked on him.

"Here. This help." She handed him an 800-milligram ibuprofen tablet and a glass of juice, which he took from her after popping the pill into his mouth. He could only use one hand. He downed the pill with the first gulp and proceeded to drain the glass. After taking back the empty glass, she held out multiple ice packs.

He waved it away. "Give me a minute." He stood, wobbly at first, and approached her. She pushed the door open wider, and he hobbled past her to go to the bathroom. His bladder thanked him as he turned back from the toilet toward the pedestal sink. He winced at the reflection in the mirror. To say he looked rough would have been kind. On the silver lining side of things, though, he was glad he still had the beard. He didn't think he could manage shaving today if his life depended on it.

Yet, he needed a shave and a haircut. Everyday brought him closer to being the Lynch of the past, and he had decided he should begin to look the part.

Upon returning to the parlor, he found that Danijela had removed the linens from the sofa bed and closed it. She sat on the adjacent couch. Lynch picked up an ice pack and thin towel from where they lay on the hassock, and began to position it on his forearm. After he placed both legs on the hassock, she repeated the process with each leg. Lynch figured there had to be an easier way, but none that sounded comfortable in the dead of winter.

"Doctor come tonight to see Raifa. He see you, too."

"I'll be fine. Give me a few more days. You'll see."

She made a face exaggerating her disbelief and her discontent with his stubbornness. "Typical man. Please. See doctor, for favor for me."

Lynch sighed, but nodded. "Where's Ibrahim? I haven't seen him since we brought Agata here."

"Busy. He go watch Darko's place. Out in country. And then he say he have something to pick up on way back. Do not know what."

Lynch hated the fact that he was laid up, that Ibrahim was carrying the load by himself. He needed to get better quickly so they could function effectively as a team while the momentum was on their side. Maybe

Danijela was right. Maybe seeing the doctor would get him up and functional again.

"I go get you food to eat." He started to protest, but she put her hand up, palm toward him to stop him, and shook her head. "I get the food. You stay here and keep arm up, leg up, and on ice."

Lynch knew better than to argue, although he felt quite capable of getting his own breakfast, or brunch at this point. He stuffed two pillows under his arm so it rested slightly higher than the level of his heart. He could feel the cold of the ice penetrating the thin towel that protected his skin from direct icing.

"That better," said Danijela.

"Yes, nurse," he answered.

Danijela smiled and turned to leave the room. Less than a minute later, he began to fidget. He really wasn't comfortable in his current position. There had to be a better way. He wanted to lie down on the couch, but heard a car door slam. He tried to jump up, but his legs needed more advance warning, and he plopped back onto the couch. His second attempt was slower but successful.

He glanced out the nearest window and saw a man looking up at the house. This was no doctor, certainly not the doctor friend described by Mike and Mary. He grabbed his handgun and made his way to the front door. He decided to hide the gun behind him as he saw the man reach to press the doorbell button, not kick the door in.

"It's okay, Lynch." Mary had walked around the corner from the dining room. Danijela followed her. "He's a friend, from church. He's here to start setting up for the video."

Lynch had argued that it would be safer to video record the women at the house than to drive them to the Southworth's church which would risk them being out in the open where they might be spotted. Mike had countered that the church had a secluded back entrance and they would be safe, and that it would be easier to move the women than to move, set-up, break down and move all the equipment again. Lynch rebutted that by saying that for their purpose, they could record it on a smartphone and didn't need a professional level recording. Mike reminded him they were going to go through the media and that the better the recording looked when broadcast, the better. They had settled in-between, with a little lighting and a quality camcorder on a tripod.

Lynch tried to place his gun in the back of his pants, but found himself fumbling it, so he "dashed" into the parlor and stashed it under a pillow. He returned to the hallway as the young man was ushered in by Mary.

"Come in, Josh."

"Hi, Mrs. Southworth. Wow, nice house. Never been here before."

Mary made the introductions, being cautious to use just first names. Lynch was not prepared for more than a few people to know who he was. The fellow showed no sign of recognition.

Josh seemed enamored with Danijela, but politely reached out to shake Lynch's hand. Lynch did the same and winced as they shook hands—and that was his good hand. It was then that Josh noted the condition of Lynch's forearms.

"Whoa, man. What happened to you, dude?"

Lynch gave a subtle shrug and replied, "Run in with a dog. A *big* dog. It's getting better."

His last comment earned him a glare from Danijela. She whispered, "Get your ice." He knew she was right and had his best interests at heart, yet he ignored her and addressed the young man.

"So, Josh, you do understand that what we're doing is 'top secret,' right? You can't tell anyone you're working on this. *Anyone.* To talk about it would not only risk the lives of the women you'll be recording, but possibly yours as well."

Josh gave him two thumbs up. "Understood, man. Lips are sealed and all that. Love doin' the work of the Lord, man." He smiled. "So, where are we makin' this shoot?"

Mary stepped into the library, across the hall from the parlor. "We thought this room would work best. We can close the double sliding doors behind the loveseat and the women could sit there."

Josh surveyed the room and nodded. "Yeah, that'll work. I'll put a screen up to cover that big front window, so no one can see in from the front of the house. Camera can go here. And I'll use two small light umbrellas, one on each side, to give us the light we need." He looked around again and nodded, satisfied. "Yeah, that'll do it. Sweet room, by the way. Bet it's nice sitting in here with a fire in the fireplace."

Mary smiled. "Yes. Yes, it is. Thank you."

"So, when is this production going down?" Josh looked at Lynch. "I've got everything I need in the car, except a screen big enough for that window."

Lynch wasn't sure what to say. His injuries had delayed their plan for a quick strike on Darko's estate.

"We had planned on tomorrow evening, but that's kind of up in the air now." He held up his left forearm as an explanation. "How much notice do you need? What's your schedule look like for the week?"

"Dude, for this, I'll stop whatever I'm doin' and scoot on over here. I can set things up now, while I'm here. Even the camera. I won't need it until this weekend. That way all we need to do is set up the big screen before we start. That sound like a plan?"

Lynch nodded, pleased that the young man was so flexible. Now, if they could somehow rescue one or two more women before starting.

As Josh began to set up his makeshift "studio," Danijela forced Lynch back onto the couch. This time, she had him lie down with his left side near the edge. She moved the hassock next to him, propped his arm on top of two pillows on the hassock, and applied new ice packs. She also plumped up a pillow and placed it under his legs and feet.

"There. You stay. I check on you in hour or so."

Lynch used the remote to turn on the TV and scan for something to watch. The pillows and his arm partially blocked his view, but he knew better than to remove one of the pillows. As he learned the day before, Danijela had some sort of psychic connection with those pillows. If he tried to remove one, she suddenly appeared at the door.

By three o'clock that afternoon, Lynch was

beginning to worry about Ibrahim. They'd had no word from him, and he hadn't returned. Lynch assumed he was taking his time and being cautious while staking out the country estate, but he had expected the man to call in once or twice to let them know he was okay.

Lynch had already watched one old Bogart film on TMC, a U.S. Open doubles match, and a recording of the second half of the previous day's Rams game, which he had missed due to Danijela's persistent "nursing." Her attentions had continued all day this day as well, and he was getting a little flustered with her persistence. Still, he knew she cared. He just hated being on the sidelines and tried hard not to take it out on her.

He heard a heavier footfall in the hallway, and Mike appeared at the doorway.

"Where've you been all afternoon?" asked Lynch.

"Ibrahim called at lunchtime," replied Mike. "I've been out getting some things he requested."

"Like what?"

"Hamburger, Benadryl, nylon rope, some chain, and—um, pet supplies."

Lynch didn't like the way he'd added the last item. "Pet supplies? What kind of pet supplies?" The more he thought about it, the less Lynch liked what this implied.

"Maybe I should let Ibrahim discuss this with you. How's the arm and legs?"

"Don't change the subject, please. What did Ibrahim say?"

Mike hesitated.

"Dogs. It's more dogs, isn't it?" All of a sudden, it added up. Hamburger, Benadryl, and chain.

Mike tipped his head back and forth. "Yes—and no.

Yes, dogs, but not more dogs. Ibrahim said they moved the three guard dogs you two encountered at the last house out to Darko's estate. So, he asked me to get three heavy chain chokers and three large muzzles, in case you need them."

Lynch took a deep breath and sighed. "They'd better be three really sturdy muzzles and chain tough enough to tow a tank." He shook his head. "Why do they have to use dogs? I like dogs. I don't want to hurt a dog. It's just doing what it was trained to do."

Mike shrugged. "Yeah, well, I like animals, too, but it seems these dogs had no concerns over killing you." He placed a hand on Lynch's shoulder. "At least Ibrahim is trying to avoid hurting the dogs. He hopes to feed them enough Benadryl to knock them out and be able to secure them, so you don't have an encore mauling." He started to leave the room, but turned back. "By the way, what about the people there? Do you have the same concern about them? If one of them points a gun at you, are you going to toss a Benadryl at him?" He paused. "Dinner'll be ready shortly."

Lynch sank back into the couch. Mike's point was well taken, especially coming from a career warrior. Why did so many people seem to put a dog's value higher than that of a person? The simple answer to Lynch was that a person had free will and reaped what he sowed, while a dog had instincts and training and performed as expected with that training. But then, a guard, or a soldier for that matter, was also expected to live up to his training. Was there that much of a difference?

Lynch didn't want to wrestle with the moral

conundrum Mike had just dumped in his lap. He could smell garlic and spices, and his stomach growled in response. He stood up from the couch and took a few steps. His legs didn't ache as before. He opened and closed his right hand. That arm, too, seemed better. Maybe the rest and tender loving care forced upon him by Danijela had helped. He could even move the fingers on his left hand, a little. That arm was going to have to improve dramatically before he'd feel comfortable tackling the estate being scoped out by Ibrahim.

He walked out to the kitchen where Mary and Danijela bustled about preparing their meal. Even Raifa and Agata sat at the counter opposite the cooktop and watched. Both women looked remarkably more at ease.

"Smells wonderful."

"Nothing fancy. Lasagna and garlic bread," Mary replied.

"Thirty minute. Go back to couch," said Danijela. "I bring more ice." She tried to shove him gently out of the room.

Lynch resisted. Through the window over the sink, he saw headlights, and then they were gone. He approached the window with caution, wishing he'd brought his handgun with him from the front room. As he glanced outside, he saw a huddled figure dart past the side of the house, heading toward the front.

Lynch found his legs responding better than he'd expected as he rushed to the parlor and retrieved his handgun from under the pillow. By the time he flicked off the safety, the doorbell began a frantic chime.

He beat the women to the door to find Ibrahim there with another young woman in his arms. He had

292

carried her from the car to the door, which explained the strangely shaped figure he'd seen. He opened the door to them and helped Ibrahim inside with the girl.

Together they laid the girl on the couch that Lynch had occupied for the past two days. He helped remove the blankets wrapped around her and saw a dark-skinned female who looked no older than fourteen. A kid, emaciated and scared, and dressed like a hooker. Track marks lined both forearms. Like Agata, when Ibrahim took her she probably didn't know what to expect. Lynch stepped back and let the women take over. They would have a better chance at comforting and reassuring the girl.

He pulled Ibrahim to the next room.

"Why didn't you tell me you were going after another girl?"

Ibrahim shrugged. "Was not original plan. Beside, even if it was plan, what good it do? You not able help."

He had Lynch there.

"I scout Darko place in country most of day. On way back, I decide to drive through downtown. I see Keisha. I know Keisha. She lured into prostitution through Facebook. That becoming more common. I also know pimp use drug, heroin, to keep her in line. Anyway, I not see pimp. She see me and first start to run away. Then she stop, and run to car. She tell me word is out on street to report if they see me. Then, she realize I can help her escape, and here we are."

Lynch looked into the other room and saw a ragged teenager with glazed eyes showing no hope. How long would it take those eyes to brighten? At the moment, though, he saw that she was shaky and sweating, despite the chill in the room. Her pimp obviously kept her on a "short leash." He approached Mike.

"When is that doctor friend of yours coming? You might want to warn him we have a teenage girl starting to withdraw from heroin."

Mike sighed. "Not quite what Mary and I signed on for, but we're here to serve. I'll give him a call." He left for the kitchen, to make the call outside of earshot.

Lynch returned to Ibrahim. "So, I hear our favorite animals are eager for a rematch."

Ibrahim frowned and nodded. "So soon. They will remember us."

That idea sent a chill through Lynch.

"But we have other worry now."

Lynch did not like the sound of that.

"When I get there, place appear empty. Nobody. No light. I see dog kennels, but not dogs, so I make noise along fence. Dog come running, barking, angry. But no response at big house or guardhouse. Again, empty. I retreat, let dog get quiet, and then start looking for best way in." He paused and lifted his nose in the air. "Is food ready? Very hungry."

In the kitchen, they found Mary cutting the lasagna. The garlic bread sat inside a towel in a basket. Plates, silverware, and glasses sat on one counter.

"Help yourselves, fellas. You know where the ice and drinks are. Coffee is made, if you want some. I had hoped we could sit and eat together, but we'll be upstairs with Keisha. Oh, and the doctor is on his way, so don't be surprised by a visitor at the door."

The men served up their food, claimed ice water to drink, and sat down at the main table in the dining room. Ibrahim charged into his food as if he hadn't eaten in a week.

"So," Lynch started to say with his mouth half-full. He continued only after swallowing. "What's this other worry?"

Ibrahim nodded, but didn't answer with his mouth full. He took a drink after finishing that bite and replied, "About ten o'clock, limo pull in. All seven girl from main office pile out. Guard follow. Driver also stay. Men I not know."

Lynch didn't understand the problem. They had anticipated a couple of guards, and this meant more women to rescue, more evidence, more testimonies.

"These are women I tell you about. Beautiful, smart. Darko control by fear."

"Okay, so what is the problem?"

Ibrahim's brow furrowed. "Darko bring them to estate for only two reason. One, he plan big party. His big party like orgy. Under circumstance, I do not see this as reason."

"Okaaayy, so . . ."

"Second reason. He regroup. Bring girls to best location to protect. Will bring other girls in, too. The girls in homes like one we raid. Pimps take girls off street. Once all girls protected, he have guards all come to estate, too. It likely he has reinforcement coming, if not there already. If we go to estate, we find much more resist, big fight now."

Thirty-nine
❧ ✦ ✦ ☙

After dinner, the three men sat in the library discussing the upcoming video interviews and how best to utilize those testimonies. Danijela poked her head around the corner, looked at Lynch and frowned. She walked straight to him and reached out for his right hand.

"Come. You must lie down. Keep arm and leg up if you wish to be better."

Ibrahim watched her and felt concern rise up within. Would she be as attentive to him? He hoped so, but still he wondered. He knew of the confusion in Lynch's heart. They had discussed it outright. But how did Danijela feel? A small voice in his head told him to tell her how he felt. Yet, such a conversation with a woman was foreign to him. He did not feel "Americanized" enough to be that direct. In his culture women were restricted, possessions, the weaker gender whose fate was controlled by the men in their lives. In his parents' time many marriages were still arranged, although such a thing would never be presented to him now, even in his homeland.

How? How does one go about telling a woman that you love her? His mind had agonized over that for months now, even before rescuing her from the councilman. He had thought that the very act of rescuing her would show her how he felt about her. Had it not been enough?

He watched Lynch literally get pulled from the

conversation, despite his protests. As soon as Lynch was out of sight, he looked at Mike and nodded.

"You still sure you want help me tonight?"

Mike nodded back. "Of course, I'm sure. Like I said earlier, we'll be a lot more effective together than your going by yourself."

"Then we go now. Keisha tell me corners her friends work and where most like to hide."

The two men left the library and walked through the kitchen. They grabbed their coats and left through the garage, where Lynch would not see them. Neither man liked excluding Lynch, but each acknowledged that he'd not be helpful and that it was more important that he take time to heal. The chances increased hourly that he'd be forced to fight at less than 100%. Why lessen his odds any further?

Fifteen minutes later, Mike's SUV cruised along Market Street, not far from St. Louis' Union Station. Ibrahim had shifted into the back seat, out of sight. Mike's plan was a good one. The girls would not know his face. He could get their attention in seconds flat, while Ibrahim's presence might set off alarms throughout Darko's network.

Ibrahim scanned the side streets as they passed by. Market Street was a busy thoroughfare, and its prominence in the city's tourism trade meant the police kept a close eye on any and all illegal activity on it, especially after the recently passed city law on prostitution. Unfortunately, that law was flawed and made no provision for assisting young girls or others caught up in the web of sex trafficking against their will.

"I not see any working girl," Ibrahim stated as they

passed the old train station.

"It's not that cold tonight, either," replied Mike.

Unlike "The Stroll" of South Broadway, the girls who worked Market Street were quite discreet and often kept to the side streets where they could watch for clients. Only when a potential mark appeared would they emerge from the shadows to make their proposition. Many worked the bars in the restaurants and hotels that lined the street, where a little cash, slipped into the hands of the bar staff, caused a form of institutional blindness to fall over the personnel.

A similar loss of sight fell over the staff of some nearby hotels where Keisha's pimp would rent rooms for the night and, in turn, expected Keisha and her "co-workers" each to turn a dozen tricks or more that night. He rotated hotels so as not to wear out his "welcome" at any one. Her pimp had moved here because their activity on South Broadway had become too well recognized by the authorities, and the riverfront hotels, like the Millennium and the Hiltons, had started training its staff to recognize and call police about sex workers.

A few blocks west of Aloe Park, they turned north onto Jefferson. Ibrahim hunched forward between the front seats, scanning the streets. He pointed to three women leaning against the wall of an alcove of one building.

"Is mother and her two daughter. Police know well. Not part of Darko network."

"There are more strollers up ahead," said Mike.

Ibrahim nodded and took a close look as Mike crawled past.

"Do not go so slow. Attract police as well as girl. Take next right and double back to train station. These are not Darko's girls."

Ibrahim directed Mike to return to Market Street, heading east this time. Up ahead, on the opposite side of the street near the sand volleyball court on Memorial Plaza, he saw two young women, spike heels, skin-tight short dresses beneath fake-fur coats, their boobs preceding their strut.

"There." He pointed them out to Mike. "Is Keisha's friends, LaToya and April." He did not know these girls, but Keisha had affirmed their desire to get out, to get off the streets. Both were controlled by addictions that had been forced upon them by the pimp. Neither one looked springtime fresh. "Ah, there is pimp. He watch close." Ibrahim pointed out a tall, skinny white male 40 feet away, leaning against a tree trunk with a cigarette dangling from his lips. Everything about his body screamed meth user.

Mike drove on by, but used the next intersection to make a turn and position himself on an intersecting course with the girls. The SUV eased up behind the girls as they turned onto 17th Street away from Market, and halfway down the short block, Mike quickly pulled to the curb and hit the button to power down the passenger-side window. Both girls quickly sidled up to the window.

"Hey, sugar."

One of the two produced a cigarette and held it out. "Got a light?"

"Are you looking for some fun? We—"

Mike didn't smile. He simply stated, "Keisha sent

us. Do you want out?"

Ibrahim rose up in the back seat, and one of the girls eased back from the car. Her gaze began to flip from the car to the pimp and back again. She looked like someone watching a tennis match with the nervous twitch of the Energizer Bunny. The other girl didn't hesitate to open the front passenger door.

A flicker of movement to his right caused Ibrahim to gaze back toward the pimp. He was not surprised to see the man running toward the girls. He pulled both young women back and began to stick his head into the window, yelling profanities. Ibrahim used the opportunity to push open the rear passenger door, slamming the man in the hip and knocking him to the pavement. In one fell swoop, Ibrahim hit him with the tip of a stun baton and watched him stiffen and then go limp.

Both girls darted into the back seat as Ibrahim pulled the man over to a nearby park bench. He took a quick glance in both directions. The security cameras on the nearby post office building were far enough away to cause no problem later. Satisfied there were no observers, particularly police, he frisked the man's pockets. He found two syringes, each loaded with the man's drug *de jour*. Without hesitating, he jabbed and unloaded one into each of the man's thighs, right through his trousers. He had no time to hunt for scarred veins. He placed one spent syringe on the bench near the man's right hand, and the other in the man's hand before rushing back to the vehicle. He would be out for quite some time, and if he became hypothermic or died before someone discovered him, so be it. He deserved it.

Yet, as they sped away toward the closest highway ramp, Ibrahim felt a twinge of remorse. He had acted as he once had. He shook his head and silently asked forgiveness, before pulling out his disposable cell phone and dialing 9-1-1 to report a man in trouble in Memorial Plaza near 17th Street.

The doctor arrived carrying a traditional black bag, but Lynch suspected it carried little more than intravenous supplies and medications to calm the girl's withdrawal. In a sense, the bag seemed a throwback, and it struck him as unusual. He couldn't ever recall seeing a doctor carry a black bag, except in old movies where doctors were portrayed making house calls. Then he realized he was actually remembering those things, that doctors once carried black bags and made house calls. He smiled at the thought that his memory continued to improve.

Danijela had been sitting with him, watching a movie on the Hallmark Movie Channel, when Doctor Deloitte arrived. Guarding him might have been the better term. When the doorbell rang, he had started to rise only to find her hand pushing him back onto the couch.

"Is only doctor, not attack from front," she had said.

He sighed and resigned himself to couch potato status once again. He hated it. How could people just lie on a couch like this, or even sit in one place, watching hours of television? It was mind numbing. Yet, it did seem to help his memory, just as Danijela had first suggested back at the cabin. The cabin. Had they watched it burn only one short week earlier? It seemed a lifetime ago already.

Lynch listened closely for activity on the first floor and hearing none, rose and went to the bathroom. Danijela remained upstairs, so he sneaked into the kitchen and rummaged through the refrigerator. He found an apple and felt tempted to snatch a beer, but decided not to incur the wrath of hurricane Danijela. He heard footsteps on the back stairwell and wondered if he should make a break for the parlor. No, these footsteps were lighter.

Mary stepped down into the kitchen from where two steps up led to a small landing at the base of the back stairs.

"Danijela still upstairs?"

Mary laughed. "Yes, she is. You're safe for now. Still hungry? I can heat up some leftover pasta or something."

He smiled. "Am I that obvious?"

"Which part? The 'can't stand watching Hallmark movies' part or the 'itching to get into the battle' part?" She smiled. "You're as bad as my husband."

"Speaking of which, where are Mike and Ibrahim?"

She didn't answer right away, and a slight frown made her mouth sag. "Out trying to find Keisha's friends. The other two girls being held by their pimp."

Lynch's countenance fell. He *was* anxious to return to the action, and he wasn't sure why. He admitted to liking the success of their previous rescue and the adrenaline rush that came with it, even though the monster dog almost won. Yet he hadn't felt like that with Danijela at the cabin. Was this one more facet of him coming to the surface?

Mary gave him a wan smile. "Your back-to-the-battle side is showing." She put her hand on his arm. "Lynch, you've got to give your body time to heal. If you don't, you put not just yourself, but others at risk, too. I know Ibrahim doesn't want to tackle that big estate without your help, so he's trying to make some easy rescues while you heal."

Lynch nodded. "I know. And every girl he brings out is one more saved. I just want to help and to move this along to a point where I can return to the land of the living. I need to re-establish my life and move on, wherever that might take me."

Mary nodded. "I can understand that. Mike and I just continue to pray that Christ becomes the center of that life for you. That doesn't magically make life any easier. In fact, sometimes it creates more problems than it solves, but having true faith in your life sure casts out the fear."

Lynch stood and gazed out the window, thinking about her comments.

"So, hungry or not? I need to get back upstairs to help."

Lynch returned his attention to her. "Thanks, but, uh, I'm fine." He watched her scurry about the kitchen gathering items to take upstairs.

As she took the first step up to the back stairs, she turned back to him. "Now, I suggest you get back to our couch before Danijela finds you out here." She laughed and continued on her way.

He took a bite from the apple and started back to the parlor. He thought about her comment on faith and fear. She and Mike seemed perfect examples of that faith. They had no fear in taking in a bunch of strangers. In fact, their home was about to become a women's dormitory and detox center. With just two bathrooms. Yet, they took it all in stride with no concern about what could happen should this guy, Darko, discover what they were doing. True, the odds of that were slim, but with each new girl, the risk increased. All it would take is one of them changing her mind in fear of what could happen to her for leaving. One quick phone call could expose them all. The Southworths were smart people. Surely they knew that risk, and yet they continued, unfazed. He wanted that kind of faith and confidence. Maybe he'd had it before. Still, it didn't seem familiar. He certainly wanted it now.

The wood floor above him creaked under the weight of footsteps, so he hurried back to the parlor. He sat down, but made sure to put his feet up on the hassock. The sounds of a second and then a third person walking above echoed down the main stairwell, and shortly the stairs squeaked as they descended. A moment later, Danijela peered around the corner.

"Hey, how you get apple? You supposed to rest on couch."

Lynch rolled his eyes. He started to make a comment about the servants forgetting him, but realized the bad taste of such a comment, even as a joke, under the circumstances. "I had to go to the bathroom, so I got it while I was up. I came right back here. Promise." He crossed his heart.

Danijela crossed her arms over her chest and gave him "the eye." He'd seen that look a lot lately. He

304

wanted to laugh at it, but knew better. That would have been like answering the question, "Do these jeans make me look fat?"

The doctor appeared behind her, followed by Mary, who took a look at Danijela's face, looked at him, and then bit her lip to hide the grin.

Doctor Deloitte walked into the room and up to him.

"So, the ladies tell me a dog did a number on you." His face said 'gravitas,' but his eyes spoke mirth.

"If you want to call a 250-pound mastiff a dog, yes."

"Ah. I see your point. The young lady there left out that part." He glanced back at Danijela, who shrugged innocence. "And this monster got both legs and forearms?"

Lynch described the makeshift protective gear they had improvised as the doctor examined his right lower leg.

"Can you move your foot up and down?"

Lynch complied. "The legs are much better, thanks to the rest, ice, and elevation. Same with the right forearm." Danijela smiled and nodded.

"Any calf tenderness when I squeeze?"

"Not so much today. I can walk without pain now, but I've not been allowed off this couch much, so I don't know how they'd do with a long walk or running."

Danijela looked smug now and the amusement returned to Doctor Deloitte's eyes. "Ahh, I understand."

Lynch could almost hear a subtle chuckle behind that comment. The doctor examined the other leg and moved to the right forearm, again checking for mobility, swelling, and tenderness. As he took Lynch's left forearm, Lynch winced. The doctor looked more serious.

"Can you roll up this sleeve any farther?"

Lynch struggled with the task, so Danijela stepped in and finished it to the doctor's satisfaction.

"Make a fist. Move your hand up and down. Wiggle your fingers."

Lynch responded to each command, although slowly.

"Does it hurt to do those movements?"

"Yes, but not as bad as yesterday or this morning."

The doctor gave his forearm a gentle squeeze that felt like a vise grip had grabbed hold. "Tender?"

"Ummm, some," Lynch lied.

The doctor had been watching his face. "Yeah, right." He reached into his black bag and pulled something out. Lynch couldn't see what it was at first. A moment later, the doctor was bending a paperclip, unfolding it. "Time to break out the expensive test equipment." The ends of the metal now sat about a quarter inch apart. "Close your eyes and tell me if you feel one point or two."

The doctor now moved along each fingertip and tested them. Lynch responded with what he felt, confident he had answered each correctly. The doctor then pulled out a Q-tip-like thing and pulled the cotton tip loose and into a long, soft wisp.

"Put your other hand out here as well. I'm going to tickle one hand and then the other. Tell me if the left hand feels the same as the right."

As the doctor did so, Lynch could honestly state that they felt pretty much equal. At least the left hand wasn't totally numb or anything. The doctor then pinched several fingertips and watched the nail beds.

"So, you say the pain and swelling have improved."

Lynch definitely thought so and replied, "Yes. Why?"

" 'Cause you may have dodged the bullet on this one. Crush injuries like you suffered can produce what we call a compartment syndrome. That's where the injured muscle swells to a point where it has nowhere else for the swelling to go, and the increased pressure inside that muscle compartment damages nerves and cuts off blood flow."

Lynch definitely did not like the sound of that. Maybe he shouldn't have been so judgmental of Danijela's persistent care.

"Usually, these kinds of acute injuries don't respond well to just anti-inflammatory meds and local care, but in your case, you're bucking the odds."

"So, I should keep up what I'm doing?"

The doctor nodded, and Danijela's smugness ratcheted up a notch.

"If it suddenly starts to worsen, more pain with use, more tender, the development of any numbness, get your butt into an emergency room."

"That bad?"

"Yes. If it worsens, you'll need surgery or you'll lose the arm."

Forty
꽃◆◆꽃

Darko's "cage" seemed to be shrinking around him. He could no longer concentrate on business and used the ruse of a transformer problem to close the company until he could sort out friends versus enemies and deal with the latter. As the Bosnians had done during the war, when faced with two fronts, he decided to take time to regroup.

He paced along the wall of windows overlooking his backyard's pool and entertainment area as twilight gave way to dusk. The automatic floodlights had popped on and created new shadows that fought those naturally produced by the setting sun. The season's dormancy of the gardens did nothing to lift his spirits, but had it been late spring with the gardens in full bloom, he still would have found little time to enjoy the beauty of them. The tall evergreen arborvitae hedge that provided absolute privacy from prying eyes in the summer now became a source of concern. He mindlessly watched the dogs meander from food bowls to water and back. At least he could trust that they had that back acreage, with all its blind spots, covered for him.

"They are here," announced Risto upon entering the room.

Darko turned to face him. "Good. Secure them downstair, as we talk about before."

The basement's rooms would be crowded, but not unwelcoming. The women from the office were already there. Now the women held by his most prestigious clients would join them. He would no longer need to guard any private homes and could concentrate his manpower here while looking for Ibrahim. How the man had continued to escape his network of informants remained a mystery. Had he also avoided hearing the news that would bring him back into Darko's grasp?

"Whores are lock down. Pimps not happy."

"Tell them unhappy better than dead."

Risto nodded. "Not able find Joey P. Word on street is girls gone; Joey P in hospital."

Darko took a deep breath. Was this Ibrahim at work again, or Joey P being stupid?

"Ibrahim?"

"Not know."

Darko felt miffed that Risto had failed to find the answer to that question before coming to him. Admittedly, the man had been busy. "Find out. And find Joey P. Take him to warehouse and call me when there. I will myself question."

He nodded. "Already call contacts in downtown hospitals. Hope have answer soon."

Darko returned his gaze to the back. He saw Goran walk toward the dogs and use his whistle and hand to command them to sit. They obeyed immediately and the man proceeded to fill their food and water bowls. Darko, himself, could never be so trusting.

He heard the light footfall of his wife, but did not turn to greet her. A moment later, her hand rested on his arm.

"How can I help?"

He shook his head. "Can you find Ibrahim, or

women he take? No, *moj najdraži*." He sighed. In truth, as the situation soured, he trusted her no more than the dogs in the backyard. Yes, he had given her a life of plenty and of pleasure. Yes, he had confided in her and took her council seriously. But, did that ensure her loyalty? Would she turn on him to keep her own freedom?

"Well, I help in my way. Host dinner party for best client. You say when."

Darko thought about that for a moment. Perhaps that would go a long way in calming these clients' fears. A morale booster. Or, would it produce a false sense of normalcy? Then he thought about the second front facing him, Richard. Maybe this could be the avenue best suited to testing the man.

He turned to Sonja and embraced her. "Yes, my dearest. A party. Saturday night."

She smiled and kissed him. "Only five day to plan. I must get busy."

As must I. He watched her walk from the room and grew curious. He had seen that look on her before. Maybe thoughts of planning the party flooded her mind, but for some obscure reason he suspected she had more than a party on her mind.

He proceeded to his office. His first call would be to Richard. He looked up the man's home phone number and dialed.

"Richard, is Darko."

"Yes, sir. What can I do for you?"

"We still have electric problem at building so plan work from home. Can you do that?"

"Sure can. When the power went out this morning,

my UPS kicked in, and I moved my work files to a flash drive before powering down. So I have them with me. Is there something specific you need?"

"For work, no. Continue what you do. But I, actually Sonja, too, request your presence at our home in country Saturday night. We have dinner party for several client. Want you be there."

"Um, sure. I don't have any plans."

"Good. Dress is business casual. Oh, and Irina be here, too." He smiled for the first time in several days as he added, "And maybe she arrange her two friend be here, too. For after-dinner party, yes? I ask her for you?"

He wished he could see the young man's face at that moment. That alone might have been all the test Darko needed in deciding where the man stood.

Richard had not been prepared for Darko's call. He had, in fact, taken time to work from home that day, with his files on the flash drive. He had also taken time that afternoon to drive back to work and circle the area in his car. Nowhere did he see utility workers replacing a transformer in the vicinity of the warehouse. The streetlights worked. Other businesses had lights. Only the import warehouse appeared dark. Perhaps they had an internal electrical failure. Yet, if that were the case, why wasn't there a fleet of electrical contractor trucks in the lot? Darko was not one to procrastinate fixing a problem that would cost him money.

No, he did not understand Darko's closing up shop, much less blaming it on the ruse of an electrical failure. Something fishy was going on, something that required moving the women.

In addition, he still tried to make sense of the man with the gun who had confronted him two nights earlier. The man did not identify himself, but spoke with the same accent as Darko and Risto. He had demanded to know who Richard was, who he worked for, and what he had been doing in the warehouse. The guy had such an intense look about him, not to mention the handgun pointing at Richard's head through the window, that Richard saw no benefit to lying to the guy.

He just hadn't told the whole truth. He'd omitted the part about being in the women's quarters.

Then, the man had asked if Richard knew what kind of man he worked for. His answer, "I'm beginning to find out" was countered by a warning, "If you value life, act normal. Act suspicious of nothing."

Then the man was gone, and Richard found that acting "normal" would require Oscar-winning talent.

Five minutes after ending the call with Darko, his burn phone rang. That was as bizarre as Darko calling him. His handler never called.

"Give me a minute."

Richard grabbed his coat and walked outside to a bench in the park down the street. This time he was careful to pay attention to his surroundings. He felt as if a dozen eyes now watched his every move and that his car was bugged, like his apartment.

"So, you've been invited to the country estate. We need to talk," said the voice on the other end. No "hello." Just straight to the point.

"What? Are you tapped into my home phone?" Richard didn't like that intrusion one bit.

"No. We're tapped into his. Something screwy is going on that we don't have a complete handle on yet."

"That makes two of us, but I'm the one on the front line." Richard now wished more than ever that he'd taken a job flipping burgers back home.

"I think we have a line on the guy you met two nights ago. Word on the street is that Komarčić has a defector. Someone, or more than one someones, rescued three girls from a pimp today. The pimp ended up in SLU Hospital with a heroin OD. It was an injection in the muscle, not a vein, so its effect will be slow and long. Mostly sedation, but no high. The girls have vanished, and word is out that this guy has them."

"So, who is this guy?"

"All we have is a first name, Ibrahim. We don't know if he's trying to compete with Komarčić or trying to bring him down, for whatever reason. We hope it's the latter and that we can get his cooperation."

"Well, either way, from what little I saw, this guy is prepared to play tough."

"He must know Komarčić well, then. We want you at that dinner party, too."

Richard wasn't sure he heard that right. "Um, do you know what that means? You heard the whole conversation, right?"

"We did."

"And you want me to play along?"

"Fully."

"And you understood the part of the conversation about Irina and two friends?" He explained Irina's invitation to a foursome and heard several distinctly different chuckles on the other end.

"What? You have a problem with that? I have some agents here who'd love to trade places, go under cover." There were several snickers at that last line.

"Not funny." Richard now had a better understanding as to why sex trafficking was such a poorly documented crime. Prostitution was considered a low priority offense by too many police departments. Even these federal agents made jokes. Was it not for the fact that increasing numbers of under-aged victims were falling into the snares of these traffickers, the crime would hardly be on the authorities' radar.

"Really. Not funny, and I'm not that kind of guy." He didn't think he could pull it off. He'd never been a player. Like Clive had said, he was that 'helping out little old ladies, retrieving kittens in trees' kind of guy. He'd actually be embarrassed to find himself confronted by three naked women who had just his pleasure in mind. He could almost feel himself blush at the thought.

"Okay, okay. You're right, not appropriate, but we want you there. We'll be positioned down the road, but we need to figure out some way that you can signal us if you need help. We can't wire you because that chief of security guy of his will scan everyone coming in the door and likely require all cell phones be left at the door. Which means you can't take this burn phone to the house. Leave it in the car, hidden somewhere."

"Can't you, like, just get a subpoena or warrant or whatever and just raid the place? He's already told us one of the women will be there. They're probably all there." Richard could not see why they faced so many obstacles and delays over taking Darko down.

"Look, we've tried to get a warrant, but the judge still doesn't believe we have enough. Irina and the others are adults, so without one or more of their direct testimonies, we have nothing but suspicions. If even one of them, just one, was a minor, we could arrest him immediately. But none of them are. The fact that they have sleeping quarters at the warehouse isn't necessarily against the law. Actually, we discovered they're in compliance with the zoning laws. Believe me, we've looked at it from every angle."

Richard wanted to stand up and pace, but that might call attention to him. No, actually he wanted to go inside where it was warm. And then pace.

"Let me think about it, and if I can come up with some sort of signal, I'll call."

He hung up and returned to his apartment. He kicked himself at the realization that he'd lost the opportunity to get the information needed. At the time, when he was with the women, he could have recorded two or three of their statements on his smartphone while waiting to make sure the coast was clear for him to leave. That could have convinced a judge to issue a warrant, and this whole charade would be over now.

Without assurance that their loved ones were safe, none of the women would have talked. Now they were gone, and he hadn't collected a single family member's info. He had been so concerned about getting caught, he couldn't think straight. True, the women had no paper or pens, but he could have *recorded* the names and locations. Some spy he was. And in five days, he would be heading right into the middle of the lions' den.

Forty-one
❦ ◆ ◆ ❧

Lynch awoke early the next day and proceeded to make coffee for the rest of the house. His legs felt considerably better, and he'd slept without interruption or pain. He also discovered while making the brew that his left hand's functioning had dramatically improved as well, although still quite sore with use and not with the dexterity he'd like to have. Still, at the rate he was progressing, he might be ready for action within a couple of days.

With a mug of joe in hand, he returned to the parlor and folded up the sofa bed. He sat on the couch mulling over the recent events and made a decision. This would be the day he would search out this Chief Dandridge and contact him by phone. He was not yet prepared to return to the land of the living, and he could only hope the man would honor that desire. If not, he would have to play whatever cards were dealt him.

They now had six women prepared to provide testimony against their captors and Darko Komarčić. Ibrahim was prepared to testify against his former employer and call out dozens of pimps by name. So, if Dandridge publicly outed him, the show would go on as planned. However, not until Komarčić and his minions were in jail, and his operation shut down, would he consider Danijela safe.

He heard stirring upstairs, and soon the noise of footsteps could be heard. As the stairs began to creak, he expected to see Ibrahim first and was surprised to see Mike in the hallway outside the parlor.

"I expected Ibrahim to be first down. The smell of brewing coffee always seems to draw him." Lynch smiled and held up his mug. "It's all ready for whoever wants some."

Mike nodded. "Ibrahim isn't here. He left about four a.m. to watch the place in the country."

Lynch frowned. The man was taking a risk going there alone. Lynch would have been happy to have accompanied him. He didn't need full use of his left arm simply to play observer.

Mike turned toward the kitchen and a moment later returned with a cup of coffee.

"I've decided to reach out to Albert Dandridge. Today, if I can track down a phone number."

Mike ran his hand through his hair and furrowed his brow. "Please be careful and use a disposable phone. I still have a bad feeling about this."

This time Lynch didn't dismiss the man's reservations. He had learned firsthand what Mike Southworth was made of. He would take some basic precautions.

Mike paused and then looked Lynch directly in the eyes. "I hadn't mentioned this before because I wasn't sure it was my place, but I have a contact you might want to consider. She's a detective from St. Charles. She and her family go to our church, too. Her husband's a musician and FedEx guy. Anyway, I took the liberty to make some discreet inquiries. She's on the Major Case Squad investigating these dead girls. I'd trust her with *my* life."

As he considered this, a commotion started and became louder upstairs. A minute later, LaToya came running down the steps and made it to the front door before Lynch intercepted her. Mary and Danijela chased after her and pulled up short as they saw Lynch.

"Whoa, ladies, what's up?"

Mary took a deep breath and replied, "She wants to leave. She's beginning to have some withdrawal symptoms, and she's afraid her pimp will hurt her."

"LaToya, can we talk about this first?"

Lynch tried to sound reassuring, to make her confident that she did indeed control her destiny now, but he knew that letting her go could be disastrous. Back on the street she would be forced to give Risto the information he needed to find them. They would have to find a new safe house, and the Southworths would be in grave danger.

"LaToya? Please?" He smiled and pointed toward the couch with his hand.

The girl's eyes bounced from one person to the next, her breathing accelerated. A small bead of perspiration appeared on her brow, despite the slight chill in the house. Finally, she walked into the parlor and sat down.

"LaToya, we can help you through the withdrawal as well as anyone can. You've seen how we're helping Keisha through it. Please don't leave," said Mary.

"Joey P w-will beat me. I gotta go back. Make it up to him."

Lynch saw the fear in her face.

"Not if you don't go back. We can help you get home, and we have friends who can help you get your education, your G.E.D. if you want that, or training in something else. Do you *really* want to go back to your old life?" Lynch paused. "Besides, we think Joey P is in the hospital. You go back now, you'll end up in Risto's clutches, and he'll force you to tell him where we all are. That puts all of these good people here at risk."

LaToya's facial expressions revealed her mental processes, as slow as they appeared.

"I-I don't want to go home. My step-dad sold me to Joey P for drug money in the first place. I go back, he just do it again. Ask for more money if he knows they's lookin' for me." She shook her head. "No, thank you. Don't want to go home, but I would like to finish my schoolin'. I knows I need to do that."

"So, you'll stay? Please? We just want to help you," said Mike.

"I-I don't know what to do. I-I need to step outside for a smoke," she replied as her eyes nervously darted from one person to the next.

Lynch took a deep breath and shrugged. What could they do? If they forced her to stay, they were no different than her other captors. They had to show her some trust, if they were to gain *her* trust.

"Sure. Go grab a smoke. The front door will be unlocked when you need to come back in. We'll be fixing breakfast," said Mike. The look on Mike's face reflected his understanding of the situation, as if he'd read Lynch's mind.

Lynch nodded. "Let us know if we can help with anything."

Mary stood and unlocked the door, opened it, and stepped aside to let her go. LaToya stopped in front of

Mary and looked intently into the woman's face. She then pulled a pack of cigarettes from her coat pocket and stepped onto the wide front porch of the home.

Lynch resisted the urge to stand in the window and watch her, but he did glance outside and saw her sitting on the porch swing, gliding slightly back and forth, cigarette in mouth. He moved into the library, where the window looked out upon the side of the porch opposite the swing. Danijela followed.

"You think she stay?"

Lynch didn't know. People did strange things, made irrational choices. He shrugged.

"If she go, we need find new place."

"Yes, we will, and the Southworths will need to contact the police for possible protection. This could become a real mess. A dangerous mess."

Tears welled up in Danijela's eyes. "They good people. Do not want to see get hurt, or lose home."

Lynch embraced her, to comfort her. He glanced out the window in time to see LaToya walk off the porch. He expected her to run, but instead, she tossed her cigarette to the brick walkway, ground it under her heel, and came back to the front door. He breathed a sigh of relief.

Forty-two

Darko had received the call from Risto shortly after lunch. Joey P had signed out against medical advice from the hospital, according to their contact there. Risto had located him within half an hour. Darko, in turn, had taken his time going to the warehouse, where Risto had the pimp secured. There was always something quite intimidating about being bound to a hard chair, in a dark room, not being sure what fate had in store for you. For most, the fear instilled by the wait was all Darko needed to get the information he wanted. Only the really stupid and the really cocky ones, who turned out to be the stupidest of all, tried to resist. In the end, Darko always got what he needed.

Joey P proved to be the exception.

Darko walked out of the closet-like room located off the back corner of the security office at the warehouse, shaking his head. He heard a muffled scream as Risto took a turn. The man was expendable, and the Mississippi River ran fast in its present low-water state. The body would likely make it past Cairo, Illinois, before being discovered. If it was ever discovered. Risto was a David Coopersfield, or was it Copperfeld? Whatever. He was a magician at making bodies disappear. Poof! Magic! Gone! Only when Darko needed to make a point was a body left for discovery.

He walked toward his office, making a detour here and there to check the limited access rooms. All remained secure. He turned toward the women's dorm and was taken aback to see the door wide open. All the women were gone, but the quarters should still have been secured. He could not afford to have unauthorized eyes absorbing the images of that place. As he neared the doorway, he heard a familiar voice beyond and felt a surge of relief. Sonja!

He walked into the quarters and saw his wife standing at one of the bedroom doors.

"*Moj najdraži?*"

Sonja startled and turned toward him.

"Beloved, you surprise me." She smiled and embraced him. "I have little surprise for *you*," she whispered in his ear.

She backed away and allowed him to gaze into the small room. A young woman lay unconscious, on her side, facing away from him, on the shabby twin bed. Darko walked over to it and turned her onto her back. She looked familiar, yet not. He looked at his wife with that question in his eyes.

"You not recognize?"

Darko shook his head and turned to look at their "guest."

"Hint. You hunt him."

Suddenly his mood lightened. He did indeed know who she was. She had matured since he last saw her and had changed her hair color. He walked back to Sonja and kissed her.

"Yes, we keep her here. He think she will be at estate. Good think."

Smiling, he left the women's quarters. That sense of foreboding which had covered him like a shroud all week now had an edge pulled back, allowing a single ray of light inside.

Lynch sat in the parlor, his left forearm wrapped in cold towels while his right hand fondled his handgun. He could hear Mike and Mary whispering in the dining room, while Danijela was with the other women, as they all tried to work out their statements for the camera.

Lynch stood and walked into the dining room. His hosts stopped talking and looked up at him.

Mike nodded in greeting. "Sorry if our discussion in here disturbed you. We were trying to keep it down. How's the arm?"

Lynch shrugged and followed that with flexing his left wrist and opening and closing his hand. "Getting there."

"Look, Mary and I were discussing two things. One, well, we both think your contacting this retired police chief is a bad idea. Just say, we have a bad feeling about it. Nothing objective we can point to. The second thing is what to do with this video after we've recorded the women."

Lynch pulled out an adjacent chair and sat down. "I, uh, don't know what more to say. On one hand, I don't know how well connected this Darko character is. If he has judges, police officers, and county councilmen in his pocket, who can I trust? Yet, I feel like I have to contact someone. If I call my old boss, he's going to demand I come in, and if I don't, I'll have zero chance of regaining my old job. I remember working closely with this Chief Dandridge. I think he can be trusted, and since he's retired, he can't force me in. Does that make sense?"

He could feel Mary's penetrating gaze on him again.

"And I feel like I need to do this *before* we try to raid Darko's place."

"Why?" asked Mike.

"To cover my tail. Well, kinda. I can't go in as a lawful police officer. I know that. Dandridge couldn't give me that kind of authority anyway. Not anymore. But someone with official standing, even if just retired, needs to know I'm alive and well and what I'm about to do. If things go south, they'll know what was going on. He'll know what happened to me, so that my parents can be told."

"We could handle that part, but I pray nothing *goes south*, as you put it."

Lynch contemplated that last comment. The Southworths would actually know more about his "rebirth" than he could comfortably tell the Chief over a brief phone call, but he would still feel more confident if someone connected to the police knew what was happening. Still, their unease seemed to be rubbing off on him. Was he doing the right thing?

"Thank you."

"I can still contact our detective friend. She might be more help than you think," Mike stated.

At that moment, Lynch felt a sense of peace wash over him, which surprised him. Until that moment, his instincts had said to contact the Chief. Now? Maybe their detective friend *was* the way to go. He was so used to acting on his gut feelings that this change in course seemed foreign. No, he decided. He would trust his initial instinct and contact the older policeman.

Mary's scrutiny persisted. "Do you *want* your old job, Lynch?" she finally asked, just as Lynch began feeling uncomfortable under her stare. "I'm sorry, but I just had this thought that you might have been moving toward a new career before your injury."

The question caught Lynch off-guard. He had assumed he would. He had chosen the career. It was what he knew. Well, once knew, but that knowledge was coming back steadily. Yet, after her question, something began to gnaw at the edge of his consciousness that maybe he shouldn't be concerned about his old job. Had there been some kind of change brewing in his life, just before his accident? Now he felt further unsettled.

Mike brought the conversation back to his earlier statement about the video. "Josh should be here in a couple of hours. We can record all the women here, as well as Ibrahim. He said it would take him a day or two to edit it and make it production quality, or something like that. We were talking about the timing of releasing the video. Any thoughts?"

Lynch shrugged. "At first, Ibrahim and I had talked about raiding Darko's place to rescue another woman he thought would want to testify against the man. Now, we have more women than we'd first thought possible."

"And there's the issue of Darko regrouping."

"Yes. There's that as well."

"Why not record the women, release the video, and let the police take it from there?" asked Mary.

Lynch nodded. "With my body all beat up, believe me, I've thought about that. I suggested it to Ibrahim, but he insists we need to free the women at Darko's estate. He changes the subject whenever I ask why."

Mary responded, "I overheard him say something to Danijela. He feels somehow responsible for these women, like he has to personally guarantee their freedom."

Her husband nodded in agreement. "I know he's been taking it very hard about the women Darko had killed, and that one woman's family. He doesn't want anyone else hurt and he feels he's the only one who understands Darko and Risto well enough to succeed without more deaths or injuries."

Lynch felt he couldn't have assessed the situation any better.

"Hey, look, I need to make my phone call. I know, you both have a bad feeling about this, but I'll be careful, and I won't divulge too much."

The couple looked at him without saying a word. They'd made their position known. What more could they say? Nothing they could say would deter Lynch from revealing himself to the Chief.

"I, uh, well . . ." He dug out a prepaid cell phone from his pocket and held it up. "I'm calling on this. Like we agreed, only your routine calls on your home phone."

Lynch donned his coat, stuffed the phone into a pocket, and left the house. He had made up his mind to make this call, but now that the time had come, he wasn't sure what to say. Would he recognize the man's voice? Maybe it would be better if he didn't. That, at least, would bolster his claim of amnesia. Surely, the man would want to meet up with him. How would he brush that off? And how much should he say about what he was involved with?

He walked briskly in the cool weather and fifteen minutes later he found himself in a park, taking a paved walking path around what appeared to be a six or seven acre, egg-shaped pond, with a small decorative lighthouse in the middle. No one else appeared to be on the trail, so he pulled out the phone, followed by a piece of paper holding a phone number. The number came from memory. He hoped it was correct. He wouldn't know what to do if someone else from his past—his parents, or the woman, Amy—answered.

On the second ring, a gruff male voice answered. "Dandridge."

Lynch sighed in relief and amazement that he'd recalled the man's phone number. Yet, he found his tongue twisted in icy knots as his mind raced to find the words he needed to say.

"Hello. Is someone there?"

"Is this Chief Albert Dandridge?" asked Lynch. Now the silence echoed from the other end of the connection. After a moment, Lynch continued, "Do you recognize my voice? Do I sound familiar to you?"

"Lynch?" The Chief seemed to choke on the name, as if asking if this was some cruel joke. "Son? Is that really you?" Lynch sensed tears of joy on the other end, although he had no memory of ever seeing the man shed a single lachrymal drop.

"It's really me, Chief. I don't remember everything, but things are coming back to me. Like your name and phone number."

"Where are you? I'll come get you."

"Um, not right now, sir. I need you to keep this

under your hat for a little while. Please. Don't tell anyone else yet. Not my parents, not anyone. I'll come in when it's the right time."

The Chief didn't reply right away. "You need medical care, Lynch. Let me come get you."

"Not yet. And I've seen a doctor, just last night. I'm fine. The amnesia's clearing." He proceeded to give the Chief a *Reader's Digest* version of his story, but found himself stopping short of mentioning names or what he'd stumbled into. The Chief already knew Danijela's name and had been to the cabin, but Lynch once again felt the same unease as the Southworths. How had he connected the cabin to Danijela? He hadn't mentioned Ibrahim, or had he? He hadn't divulged any information that tied him to her or that place. Nothing at the cabin tied them together. So, how did the Chief end up there?

Another disturbing thought came to mind. The Chief had recognized his voice just then. And that other detective, Janick, also seemed to recognize his voice. Was one, or the other, compromised? If so, which one?

"I, uh, need to help this lady. She saved my life, and I owe her. Promise me, Chief. Don't say a word to anyone about me until I say so."

"I can't make that promise. You need to come in."

"No, sir. I'm not ready. I need maybe two weeks."

He heard a deep sigh from the other end.

"Okay, Lynch. I'll give you *one* week. After that, I tell Halbert and Janick, and they'll put the word out to find you. One way or the other. Stay safe. I'm looking forward to seeing you."

Lynch had completed his second loop of the walking trail by the time the talk ended. Overall, the conversation had not gone like he'd expected. Why had he held back? He hoped one week would be enough time.

As Lynch's thoughts about the discussion ended, he noticed something. He had walked over a mile, and his legs didn't hurt. He decided to put them to a test and began to jog back to the house. His return trip took half the time of the first leg, and he felt no pain. His legs were ready. Now he needed to focus on the forearm and hand.

Lynch arrived back at the house just as Josh pulled into the driveway. He assisted the young man with the large screen to block the window and watched as the videographer tested his lighting and sound. By then, the women had congregated to the front rooms, watching as well. All of them, except Danijela, appeared nervous. He smiled as Danijela moved between them, whispering encouragement. The translator arrived, and it was decided that Agata would go first, so as not to tie up too much of the volunteer's time.

Halfway into that video session, Ibrahim burst through the front door. He grabbed Lynch and dragged him into the kitchen. Mike followed.

"You are better, yes? Good to go?"

Lynch looked at the man. His eyes seemed crazed, his breathing erratic.

"Ibrahim, I can't hold anything heavier than a couple of pounds in my left hand. And I'm lucky if I can squeeze a wet sponge."

"Is good enough. We must go. Tonight."

"Whoa, Ibrahim," Mike said, inserting himself into the conversation. "Lynch isn't ready. A few more days maybe. Has something happened?

Ibrahim paced the kitchen with a frantic energy, running his hand across his head as he did. He kept shaking his head back and forth, breathing heavily. "They find her. Take her." He stopped and looked at both men squarely. "They use her cell phone, send photo. Darko have my sister."

Forty-three

Amy dialed Richard's home phone number yet one more time. She avoided calling his cell, but if his landline also had Caller ID, she risked appearing desperate and needy after this eighth attempted call to apologize. In truth, nothing could be further from the truth. She had come to terms with being friends and letting God handle the future. She didn't want to burn that bridge needlessly when a sincere apology might be all it took to douse the flame.

The previous seven calls had ended with her hanging up as Richard's voice mail clicked on. She didn't want to leave a message. That would seem too impersonal. However, it was now late, and she would be working late the following day with a long, late afternoon class for the paramedics. As his voicemail answered her call, she made a last minute decision to leave a message.

"Richard, this Amy. I'm sorry I've missed you again. I've tried several times to reach you. I, uh, I want to apologize for the other night at dinner. I had no right to bring up the Europe Night Club or to put you on the spot, and I'm truly sorry. I admit I had too much to drink before you arrived and that played a part, but it shouldn't be an excuse. I really had a good—"

The constant ringing of her front doorbell interrupted her.

"Just a minute. Someone's at my front door, and it seems urgent. Back in a second."

After the incident three nights earlier, she remained hesitant to respond. She decided to leave the phone line open by not hanging up. She glanced out the door's peephole and saw an attractive woman, maybe 40, with long, dark silky hair and stylish dress. The woman looked scared and started pressing the doorbell's button repeatedly again. Amy left the security chain in place, but opened the door.

"Yes? Can I help you?"

"She need help. They say you nurse. My sister, in car, collapse. Not breathe. Quick. They say you nurse. Please help!" The woman kept pointing to a car parked in front of the house two doors down.

Amy went into emergency mode as soon as she heard the woman's hysterical plea.

"We need to call 9-1-1."

"Already call. On way, but she need help now! Quick. Please!"

Amy set the phone down on top of an adjacent table, grabbed her coat, and released the door. She ran after the woman, toward the car. Upon reaching the car, she saw a figure lying on the back seat, not moving. The woman pulled open the door and Amy leaned inside to assess the distressed sister.

Immediately a warning flag arose in her mind. The "sister" was a dressed mannequin. At that point of realization, she felt a jab into her back, followed by a lightning bolt shooting through her body. She fell forward on top of the dummy and was barely conscious of her feet being tucked into the vehicle and the door closing. A moment later, she felt a sharp stab into her upper arm, and within a minute her thoughts dissolved into a kaleidoscopic whirl.

Richard had been avoiding Amy's phone calls. That alone had required Norse god-like resolve, but tonight, when she actually started to leave a message and apologize, all of Asgard had been required to restrain him from picking up the phone. At the most basic level, he had never held her comments against her. What she had seen at the nightclub had happened. It was what it was, and he held no illusion about how it looked. He also had no doubt about the confusion that had created in their relationship.

His greatest dismay was in being unable to open up to her, to show her who he really was and why he had to act like he had. Like Clark Kent to Superman, or Peter Parker to Spiderman, he felt a need to protect her from potential harm by taking on a false identity. The only problem was he couldn't hide in a colorful Spandex crime-fighter costume behind a mask. His only recourse to protect her now was to take on a cold persona, pretend her comments had driven him away, and avoid her until everything was over.

All of his reasoning fell apart as he overheard what transpired at the end of her message. He gave her five, then ten, and finally, fifteen minutes to return to the phone, but she never came back.

He reached for his landline phone only to realize he couldn't risk using it. He grabbed his coat from its hanger and fumbled through the pockets to find his throwaway cell. He dialed the only number stored in its memory.

"Yes."

"I think they've taken Amy Gibbs. You need to contact the St. Peters police and send a cruiser to her address." He proceeded to explain what he'd heard and her failure to return to the phone.

"And you think Komarčić took her?"

Richard heard his handler talking with someone in the room with him.

"The woman's voice sounded familiar. I still haven't placed its owner, but the accent was definitely Eastern European and the same accent I've been hearing around me since I started to work for him."

"That certainly would put a new priority on this case."

"You think?" Richard couldn't help hide his discontent.

"Hold on. Cruiser's just pulling up. Front door is wide open."

Richard picked up his regular cell phone and listened with the other ear. The line remained open, and he could hear two men enter the house.

"Tell 'em I still have an open line on her phone. It should be near the front door because I can hear them."

A moment later, through Amy's phone came, "Hello?"

"Is she there? This is Richard Nichols. I called in her disappearance on another phone when she failed to return to the phone. Who am I talking with?"

The officer identified himself, and Richard again explained what had happened. "Is she there?" Richard began to pace around his living room.

"No one here, sir. We've found her purse and car

keys. Cell phone is in her purse. Wallet's still there."

Richard heard more voices in the room with the officer.

"Sir, we'll take it from here."

Before Richard could protest the line clicked off.

"You still there?" he asked into the throwaway.

"One sec," came the reply. After a moment, his handler came back on. "All right, we've got people on this one. If we can show that he did actually take her and we can place her at any of his properties, we'll have no problem getting a warrant."

"Wait a minute, what—"

"Look, we gotta determine what really happened here. We'll work as fast as we can. In the meantime, you need to continue your charade. Work from home, go to the party, whatever. Play ignorant here. We're on it."

Richard stopped in his tracks. How in the world was he going to do that? He was about to protest and quit, but how would that solve anything if Amy really had been taken by Darko? No, he saw that his handler was correct. If Darko had Amy, his only chance of helping her was to play into Darko's game and get access to his estate via the upcoming party. However, he'd have a few surprises of his own.

Forty-four

❧ ♦ ♦ ❧

Lynch and Mike calmed Ibrahim down long enough for the three men to move to Mike's study on the second floor. Mike grabbed an extra chair from an adjacent room and moved it in so that all three men could sit. Yet, Ibrahim refused to use it and paced beside Mike's desk.

This was not what the "team" needed. Lynch was not 100%, so he, they, needed Ibrahim to remain calm and able to think quickly.

"Ibrahim, please, you need to calm down," said Lynch. "This is exactly what Darko wants you to do. If there was any move he could make to throw you off-balance and make you act impulsively, this is it. Think about it."

"Lynch is right," added Mike. "You can't think straight if you're like this. And you need to be on the top of your game if we're going to rescue your sister, as well as the others."

Ibrahim stopped walking and looked at both men.

Mike continued, "Until now, you've been one step ahead of Darko and Risto. Now, Darko has turned the table."

Ibrahim nodded and finally sat down.

"Thank you," said Lynch. "You were beginning to make me nervous, too." He felt his heart rate begin to slow.

"She is sister. I have only mother and sister. No other family. You be nervous, too, if you walk in my

336

shoe."

Both other men nodded.

"Agreed," said Mike, "but we need you level-headed and calm if we want to see this changed."

After a moment's silence, Lynch continued. "So, how do you know for sure they have her?"

"They call my mother on her cell phone. Send picture."

"Okay, and is there any clue *where* they have her?"

"At estate. Where else? They move everyone to estate. Easiest to keep her there."

Mike shook his head. "That's an assumption on your part. She might be there, or she might not. But that's for sure where they'd want you to come."

"Where else could they keep her?"

Ibrahim looked pained, as if impatient with the inaction. "At the warehouse. Maybe a private home. A motel room."

Lynch contemplated this and said, "I doubt it'd be at a private home. Darko's clients might be scared, but they'd balk at being a party to kidnapping. Plus, too many people around most motels. She could raise attention in lots of ways. Can we check out the warehouse somehow, without being obvious?"

Ibrahim stood and began to pace again. "Not know. I cannot just walk in. If she is there, guard will be told to watch for me, even if they expect me go to estate."

Silence engulfed the room. A few minutes later, Mike stood and gazed out the window.

"From a military perspective, we simply don't have the manpower to open another front, so to speak. If you make your move against the estate and your sister isn't there, it stands to reason they'll kill her to spite you. If you make a move against the warehouse, the same thing goes. Either place, they'll be waiting for you, and you run a good chance of getting injured. Then all of the women might be hurt, or killed, and you'll be out of commission. We need more people."

Ibrahim started to say something, but stopped.

Lynch knew Mike was right. Perhaps he'd been too self-centered when he chose not to go to the police and make his status known. Yet, in his heart, he knew that he'd made the right move. Then. Circumstances had changed.

"Mike, call your friend, the detective from St. Charles. What's her name?"

Susan. Susan Prichard. What do you want me to tell her?"

Lynch thought about that a bit. "Don't use my name. Just, um, tell her about your involvement with that ministry that deals with trafficking and that you have several women about to make video statements about the trafficking ring and their captors. Invite her, but her only, to watch the video session, if she can make it. Tell her she's not to involve the Major Case Squad yet."

"And when she asks why?"

"Say you'll tell her when she comes."

"*I'll* tell her, or you'll tell her?"

"We'll play my part by ear."

Mike returned to his desk and pulled out a booklet from the top left drawer. Lynch could see that it was some sort of church directory from the cover page. Mike dialed a number and waited.

"Russ? Hey, it's Mike Southworth, from church. Is your wife there?"

Lynch strained to hear the other half of the conversation, but couldn't. He motioned for Mike to put it on speaker. Mike shook his head.

"Look, could you have her call me? It's important and has to do with the case I hear she's working on. . . . That's right, those murders. . . . I can't really give you any more info. Please have her call me. Here's my number." Mike relayed his phone number to the man. "Oh, and Russ, please don't mention this to anyone else. Nobody. OK?" Mike nodded, as a sign that Russ had agreed, and hung up.

He glanced at the other two. "That was her husband. He's going to call her."

Thirty seconds after he stopped talking, the phone rang. Caller ID announced "Susan Prichard." This time Mike put the phone on speaker.

"This is Mike. You sure didn't waste any time calling." He chuckled.

"Colonel, if you've intel to break this case, I don't have time to procrastinate. What do you have for me?"

"First, you have to promise me something."

"Oh?"

"I have no desire to obstruct your investigation, but we have some really sensitive issues here and women who are afraid of the police. We need you to come on your own, no others in the MCS are to know about this yet. And you can't ID yourself as a police officer, or these women will bolt. Can you agree to this?"

There was a pause on the other end.

"Let me call you back." The line went dead.

Mike looked as surprised as Lynch felt, as his eyes widened and he shrugged his shoulders. Had she cut them off because she was already directing the MCS their way? Lynch pondered other reasons why she might have hung up as Ibrahim resumed pacing. Two minutes later, the phone rang again.

Mike glanced at the Caller ID and said, "It's her." Then he answered and put the call on speaker.

"Sorry about that. I was in the middle of the MCS work room and couldn't talk freely."

"Not a problem. I understand. So, can you agree to our, um, terms?"

A sigh could be heard from the phone. "It's not how I'd prefer doing this, but I agree. What have you got?"

Mike began to explain how he and Mary had gotten involved with Desert Well Ministries and Crisis Aid International and had volunteered their home as an emergency shelter. He proceeded to tell her about the night Danijela arrived, followed by the others, without using any names.

"What night did that first woman arrive?"

Mike gave her the date, and there was a pause.

"This woman's name wouldn't happen to be Danielle or something, would it? Lt. Janick received a call about the first murder, and the caller mentioned the victim was a friend of this Danielle. No wait. Danijela. It's Danijela. We traced a possible location for this person, and that same night that home exploded in a supposed gas leak. The arson investigator found that the gas line had been purposefully disconnected. Then, all of a sudden, the next night a strange woman shows up at your house. Tell me this is a totally insane scenario and my story and yours are unrelated."

Lynch nodded and mouthed, "This lady's sharp."

Mike raised his brow. "Yes? No?" he whispered back.

Lynch nodded again.

"You're right, Susan, that's totally insane. But insane or not, Danijela is here, and she witnessed the arson. She'll be recording her story second, in about 30 minutes, and I think you'll want to hear who's involved."

"You still live in Ferguson, right?"

"Yes, same house as forever."

"I'll be there in fifteen minutes."

The men could hear the excitement in her voice. Mike was about to sign off and hang up, when she asked, "A man by the name of Jusuf didn't happen to come with her, did he?"

Lynch began to wave his arms and vigorously shake his head.

"No, Susan, no one by the name of Jusuf came with her."

Lynch nodded. The sincerity and truthfulness of Mike's reply came through. He had no need to lie. No one named Jusuf came with Danijela.

Her reply, though, came through with an edge of suspicion. "Okay, because there have been rumors floating around about this man named Jusuf. So, if a guy named Lynch is there, tell him I look forward to meeting him again."

Forty-five
❦◆◆❧

Amy awoke with her head spinning and the word "magnet" swirling inside. As she became more aware of her surroundings, she became more puzzled. What in the world had just happened to her? The vague recollection of running out of her home to help someone in a car floated into her consciousness. Then what? Nothing, until waking up in this room.

She glanced around and realized just how bizarre the room appeared. Had she also been transported back in time? The colorful, high-poster bed with its rich, silk bedding and pillows, plus sheer curtains hanging from its canopy, seemed from a different, distant era. Outside the gauzy cocoon, subtle light from antique brass lamps revealed ancient tapestries depicting scenes that were not exactly suitable for prime-time viewing. Amy blushed as she pulled the curtain aside and took a closer look at the nearest wall hanging.

That's when she realized that her attire matched that of the image. How? What? Who? At first, she felt embarrassed that someone had undressed her and put her in this garb. Yet, the more she thought about the personal violation of that task, the angrier she became.

She lowered her legs over the side of the tall bed. The silky harem pants—she could think of no other term for them—offered no resistance, as if friction did not exist between the see-through material of the clothing and the silk linens. Had she not been careful, she might have slid over the side and fallen to the floor, but she managed to stand, albeit wobbly on her feet.

Although still unsteady, she managed to walk toward the closer of two visible doors, only to find it locked. She raised her fist to pound on it, but stopped at the sound of a voice behind her.

"Will do no good," said the feminine voice.

Amy turned to find two beautiful young women, who apparently had emerged from the other door. The woman who spoke seemed familiar and was dressed as she was. The other woman wore little more than expensive lingerie. Amy's bad dream seemed to devolve toward becoming a nightmare. She didn't need a new nightmare.

"You are Amy, yes?"

Amy refused to acknowledge the question.

"We not hurt you," said the second, skimpily clad woman. "I am Miloska and this is Irina. We are here for Richard, too."

At the mention of Richard, she realized that the first woman, Irina, was the woman from the nightclub. Yet, it was the words "*for* Richard" that sank into Amy's foggy brain. Following that night at Europe Night Club, she had berated herself for "falling" for Richard only to discover that he was a player. Macy had been right about being on the rebound. Yet, his demeanor and actions were anything but those of a womanizer. His explanation fell short, but she knew deep inside that he was withholding something, the truth perhaps, for a reason she did not understand.

For days, she had mentally vacillated between the good and bad possible explanations born of her own imagination. Now, the worst of those possibilities seemed on the verge of coming true.

"We also apologize," Miloska continued.

Amy gave her a questioning look, and the woman pointed to her outfit.

"We were instructed to dress you properly," said Irina. "No one else has touched you or seen you. I know how I would feel, to wake up like this. So, we want you to know it was us, and we apologize for taking the liberty."

Amy felt the anger rise. They had no right to "take the liberty," as the woman stated. She started to protest, but Irina spoke first.

"Is my fault. I promised Richard a foursome. I thought it was in jest, but Darko took it seriously. I did not foresee an outsider being taken for this."

Amy's eyes widened. A foursome? She took her Christian beliefs seriously and had yet to find the right man for a twosome, within marriage. There was no way she would participate in Irina's perverse proposal. She had to find an out, a means of escape. As for Richard, why had he involved her? Their relationship was now history in her life. If he lived long enough.

Irina bowed her head and her voice shook. "You must understand. We do this to survive, and to protect families. If we disobey, we end up organ donors, like our friends."

Fear joined Amy's anger. The woman she had cared for. The other two cases being investigated by the Major Case Squad. The implications staggered her, followed by "why me?" What had she done to deserve this, particularly on top of dealing with the monster known as the L.A. Rapist? Did God now hate her?

No, she knew that last thought was wrong. God loved her. And He had also promised that *all* things would work for good. The problem was that man could not envision *how* He would do that in each and every case, and that uncertainty typically led to fear.

Amy had had her share of dealing with fear. She had proven herself against the L.A. Rapist, she would not give in to fear this time. At that moment, she made the decision to trust Him.

Forty-six
❧ ♦ ♦ ☙

Clive arrived mid-Friday afternoon, along with Hassle. Richard had not been able to reach the others. As the sky darkened and brought with it the smell of another impending snow, the trio clambered into Richard's new car and drove about a mile to a small craft brewery east of Lafayette Park. Even though they preceded the Friday night dinner rush, the place was already filling with Happy Hour regulars. The hostess led them to a table about midway to the back.

Richard looked at her and smiled, "Would you have anything more private toward the back?"

She gave him a curious look before glancing at her table chart. "Um, sure."

She led them to a table for four in the far back corner.

"Perfect," said Richard as the other two took their seats. "Thank you."

After perusing the menu of house-brewed craft beers, each man ordered and made small talk until the draughts arrived.

"Okay, so . . ." Richard hesitated. He knew his limits and the need for discretion, but his need for help overrode those limitations. His handler would not be pleased, but he'd deal with that later, should the need arise.

"Yeah, man. What's the emergency?" Clive asked as he leaned backward onto the back two legs of the chair and smirked. "Need a boys' night out after working surrounded by all that estrogen?"

Richard shook his head and started at the beginning. "That dear, sweet cousin of yours may think she did me a big favor, but I'm in hot water up to my eyeballs now."

Clive raised his brow in surprise, while Hassle leaned forward to pay attention.

"Her friend, the guy she put me in contact with, is an FBI agent." He leaned forward and beckoned Clive to get closer. As soon as Clive joined the other two over the table, Richard lowered his voice and continued. "The FBI has been watching the guy I work for almost a year, but they weren't able to infiltrate his organization. At least, not successfully. The one man who tried remains unaccounted for. When they learned that I had the marketing and social media skills that Darko was looking for, combined with what they learned about my military background, they approached me about becoming a mole in the company. When I agreed, they had me apply for the job, knowing that I'd probably pass Darko's security screen. I did, and . . ."

He continued by telling his friends what he had learned, of the tenuous trust he had earned, and the upcoming party. He ended by telling them of Amy's abduction. He could see the rage building in Hassle. Hassle and Amy had much in common, and Richard knew that Jim would help in any way asked of him in order to free her. Clive was less likely to go beyond the call to rescue her, but he had other skills that Richard needed.

Hassle took a deep breath and rubbed his temples

with his hands. "What do we do? Do you have a plan?"

Clive scratched his head and asked, "Why doesn't the FBI just move in? Sounds like they have the goods on this guy now."

"Because at the first sign of trouble, Darko will eliminate any and all witnesses. That includes me. There has to be someone on the inside, and right now I'm stuck with that job."

"Lucky you."

Richard frowned at Clive. "Yeah, lucky me."

Hassle finished his beer. "So, back to my first question. Do you have a plan?"

Richard waggled his head and gave a subtle shrug.

"I have some ideas, but I'm lacking good intelligence. I don't know where the women are housed, other than they're being held at Darko's country home. I have that address and have looked at it on Google Maps, but that's as far as I can get. His chief security guy, Risto, is as bad as they come. Well-trained and, as far as I can tell, brutal and remorseless."

Richard finished his beer and held up the glass for another. After the waitress brought another round, he resumed.

"I'm pretty sure everyone entering Darko's place for this party will be searched, car and all. I don't know if there'll be a manual frisking or just a wanding. Probably both. Risto will check for wires, too. He's thorough and as paranoid as the boss."

"Won't your fibbies be monitoring this party? They'll be there, right?"

Richard made note that Clive's focus appeared to be on having the authorities handle this problem.

Maybe he was right, but something seemed off to Richard, something he couldn't quite put a mental finger on.

"I've been assured they'll have a team just down the road, but . . ."

Clive groaned. "There's always a but."

"I was going to say, but they're Feds. They can't act without a warrant. I don't know that they have one, and I want someone, two someones, whom I fully trust covering my tail." He pointed to both friends as he said that.

"I'm game," replied Hassle.

"May I point out that we're civilians now," answered Clive. "We have no authority here and could get into big-time trouble."

Richard nodded. "Don't think I haven't considered that. *I'm* the one who'll be on the inside. I need some way of defending myself and Amy, and any of the other ladies I can corral."

Clive seemed appeased, yet reticent.

"Look, Clive, these guys are as bad as any Taliban we fought and killed, but we're not in Afghanistan, and I respect our laws. I'm not looking to kill anyone, just save some."

"I hear you, Thor. Will you at least run this by your handler and see what potential risks we'd be taking?"

Richard answered without hesitation. "Nope. I don't want them to know about you, and I have no plan to put you in harm's way, or between them and Darko where they might confuse you with Darko's guys."

"Why not tell them?" asked Hassle. "I kinda have to agree with Clive on this one. We'd be in a better position legally if they knew ahead of time we're with you."

"Because something just doesn't feel right. I gave them enough intel to raid Darko's warehouse before they moved the women, but they didn't, and I don't know why. Darko's the kind of guy who covers his bases. Maybe my handler's on the take, or the judge refuses to issue a warrant because he's in debt to Darko. I don't know, but something's as hazy as a burning poppy field in Helmand Province and inhaling makes folks do funny things."

The other two men looked at each other for a moment, before Hassle nodded again. "As I said, I'm game. I've met Amy and her father, and there's no way I'm going to stand by and let them do whatever they want to her. C'mon Clive, you've seen how the Taliban and warlords misuse women. You can't sit by, knowing what's happening here. And if it's like this in St. Louis, imagine the level of trafficking in Chicagoland."

Clive let loose a long sigh and finally nodded. "Okay, I'm in."

Richard released the breath he'd been holding. "Thanks, buddy. Okay, you two, here's what I need you to do."

Forty-seven

Lynch didn't wait for Susan to arrive and took Mike's car to run an errand. Forty-five minutes later, he returned and noticed the different car parked outside the home. Using the garage door opener in the car, he waited for the door to lift, pulled into the garage, and entered the house through the kitchen. Mike stood at the counter pouring a cup of Starbuck's best from the coffeemaker. The aroma stirred around Lynch, making him salivate.

"If that's that Yukon Blend you like, pour me a cup, too, please."

Mike looked up and raised his brow in surprise.

"Lynch?" He scanned Lynch from head to toe. "Whoa, you clean up nice." He handed him the cup he'd been pouring and grabbed a second.

"Yeah, well, I decided if I'm about to re-enter the land of the living, I need to look like my old self. Have to say, I got my money's worth from that barber."

Mike laughed. "If it was my barber, he'd have done it for free just to clean that mop of hair from your head and the Duck Dynasty beard from your face."

Lynch smiled and took a sip. "You're too kind. The beard was way beyond Duck Dynasty. It screamed homeless barbarian and you know it." He used his free hand to stroke his clean jaw line. "Gotta admit, this will take some time to get used to, not to mention the time I'm going to have to spend shaving every morning. And my head sure was cold coming out of the barbershop."

Mike grinned and nodded. "You look good."

"Spoken like the military man you are." He took a deeper drink of coffee. "I take it your police friend is here. I saw a strange car outside."

Mike nodded. "She's in the library. Danijela finished her testimony about five minutes ago, and now Keisha is taking her turn.

At that moment, Danijela's voice came from the adjacent butler's pantry. "Coffee smell good and I hear Lynch voice. He back?"

Mike nodded, as he was positioned to see her coming. She would not see Lynch until she entered the room, and as she did, her brow shot up and eyes widened.

"Ohhhh," she squealed, a big smile lighting up her face. "I love, I love." She ran to him and stroked his clean face several times before planting a kiss on his cheek.

Lynch blushed.

Mike extended a cup toward her, but she waved it off and grabbed Lynch's free hand. He almost spilled his coffee as she tugged at him to follow her.

"Coffee wait. Come, come. Meet Susan. I like her already."

Lynch planted his feet, and the two came to a sudden stop. He wasn't sure if he was ready for this. "Not yet. Let her hear another testimony or two. If I go out there now, she'll end up focusing on me, not you ladies. And it's your stories she needs to hear, not mine."

Danijela gave him a pout, but nodded as she released his hand. She took her cup from the counter next to Mike and said, "I go back. Will let you know when is time."

The men both took a drink as they watched her exit the kitchen.

"Is that the only reason?" Mike smiled as he asked that.

Lynch stared at him and furrowed his brow.

"Do I sense a little bit of, um, fear might be too strong a word. Apprehension?"

"I'd be lying to say I'm not uneasy about this. I don't know what's in store for me."

Mike nodded. "None of us do. On any given day, at any given minute, we don't know what the next minute has in store for us. A guy my age could be sitting on the couch watching TV one minute and dead the next. You might feel great and the doctor gives you bad news. One second you're just a married couple, and the next you're going to be parents. All of life is uncertain."

Lynch pondered that for a moment. Mike was correct in stating the obvious, yet putting that into words gave life a different perspective.

"You know, I haven't forgotten your earlier comments about the uncertainty of life," said Lynch. "And I've watched you, and Mary, and Ibrahim. You're all willing to put your lives on the line for what is right."

Mike nodded. "Because we believe in what is right, and Godly. It's not always easy, but we know there's something better after this life, for those who believe in Christ and accept Him as Lord. The world wants to believe that all paths, all religions, lead to God and that every good person goes to heaven, nirvana, paradise, or whatever name you want to give it. But the Bible says the opposite. No one may come to God except through Christ. No one. If you wait one second too long to do that, you will never get that chance. There are no do-overs."

Lynch sat down on a stool at the breakfast bar and cradled his coffee mug in both hands. Do-overs. Wasn't that exactly what he was getting? He understood what Mike meant, no second chance after death. In his case, was he really getting a second chance? His memory had largely returned in terms of recalling certain events and people, but not so much in terms of his emotions, hopes, and dreams. In his prior life, had he sought a second chance? Had he had such regrets that he needed a do-over? Moreover, if he had, where had he stood in correcting the situation? As he mulled this over, thoughts of Amy came into his mind. Was he in need of a replay with her? Had he wronged her somehow? And what about now? He had strong feelings for Danijela. Would he have similar feelings for Amy once they re-united?

Confusion reigned.

"You know, Lynch, God is not a god of confusion. The Bible states that He gives us a sound mind, that He is the author and perfector of our faith, and that only He can make us whole."

Lynch's eyes widened. Had Mike just read his mind? Of course not. Suddenly, it was as if God was speaking to him directly through Mike, as if God now reached down from heaven beckoning him to accept the gift of grace He offered.

"Mike, I want what you all have. And I want to be whole."

"Then, let's pray."

As Danijela returned to the kitchen 30 minutes later, Lynch found a new strength rising within. He had been overwhelmed with a sense of God's love, to the point of tears flowing down his cheeks. Mike had simply nodded and said, "Happened to me, too."

Danijela looked at both men and questions could be seen in her eyes. "Okay, what happen? I tell something happen while gone. You okay, Lynch?"

Lynch smiled. "Never better."

Mike eased away from the counter where he'd been leaning and said, "C'mon Lynch, it's time for your resurrection."

The three walked through the dining room into the main entry hall. Lynch could sense Danijela's curiosity like a drill boring into his back. He chuckled inside at the thought.

As they came to the doorway to the library, Agata came through it and embraced Danijela. The translator followed and then Keisha.

"Agata wants to thank you all again for saving her and Danijela in particular for all of her kindness since she's been here, and for her encouragement in making this video."

The hug lasted longer than Lynch would find comfortable and he prepared himself for the same, but the four women moved into the parlor and he felt spared. Mike peeked through the partially closed door to see them setting up for the next woman's testimony. He nodded his head toward someone in the room.

"Susan, can you join us for a moment?"

As soon as the detective came into view, Lynch recognized her. He had met her at a conference several years earlier. A tall brunette in her late thirties, Lynch's first impression back then had been chauvinistic: she was too attractive to be a grunge detective. Yet, she was working with the MCS, so she had proved her mettle to her superiors.

In fact, she proved it to him right then, with her poker face and calm demeanor.

"So, Lynch Cully *is* alive and well." She extended her hand to him.

She showed not the least bit of surprise. She played her cards close to the vest just as Chief Dandridge had once advised him.

"Obviously alive. The 'well' part has taken some time."

Mike put his hand on Lynch's shoulder. "He has quite the story, but I can assure everyone here that in this rebirth, so to speak, he's born again in every sense of those words."

Happy murmurs arose from the parlor and library. Ibrahim emerged from the library to shake his hand. Mary and Danijela jostled each other for the first hug. Even Susan smiled for the first time.

"Praise God," said Mary.

Lynch felt surprise that the attention didn't cause embarrassment, but brought with it a spirit of welcome.

"Why don't we go upstairs to my study," said Mike. "There's a lot to talk about. Ibrahim?"

"I stay here. Help video and give my story last."

Lynch saw no reason for Ibrahim to sit in, unless

their discussion moved on to needing details about Darko's estate. Lynch recalled most of what Ibrahim had told him, and if a question came up that required more info, they could retrieve Ibrahim within a minute. Besides, they didn't need Ibrahim's distress about his sister leading them astray from the more vital points.

Forty minutes later, Lynch leaned back in his chair, placed his hands behind his head, and stretched. Susan's professionalism had faltered once or twice, with her emotions emerging as he told his story. Now, he waited for her to speak.

She scrutinized him and appeared to choose her words carefully. "So, why did you contact me? We've only met the one time, and Janick already believes you're alive. I was with him when Jusuf, you, called. He's already conferred with Colonel Halbert and Chief Dandridge. They've been looking for you."

Lynch eased forward, despite the unease he felt at that revelation. That now placed his old boss into the ring of suspicion, too. "If I called Janick or walked into the department, I'd be escorted to a hospital for medical testing, which I don't really need. I owe a debt to Danijela, and I don't want to risk being removed from this case until I know she'll be safe." He paused and watched her reaction. She revealed nothing. "Actually, I talked with Chief Dandridge earlier today. I convinced him to keep this in confidence until I was ready."

She took that news calmly, too.

"What I didn't tell him, was what I was involved with here. Something inside made me hesitant. We called you because Mike suggested it, and I've grown to trust his instincts."

This time she looked surprised.

"You didn't confide in the Chief?" She paused this time, apparently watching his response. "I was always under the impression you two were like this." She crossed her right middle and index fingers.

"Maybe. It's stuff like that I have a hard time remembering. Events, dates, names—those are the things coming back to me."

She responded with a subtle nod.

"You do realize I should call this in, arrest Ibrahim on the spot, and get the MCS moving on these women's statements?"

Lynch nodded in return. He began to have second thoughts about contacting her. Maybe she was more "by the book" than he'd hoped.

"But you won't."

Lynch turned, surprised to hear Mike speak up.

"You won't because you know that Lynch's hesitation to tell the chief everything has more behind it than meets the eye. You also know that to do what you say will jeopardize every woman still under this Darko's control because we don't know who's on the take with him. We know at least one local judge was corrupted by this character. How many others might there be? You'll need warrants, and the wrong judge could mean a death sentence to these women."

"Not to mention putting your friends here, Mike and Mary, in jeopardy," added Lynch.

Susan did not reply.

"How would you feel if the wrong person got wind

358

of this and notified Darko, who then ordered hits on your friends?" He watched for her reaction and realized he'd hit the right nerve.

Lynch continued. "I know you're thinking you can take this to a female judge, that a woman would be sympathetic. I thought that, until I saw an internet article about a woman judge whose housekeeper was an illegal alien she kept as slave labor. Not all trafficking is about sex. Do you know the local women judges well enough to gamble these women's lives?"

"So, what do you want me to do? *You* called me. You've told me your story, and I've heard two of the women give statements. Now, it's like you're handcuffing me and putting duct tape across *my* mouth."

Lynch sighed. She was right. There was one other avenue they could travel. Only now did it come to mind. If he'd thought of it earlier, they might not have had to involve her. However, her help would come in handy.

"We have a dilemma. Darko has Ibrahim's sister, but we don't know where. Ibrahim wants to raid Darko's place tonight, to save her, but he realizes the risk of moving on the wrong place. Or, for that matter, the risks of moving on the right place. We need more intel, and Ibrahim ran into a guy who maybe could help. We don't have a name, just his license plate and the fact that he works at Darko's import business but was snooping around in the middle of the night, acting very suspicious. Can you get us a name and phone number?"

Susan nodded. "Sure, that's an easy one."

"After that, check around, quietly. See if you can find a judge who's unlikely to be in cahoots with this guy. We'll need a name and contact info for some fast warrants if it comes to that. Third, if you think it's okay, you can tell Janick about our meeting. We've had our differences, but as I think about it, I know him well enough to believe he's clean. He lives alone. His apartment is a dump, and even though he can't afford a cleaning service, he'd never stoop to slave labor. Plus, his neighbors are as nosy as they come. If he kept a woman at his place, it wouldn't be a secret.

"He could still be on the dole," said Mike.

Lynch shook his head. "Don't think so. If he had a second source of income, he'd be living the lifestyle, flashing it around. He's not smart enough to keep it secret, invest it, and delay the self-gratification until retirement."

Susan chuckled. "That part I have to agree with. Okay, I won't go straight to him with this, but if I need his backup, I'll consider it." She paused. "It's Thursday night. Give me a day to find this guy you want. Maybe I'll have a judge by then, too."

"Deal, but let us contact this guy. I'm sure he'll remember Ibrahim. Not too many people are confronted by a man with a foreign accent aiming a gun at you. To have that same man find out your name and phone number, well, I think he'll cooperate faster with us than with you."

Susan smiled. "I'll pretend I didn't hear that. I could lose my badge over this, if things go badly."

Lynch stood. "Naw, I've got your back. Your name will never be mentioned if that happens. But, you know something? All of a sudden I feel like everything is going to go our way."

Forty-eight

❧ ♦ ♦ ❧

Richard and his buddies had spent Friday morning occupied by their respective tasks. Hassle's had been the easiest, and now they had a new recruit, Amy's father. Lt. Col. Gibbs had easily come up with two AR-15s with sniper scopes, and the two were off canvassing Darko's estate, looking for high ground where they could cover Richard's escape with Amy, and anyone else he could get out, should that be necessary.

Clive had set up shop on Richard's kitchen table. As afternoon approached Happy Hour, Richard watched as his friend placed the finishing touches on Thor's hammer.

"Wow, that looks just like it did before you modified it. Great job." Richard stood there, thoroughly impressed not only with his friend's craftsmanship but also with his ingenuity.

He picked up the hammer and swung it up and around in a circle over his head.

"I can't even tell if there's a weight difference."

Clive nodded. "The difference is only a few ounces right now, but once we add the juice, it'll be close to a pound heavier. I'm happy with that, and that weight change sure won't affect *your* swing. I could add five pounds and you'd still be picking it up as if it were a fly swatter."

Richard nodded. He hoped to swat some "flies" with it. The more he thought about their taking Amy, the more he realized they had done so because of him.

What other reason could there possibly be? Did Darko now see him as a threat, or did he think he could use Amy as insurance for Richard's silence? Richard leaned toward the latter explanation, as he had done nothing threatening to Darko. Or had he? Had Darko found out about his visit to the women's quarters?

"Here, give it back and I'll charge it. Then, we can give it a quick test outside."

As Richard handed it back to Clive, his cell phone rang. The number was not a familiar one.

"Hello?"

"Richard Nichols, we must talk."

He felt the blood drain from his face. The voice was one he would not soon forget—the mysterious man outside his car just a few nights earlier. He motioned to Clive to join him and placed the phone on speaker.

"What . . .? H-how did you get this number?" If this man could trace his phone number, did he also know where Richard lived?

"Is no important. We must talk. We have common enemy, yes?"

Richard's mind raced. Did they? Was this man after Darko, too? Just how much did they have in common? He took a deep breath and forced himself to be calm, as he had done in Afghanistan before every patrol or excursion outside their base. He needed to think clearly.

What should he say? If he admitted that Darko was an enemy, well, maybe the guy actually worked for Darko. Then, he might as well admit the same thing to Darko directly.

"Who are you and what makes you think I have an enemy?"

"All man have enemy. Some physical, some not. Sometime people, sometime not." The voice on the other end of the phone paused, as if to let that sink in. The man continued, "I, too, once work for Darko. Now, he is enemy. He hold my sister, just like he hold your friend."

"H-how do you know this?" Richard wondered if he was being baited. How could this man know about Amy?

"Is no important."

Clive kept shaking his head and using battlefield sign language to show his distrust. Richard felt reassured that his friend shared his suspicions.

"It is to me. How do I know you don't still work for Darko and are testing me for some reason? I like the work I'm doing. Darko has given me a good job and has been more than generous with my pay and benefits."

Thinking on his feet, Richard had decided to throw in those last comments in case he *was* being tested. In reality, he was being truthful. He had a great job. Just a not so good boss. No, make that a really nasty boss. He hated being caught in the crossfire between Darko and the good guys. Even worse, he hated Amy's being caught in that same crossfire.

"Do name Ibrahim mean anything to you?"

"No."

"Danijela?"

"No, again."

"Aida Tadić?"

This time Richard paused. What did this man know about Aida? He still did not know enough about this man to trust him.

"Yes, that name mean something. I sense it, and you pause. No reply. She not deserve to die by Risto's hand."

Richard heard two other voices on the other end, American voices, one female. There was more noise. Someone else was taking the phone.

"Richard, this is Detective Susan Prichard of the St. Charles Police. I'm currently assigned to the Major Case Squad, and Ibrahim, the man who called you, is working with me. I'm the one who traced your phone number, and it was purely coincidence at the MCS that I heard it was you who had called in a possible kidnapping of a friend. The Saint Peters Police are working on that case and have called in the FBI."

Richard still had his suspicions.

"How can I confirm what you're telling me?"

"Here's my badge number." She rattled off her number. "You can call the St. Charles Police to confirm it."

Clive nodded vigorously and slid his hand across his throat to encourage Richard to disconnect.

"Call me back in five." He hung up before getting a reply.

Lynch sat back in his chair and sighed. He had no argument with having Ibrahim make the call. That part of the plan had worked. The intimidation factor of hearing Ibrahim on the phone had gotten the man's attention. Yet, the man's level of suspicion, while not unexpected, did make things more difficult.

"I   guess   he's   actually   calling   the   police

department," said Susan. "I always figured just giving my badge number was enough reassurance for most people."

"Probably. For some reason, though, I don't think that's going to reassure him as much as we'd like," replied Lynch.

Susan nodded. "Maybe. Maybe not. He's right to be suspicious. My badge number is easy enough to get. Any woman could call and use that ploy, if she had the number. In addition, this Darko guy sounds like he has the resources to get just about any info he wants. So, even if he calls the department and confirms my number, why should he trust that alone?"

"My point exactly," said Lynch.

"So, what if he not play ball?" asked Ibrahim.

Lynch shrugged. "Then we're still on our own. Reaching out to him was a long shot anyway."

"Then I get ready." Ibrahim stood and moved toward the door.

"Ready for what?"

"To go to warehouse. Is less risk."

Lynch shook his head. "I thought we talked about that already. They'll expect you to go there first. If she's there, they'll have her well guarded."

Ibrahim nodded. "Yes. As I would do. But is still less risk than going to estate right now. I will go with, without help. She is—"

The ringing of Susan's cell phone interrupted him.

Susan furrowed her brow as she looked at the phone. "It's my department." She accepted the call. "Prichard."

A smile crossed her lips. "Our friend is more

resourceful than we thought," she said toward Lynch. Back to the phone she said, "Yes, I'll take the call." She put the phone on speaker and placed it on the desk.

"This is Detective Prichard."

"Good. This is Richard Nichols. I figured anyone could call and claim to be you, and have your badge number. But only your department could patch me through to your phone."

"Good thinking, Richard. Can we talk you into helping us?"

"I was thinking more of asking you to help me, but we can call it a mutual thing. If Ibrahim is who he says he is, then I have to figure he's already told you all about Darko."

"He has."

"Then, for obvious reasons, you know the fewer people who are in on this the better. The Navy said it best, 'Loose lips sink ships.' How many people know about this?"

"We understand. There are four of us here. The Major Case Squad has not been formally involved yet."

"Okay. On my end, there's a team of Feds I've been providing intel to, but I'm growing suspicious of my handler. They could have acted by now, with what I've given them, but they haven't. Also, there are four of us. My friend's father, retired Army, two Army buddies of mine, plus me."

Lynch smiled. This guy was *a lot* more resourceful than he'd expected. Susan, however, looked dour.

"Whatever you guys are planning, you realize you run a risk of breaking the law. I can't ask you to do that. I think we—"

"You didn't *ask us* to do anything, detective. We're set to go, with or without you."

"But, you need—"

"No, detective, we've thought this through. My friend is in trouble, and we're prepared to get her out. And if we get into trouble, we're prepared to make the Feds and local police look like fools in the press. Once the full story gets out, no jury I know of is likely to convict us of anything."

Susan started to answer, but Lynch stopped her. She put her phone on mute.

"He may or may not be right," said Lynch, "but let him keep on thinking that. We need his help, and if he starts having second thoughts, we might not get it."

Susan nodded and resumed the call.

"Okay. So what can we do?" she said to Richard.

"I'm not sure. Here's where we stand. Darko's having a big party tomorrow night and I'm invited. I suspect he plans to test my loyalty. I have a plan to free my friend. That's as much as I want to tell you."

Lynch raised his eyebrows. Tomorrow night didn't give them much time to prepare, but Ibrahim was champing at the bit. Maybe it would be best to channel that energy sooner, rather than later.

"We can help. Ibrahim knows the estate and house well, but we might need more time."

"Don't have more time. Tomorrow's the big show. I didn't set the date."

Susan took a deep breath and looked at Lynch, then Ibrahim. Both men nodded.

"So, again, what can we do?"

"Not sure. Ibrahim mentioned his sister. What's

with that?"

"Darko took his sister to flush him out. We were hoping you could help us pinpoint where she is. That's why we called in the first place."

There was a pause on the other end.

"I'm not sure how I can help."

"We suspect she's being held at the estate or at the warehouse. If it's the latter, we'd like to get her out before taking on the estate."

Lynch heard a murmur of voices from the other end, before Richard replied, "How soon can you meet me there? At the warehouse."

Lynch signaled 30 minutes.

"Thirty minutes, at most."

"See you there," answered Richard and the line disconnected.

Lynch was about to say something, but Ibrahim was already up and out the door.

Forty-nine

Amy's initial anger had slowly devolved into boredom. She and the other women had little to do. No, make that nothing to do, but at least they had not been disturbed. She'd been fed and the food was good, even if the company held a lot to be desired.

Amy paced across the room for the hundredth-something time that day. She again tried her hand at opening the door, to no avail. At least in a real prison, the inmate had access to reading material to combat the monotony. Here, she had no interest in the porn available in the room, and no one responded to her request for a good book. And forget television. One of the few things she had pulled from Irina was that the house had no television, except for a large screen in the master bedroom, which played only DVD's and other homemade video. Amy had no desire to see that setup, and the thought of what they might watch sickened her.

Amy glanced back across the room to where Miloska napped on the bed. The woman had not spoken another word to her since introducing herself and Irina upon Amy's awakening. Amy had caught the two women speaking to each other, in a foreign language, but both quieted when Amy would approach.

Two hours earlier, an armed thug had opened the door and commanded Irina to follow him. Amy felt grateful that he hadn't come for her.

She looked again at Miloska. Maybe she had the right idea. Napping would kill some time, but would she be able to sleep that night? Amy sat on the edge of the bed, away from Miloska, and as she contemplated lying down, the door opened and Irina walked into the room. Amy caught only a brief glimpse of the man who had escorted Irina back to the room. He was different from the first man, but to say more than that, she didn't have enough information to work with. Could either of them be bribed, or somehow convinced to help her? Unlikely.

Irina saw her on the bed and nodded. "Ready for a nap?"

Those were the first words from Irina this day. Was the woman ready to talk? Amy needed more information. She needed to talk with Irina or anyone else who could help. Even the smallest tidbit of information about the house—its layout, the property, anything—could come in handy if an opportunity arose to run for it.

"Irina, I need your—"

The woman cut her off with her hands. Amy noticed her position in the room and how she kept her hands directly in front of her. Keeping her arms still and moving her hands from her wrists only, Irina kept pointing over her left shoulder. Amy kept her head faced forward and glanced up with her eyes. Of course! Why hadn't she noticed it before? A camera lens, partially hidden above a tapestry. Irina had placed her body between the camera and Amy, so she could signal without being spotted.

"Come. I need to show you how to get ready." Irina moved toward the bathroom and motioned for Amy to follow.

"Ready for what?"

"Come with me."

Amy had explored the bath area. Besides a large whirlpool tub lined with candles, she had found a large shower enclosure, a fully stocked, well-lit cosmetic bar, and a walk-in closet area stuffed with kinky costumes and elegant gowns from size six to sixteen. The camera she discovered above the tub was not connected to the coaxial cable coming out of the wall.

By the time Amy joined Irina there, the other woman had turned on the shower and steam from the hot water rose up and over the enclosure's glass walls. As Amy entered, Irina put her finger to her lips.

"Must whisper. Even with the water running, Darko's microphones are sensitive. Give the water a minute and the camera lens will steam up." In a normal voice, she continued, "What size are you? Tomorrow night, we are expected to join Darko and his guests for dinner. After dinner, we will be with Richard."

Amy shook her head, "I'm not—"

"What size are you?" Irina asked again. After asking, she glanced toward the camera.

"Twelve tall."

Irina walked into the closet area and pulled out several size twelve gowns. "You can try these on later." In a whisper, she said, "The camera's almost ready."

Amy whispered, "I didn't think the camera was connected."

"That's the old coax. He upgraded them to wireless with USB connections," Irina replied. She looked again at the camera and smiled. "Okay, the lens is covered. Take one of these out to the mirror and hold it up to yourself." She extended two gowns toward Amy.

"Seriously, I'm not going along—"

"Amy, humor me. I don't want to see you involved anymore than you do. But, unless you want to get hurt, play along. You can't get out. The grounds are patrolled by dogs. You wouldn't make it to the front gate."

Amy thought about that. She had wanted information. She hadn't expected it to look hopeless.

She did as Irina instructed, holding each dress up to her body. She glanced at the labels. These were high quality eveningwear. "I don't know. What do you think?"

Irina came out and wiped the mirror with a towel.

"Maybe a different one," she replied.

Amy followed her back to the closet. "Won't he get suspicious with the camera being fogged up?"

Irina shook her head. "Happens all the time, but I wanted to make sure we could talk." She reached up to her bra top and pulled out a cigarette lighter. "See where I'm hiding it. We might need it."

Amy furrowed her brow. What could a lighter do, start a fire and kill them from smoke inhalation?

"Don't blame Richard. Believe it or not, he's trying to help us, and he can't do that if he's dead, too. Our best chance to get out of this is to play along during dinner and hope he has a plan for afterward."

Amy felt chagrined. She had been thinking the worst about Richard and that his after dinner plans included the three of them for dessert. Now, maybe she saw a ray of sunshine breaking through the gray clouds. Another thought came to mind.

"Irina, did you know that Richard was called Thor in the Army?"

Fifty

❧ ✦ ✦ ☙

"Are you sure about this?" asked Clive as Richard parked his car outside the warehouse.

"You said we needed to test it, right?"

"Yeah, but I thought maybe aiming it toward a tree or something. What if it doesn't work as designed?"

"It'll work. I have every faith in your skills, old buddy."

Clive shook his head. "I don't know about this."

"Relax. Trust me."

"I've heard that before."

"Look, just pretend I'm showing you where I work. Go with the flow. Thor will take care of the rest."

"Maybe I should be armed."

"C'mon, let's go. Just act normal."

Clive took a deep breath and exited the car. He followed Richard toward the man-gate where Richard swiped his key card and opened the locked gate. A minute later, he repeated that action of the man door to the loading area. As they entered the building, a young man Richard had never seen emerged from the security office.

"Hey, no one's allowed in here. We're closed." He made no secret that he was armed, although, in Richard's way of thinking, his first mistake was in not having the gun in his hand.

Richard quickly realized he needed to change his tactic. The man obviously didn't know him either.

"I work here, idiot. How else would I have unlocked

the door and just walked in?" He glowered at the man. "Who are you and where is Risto? I was told to meet him here." Richard's tone was aggressive and intimidating, which along with his size and build achieved what he wanted. The man looked unsure and uneasy, but still made no move for his weapon. An amateur.

"I am Rico. No one told me . . ."

"Do we have to tell you everything?" Richard's heart raced, but he kept up the act. He took several steps toward the man, who reacted by taking one step back.

"No, of course. Who's that?" He pointed to Clive.

"He's with me. You don't need to know who he is."

This time the man began to look concerned, and his hand inched closer to his holstered weapon.

"What's that in your hand?"

"A souvenir."

"A what?"

"A souvenir. I worked security for Marvel, when they made the Thor movie. I got this hammer prop as a reward. I came by to secure it in my office."

Now the man relaxed and actually smiled. "No kiddin'. Thor's hammer?"

"Yeah, kid. Thor's hammer." Richard walked right toward the guy. "See? Pretty realistic, huh?"

By this point, Richard was in striking distance and before the man's eyes could widen, he encountered Thor's hammer up close and personal. He hit the floor with a solid thump.

Richard smiled and brushed the top of the hammer. "Yep, nice fly swatter."

Clive stood there with both hands on his hips. "Really? Did you just say that? What happened to showing my friend my office? What happened to testing my additions? Q would be proud, you know. Bond never had such a hammer."

"Save it, Clive. Help me secure him and put him someplace safe."

"You know, you didn't need my additions to do what you just did."

Richard nodded, and the two men bound the unconscious guard with hefty zip ties and dragged him into the room off the security office. As they dumped him there, both men looked around.

"Whoa, glad I'm seeing this room with you and not at the whim of that Risto character. I don't want to know what happened in this room." Clive eased back to the door.

Bloodstains surrounded a metal chair, which had one leg connected to the negative pole of a car battery. A small table next to it held a variety of garden and surgical tools. Richard, too, did not want to know what they'd been used for.

"C'mon. Let's check the women's quarters. If they have Ibrahim's sister here, that's where she'll be."

The two men hurried down the hallway and headed toward the locked door.

"With a little luck, my alterations to the door are intact." Richard counted on the idea that anyone coming to open the door would simply use his key fob or whatever else he used to open electronically the lock before getting to the door. After all, it was locked, right? Who would think to check the latch?

As they turned the corner toward the door, Richard noted the red light blinking. So far, so good. The next step would be critical. Was there a guard behind the door? The lady or the tiger? Or both?

"Time to see if this hammer is up to the task," Richard whispered.

He eased open the door. The lights were on and the static-laced noise of the old television set could be heard from the central living area. Someone was indeed home. He motioned Clive to hang back and crept down the hall. As he came into view of the dilapidated dining table he saw another strange male face, but this time he had no delusion of pulling off the same deception. He charged ahead, but his hand rested higher up on the hammer's handle.

The man started and reached for the handgun resting on the table in front of him. As the man turned toward him, Richard pressed a hidden button on the bottom of the hammer's head and a stream of fluid spewed across the remaining ten feet between them. With a slight tweak in his aim, Richard easily doused the man's face and the guard's hands flew to his face as his mouth screamed in agony. The gun fell to the floor and Richard jumped on the guy, pinning him to the ground. As the man started to put up a brief fight, the hammer took down its second fly.

Clive rushed in to assist, and a moment later, their second conquest lay there bound by zip ties. Clive looked around and found a scratched-up Tupperware pitcher. He walked into the bathroom and filled it with water, which he then poured over the man's face. He repeated that action two more times.

"Don't want him blind for life. Our taxes would just end up supporting him."

Richard nodded, but he wasn't sure society would be better off with this guy having full visual capacity. "That Grizzly Bear Spray took him down immediately. Good stuff. And the hidden dispenser worked just like I knew it would. I never doubted your design or craftsmanship. Maybe you should branch out from graphic design. I bet there's a market for things like this in the world of security."

"Sure. I can sell Thor's hammer at 'QVC' or hawk it on 'As Seen on TV.' I'm sure they'll sell by the thousands." The skepticism in his voice was clear.

The two men turned as one as they heard a muffled commotion coming from the bedroom furthest from the table. Richard entered the room first and found a woman—twenty-something by his guess, with long, dark hair—hog-tied and gagged, lying on the bed, her back to them. He touched her and she began to struggle. He managed, with difficulty, to turn her over to face them.

"Ibrahim sent us. Shhhh . . ."

She gazed into his face, and he saw the black eyes, the split lip. She winced as he again touched her shoulder. The bruise there was covered by her shirt. She had been worked over by someone who knew how to prolong the torture.

"He'll be here any minute. Let me untie you, and we'll get you out of here."

She nodded and relaxed.

Two minutes later, as Clive led the way, hammer in hand and his finger on the button, Richard carried the woman toward the loading area and the door leading to her freedom. As soon as Clive opened the door, three people rushed toward them. Since one was a woman, Richard assumed they were Ibrahim, Detective Prichard, and the man whose name he did not know, but whose voice he heard behind the scenes during the phone call.

"*Sestra, jesi li dobro*?" Sister, are you okay? The man took the young woman from Richard's arms, stroked her hair and carried her away.

"I'm Detective Prichard. You must be Richard Nichols."

Richard nodded and extended his hand. As they shook, he said, "This is my friend, Clive, a.k.a. Q. Thanks to his artistry and ingenuity . . ." Clive held up Thor's hammer. ". . . we have minimal casualties. Two men, secured with zip ties are inside. You might want a crime scene unit here. When we moved the first guard into the room off the security office, we found some grizzly stuff. Something else took place in that room and it wasn't pretty."

Richard noted the man who accompanied Ibrahim and Prichard and thought he looked familiar. The man appeared to be scrutinizing him, sizing him up.

The detective replied, "I guess I need to say good job. I thought this was going to be a team effort, but you obviously didn't need us."

Richard shrugged. "It helped that I work here, remember? I have the keys to the building and have been here long enough to see how they can operate. I don't know how all this goes, but on TV I'd have to stick around and give a statement or something to the police.

Do we need to do that?"

Prichard shook her head. "Not tonight. I'll get someone I trust to pick up the two men, and we'll put a surveillance team or two on the place, in case they have a relief crew coming in. We'll lock the place down until this whole thing is tied up. Then we'll work the crime scene."

"Look, we'd like to talk with you about tomorrow night." It was the unidentified man speaking.

"And you are?" asked Richard.

"That's not important right now. We need to know what your plan is and how we can help. You were correct on the phone when you said you have the best opportunity by being inside. There must be some way we can assist."

Richard gazed at the man. He didn't like the man's choosing to remain anonymous. Worse, he didn't like the fact that the man looked so familiar but he couldn't put a mental finger on why or where.

How much should he share? He made a snap decision to tell the truth, just not all of it. He wouldn't compromise Hassle or Lt. Col. Gibbs. He wouldn't have exposed Clive either, but they hadn't gotten outside in time to let Clive melt into the side streets before this trio showed up.

"To be honest, I'm winging it. I don't know the floor plan of the place, how it sits on the property, where the women are being held, or anything. I know their security chief won't let anything slide, so I'll have no chance of slipping a gun in with me. I'm hoping to be able to get my trusty hammer in, to 'entertain' them, you might say."

The man looked incredulous as he stared at the hammer.

"Don't let its stage prop appearance fool you. It'll pass through any metal detector and will pack a punch when needed. Just ask the two losers inside."

"What about dogs?"

Richard had forgotten about the dogs. Now, he wished he could still forget them. They weren't just dogs, they were beasts from Hades.

"Um, I forgot about the dogs. I saw them outside here the other night." He paused. "I'm pretty sure I can disable them, but—"

"No buts on these dogs. They'll take you out if you don't take them first. Tell you what, we'll deal with the dogs and any other guards we can disable outside. That'll help free up your escape route. We might be able to help in one other way. Can we text you on that phone?"

"Sure."

"Keep it on tonight. You'll hear from us."

Fifty-one

❧ ♦ ♦ ❧

"Quit pacing!" Hassle motioned with his hands for Richard to stop.

Richard stopped long enough to look at his friend and replied, "What did I do before every patrol we made in Afghanistan?"

"You paced," said Clive. "And then you'd go off to a corner of the compound and throw up. Your nervous stomach was the talk of the company. So, you gonna go into the corner of your living room and barf?"

"No. I thought I'd wait and do that part at Darko's place. Make it symbolic." He resumed wearing the carpet thin, only to stop at the other end of his living room. "Sorry. It's my way of . . ."

". . . letting off steam!" Hassle and Clive said in unison with Richard.

"We know," said Hassle. "Neither of us would need a job if we had a buck for every time you told us that overseas." He grinned and checked his watch. "Colonel Gibbs should be here any moment, and we'll be heading out. You know where we'll be set up, right?"

Richard nodded. "And Clive will be nearby with the backup getaway car. Yeah, I know where you'll be. What I don't know is if the Feds will be there, or how we're going to team up with Ibrahim and Nameless." He had taken to calling the stranger that name out of a lack of any other moniker. He still hadn't placed why the guy looked so familiar, but then, his mind had been preoccupied.

Despite trying to will his body to sleep the previous night, he hadn't succeeded. About one a.m., his phone chimed with a new text message, and Nameless had come through. Attached to the message were three JPEG files, each holding a detailed sketch of some aspect of Darko's estate—the grounds with notations on gates, security cams, and more; the main floor of the house; and more importantly, the lower level with its holding rooms and a place called "The Harem." Ibrahim suspected that Amy would be held there. Richard had been up until three a.m. memorizing the details. Only then had he been able to fall asleep.

Clive pointed to his attire and asked, "Is that what you're wearing? From the looks of the floor plans, I expected the invitation to be white tie or something. The place would sit well with the pashas of the Ottoman Empire."

"I was told just business casual. This is what I've got."

"Maybe we should take you shopping on the way out there," replied Clive.

Hassle laughed. "But I'm sure he's got his Mickey Mouse boxers on to impress the ladies afterward."

"Not funny," answered Richard. He had given in and told them about the proposed foursome, and until now, they had been circumspect in their comments. He knew he'd be the brunt of their humor before the day was over. *Their* way of letting off steam. He didn't push them.

The doorbell rang, followed by the sound of footfall on the stairs.

"Must be the colonel," said Hassle. "I told him just

to come on up." He got up and opened the door to the apartment.

A moment later, Amy's father appeared at the open doorway. He looked as if he hadn't slept all night. Richard surmised that he hadn't. He knew he wouldn't have slept had *his* daughter been kidnapped.

"Sir, are you okay? Are you sure you want to go with us?" asked Richard.

"Of course I'm going. I'm surprised you'd even ask me that," he snapped back. "Sorry, I haven't slept and I'm running on caffeine." He looked at Hassle. "Hope you don't mind if I power nap while you drive. I'll be okay."

Hassle nodded and stood up. The colonel tossed his car keys at the younger man.

"We can take my car. All our gear is in the trunk, and we don't have to look suspicious moving it to another vehicle." He smiled, but the effort came off half-hearted.

Richard knew this whole thing was taking its toll on the man.

"Colonel, I'm really sorry about this. It's my fault and—"

"Nonsense. It was this Darko character's choice to involve my daughter, not something you did. Now, he's going to find out what kind of father, and friends, she has."

Richard noticed he'd already become more animated, more alert. Every soldier who'd been on a front line could recognize the adrenaline rush. He gave the colonel and Hassle a fifteen-minute head start, and then he and Clive moved out as well in their separate vehicles.

Lynch and Ibrahim drove past Darko's estate just after noon that day. Mike had wanted to join them, but Lynch had tasked him, along with his wife, with making sure the video testimonies were completed and compiled into a suitable format to present to the media as well as law enforcement. Should he and Ibrahim not return, he needed to know their efforts would not have been in vain.

Just beyond the property boundary, an old farm lane came off the highway and skirted the south side of Darko's land. Ibrahim pulled off the main road and nosed up to the chain that closed off the gravel lane. He jumped out of the car, grabbed a chain cutter from the back seat, and dropped the barrier within ten seconds. Remembering the chain at the old man's river cabin, and with the car on the other side of the barricade, he placed the chain onto a rusty nail to give the appearance it was secure. From there, he drove slowly down the lane for about half a mile and pulled off into a widened spot covered with gravel.

"From here it is half-hour walk to fence," Ibrahim stated. "At place where you can see fence, must start to look for security cameras, too."

Lynch nodded. They'd gone through this before. He retrieved his gear from the car's trunk and checked his cell phone for a signal. He hadn't expected one and seeing zero bars did not surprise him. That made communications a problem. They hadn't been able to obtain any other form of short-range com equipment on short notice.

"We'll need to stay within sight of each other," he said as he held up the phone. "No using these out here."

Ibrahim nodded. "As I expect. Better we stay together anyway." He tucked his 9mm handgun into its holster and shouldered his pack. "Ready?"

"Lead the way."

Ibrahim eased off toward the north, following a dry creek bed part of the way. They were in no hurry as they had hours before the dinner party. Their goal for the afternoon was to monitor the security patrols to see if they held to strict timing, routine paths, or any other form of regularity that would make them easier to predict. They were also on the lookout for the dogs. Lynch especially wanted no additional run-ins with any one of the beasts. This time, as much as he disliked the idea, he was prepared to shoot and kill if necessary.

Thirty minutes later, Ibrahim slowed down and pointed toward a tree. Lynch saw a camera aimed parallel to the ten-foot-tall chain link fence he also saw for the first time. He moved with caution toward the tree, but behind the camera's field of view. He noticed a detached coaxial cable and thinking the camera was out of commission he reached for it. Ibrahim stayed his hand.

"Not yet touch." He fingered the dangling cable. "From old system. Now is wireless." He pointed to a box attached to the tree above the camera. "Battery and transmitter. We disable in two, three hour. Might bring man out to fix." He then turned and pointed farther along the fence behind them. "There is next camera, but range not so good. Can detect us moving here, but not give clear image. From here, we go straight toward fence and use camouflage."

Ibrahim pulled a winter-forest camouflage sheet from his pack and draped it around his head and body. Lynch copied his action.

"From here to fence, move slow, stop. Move again, stop. We stop ten foot from fence and sit and watch. Should have full view of open ground and back of house."

After a painfully slow stop'n go toward the fence, Ibrahim sat on the dry leaves, covered with his sheet. Lynch started to sit next to him.

"No. Move away. Camouflage become more noticed if we together."

Lynch moved five, six feet away and sat. No sooner had he done so, he saw movement to his left and watched as Ibrahim pulled his sheet around him, hiding his face. He quickly copied and watched as a man and dog walked close by. The dog stopped and stared their way, but the light breeze was in their favor and after a moment, the two moved on. Lynch made note of the time.

For the first time, Lynch had the opportunity to see and study the house, if one could call it that. He'd only seen pictures of homes that big.

"Wow, how big is that place?" he asked when he was sure the dog was out of hearing range.

Ibrahim opened up the sheet to expose his face. "Twelve thousand foot square. Six acre to back. Yard and flower garden. Is beautiful in summer. Not so much now and we must run cross it, wide open."

As Lynch surveyed the area, he saw some hedges

they could use for cover and one larger line of evergreens close to the mansion they could definitely use to their advantage. However, he realized, if he saw that as an advantage, he knew a well trained security team would have it covered somehow, knowing it as a weakness. He and Ibrahim discussed their options and timed the single patrol as the afternoon crawled by and the light began to wane. According to Ibrahim, they would let the dogs run loose soon, and the guard would move to watch the house.

"Now," said Ibrahim. "Cameras not so good in low light, but infrared kick on soon. Run and pull wire from battery. I work on first dog."

Lynch saw him pull a bacon-wrapped "treat" of hamburger and Benadryl from his pack. As Lynch performed his task, he saw Ibrahim begin to cut a small section from the chain links. The hole was large enough to move his arm through and allow Ibrahim to toss the treat onto the path used by the patrol. Lynch checked his watch. If Ibrahim was correct, the final patrol would be there soon.

Their jobs completed, they moved back into position to watch and wait.

Right on schedule, the man and his Bandog came into view to their left. About 30 feet away, the man's radio chirped, and he lifted it to his head. Lynch couldn't hear what was said, but saw the man nod. He released the dog and gave some command that sent the dog into circling the area. The man came to within fifteen feet of them and lifted binoculars to his eyes. Lynch watched him gaze right over them toward the camera. He then radioed back to the house in his native language and called for the dog.

Lynch had focused on the man and didn't see the dog until it approached. It stopped and began to sniff and nose around the ground. Lynch watched as it found the "treat" and took it in its mouth. The man began to scold it. Lynch assumed he was trying to stop the dog from eating whatever it had, but he was too late. The dog consumed it in two gulps. The man continued to berate the animal, while Lynch prayed silently that the treat would accomplish their goal—one drugged dog. Just two to go.

Fifty-two

❧ ♦ ❧

Amy gazed at her image in the lightly fogged mirror. She had to admit that she looked good. Miloska was a master with makeup, and Irina could handle hair like the best salon stylists. The gown? Well, only while playing dress-up as a little girl had she ever envisioned herself wearing such a garment. A one-of-a-kind Givenchy was not in her budget. Irina's requests that she "play along" didn't fit her either. In a sense, though, the person staring back *wasn't* her.

Amy had struggled with Irina's request all night long. She couldn't convince herself that she was a good enough actor to play a role. Nor could she convince herself that playing along would be to her advantage. The only thing she had convinced herself of was that Richard wasn't the bad guy. In fact, she expected he had contacted the police after her disappearance during their phone call. In an all-too-brief dream, she saw him coming with a fall cadre of officers to rescue her.

As she daydreamed, she heard the door open and a male voice say, "Come!"

She hurried to the bedroom to see Irina and Miloska heading toward the door. Irina stopped and faced her.

"Darko just wants the two of us right now. He does not trust you to behave during dinner with his clients."

"What? Why am I all dressed up then?"

"He will call for you after dinner. Please. Think again about what I ask of you."

Amy saw the pleading in her eyes. She started to reply, but stopped. Nothing she could say would change anything right now. She gave her head a single nod and watched as the two women left the room.

No sooner had the door closed than she was at the door trying to open it, hoping the goon had failed to close it tightly. No such luck. In disappointment, she resigned herself to wait and sat down in the only comfortable chair in the room. She would wait, but when called she would . . . she would . . . she would what? She hated the loss of control. Then she thought, *If I've lost control already, why not really lose it when the time comes?*

Richard pulled his Lexus up to the guardhouse and saw Sergei through his window. He powered down his window and nodded to the man, who in turn, left the small building and walked around the car, peering into the windows. He came up to the driver's window.

"Evening, Sergei. Haven't seen you at the warehouse recently."

"Trunk."

Despite the winter evening's chill, a bead of sweat appeared on Richard's forehead. He complied and pulled the release for the trunk's latch. Would Sergei question its contents, his hammer?

Richard heard the lid slide open and just as quickly close. He sighed in relief. So far, so good.

"Drive to main parking and find spot. Risto meet you at main door."

With no further word, the man slipped back into

the guardhouse and sat stone-faced looking out the window. In reflection, Richard realized he'd never gotten much more out of the man at work either. He also recognized that leaving his hammer in the open in the trunk was less suspicious than trying to hide it, as he had first contemplated.

The drive to the house took another two minutes, and Richard's first glimpse of the place took his breath away. Sure, he had seen sketches of the floor plan, but they hadn't prepared him for the immensity of the "home."

A half dozen other cars sat parked outside the five-car garage. Richard recognized none of them from work. That meant he was likely the last one to arrive, even though his car's clock showed him to be five minutes early. He felt glad he hadn't decided to be fashionably late.

After parking, he found his way to the massive, double front doors, which opened as he neared. True to Sergei's word, Risto stood there with a hand-held metal detection wand. Only once before had he been "wanded," so he knew to keep his car keys in his hand for quick inspection. He carried no coins in his pocket, having suspected this would happen.

"Good evening, Risto. Am I the last to arrive?"

The security chief looked as pleasant as Sergei and just as talkative. He moved the wand up and down over Richard's body. It beeped only near Richard's hand, which he opened to reveal the keys.

"Open coat."

Richard complied and Risto frisked Richard's chest. With no further words, he simply nodded with his head, pointing the direction Richard was to walk. For the second time, Richard felt relief. Risto had allowed him to keep the keys.

Transfixed by the artwork and antiques, Richard walked ten feet into the hallway before seeing Irina and Miloska next to him.

"Is impressive, yes?" asked Miloska as she relieved him of his outer coat. He followed her with his eyes to see where she stored it. In an emergency, he could do without the coat, but he preferred not to leave it behind. That coat was his favorite. He turned far enough to see Risto scrutinizing them. He immediately placed his arm around Irina's shoulders and leaned over to kiss her on the neck.

"Hmmm, can't wait for dinner to be over." He hoped he spoke loudly enough for Risto to hear and that he sounded convincing.

Irina responded in kind, putting her arm around his lower back and squeezing close. "We have a special treat for you. You better eat well to get your strength up." Leaning up to kiss his ear, she whispered, "Darko has friend of yours here. She is not happy, but she is okay."

Richard did not respond. He was afraid of tipping his hand, exposing the fact that he already knew Amy would be there.

Darko and Sonja watched Richard and the women on a video feed into his office. The man's body language seemed tense, but not exceptionally so. Still, Darko wondered. More importantly, he now realized he might

392

have made a mistake in bringing the Gibbs woman here. His grapevine told him the FBI was now involved in her case, and his reach didn't quite grasp that high.

"So, *moj dragi,* what do you think?"

Sonja watched Richard with the women for a moment longer and replied, "He look nervous. Something is up."

Darko laughed. "Is maybe nervous about being at boss house for dinner with important people. Maybe nervous about Irina plan for him. Maybe—"

Sonja cut him off. "Maybe nervous because he is spy on us."

Darko shook his head. "*Ne, on ne može biti špijun.*" He cannot be a spy. "Risto has run check on him three time now. We have tap on phone. I just cannot believe he has such secret life."

Sonja shrugged. "Then is time to join guests."

With that, she turned and left the room. Darko watched her leave and picked up a portable radio. "Risto, let dog loose and bring men to house."

"*Da,* Darko. We have new problem."

Darko did not want to hear about new problems. He had a party to host, clients to placate, and ladies to enjoy.

Risto continued, "New men at warehouse do not answer phone."

Fifty-three

"Come, is time to set bait," said Ibrahim.

He stood and walked toward the fence. From the hole he'd previously cut in the links, he tossed several more meaty "treats" in front of them. He glanced to their left and moved a bit. Lynch saw that he was looking for the camera to that side of them.

"Still not on infrared. We must act fast."

He banged the chain cutter across the fence, making as much noise as possible. Lynch wondered what he was trying to accomplish, until he heard the barking. No human near the house could have heard the racket Ibrahim had made, but the dogs had no such trouble with the distance. As the barking came closer, Ibrahim sat back down and pulled the camouflage around him.

Soon, a Bandog and Lynch's "pet," the English Mastiff, appeared. They walked in a roaming pattern at first, but then the mastiff caught a scent and charged toward them. He stopped 20 feet away and began to "hunt" with his nose, just as the first Bandog had. The other Bandog quickly joined the mastiff and within minutes, both had found not one but two treats apiece. Then, the mastiff exerted his alpha dominance to claim a third treat the Bandog had found.

Lynch watched both dogs as they began to work the area to his right and follow the fence line until he could see them no more. Ibrahim uncovered and stashed his camouflage sheet in his pack. He moved to the fence and, more quietly this time, finished cutting the hole in the links so they could fit through it.

"Good sign only two dog come. Mean first dog sleep somewhere."

Lynch liked that idea, but also knew the first dog might simply be restrained somewhere. He hoped Ibrahim was right.

"Come. Move quickly now." Ibrahim slid through the hole in the fence and waited for Lynch.

"Don't we need to wait for the drug to work?" Lynch had zero desire to encounter those dogs again.

"No time. Must get half way to house or camera find us."

The two took off running, and Lynch repeatedly glanced toward his right, the direction the dogs had wandered. He ran to keep up with Ibrahim, trying to ignore the potential canine threat.

As Ibrahim finally began to slow the pace, the potential threat took a turn to reality. In the waning light, a guttural growl rumbled toward them. Two four-legged forms emerged from behind a hedge, bounding toward them. Ibrahim and Lynch turned as one toward the menace as Ibrahim muttered something in Bosnian that Lynch didn't need a translation to understand.

Suddenly, the smaller of the two animals stumbled and its attempts to stand faltered. After its fourth try, the dog settled to the ground and lay still. The mastiff slowed, but continued toward them.

Both men sprinted toward the tall hedgerow close to the large patio. Lynch knew instinctively what Ibrahim hoped to achieve there. The hedge could cover their flank and give them, together, better odds against the monster chasing them. The beast continued to gain ground, to the point where Lynch could hear it breathing behind them. He didn't think they were going to make it to the evergreens, but then the breathing seemed farther away.

As they reached the hedgerow, Ibrahim turned first and faced the dog. Lynch tensed as he followed suit, and upon turning, he saw the animal 20 feet away advancing slowly on them. Hot breath accompanied each growl, looking as if it was exhaling smoke. Ibrahim drew his handgun. and this time, Lynch didn't stay his hand. Yet, instead of lunging for the gun, it sat down and rolled its head. The next growl sounded mute compared to those just a minute earlier. With that, the dog lay down and rolled onto its side.

Lynch raised his hand and offered a 'high-five' to Ibrahim, but the man ignored him. He then pulled his pack around to retrieve a muzzle and ties. Ibrahim stayed his hand.

"No time. They sleep for hour, maybe more. Go to door by patio, as we discuss. Watch for guard. I go to garage and enter there. Trouble, shoot twice to warn."

Richard followed the two women down a long hallway toward voices, male and female, coming from a room somewhere farther along. Several rooms opened onto the hall, and as Richard glanced inside each as they passed by, he saw opulence he could only have imagined at one time. Darko had money to burn, and it didn't appear to stay in his pocket long enough to singe a leg.

After passing a large formal dining room filled with ornate French antiques, Irina turned into a room filled with talk, bustle, and the clinking of glassware.

"Ah, Richard. Welcome."

Darko appeared from behind him, accompanied by his wife. Irina slipped by and moved to the bar, while Darko clapped his hand on Richard's shoulder.

"Good evening. This place is, well, amazing. I can't think of a better word. I thought the antiques at work were beautiful, but you definitely have the best for yourself here. I feel like I've been transported to a European castle, minus the tourists." He grinned.

Irina approached him and handed him his favorite beer. He thanked her as she kissed him on the cheek.

"Warsteiner is a good beer, but we have other if you like," said Darko. "In fact, my bar stock is better than most restaurants in city. Whatever you like, Irina will arrange for you."

The young woman smiled and nodded. Richard had no doubt that under Darko's watch, or Sonja's, that each woman's task at this party was to cater to her assigned man. He glanced around the room and saw ten other men of varying ages, each with a beautiful woman fawning over his needs. All of the women from work were there, plus several he'd never seen.

Oddly, there was one man sitting off by himself. He was easily the oldest of the group and seemed uneasy with what transpired around him.

"Come, Richard. Let me introduce you around and then dinner will be served."

Darko whispered in Sonja's ear, and she walked over to the man sitting alone by the window. Richard saw him shake his head at whatever she said. Darko then took hold of Richard's elbow, led him to the nearest group, and began with introductions. With the overt sexuality on display, Richard had a hard time concentrating on names. However, by the end, Richard had met a state senator, a court-of-appeals judge, the CEO of a large realty group, a senior vice-president of a major local bank, two men whose occupations were only hinted at—police white-shirts, the head of a well-known, secular non-profit organization, and two who were senior businessmen. At the end, he met the man by the window—Al, occupation, retired.

Darko moved to the center of the room while Sonja opened the large doors to the adjoining dining room. "Dinner is ready. Please, come. Let us eat."

Irina found him and took his arm. Miloska tried to assist Al, but the man rebuffed her.

"What's wrong with him?" Richard whispered into Irina's ear. She shook her head.

As they turned away from the windows and toward the dining room, a swirl of movement outside in the yard below caught Richard's eye. He glanced back in time to see the large dog he had seen at the warehouse collapse onto the wintry turf. Then he quickly turned toward the dining area rather than draw attention to events outside.

Lynch watched Ibrahim steal across the backyard by moving right up to the house and rushing past the darkened windows of the lower floor. As Ibrahim passed one set of ground-to-ceiling windows, the lights suddenly flashed on revealing an indoor pool with doors opening onto the patio. Despite the steamy windows, Lynch could make out two men as they inspected the room, tested the water, and counted what appeared to be towels. Obviously, someone planned to use the pool after dinner, with or without swimming suits. Lynch didn't want to hang around to find out.

He would have to be careful now. The door he was to use opened into a room adjacent to the pool. The slightest noise would attract these men, and that would present an obstacle Lynch didn't need, or want.

Hoping that the condensate fogging the windows of the pool enclosure would block him from view, he ran to his target only to find it locked. Not unexpected, but Lynch had wished to find it otherwise, to save him the time of trying to pick it. As he pulled out his pick set and kneeled in front of the door, he heard the men's voices rise. He quickly looked about. Had they seen him?

He scrutinized the area to discover one of the dogs lying inert at the closest edge of the patio, well within view of the windows. He eased far enough away from the building to see those windows and saw one man pointing toward the dog. The second man started to run toward the doors, but the first man stopped him and pointed Lynch's direction. A second later, the lights in windows above Lynch's head came on. They were going to use the door where Lynch sat rather than open the poolroom to the outside temperatures.

One man he could likely handle, having the element of surprise on his side. Two men would turn the odds against him. Lynch eased back into the shadows and waited.

Fifty-four

After sitting at his assigned seat, Richard sat there amazed at the china and cutlery until he realized that with four forks, three spoons, and two knives set next to the large plate, plus a separate fork and spoon set above the plate, he was out of his league. He had once been told that when one encountered such a setting, one always worked from the outside toward the plate. The great-aunt who had instructed him so, always spoke of 'one' did this or 'one' did that. As if 'one' had forgotten how to tell a girl from a boy, a 'she' from a 'he.' She also held her little finger away from her teacup. She was one crazy old lady, but that's when he had learned how interesting seniors could be. Clive teased him about being the Boy Scout and helping out little old ladies. If Richard could blame anyone for that tendency, it would be Great-Aunt Tessie.

As the first three courses arrived, via a haggard-looking trio of young women whom Richard suspected were also unregistered aliens, he managed to keep up. When in doubt, he followed Irina's lead. From the silverware, he had expected a seven-course meal, or maybe eight. He couldn't remember if dessert counted as a course. He had also expected dinner to take quite a bit of time. After all, these were refined men in his company. Men used to the finer things. Men who would savor the food before them.

Wrong! These men had appetites that didn't include food. They rushed through the smoked trout with watercress and apple slices appetizer, the vichyssoise, the whatever-it-was salad, and the raspberry sorbet. They seemed to slow down for the fifth course, lemon-orange Orange Roughy. Nevertheless, it wasn't until the main course of roast lamb with shallots, mustard, and mint that they truly took pause to enjoy the meal.

As they enjoyed the succulent lamb, Irina leaned over to Richard and whispered, "I look forward to seeing your hammer."

Richard choked, and that caught the attention of Darko.

"What is wrong, Richard? Is the lamb not prepared well?"

As Richard sipped the fine chardonnay to regain his composure, Irina took the lead and raised a hand. "No, no. I say something to catch him off-guard. Darko, did you know Richard was called Thor in the Army? He even has a hammer."

Darko laughed and raised his wine glass. "To Thor, then. Do you have this, um, hammer with you?"

By then, Richard was able to play along. The only way Irina could have known about the hammer was via Amy, but there was no way she could have known about its modifications. Still, he couldn't have played it any better. He now had his excuse to retrieve the prop from his car.

He dabbed his lips with his napkin and then said, "In fact, I do, Darko. It saved my life in Afghanistan. Would you like to see it?"

Darko smiled and emptied his glass. "Ah, I sense good story. Yes, yes, we must see great hammer of

Thor." He laughed again and nodded toward Risto.

Following a decadent dessert—a chocolate tart with a semisweet chocolate filling, topped with chocolate mousse and broken shards of dark chocolate, and served with a red raspberry sauce, the dessert dishes were cleared. Richard arose and walked around the table toward the main hallway. Risto joined him and followed him to his car. Upon opening the trunk, Risto inspected the trunk's interior and looked at the hammer. At the main door, he stopped Richard and used his wand on the prop. Apparently satisfied that it was harmless, he escorted Richard back toward the dining room. Halfway there, his radio squawked and he left Richard in a hurry.

Lynch had reached into his pack and retrieved the stun baton he had used on their previous "rescue." He didn't dare rise up to see how many men he now faced. If he could see them, they could see him. He had one simple option—to take them one at a time. At least the first one would be easy.

As anticipated, the door opened and Lynch found himself behind it. As the man stepped outside, Lynch tagged him with the baton and saw him fall, blocking the door. The second man began squabbling.

"What? You slip? Get up!" The man reached down to assist his comrade.

Tag number two.

Lynch pulled the second man off the first and dragged him around behind the door. He quickly zip-tied the man's wrists and ankles, and duct-taped his mouth. The first man came next and as he secured the man's extremities, he thought things seemed to be moving a little too smoothly. They had no idea how many men guarded the place, but he had already taken two out of commission and now had open access to the building.

That's when he saw the red dot of a laser on his arm, moving toward his chest. He ducked behind the fallen men and watched the dot search for him.

"Drop weapon! Come out!"

Lynch waffled. If he gave up now, would the man simply shoot him and not even bother with questions? Could he buy some time, function as a decoy to allow Ibrahim time to gain access? Of course, buying time worked both ways. He might soon find himself confronted by a whole squad of men.

He decided. At the moment, they were at a stalemate. Lynch would leave it that way. The guards would focus on him, not knowing his numbers, and that would draw them away from the other end of the house. He would also have an opportunity to determine the enemy's strength.

"No! Drop your weapons and put your hands behind your head. Police!" yelled Lynch. ""We have the place surrounded!" That worked in the movies.

"Ha!" came the reply, followed by a single gunshot that shattered the glass above his head.

Well, that didn't work, thought Lynch, but he stood his ground. The man would have to come through the door to get him. Guards coming from the outside would be visible well before they could reach him. He set his baton by his side and pulled the 9mm Mike had given him. Time to wait . . . and hope Ibrahim had made better progress.

Richard returned to the dining room to find the others had returned to the adjacent room where after-dinner drinks flowed and cigar smoke clouded the ceiling. He had his hammer. What next?

Did he wait until Irina led him to wherever and make a move then? In the back of his mind, he didn't think Darko would let events go that far without some other test. Moreover, Risto's sudden disappearance concerned him. Had they detected his outside backup? Worse, had they neutralized them?

He turned away from the table and wandered into the drawing room, hiding the hammer behind his back. He drew upon every reserve of boldness he had to continue.

"Ahh, Richard. Nice try, but you cannot hide it behind back." Darko laughed. He seemed merry and relaxed, but Richard still saw an edge in his eyes. The man could act better than Richard. Time to up the game.

He flipped the hammer out and laid it across both hands in front of him, as a magician would present a prop. "Ta daaa . . ." He motioned for Irina and Miloska to join him. "My assistants, please." He was winging it now. "This is the mighty and mysterious Hammer of Thor. Let me tell you how I came to possess this wondrous thing."

Richard started to tell his audience of the details leading up to that fateful foot patrol that would earn him the call sign of 'Thor.' He had barely begun when

Darko interrupted.

"Wait, wait. We have one more guest who would like to hear story." He snapped his fingers with the same melodramatic flourish as Richard's presentation of the hammer.

Sergei appeared at the hallway door, pushing Amy in front of him. Her appearance surprised Richard, even though he knew she was there. "Amy!" He glared at Darko. "Darko, what is she doing here? You have no right to—"

"Amy? Amy Gibbs?" The old man, Al, spoke. "Darko, what's the meaning of this?" He walked toward Darko, possessing the swagger of a younger man.

Darko's merriment dissolved into the smoky atmosphere above. He picked up a radio from a nearby table and called his security chief. "Risto. Come to drawing room."

Richard could not hear the reply, but it displeased the boss.

"Darko, again, why do you have Ms. Gibbs here?"

Richard glanced at Amy, who appeared unharmed. He would make sure she stayed that way. Amy looked at him only briefly, but he couldn't make out the emotion behind those eyes. Did she blame him? He would understand if she did. He blamed himself.

Amy's gaze moved to Al. "Chief? Chief Dandridge, w-what are you doing here? A-are you part of this?"

Richard could discern her feelings now. Disappointment and sadness, as someone she held in high esteem now fell from grace and light now exposed a dark, hidden secret. Tears fell across her cheeks.

* * *

Lynch sensed more than saw the man approaching. He scooted on his butt along the edge of the building away from the door and broken glass. The two men stirred, but their restraints held. He saw no need to deal with them again as they wouldn't become alert until this game of cat and mouse played out.

Through the broken window, he heard the man's radio crackle and heard the name 'Risto.' *So that's who I'm up against*, he thought. He would have to be on full vigilance. He looked farther along the building and saw no quick escape. His quick glance up revealed something more, a security camera. With a smartphone, Risto could watch his every move. He needed a more defensible position, and he needed to take out that camera. Did he risk a shot? Maybe it was time to fire off two shots to alert Ibrahim. His magazine held eleven and he had only one spare.

He aimed at the camera and squeezed off one round. Missed. He aimed again and heard the growl. He quickly brought his gun around to find the Bandog that had been lying near the patio charging him. Its feet stumbled, but its determination did not.

He fumbled around the ground near him searching for the baton. Distracted by the animal, he failed to see the large man appear to his left.

"Drop gun." To the dog he commanded, "*Čuvati!*" Guard!

The animal stopped, but stood alert to Lynch's every move. As Lynch moved his gun hand, the beast growled louder. At least the dog wasn't attached to his forearm.

Lynch flipped the gun around and lowered it to the

ground. The man kicked it away.

"Throw baton away."

As Lynch complied, the man's radio came alive again. He shook his head and frowned, but the boss called, or so Lynch assumed.

"Stand slow. Make wrong move and I shoot."

Lynch nodded. He knew the man would prove true to that word. Silently, Lynch prayed that Ibrahim had fared better than he had.

Lynch stood slowly and the man pushed him toward and through the door.

"Straight to door, left to stair."

Lynch did as told and soon found himself in an ornate main hallway, with voices coming from a nearby room.

"You've gone too far this time, Darko. You *have* to let her go, or else."

"Or else what, *chief*?" The last word spit from the man's mouth.

Lynch felt Risto's gun push into his shoulder. "Stay here. Sergei!" Another man emerged through the doorway. "Watch him. Shoot if move."

Lynch leaned up against the wall and crossed his arms, but that did not last long.

"Face wall."

Lynch complied.

"Forehead on wall. Take step back."

Lynch did as told and found himself in a slightly off-balance position. No doubt just what Sergei wanted.

"Hands behind back."

Again, he complied. What choice did he have? The man was just far enough away to give him the advantage. Any sudden movement by Lynch would result in a bullet flying his way.

With his hands behind him, Sergei placed a zip-tie around his wrists. Now, he really felt off-balance. He had no trick up his sleeve, only trust that the cavalry would come to the rescue. Then, words that Mike had spoken to him before they left came to mind, and he said a quiet prayer.

Darko's demeanor grew to match his name. His earlier misgivings at having taken the Gibbs woman now blossomed to full-blown regret. Of course, he'd no way of knowing the old police chief knew this woman. Yet, now he had two loose ends and only one path of recourse, to eliminate both. That, however, was not something he could do with the others present.

Yet, as he scrutinized the woman and tried to think of the best way to remove the two without the suspicion of the others, he realized she would become an attractive addition to his harem. Of course, drugs would be required to tame her, but that was no obstacle.

"Risto, escort lady and Chief Dandridge to private room for private visit."

Risto motioned to the old man to follow, but the Chief did not budge.

"Let her go, Darko. She has no role here," the Chief continued.

Richard agreed, "Please, Darko. If this somehow pertains to me, let her go. You will have no problems from me."

Darko's tone softened. He had to sound reasonable, convincing. "Chief, we will discuss in private. In meantime, our friends wish to make use of facilities here. Please go with Risto."

Lynch knew that voice. He had spoken with Chief Dandridge only two days before. *What is he doing here?* he wondered. Had the Chief sold him out? He racked his brain. Had he mentioned Darko? No, and although he had not mentioned Danijela, but only that a woman had saved his life, he knew the Chief had been aware of her. Likewise, he'd made no mention of human trafficking, or of Ibrahim, or the cabin. Or had he? Risto had showed up and destroyed the cabin only after the Chief had been there. Then Lynch realized that the name Danijela, added to Ibrahim's name on the property record, was all that the Chief, Risto, or Darko would need to do the math. Mike's reservations about contacting the Chief had been on target.

One question remained in Lynch's mind. Who was the woman in the center of this contention?

Lynch heard the footfall of three people come into the hallway. One was distinctively female, as the sound of heels on a hard surface echoed through the hallway.

"How did you get here? How in the world did you get involved with this?"

Lynch could hear the Chief, but only swirls of movement reached his peripheral vision.

"Don't talk to me, Chief."

Lynch could swear he knew her voice, too. But how?

"Amy, I-I . . . it isn't what it seems. I don't—"

"You don't what, Chief? You don't inhale? You never had sex with that woman? What? No matter what you *didn't* do, you *did* turn a blind eye to all of this. That makes you just as bad."

Amy? Was that the Amy of his memories? No wonder the voice sounded familiar. A flood of memories eddied through his mind. He remembered. All of it. All things that once eluded him now came back.

Lynch heard some scuffling.

"Hey, let her go!"

"Sergei, drug her. Take her back to room."

The commotion grew as Lynch imagined Amy fighting back. He eased his feet forward. He needed to get back on balance. Hopefully, his captors were distracted enough to give . . . him . . . the time. Within seconds, he was fully mobile. He turned and lunged toward Sergei.

"Lynch!" cried the Chief.

"Lynch?" Amy's eyes widened, before she fell and collapsed to the floor.

Risto fired a shot toward the woman, but Lynch caught it in the shoulder. The burn could not compete with his desire to protect Amy. He moved to cover her body. As Risto changed his aim, Lynch saw the Chief lunge for the man.

"Lynch! No!"

The shot echoed down the hallway as the retired police chief fell to the floor. Suddenly, Risto fell as well, blood coming from a well-placed hole in his forehead, the back of his head missing. The echo had been Ibrahim's.

410

Sergei had no time to pull his gun again before he, too, fell from a well-placed gunshot.

Richard had watched the Chief and Amy leave the room, unsure what to do. Yet, his hand inched closer to the release button and his mind began to calculate the distance between him and Darko. He took a few steps forward, as if to follow Amy, but in reality, he sought to close the distance.

As gunshots bounced around the hall outside the room, Richard saw Darko reach for a wooden box on a nearby shelf. As his boss pulled out a handgun, Richard released the grizzly spray and caught Darko fully in the face.

"Awrrrlll!" Darko's shrieks filled the room, and his gun dropped to the floor. The others ducked for cover. Several of the women ran for the dining room door. Richard raced for the gun, but Sonja beat him to it.

She raised the gun and fired at him. Instinctively, he raised the hammer and felt the impact of the bullet on the Kevlar. She fired again, with the same effect. The third time, her gun misfired and jammed. Richard's right hand slipped down to the end of the hammer's shaft and twisted.

The end of the shaft fell away and a ceramic throwing knife fell into Richard's hand. With a quick throw, the blade righted itself just in time to pierce Sonja's chest. Her eyes reflected the pain as her hand went to her chest and felt the blade. She pulled it free, only to collapse with it to the floor.

Richard ran to the hall and witnessed the carnage

around him. A man, his hands bound behind his back, hovered between the Chief and Amy. Profuse bleeding soaked the shirt and coat about his left shoulder. Amy appeared uninjured and began to stir. Knowing she was safe, he ran back into the room and tied up Darko with an electric cord. His knife in hand, he returned to the hall to cut loose the man's bonds.

He heard sirens in the distance. Richard looked around and snorted. "*Now* they show up."

With his right hand free, the man, Nameless, knelt over Al, the Chief. "Chief, stay with us. Stay with us."

The Chief fought to speak. "I . . . didn't . . ." He struggled for another breath. ". . . sell . . . you . . . out." Again, he labored to take in air. "I never . . ." At that, what breath he had wheezed from his mouth and his eyes glazed over.

Nameless tried to apply pressure with his right hand, but with his left arm useless, he couldn't seem to manage.

Richard knelt next to him and felt for a carotid pulse. There was none. A quick glance at the Chief's eyes revealed he had already departed. Richard shook his head. He'd seen enough death on the battlefield to recognize it now.

Amy sat up and looked their way, but Richard saw that he wasn't the target of her gaze.

"Lynch? Is it really you?"

At that, Richard knew that Nameless had a name, and had returned from the dead.

Fifty-five
❧ ✦ ✦ ❧

As police flooded the mansion, Richard returned to the drawing room and picked up his hammer. Once again, it had saved his life, thanks to Clive's alterations. Unfortunately, the hammer itself would have to be retired. The impact of two rounds from a short distance had shattered the Kevlar. That side of the prop felt so soft Richard wondered if he could poke his finger through it.

As uniformed officers escorted Darko away, a tall, dark-haired female police officer approached him.

"Richard, . . ." She extended her hand to him. ". . . once again, I seem to arrive after the action."

He shook hands with her and asked, "Is it over?"

"Look around. What do you think?"

He nodded. "I guess we won this battle, but someone else will move in, fill the void left by Darko." He hated to admit that. The idea sounded so pessimistic, but he was right.

The detective nodded and frowned, confirming that he was correct.

"All we can do is keep fighting, keep exposing the dark. Today, though, look at the number of lives you'll have helped change. Focus on that positive."

Richard nodded and looked toward the hallway. He didn't feel positive. He owed Amy an apology, yet he didn't want to face her. Lynch was back, and he felt as if he'd lost something valuable. No, *someone* valuable. He had lost more than a friend. He'd fallen for her, and he

413

dreaded the prospect of losing her.

He nodded at the detective and wandered toward the hallway. A paramedic crew had Lynch on a backboard, and one medic was placing an IV line into his right arm while a second applied a pressure dressing to his left shoulder. Several officers came up to him, eager to shake his hand, but being unable to, they congratulated him and welcomed him back to the fold. A baby-faced, red-haired officer in plainclothes approached and smiled as Lynch caught sight of him.

"Saints begorrah! He fooled the Devil and the dead do rise!" he said in a perfect Irish brogue.

Lynch laughed. "Well, if it isn't Famous Seamus. Are you still making the talk show rounds?"

The officer laughed as well. His brogue gone, he replied, "Nope, back on the mean streets with homicide. Susan called me and asked for help. I guess I should be flattered she finds me honest and trustworthy."

"She must not know you like I do."

"Yeah, right. Which arm should I punch?"

Famous Seamus looked at Richard, as he stood there hammer in hand. He stepped toward Richard and extended his hand.

"And you must be Richard Nichols. I'm Sergeant Seamus O'Connor. We owe a lot to you. Can I buy you a pint or two later? Guinness, of course, at this great little Irish pub I'd like to introduce you to."

"Thanks, but the guys who backed me up will want to come, too."

The brogue returned. "And when did an Irishman ever turn down new friends to drink with?" The detective turned back to Lynch and said, unaccented,

414

"See you later, Wonderboy. I'll stop by at the hospital. I've asked the paramedics to take you to Barnes. Sarah's on duty in the E.D. She'll make sure you get the best." At that, Seamus turned to join Detective Prichard in the drawing room, but stopped and looked back at Lynch. "By the way, Lt. Janick knows you're alive. You can expect him at the hospital, too." He shook his head. "Never expected Batbrain and Wonderboy to be a team again." This time he turned and walked into the other room.

Richard looked around and saw Amy walking around the corner at the far end of the hallway, escorted by a female paramedic. He started to follow, but Lynch raised his good hand and stopped him.

"Seamus is right. We owe you on this one. Your intel was what we needed to convince a judge to get warrants, not to mention your rescuing Ibrahim's sister. If she'd still been in Darko's clutches, Ibrahim might not have showed up when he did. I wouldn't be talking with you, and Amy wouldn't be walking down the hall. I'm Lynch Cully, by the way. Thank you." He extended his hand, IV and all.

Richard shook his hand, gingerly. "You're welcome. I guess I just see it as being in the line of duty."

"Hey, can you guys give me a couple of days? I want to join you for those beers, but I don't expect the doctors will be letting me out tomorrow."

Richard smiled. "I'll see if my buddies can stick around for a while."

He followed the paramedics and gurney outside where the parking area looked like a scene from a TV cop show—lights flashing, officers milling around, police tape barriers, and one area cordoned off with a MedAir chopper waiting for Lynch. The MedAir crew surrounded Amy, along with her father. Hassle and Clive stood a few feet away.

He walked up to his friends and presented Clive with the hammer.

"It took two rounds and saved my life again, along with the spray and the knife. Your ingenuity saved my life, twice now, ol' buddy. I am forever in your debt."

Clive smiled. "Like the sound of that, and you can name your firstborn after me if you want, but right now, I'd like you to introduce me to your co-worker over there. That one, with the coal black hair."

Richard laughed. "That's Ivanka. Promise me no shenanigans, though. She, *all* of them have been through a lot."

Clive crossed his heart.

Richard took a step toward Amy and heard Clive behind him say, "He said his co-workers were gorgeous. Hassle, look at those ladies. I'll never doubt him again."

Amy looked amazing. As he stepped closer, she excused herself and joined him.

"Amy, I . . ." He paused. "I'm sorry. I honestly don't know how you got involved in this. I didn't have any—"

Amy put her finger on his lips to hush him. "I know you didn't. We're good. Really. My dad made a comment that sums it up. Folks need to take responsibility for their own actions and quit trying to blame others. You didn't make Darko kidnap me; he did it on his own and he'll pay for it." She placed her hand on his arm. "Like I said, we're still good."

Richard watched as the MedAir crew lifted Lynch's

gurney aboard and secured it in place.

"Excuse me a moment," said Amy.

She walked over to the aircraft and took Lynch's hand. She talked with him briefly and stepped back from the chopper as its pilot powered up and the blades began to circle. She walked back to Richard's side, where her father joined them.

"I thought you might go with him," said Lt. Col. Gibbs.

"Can't, no room and, to be honest, I'm not about to go looking like this. I need to find my real clothes and the detectives need my statement. I will need a ride home, though."

"I've got my car, and Hassle said he's heading back with Clive," replied her dad.

Richard saw an opportunity and did not hesitate to take it. "Sir, I have to stick around to give my statement, too. I'd be more than happy to give her a ride."

"Thanks, son, but I'm in no hurry. I can stick around."

Amy gave her father a look. "Dad, you go on. I can ride with Richard. We'll call as we leave, and maybe you could get some Greek from Zorba's and have it waiting for us. Thor might have eaten, but I'm starving."

The colonel looked at his daughter, then at Richard, and again at Amy. He nodded. "See you soon."

Richard's heart leapt—well, a little. Maybe he hadn't lost her yet.

Fifty-six

❧ ◆ ❧

Lynch returned to his room shortly after breakfast time, feeling groggy, hungry, and disoriented. His surgery had started around one a.m. and lasted longer than anticipated. He woke up in recovery to find his parents there. Doctor Sarah Wade had insisted he call them from the E.D. After all, she argued, it was only proper that they get the news of his return from him, not the news media. She then pulled some strings to get them into the recovery unit, where two out of three of them held a tearful reunion. He had been too drugged to care at that point.

As an orderly wheeled him down the hall, he had no problem spotting his room. The staff had taped balloons to both sides of the doorframe, and a botanical garden's worth of flora lined both sides of the hall. As he came closer, he saw a sign posted over the door reading, "He's ALIVE!" Lynch wondered who would claim responsibility for that.

Expecting a room full of people, he was surprised, but also happy, to find his room empty. A nurse greeted him inside.

"You've got a whole horde of people wanting to see you. We shoved them all out until you're settled and ready for them. You just let us know, and we'll let them up a few at a time."

"Thanks. You can let my parents up now. I'll let you know when I'm up for more."

Finally feeling coherent, he spent the next hour

418

telling his parents about his travails of the past few months. His mother cried a lot, while his father sat there silent but shaking his head occasionally. Next came a crew from the police department—Colonel Halbert, Lieutenant Janick, and a small handful of other detectives. Halbert delivered bittersweet news, they'd filled his position since he had been presumed dead, but he was eligible for full re-instatement as a police officer within the state as soon as the doctors cleared him. Janick told him he would personally go to the Ladue council about adding a new full-time police position so they could put him back on the force. Lynch held back his reservations about returning to active duty. He had a new career in mind.

The rest of the morning filled with well-wishers and phone calls. Even the governor called to wish him the best. However, the people he longed to see most hadn't shown up. As lunchtime approached, the nurses shooed everyone out and brought him a tray of clear, tasteless broth and green Jell-O. While he picked at the "food," Sarah Wade walked in.

"Hi, Lynch. I had the nurses put everyone else on hold until later. I thought you might want to see these people next." She grinned.

In walked the Southworths, Danijela, and Detective Prichard with Ibrahim. Lynch had suspected that Ibrahim would not remain a free man, but hoped that his role in breaking up the human trafficking ring would serve well before any judge.

Danijela extended a foil-covered treat toward him. "I bring cake. To celebrate. You will like."

Sarah laughed. "Not today he won't. Sorry, but until

you're back on a regular diet, no cake."

Lynch looked at her pleadingly, while Danijela winked and gave him a conspiratorial nod.

"Are we in time?" asked Mike. "Where's the remote?"

"What's up?" asked Lynch. He untwisted the cord from the bed rail and handed the remote to the man. The appearance of a prominent local news anchor answered that question.

"We have breaking news that a major human trafficking and smuggling ring based in South City has been broken. We have video testimonies from several women recently rescued from that ring. I must warn you that much of what you are about to hear is disturbing."

For the next five minutes, highlights of the women's testimonies filled the broadcast. Everyone in the room watched, spellbound. When the video finished, the news anchor reappeared to announce the resurrection of Detective Lynch Cully, once thought dead at the hand of the L.A. Rapist, and his role in breaking up the trafficking ring. Silence ruled the room for the next two minutes, as Mike placed the continuing newscast on mute.

A nurse interrupted the quiet. "Colonel Southworth, there's someone out here asking for you."

Mike gave Lynch a wink and left the room.

Lynch looked at Danijela and said, "A week ago, I asked Mike and Mary to do something for me. Well, for you, really. Close your eyes."

Danijela gave him a look of suspicion, but complied. Mary Southworth took hold of her shoulders and turned her to face the door. A moment later, a middle-aged couple and a teenage girl filled the doorway.

"Okay, you can open your eyes."

Danijela's eyes widened and her torrent of tears could only be matched by those of her mother, father, and sister.

"*Mati! Otac! Dijana! Hvala, Bogu!*" She ran to their arms and a babble of Bosnian followed.

After five minutes, Danijela separated from her family and walked over to Lynch's bed where she leaned down to hug him. "*Hvala*," she whispered in his ear.

At that moment, Seamus O'Connor walked in. "Hey, I found two stragglers outside."

In walked Amy and Richard in time to witness Danijela thanking Lynch and kissing him on the cheek. Lynch could not describe the look on Amy's face, until he glanced around and saw the same look on Ibrahim's face. Then, as Amy placed her arm around Richard's waist, he knew firsthand the same painful confusion. Just what kind of reality show had he woken up to? Lynch-Danijela-Ibrahim. Danijela-Lynch-Amy. Lynch-Amy-Richard. Did they all see what he saw? For once, he regretted his unique ability to see patterns. Two women and three guys. At least one guy was going to lose out. Maybe all five of them would.

Lynch wanted to bury his head in the pillow and return to his life incognito.

Before anyone could speak, Seamus' cell phone rang, followed a beat later by Susan's cell. Ten seconds later, Amy's phone chirped. Simultaneously, their faces took on an ashen pall. Seamus lowered his phone and spoke first.

"I'm sorry, but we need to leave right away. The MCS has been placed on emergency response."

"I've been called to work, too," said Amy.

Susan was already escorting Ibrahim out the door as Lynch asked, "What's up?"

Seamus took a deep breath and replied, "A school shooting. Automatic rifle fire. Multiple gunmen. Unknown number of casualties at this time."

Sneak Preview:

THE SILENCED SHOOTER

Prologue

❧✦✦☙

An omen? Abdul Aleem Malik Fawaz exited the black government sedan and straightened the *kuffiyeh* covering his head as he glanced at the residence to his left. The building's planners had designed it first as the Presidential Palace, but budgetary constraints were common even in that day. He recalled his first visit there and how disappointingly small the building seemed compared to its reputation. This evening its façade glowed a dull orange, reflecting the brilliant sunset to the southwest and reminiscent of the desert sands. The effect made it seem even smaller.

The sun setting on that building. Was that an omen of what was to come for the country as well?

Today, he wore a charcoal grey suit rather than his customary *thobe* and *bisht,* robes appropriate for his role as a Senior Fellow. Today, he had an important meeting at the highest level. Today could possibly mark the beginning of a new era, the time for the emergence of a new world order ordained long ago. Yet, at no time had the pieces been in place to make that happen. Until today.

Fawaz accepted his briefcase from the driver and turned toward the main doors to the lobby of the building where his meeting was to take place. He entered the building and welcomed the warmth and the respite it provided from the frigid January day.

"Credentials please," requested the security officer clothed in a dark blue, wool suit. The lapel mic and earpiece of his communication device were not obvious, unlike the bulge of a handgun inside his jacket.

For the second time, Fawaz presented his creds. At the gate, the car had undergone a thorough inspection. This time it would be his person, his travel mug, and briefcase, so he handed those items to the officer without a word. He'd been here often enough to know the routine.

The officer in turn lowered them behind his desk and ran them through the scanner Fawaz knew was there. The man glanced at the monitor before him, and raised the case again to place it on top of the desk. He lifted the mug, opened the travel lid and sniffed. Satisfied that its contents were innocuous, he handed it back to Fawaz and extended a white plastic tray toward him.

"The contents of your pockets, please."

Fawaz emptied his pockets to reveal only two items, his wallet, and a chain holding two keys, one to his apartment and one to his office.

"Step over here, please."

Fawaz moved into the whole body scanner, similar to those used at some airports. The guard frowned.

"Please step back. What is in your coat pocket, sir?" He again extended the tray toward the Fellow.

Fawaz sighed. He'd forgotten the ornate, and expensive, pen his sister had given him to celebrate his promotion to Senior Fellow. He removed it from his jacket's inside pocket and placed it in the tray. A second officer appeared from a doorway behind the desk.

"So sorry, I forgot it was there."

The second officer inspected and scanned the items in the tray, while Fawaz returned to the body scanner and successfully passed through. He reclaimed his personal items, and without words, followed the second officer. They already knew whom he was to meet.

The guard ushered him directly into the office of Roberta Faris, an advisor on national security affairs. She was the third such advisor in her position and had the ear of their leader, but she was the first to embrace Islam openly. Her predecessors had been secularists, with no religious leanings, unless one viewed human secularism as a religion unto itself. She had been the one to recommend Fawaz for his promotion, and for that, he overlooked the fact of her gender.

"Abdul, it is good to see you again." She extended her hand, which he shook before taking the chair across from her where she motioned him to sit. In the past, she had relegated him to the wooden chair across the desk from her. Today, they sat as equals in an informal sitting area.

"I read your report, and Imam Mahdavi has confirmed your conclusions. Have you anything to add?"

Fawaz nodded. "Indeed, I do. There were names and locations I did not feel comfortable placing in writing."

"I understand. Please keep them to yourself right now."

He gave her a questioning look.

"I think you understand why I ask that."

He did. Plausible deniability. The United States' CIA had coined the phrase during the Kennedy administration, and it again became "popular" during the Iran-Contra affair of the 1980s. The concept rarely, if ever, worked, so he was surprised that Faris would even think to rely upon it.

Nevertheless, who was he to question a superior, someone who had direct influence on his career?

They discussed his written report, and he offered three distinct courses of action to initiate their response. All of them focused on the political aspects of the problem, as requested. It was, after all, an election year for the United States. The man they worked for was the consummate politician, who saw governing as a game of politics and himself as the ultimate competitor. To Fawaz, it appeared that the man's need to win superseded the needs of the people. Yet, that flaw, that lack of true leadership, fit perfectly with the goal of Islam, to make the world an Islamic state. The man's popularity polls had plummeted and his standing among world leaders had become fodder for the European tabloids. The man was a classic narcissist, who continued to believe himself infallible. Yes, Allah could use him.

Ms. Faris nodded and looked thoughtful as he laid out his case and recommendations. At the end of his presentation, she stood, walked across the room, and proceeded to place his report in the shredder behind her desk. She turned back to him and said, "I expect you to remove all traces of this report as well. Shred any hard copies and wipe clean any electronic versions, as well as any correspondence pertaining to it."

Fawaz nodded. He had expected as much and would comply. Mostly. Direct order or not, he would make sure he had personal insurance. If he would somehow end up in a U.S. Federal Court, he would need leverage, and he knew these people well enough to know how rough they played. There were few places in the world where he could hide, and none of those locales were particularly hospitable or welcoming. He took a sip from his mug and with care, positioned it on the table beside him with the digital recorder's mic pointed toward Faris' chair.

Ms. Faris retrieved something from her desk and returned to the sitting area to join him. The envelope in her hand seemed thin.

"Your recommended options are all quite reasonable, but we have discussed a different course of action, in light of waning popularity polls. Here is what we would like you to do." She handed him a single sheet of paper from the envelope and watched as he read.

"I believe you have contact with people in Detroit and elsewhere who can accomplish this. Yes?"

Fawaz couldn't believe what he read. Were they really willing to take such a step?

He looked up at her and tried to read her eyes, only to see his own reflection in the ice.

"Y-yes, I have such contacts." He wanted to question her, but something held him back.

"Good. How soon can we expect it?"

He tried to think, but the potential ramifications of this plan flooded his brain. He struggled to pull his thoughts together.

"One month perhaps. It will require planning and perfect timing. I can give you a timetable, if you wish, after I've made contact with these people."

She shook her head. "That won't be necessary. In fact, the less we know the better. Just make sure it's completed before the spring primaries."

A quick note from Braxton . . .

I hope you enjoyed *Rescued and Remembered* and thank you for purchasing it. Please consider writing a review at my website, on Amazon, Barnes & Nobel, iTunes, Goodreads, or elsewhere. Reviews are crucial to Indie authors. It doesn't have to be lengthy. Just a couple of sentences will do.

Also, if you'd like to stay informed about my new books, book signings, and more, please sign up for my newsletter. You can do that at my website: **www.braxtondegarmo.com**. As my gift to you for signing up, you'll get the eBook, *And Then One Day*— the prequel to the series. Have you wondered how Lynch and Amy first met, or what led to their breakup? This is the book for you.

And did you know you can purchase signed copies of my paperbacks at my website? With shipping included in the price, ordering them directly from me is typically cheaper than ordering them online.

Books by

Braxton DeGarmo:

MedAir Series:

Looks that Deceive - 1

Rescued and Remembered - 2

The Silenced Shooter – 3

Wrongfully Removed - 4

A Zealot's Destiny - 5

Others:

Indebted

The Militant Genome

ABOUT THE AUTHOR

 Braxton can't lay claim to wanting to be a writer all his life, although his mother and seventh grade English teacher were convinced he had what it would take. A bachelor's degree in Bio-Medical Engineering led to medical school and a residency in Emergency Medicine. He served for a decade in the U.S. Army Medical Corps with tours such as the Chief, Emergency Medical Services at Fort Campbell, KY and as a research Flight Surgeon at Fort Rucker, AL. Who had time to write?

By the 1990s, as a civilian, his professional and family life had settled down, somewhat, and his mother once again took up her mantra, "Write a book. You're a good writer." In 1997, a Valentine's Day writing contest convinced him that maybe he could write fiction. He spent the next fifteen years learning the craft of writing.

Now, nineteen years after that first hesitant start, he has seven novels published and can't find enough time to write. As a Christian, he writes "true-life" Christian fiction (suspense and thrillers) that many call "cutting edge," as he's not afraid to take on such issues as human trafficking, racism, and more. His characters are real-life as well. As such, his books are never likely to gain acceptance by the Christian Bookseller Association. But then, he never intended to tell stories just to the choir.